# STATE OF EMERGENCY

Andy McNab

## BANTAM PRESS

LONDON • TORONTO • SYDNEY • AUCKLAND • JOHANNESBURG

TRANSWORLD PUBLISHERS
61–63 Uxbridge Road, London W5 5SA
www.transworldbooks.co.uk

Transworld is part of the Penguin Random House group of companies
whose addresses can be found at global.penguinrandomhouse.com

Penguin
Random House
UK

First published in Great Britain in 2015 by Bantam Press
an imprint of Transworld Publishers

A CIP catalogue record for this book
is available from the British Library.

ISBNs 9780593069813 (cased)
9780593069820 (tpb)

Typeset in 11/14pt Palatino by Falcon Oast Graphic Art Ltd.
Printed and bound by Clays Ltd, Bungay, Suffolk.

Penguin Random House is committed to a sustainable
future for our business, our readers and our planet. This book
is made from Forest Stewardship Council® certified paper.

MIX
Paper from
responsible sources
FSC
www.fsc.org     FSC® C018179

1 3 5 7 9 10 8 6 4 2

# STATE OF EMERGENCY

# STATE OF EMERGENCY

www.**transworldbooks**.co.uk

# 1

The inflatable bucked and kicked as it skimmed the surface of the Thames. A stiff breeze flustered the water, sculpting it into small waves that smacked the bow as the craft progressed upriver. The low cloud pressing down on the capital glowed a dull orange, reflecting the city lights on to the deserted waterway. A lone night-bus made its way across Battersea Bridge, empty of passengers, like a ghostly *Mary Celeste* on wheels.

The only interruption to the boatman's progress had been a River Police launch heading downstream to its base at Wapping. He had throttled back to tick-over and steered into the shadow of one of the few remaining Thames barges moored on the seaward side of Tower Bridge. As the launch came past he flattened himself against the hull, clenching his teeth against the cold. The launch slowed and veered so close that for a few seconds he could hear the radio coming from it – the sound of cheering. The election results were coming through. He stayed like that until the sound of the launch had faded into the night. The snow was starting again; welcome additional cover to obscure the small craft, fine flecks that swirled uncertainly in the biting wind.

All but his face was covered by the marine dry-suit. The chill sliced at his features, freezing the moisture in his nose and round his lips, a warning that whatever snow made it to the ground would quickly freeze. Already, ice was crusting along the water's edge. He decided to ignore it. Years ago he had taught himself not to worry about things that were out of his hands and focus on what he could control – and what was ahead.

Although he had never been there, he knew the layout of the hotel inside out. He had started with YouTube, and the news reports of the opening, then read all the entries on TripAdvisor – it was amazing how much time people wasted recording their visits in mind-numbing detail. From there he had graduated to a presentational CGI animation prepared by the architects, and finally the plans themselves, until he could conjure up the whole layout in his mind's eye, like a hologram. He had two entry-point options: one through the kitchens, the other the laundry. But the kitchens even at three thirty a.m. were unlikely to be empty. A skeleton crew would still be on duty, handling room-service requests and keeping the last of the revellers fed and watered. The laundry should be deserted. He had to find some-where to slip out of the dry-suit and ditch the backpack after he'd pulled out the less conspicuous overnight bag that held the kit he needed: the weapon, a Glock 9mm with a titanium suppressor and an extended twenty-round magazine – much more than he required for what he expected to be a surgical strike – a Bowie knife, smoke canisters, a mask. From his research, he knew that there was a locker room and a toilet to the back of the laundry: he needed a mirror to check himself over before he moved into the public area.

In the first plan there were to have been three of them: two for cover. He hadn't liked it. Too conspicuous. 'But who's going to watch your back?' they'd asked. He'd said he'd watch his own. He was used to it: why break the habit of a lifetime? Alone, he had complete control, no one else to consider if he had to make a change of plan. The truth was he didn't much care about his back, didn't want to be encumbered. This was his idea, his plan. 'We won't forget this, Fez,' they'd told him.

Whatever.

The hotel came into view: the 'Ice Palace'. These days, all new buildings in London seemed to acquire nicknames – the Gherkin, the Cheese Grater and so on. And Ice Palace sounded better than 'Battersea Regina' – some smartarse had already called its giant three-storey atrium the Battersea Vagina. True to its name, though, this one looked the part, all tiered glass, like something that had time-travelled out of the future. And, like all good palaces, it was surrounded by a vast fortified wall to keep out any trouble. But not the river front. Didn't the architects have any sense of history?

As the craft made its way towards the target, he reviewed his route once more. He was right to avoid going through the kitchens. Unless he could slip past the staff he would have to take down whoever was there, which would be messy and risky. He didn't want collateral: there was only one target. The better option was through the laundry. He smiled grimly as he thought of the heavy security out front, ever vigilant, never imagining the threat that was coming by river on a frozen February night.

He slowed as the hotel came into view. A giant slab of glass and concrete bordering the southern bank of the river, so new there were still traces of the last construction work. He unclipped the oars and dropped their paddles into the water. Short, shallow scoops brought the craft noiselessly up to the jetty.

Over his shoulder he spotted a lone silhouetted figure on the broad apron that separated the hotel from the river, leaning against the balustrade, the orange dot of a cigarette glowing minutely as the smoker drew on it. The figure straightened, the cigarette suspended in front of him. As he watched, he unzipped the suit, felt for the Glock. One well-aimed shot and it would be that smoker's last gasp. But before he drew down his weapon the man flicked the butt into the water, turned and ambled back out of the cold.

The craft nudged the jetty and he reached for one of the polystyrene bumpers that dangled from it, tugged it and drew the craft towards a metal gangway. The whole structure was encased in a thick glaze of ice. He struggled for grip through the waterproof gloves. The boat slid from under him and, for a few seconds, he feared he would drop into the icy river. He was out of shape: he hadn't done shit like this in a long while. After several tries he managed to haul himself high enough to get one foot on the structure. Then he kicked the inflatable away. He wouldn't be needing it. Maybe someone downstream, Gravesend perhaps, would be the lucky owner of a new boat by the end of the night. There was no exit from this, no going back now.

Half crouching, he moved swiftly along the gangway, which bucked and creaked under him. The snow was thickening: bigger, heavier flakes falling with more purpose now, already laying the beginnings of a carpet of dull white across the hotel river front. He fixed on a point some four metres beyond the west wing of the façade. From his memory of the plans he had studied, there was a ramp from which vehicles could reach the lower-level service area, bordered by a metal fence. He was just about to set off towards it when he saw the camera tower. That wasn't in the plans or the photos. It was new. Builders' plastic barriers were grouped around the base. Were the cameras live? He would stand out a mile against a white background. But then he remembered the havoc snow played with night-sights, filling the image with miniature starbursts of reflected light. He decided to risk it, moving nonchalantly with a civilian gait.

He vaulted the fence and dropped on to the ramp, paused, scanned the area for any more new cameras, any more smokers. Nothing. He moved down towards the laundry service door, unzipped the suit and took out the precious key card charged with that day's code. In his mind it was the one weak link in the plan, the only thing for which he'd had to depend on someone else. But it had given the others something to do so they felt part of it. He approached the door beside the shuttered vehicle entrance. The key reader was at eye level, just to the left. He went up to it, swiped the card. Nothing. He tried it again, pushed the door again. Then he saw the hinges. It opened outwards. One more swipe and a tug. He was in.

He moved between the vast stainless-steel machines that by day could handle the four-hundred-plus bed sheets but were now silent. It was almost completely dark, just a pinprick of blue light: the master switch for the machines at the end of the row. He took out the mini-Maglite so it was ready in his hand. The smell of trichloroethylene went straight to the back of his throat. How did the poor fuckers who worked here put up with it? Probably they were illegals who'd got in hanging on to a cross-Channel truck. After a trip like that it didn't matter what the world smelt like. He reached the end of the row and paused, considering whether it was time to step out of the dry-suit.

A flurry of rustling said panic and flight. His first thought was rats. Then, in the pencil beam of the Maglite, he saw them: what little of the woman that was still dressed suggested she was either a waitress or a cleaner, the man harder to tell in just the wife-beater that clung to his heaving chest. There was no choice. The woman was about to scream, but the sound never made it. All that came out of her throat was a gush of blood. The guy got his in the forehead. The suppressed coughs of the pistol seemed to hang in the air as they dropped, still entwined, onto the heap of clothes beneath them.

He sighed, holstered the weapon, dropped the backpack, unzipped and stepped out of the dry-suit.

# 2

**03.30**

The hotel had a network of service passages so cleaners and maintenance staff could move throughout the building unnoticed: perfect. The suit, white shirt and black tie had the right anonymous security-operative look about it. He had a fake ID if anyone queried him. And if that didn't work there was always the Glock in its polymer belt holster. The bag was more of a giveaway.

Six months ago, he would have been on the guest list, a valued comrade, a loyal brother. But he had burned those boats. Two waiters came past bearing silver trays of glasses. They didn't give him a second look. Good. He moved on closer to the room where the reception was.

'All right, Fez?'

He wheeled round. How he hated that name. He'd been stuck with it since Helmand. Something to do with the shape of his hair. Protesting had only made it stick.

He nodded at Ballard, reached for the Glock. 'You lost?'

Ballard swayed a little on his feet. His blazer was flapping open, his tie loose. 'Story of my life.' He raised his hand, too late to stifle the belch that erupted from him. 'G'night?'

He had nothing against Ballard. They'd both done two tours in Afghanistan, both seen the same shit, had been discharged the same year and joined Invicta a year later, among the first to sign up. Both of them had been through the rehab programme, only Ballard had clearly lapsed. Perhaps Fez could talk his way past.

'Yeah.' He nodded, a hand reaching round the grip of his weapon. 'Good night.'

He tried not to infuse the words with deep irony. It was good that Ballard was too shitfaced to register any surprise at seeing him, as if it was quite natural that he would be there to join in the celebrations. Maybe Ballard had forgotten Fez's sudden exit from the organization. Maybe he could be spared.

Ballard leaned closer. 'So where'sa Gents?'

'You've taken a wrong turning. Back into the main hall and left.'

Ballard looked relieved. *Go on then, fuck off.* But he didn't. He leaned against the passage wall, frowning at Fez's suit. 'So – whya you here? Thought you'd packed it in?'

He shrugged. Maybe in Ballard's alcoholic haze he would accept that as some kind of answer.

Ballard frowned, trying to focus as he stepped away from the wall, his face just centimetres from Fez's. 'Here – you're banned. Shouldn' be here.'

Nothing for it. Fez slammed a flat left hand into Ballard's chest so he fell back towards the wall, leaving enough space between them for him to draw down the weapon in his right. Keeping his left high and out of the way of the shot, he pivoted the weapon as soon as it was free of the holster and fired.

Immediately he stepped back to ensure there was no blood on him as Ballard slid down the passage wall. Shit, what now? He looked up and down the corridor, got his bearings and, gripping Ballard by the armpits, pulled the lifeless body towards the door to a store room.

He had to move quickly now. A loud pumping beat of the sort of music he loathed thumped above the hubbub of partying revellers behind the swing doors. He put his head in and spoke to the nearest couple. 'The guv'nor still in there?'

'He was 'bout half an hour ago.'

'Thanks.' He moved on through the crowd. He saw a pair of bouncers standing sentry in identical suits, little coils running from their ears into their collars, their ISA ID armbands ungainly over their jackets. They looked ridiculous, bloated by steroids and too much muscle to be useful. More like a pair of bouncy castles. They were preoccupied with a group of pissed hoorays, who were arguing loudly. He steered away from them, deeper into the throng, a heaving mass of mostly young bodies, the same age as the ones he had just dropped downstairs. He felt his pulse step up a level. Two banners had been hung across the room. One said, 'Victory!' and the other 'Tomorrow Belongs to Us'. On the stage a youth with a ludicrously exaggerated blond quiff was crooning into a mic but his voice was inaudible. He saw one of the party officials and elbowed his way towards her. She was well pissed, gyrating drunkenly against her partner.

He nodded towards the stage. 'Where is he?'

She frowned. 'Who are you?'

*And who the fuck are you?* he felt like saying.

'Oh, yeah, right. Probably gone to get his head down, I should think.' She gestured upwards. 'Been on his feet the last two nights, poor man.'

Her partner pulled her back towards him. He thanked her with a curt nod, extricated himself from the crowd and headed in the direction of the lifts.

# 3

**03.50**

Ed lay on the bed, grinning up at the chandelier. He spread his arms and legs as if making a snow angel, feeling the luxurious sheets slide under his limbs. He'd never been in a five-star hotel before, never mind the presidential suite. It smelt of new carpets and fancy soap. He glanced at the wall of window to his left, the curtains undrawn. Across the Thames, somewhere on the north side, a column of fiery smoke funnelled up from a blazing building. The river was invisible, except for a row of lights on the opposite bank, the rest obscured by snowflakes floating down, tinged orange by the hotel lights.

He smirked. Christmas had come right in the middle of February. Jennifer was in the bathroom getting ready for what was left of the night. Although he'd had the bare minimum of sleep for the last three crazy days' campaigning, the election-day adrenalin, plus a cocktail of Pro Plus and Red Bull, kept him buzzing. He glanced at the massive muted TV, churning out election coverage, the umpteenth replay of Vernon Rolt's moment of glory, the new MP punching the air, then the all-too-familiar sound bite about making the streets of Britain safe again, cutting out the 'tumour of terror'.

Jennifer appeared from the bathroom gift-wrapped in a voluptuous hotel bathrobe, her blonde hair draped about her shoulders in damp snakes.

'How d'you like me in this?' She did a twirl so the robe fanned out around her.

He grinned. 'I'd like you better out of it.'

She rolled her eyes, her attention caught by the TV. The image had cut to a heaving throng of protesters in Birmingham, pushing through a cordon of police riot shields, petrol bombs arcing above, a news reporter ducking as one of the flaming missiles came his way.

Britain might be on fire, but right now Ed didn't give a shit. He snapped his fingers to get her attention. 'Hey, it's a compliment.' He pushed himself up onto one elbow. 'Jen, babe, I've been meaning to say . . .'

'What?'

'Could you put my shoes outside?'

She groaned, picked them up, opened the door and was about to chuck them out onto the landing when they heard the first muffled thud.

She dropped the shoes, shut the door abruptly and looked at him, alarmed.

He sank back onto the bed. 'Fireworks, probably. They're still celebrating downstairs.'

'*Inside* the hotel? Like, I don't think so.'

Jennifer wasn't giggling. That was a slight problem with her – a bit too serious. They'd met only three weeks ago in the queue of volunteers for Rolt's campaign. Having just lost another bar job and with fuck-all else to do, he'd thought it might be a laugh. That, plus doing his bit for the country, of course, making a stand against Muslim extremist nutters, putting them in their place – preferably back where they came from. He'd seen her in the line and couldn't take his eyes off her – she didn't seem to mind. When they'd got talking it turned out she was heading towards her university finals in politics and was on a mission to help right some wrongs. Her father, a cop just retired from the Met, had egged her on to support Rolt. 'Dad says he's our only hope,' she'd told him earnestly. He'd nodded vigorously. Next thing he knew they were paired up on the campaign trail. Bingo.

She'd agreed they would spend election night together, and he'd pulled off something of a coup by securing the suite that had been booked for Rolt, who hadn't even shown up at the victory party downstairs. Everything had come good, except now she was spoiling it by going all serious.

Jennifer stood close to the door, listening.

He beckoned her. 'C'mon, get over here.'

There were two more thuds, louder this time. She shuddered, gripped the lapels of the robe and bit her bottom lip as her eyes welled. He sighed as she wiped away tears. They had had their share of scares during the campaign and he had put on a show of chivalry, which he reckoned had only half convinced her.

'Maybe they're chucking furniture down into the atrium. Lock the door, come to bed and let the rumpus begin.' He raised his arms in her direction and put on a sinister James-Bond-baddie voice, which seemed to go with the surroundings. 'Come, my child.'

The lights snapped off and the TV screen faded to black.

Shit, he thought. This really isn't how it's supposed to go. He levered himself up from the bed and marched towards the door. He was about eight feet from it when the lock exploded, taking a chunk of the door with it, spraying them with splinters. Jennifer leaped towards him, gripping so hard her fingernails dug into his shoulder. There was something in the air, not a smell as such but as it hit his lungs he felt as if he'd inhaled nettles. His eyes burned and filled with tears. He whirled her round and pushed her towards the bathroom, falling on top of her as he lost his footing on the wet tiles. He kicked out wildly at the door and it slammed shut. He thought of getting up to lock it, then realized it would be ridiculous after what had just happened to the other door. They huddled in a corner of the shower, behind a partition no more than three feet high, clutching each other in the total darkness. Something sticky ran down the back of his hand, too thick and cold to be blood – they must have collided with a soap dispenser.

Fuck, fuck, fuck. This was for real. Rolt's people had always said, 'Be ready. Never drop your guard.' Any jihadi just back from Syria might be out there waiting for them. But the hotel was ringed with security: they should have been safe here. Rolt had many fans, but he wasn't short of enemies sending death threats. For all his claims that he wanted to protect the patriotic Muslims, he'd pretty much alienated the entire lot of them. Ed and the rest of Rolt's team had even been given some basic self-defence tips by one of the tough guys from the MP's organization, Invicta, a jab in the eye, a boot in the balls but neither applied here. Jennifer's grip tightened on him.

'Hey, loosen up,' he whispered. And then, uselessly, 'It's gonna be all right, okay?'

'No, it's not. We're going to die, Ed. They want to kill Rolt and they think we're him,' she said, through huge convulsive sobs.

He pressed a hand over her mouth and hugged her to him.

As he held her, he raised himself half an inch to peer over the partition. Through the crack between the bottom of the door and the floor tiles, he saw a light sweep past, then back across it.

'You want to get yourself beaten up? *Killed?*' That had been his mother's response to his signing up for Rolt's campaign. She always overreacted, always went for the negative. Now he wished he had listened, given the whole thing a wide berth. 'They'll come after you. You'll be a target. Is that what you want, to spend the rest of your life looking over your shoulder?'

The light under the door reappeared, static this time. He thought he could hear breathing. Then the door burst open with such force it smashed into a glass splashguard, which exploded into pieces over them.

The light was coming from a torch attached to something. He couldn't see what or who was holding it. Someone stepped into the room and Ed ducked, but his pathetic attempt to hide was rendered useless by Jennifer's whimpering.

He could see the shape of the gunman now, his profile

contorted by something – a face mask, sound coming from it like Darth Vader. He prised Jennifer off him and stood up. What drove him he didn't know: he was beyond scared, his pulse hammering in his temples, the taste of vomit in his mouth as he opened it to speak. 'You want Rolt? He's not here. Just us. We're nothing, just – we don't even officially work for him.'

His voice was hoarse. The saliva had vanished and his tongue felt like rubber.

The torch beam was now trained directly on him. The figure didn't move. Above Jennifer's whimpering he could hear hissing breaths coming from the mask. He could see more of the silhouette now, completely still, legs slightly apart. The torch was attached to something – a gun: a very big one. Ed thought of all the things he would promise to do in return for his life. All the clients he had ripped off whom he'd reimburse, all the teachers he'd apologize to . . . His life flashed before him – the fuck-all he'd achieved so far. If he could do one thing in the time left, like save Jennifer from this . . .

Behind the gunman, back in the bedroom, Ed thought he detected another movement. How many were there?

A tiny red dot danced above the gunman's left ear. Then there were two *thunk* sounds, plus the short, sharp, metallic grinding sound of a top slide moving, and the gunman dropped to the ground in a lifeless heap, the weapon clattering onto the tiles beside him. Jennifer screamed, a high-pitched distress signal shockingly amplified by the tiles, then dissolved into convulsive coughs. Ed squeezed her to him as his bowels trembled. Were they safe? Were they next?

A second figure stepped into the room, holding a dripping towel up to his face. Ed raised his hands, but the man didn't even look at him. All his attention was on the body twisted on the floor. He reached down, picked up the weapon and lifted the mask off the dead man's face. Despite the fear raging through him, Ed heard his own voice pipe up: 'Who is he?'

The man didn't answer, but shone a phone torch on the unmasked face. A pair of empty blue eyes stared straight up out of a pale pink freeze-framed face. Ed looked away. It was his first dead body, a massive crater where the man's left ear had been. He looked back to the shooter. 'So who are you?'

Tom Buckingham reached down and replaced the mask over the lifeless face. 'Nobody.'

# 4

**06.00**
**Piccadilly, Central London**

There had been no sleep for Tom, just a swift pit-stop for a shower and change of clothes. He adjusted his tie in the bathroom mirror and took a step back. *You look like shit.*

The whites of his eyes were still bloodshot from the CS gas. He knew the drill, used the hotel hair-drier to evaporate the irritant, but it would be a few hours before they calmed down. There would be a lot of cameras around today and he didn't want to stand out, but he also needed to be on maximum alert.

From somewhere overhead came the deep pulsing thuds of a police Eurocopter, hovering nearby. He had been looking forward to a spell of much needed R&R, a break from the grind of the months under cover, but last night's attack had nixed that. Fez Randall's face flashed in front of him, his shocked eyes staring heavenwards, his mouth frozen open in disbelief. Not an aggrieved suicidal jihadi, but a former soldier, like him, a member of Invicta, like him, a blue-eyed Brit, like him. Yes, there might have been a choice. Tom could have given him a warning, a chance to disarm, but he'd nothing to go on: no tip-off, no intelligence, no prior ID, no knowledge of where the man in the mask had come from, or how he had got past the heavy security round the hotel. For all Tom had known at the time, he might have been wearing a vest full of explosive. That was why it had had to be a head job, to stop the attacker even thinking of detonating. And since homemade or low-grade military explosive was both unstable and volatile, a high-velocity round entering a vest could very well have detonated it. And even if there had been no vest, he was about to brass up a pair of innocent civilians who just happened to be in the wrong place at the wrong time.

The one mistake Tom was still cursing himself for was lifting Randall's mask in front of the couple. The woman he didn't think would be a problem, but the mouthy boyfriend . . . He just had to hope that the Official Secrets Act would do its job and keep his gob shut.

What troubled Tom far more, though, was whether Randall had had help. Was this a one-off or part of something more? And what had been his motive? Questions that couldn't go unanswered. Meanwhile, a whole new chapter in the extra-ordinary political rise of Vernon Rolt was about to open, and who knew what that would lead to? His train of thought was hijacked by a rapid volley of thuds against the door.

'Stop wanking and get out of my bathroom.'

Tom opened the door to find Jez outside in a pair of unnecessarily ample boxers, absently clutching the contents. 'You're the one who'll be abusing yourself for the rest of your life unless you get some decent underwear.' Tom stepped out of the bathroom and into the narrow corridor.

Jez raised an eyebrow at him. 'Rough night?'

'Yeah.'

'Your man got in, then.'

Tom nodded.

Jez continued to gaze at him, evidently expecting more.

Tom obliged: 'A victory for common sense. He'll do what needs to be done.' He felt Jez's pitying gaze. If he'd guessed that Tom was under cover in Rolt's organization he'd had the decency not to mention it. Nonetheless Tom sensed that his parroting of the party line fell wide of the mark, an insult to their friendship. Not for the first time he wondered how much longer he could go on with this charade.

Right on cue, a volley of sirens erupted from a fleet of emergency vehicles rushing up Piccadilly. Jez sighed. 'Well, I suppose it can't get any worse.'

*Don't bank on it*, thought Tom. But he didn't say it. Instead he gave a half-hearted and decidedly noncommittal shrug, and caught a look of renewed curiosity on Jez's face. 'What?'

'What happens to Rolt's private army now?'

Invicta was supposedly just a support network for ex-servicemen struggling to come to terms with life outside the forces, so it was a good question, all the more so after last night's incident. But Jez couldn't know that. Tom gave another shrug. 'More of the same, I guess.'

'And what will it mean for you?'

'Dunno.' A lame answer. But he really didn't know.

Jez opened his mouth to continue, then shut it again. Tom knew what he was thinking: *I thought you had more sense than to fall for that prick Rolt and his sad band of brothers.*

They went way back, the two of them. After school, while Tom enlisted in the ranks, Jez had taken the high road: Sandhurst, then the Guards. Tom knew Jez always regarded his choice to forgo officer training as a two-fingers to all the privilege he had grown up with. But it was Tom who made it into the SAS, while Jez had chucked it in after three years, succumbing to the infinitely better wedge from a private security firm started by another of their mates.

'Weather's not letting up.'

It was a good line to fill an awkward silence.

'You'd think it would calm things down.'

'Yeah.'

The spare room in Jez's ridiculously well-located third-floor flat off Piccadilly had seemed like a good idea at the time. The view of some extremely well-appointed drainage pipes crawling up an airshaft at the back of Brown's Hotel left something to be desired, but it was five minutes from the tube, and a pleasant twenty-minute stroll across the park to Rolt's headquarters in St James's. But Tom couldn't help feeling he was starting to outstay his welcome. He knew that if he didn't want to fuck the job up – not to mention get himself killed – no one could know his real purpose inside Rolt's organization, and that included Jez, who was practically in the same business. His cover had to be one hundred per cent solid. But all the secrecy had taken its toll on their friendship. One day he might be able to come clean – but when?

Tom straightened his tie. Jez half closed the bathroom door, then opened it again. 'Mind your back out there.'

'Thanks.'

'And, well, if you fancy a change of scene, let me know.'

'Thanks, mate. I appreciate it.'

The bathroom door closed. He knew his friend meant well. Tom's sudden departure from the SAS had been a surprise to Jez, even more so his emergence at Invicta, by Vernon Rolt's side. He would have liked to be honest and tell him what he was really up to, but going under cover was just that: no one could know.

Another volley of sirens brought him back into focus: a new day and new trouble.

# 5

The walk to Rolt's office was usually Tom's favourite part of the
day, but this morning, as he crossed into Green Park, all it
offered was a stark reminder of what a tense and brittle place
London had become. The snow had smoothed them over, but
Tom could make out deep tyre tracks from what must have
been a hijacked HGV gouged into the grass. There was no sign
of the vehicle that had made them, but the row of saplings
planted just a few months ago lay broken, and beside the
southern entrance to the tube, the kiosk where he sometimes
bought a paper had been completely demolished. He strode on,
looking for something positive to focus on.

Although it was morning, the few cars still had their headlights on, streaking the road with puddles of light. Above,
gunmetal clouds hung low over the rooftops of Westminster,
threatening yet more snow. The last fall had quickly gained a
dull grey crust from the slush thrown up by the traffic, which
had then frozen. As he reached the Mall, he saw Buckingham
Palace, unlit, its occupants evacuated to Sandringham, a
measure of how low things had sunk. Where once a constant

stream of tourists had come to gawp, now all that stood in front of the gates were a couple of Army Land Rover Wolf TULs and a few guards milling about, their bearskins and red tunics swapped for Kevlar and live ammunition.

He crossed the road and slipped into St James's Park. There he saw the aftermath of another of the night's battles: overturned benches and a riot shield amid a pile of charred wood from what had been the tourist information booth. Despite this, the park still clung to its austere winter beauty, a monochrome scene of black, leafless trees on an expanse of grey snow. On the frozen lake, cans, bottles and takeaway cups rolled about, blown by a sharp Siberian wind that tugged at his coat. Towards the southern side of the park a tow-truck was winching an overturned police Land Rover back onto its wheels. Crowd-control barriers lay scattered about, as if a giant child had scooped them up and chucked them around. Already stretched to breaking point, and having been repeatedly warned off getting too tough, the police had been overwhelmed by angry and determined protesters.

Meanwhile the government had been torn between keeping order and not alienating potential voters while the election campaign was on. But all that was about to change – if Vernon Rolt got his way.

Outside the building, in addition to the usual police presence, there were several reinforcements in full riot gear, visors and body armour, plumes of vapour rising from their breath in the chill of the morning. They stiffened as he approached but one of the regulars waved him forward. In recognition of the need for heightened security, Tom reached for his pass and held it out, then opened his coat. They were only doing their job. He waited while the police officer passed her wand over him, taking a little longer than she needed to. She was blonde and petite under her stab vest and other kit. In the past he would have said something, but not today: the events of last night still cast their shadow over him.

She smiled. 'Nice threads.'

He smiled back, but that was all. Under the Hugo Boss suit

and freshly laundered Harvie & Hudson shirt he felt uneasy. Four hours ago he had shot a man dead. It had had to be done to stop two more getting killed, but why had Randall been there? What exactly was his beef with Rolt?

'Hey, Tom.'

He turned as he mounted the steps and saw the reporter, Helen something from *Newsday*, the paper that had done the most to put Rolt in power. He didn't know how she knew his name, but that was reporters for you, if they were any good at their job. He was in no mood for a conversation with anyone right now and especially not the press. He had seen her before, at events Rolt was speaking at, and had noted her genuine charm, as well as an appealing mane of darkish blonde hair, which, judging by her eyebrows, was real.

'Could you give us a couple of words?'

'Which ones?'

'How about "home secretary" for starters?'

He liked her directness and she had a perky, winning way about her that amused him. Rolt's appointment had yet to be formally announced. He gave her his poker face.

'Are you able to confirm?'

He knew that was the deal, the post Rolt had demanded in return for standing. He gave her a mock-indignant look. 'I couldn't possibly comment.'

She rolled her eyes. He always made a point of being civil to journalists. Rolt loathed every one of them, tore into them whenever they caught him off guard, saw them as the enemy, even those at *Newsday*, who wrote about him as if he was the Second Coming and had helped put him where he was today.

She wasn't giving up yet. 'How about a drink later?'

He stopped. By noon the announcement would have been made. Britain would have a new home secretary, a man with no previous political experience who, only months ago, had been dismissed as an extremist and a racist.

Rolt made no secret of what he perceived as Britain's self-inflicted impotence in the face of escalating Islamist terror. As tensions between the opposing communities boiled over and the country went to war with itself, Rolt's calls for what some denounced as nothing short of ethnic cleansing had started to win support. Suddenly, with an election looming, he was in demand, his inflammatory views finding favour with an increasingly scared public. No longer the outsider, he had found himself holding the balance of power, and when the governing party came calling he could dictate his terms.

'Or dinner?'

She gave him a look that implied more than that. The thought flitted across his mind that he badly needed a night off and some distraction. As he went towards the double doors she pressed her card into his hand.

The lights were off in the foyer: no receptionists in yet. Good – he'd have the place to himself for a while. But as he mounted the polished wooden stairs, two figures emerged out of the gloom and blocked his path, a pair of thick-necked bodyguards with matching black suits and blank faces. Tom had never seen them before. Had they been sent from Whitehall? They didn't look like government issue: too steroidal.

'Morning, gents.' He gave them a cheery grin and kept moving towards them.

One – he resembled a young Arnold Schwarzenegger – raised his hand. 'Please – you stop.'

A strange guttural accent: possibly Russian, but not quite.

This was Tom's place of work. He had every right to be there. He wasn't going to stop for anyone, even if they did ask nicely. He was about to barge through them when the door to Rolt's office at the end of the corridor opened and the pair immediately turned and set off towards the person who had just emerged.

It was too dark for Tom to make out anything more than a silhouette, a short, stocky figure, a man well into his sixties, judging by the stiff movements and stoop. Now Rolt was standing in the doorway. The silhouette turned and gave him a bear hug. Tom had never seen anyone hug Rolt – he wasn't the hugging kind. It was an awkward sight, not least because Rolt towered over his visitor.

The steroidal duo came alongside their man and the three stepped into the lift, which led straight down to the private garage beneath. Rolt watched them go, then went back into his office.

Tom reached the door, waited a few seconds, then entered without knocking. There was a smell that he had never encountered before in that room: tobacco. Rolt spun round, a look of complete shock on his face. He had on a three-piece Prince of Wales check suit, and a dark red silk handkerchief in the breast pocket that matched his tie. But his face was haggard.

'Sorry, am I interrupting?'

Rolt flushed. He didn't look at all pleased to see Tom, which was interesting. For a moment nothing came out of his mouth, as if his new outfit had constricted his breathing. Then his face sprang to life. He was beaming at Tom now, the same forced grin that he had produced on the campaign trail when he had been mobbed by an adoring public, with whom he never looked at ease. Even with the grin, his eyes still seemed narrowed by some lingering worry.

'No, no, you're just – very early.'

Tom beamed back as though he hadn't registered the awkwardness. He gestured at the door. 'One of your fan club?'

Fear flashed across Rolt's face again.

'I heard the lift.'

As Tom's words sank in, Rolt's face relaxed. He rolled his eyes. 'Yeah, just an old acquaintance from my business days. Looking forward to me getting to work, kicking some *ass*.' He mimed a kicking motion with his foot and laughed at his own feeble joke.

Tom's eye fell on a cigarette butt that had been dropped onto the floor, perilously close to one of Rolt's precious Persian rugs. Strange, since he was a fanatical anti-smoker.

Rolt followed his gaze. 'Fucking cleaners.'

He reached down, pinched the butt between thumb and forefinger nails and dropped it into the bin, then wiped his fingers on a tissue.

Another awkward silence. Tom rescued him from it. 'Well, congratulations, chief. You nailed it.'

Rolt never tired of compliments and Tom dished them out regularly, to keep the man sweet.

'Thank you. Yes, I think I rather did.'

Tom added one more for good measure: 'The Party would have been screwed without you. You totally saved their bacon.'

The awkwardness gone, Rolt nodded in acknowledgement, then put his head on one side. 'I rather thought you'd be having a lie-in.'

Tom felt a flash of contempt – Rolt had no idea what it was like to kill – but he didn't let it show. Instead he shook his head mock-mournfully. 'No rest for the wicked.'

It was a line his mother sometimes used, which had always irritated him, but seemed right for filling another discomforting hole in the conversation. But that was enough. Down to business. 'So, about last night.'

Rolt groaned like a teenager and glanced at his watch. 'God, do we have to?'

Tom fixed him with a look that said, yes, they did. 'It's all pretty much sorted. I called the Security Service first. They had the whole area sealed off before the Met arrived. The spooks' own team will have dealt with the body, and in your new position you'll be able to see to it that it's all swept under the carpet. The two who were in the room are being looked after. They've been told the consequences if they utter so much as one syllable. The girl didn't see the face and the boy's been read the Riot Act.'

Rolt was visibly relieved. 'Well, that should be an end to it. Good work.' He started to collect together some papers on his desk.

'Thanks. All the same, you'll need to figure out what to say, in case it gets out.'

Rolt glared. 'So what if it does? It just confirms everything I've been saying. We have to face up to the Islamist threat here in our streets, and we have to act now – and fast.'

He sounded like one of his own sound bites. Tom had guessed he would assume the obvious. He watched Rolt's face carefully as he set him straight. 'He was one of ours.'

'Who?'

'Fez Randall.'

He watched Rolt closely as he delivered the bombshell. The look, a mixture of disbelief and disgust, that spread over his face seemed like a lot of Rolt's expressions, manufactured rather than spontaneous. Had he known this was coming? Could he have known? 'For God's sake! The man was my driver only a few months ago.'

Tom kept his eyes on him. 'One of the original recruits, number five or six.'

'Who left abruptly three months ago. Packed it all in.'

'Why was that?'

Rolt shrugged. 'No idea.'

Now his face reddened with indignation. 'And after all I did for him! He was on his way to Hell in a bloody handcart when we picked him up. Would have dropped dead long ago either from drink or drugs if it wasn't for us. What was his problem?'

Tom wasn't surprised by his show of amazement and dismay. Since the day Rolt had received the call inviting him to stand for Parliament, it was as if he had forgotten all about the men on whom his reputation had been built. Sure, he'd done good work by ploughing his fortune into helping servicemen who had fallen foul of civilian life. Many of them owed their rehabilitation to him. But he always assumed they would repay their debt to him by standing with him shoulder to shoulder, no matter where that led.

'Always was a mouthy bastard. That's why I stopped him driving for me. Bad attitude. And he'd lapsed, you know – couldn't risk having him behind the wheel.'

That didn't fit with what Tom knew. Randall had a reputation for being a man of few words, who kept it all in. As for drink, Invicta had zero tolerance of alcohol. Rolt was passionately teetotal and key to the rehab programme was getting – and staying – dry. He would have to find out if

Randall had in fact slipped off the wagon. 'Was that why he left?'

'How should I know?'

What had made him so popular with those who he had helped was the structure he provided, an orderly routine around which they could rebuild themselves and take control of their lives outside the forces. In the past he had shown compassion only for those he thought of as 'his' men, many of whom had come to Invicta when they had reached rock bottom.

The most visible enemies Rolt had made were among Britain's Muslims, whom he had torn into indiscriminately, casting them all as the propagators of terror and death. And yet this would-be assassin had been one of his own, a previously dedicated Invicta member.

'Is there anything you can think of that might have given Randall cause? Maybe when he was your driver?'

Rolt looked away for less than a second, as if something had occurred to him, but he swiftly covered it with a show of indignation and glared at Tom. 'I said no.'

'Let me know if anything occurs to you.'

'Well, he's gone so there's nothing to worry about.'

Tom's expression showed he didn't agree.

'What?'

'He may not have acted alone. There may be more.'

Rolt sighed, as if he was already tiring of the subject. 'Aren't you being a bit melodramatic?'

Tom ignored the comment. 'And we have to be realistic about the details of his demise leaking out.'

'Well, don't worry about it. Not your problem.'

He was wrong. It was very much Tom's problem.

Rolt shook his head again, apparently still stung by Randall's disloyalty. 'Takes your breath away, doesn't it? I mean, why did I bother?'

Tom didn't respond. During his time inside Invicta he had found he understood far more about its members than Rolt – a non-soldier – ever would. Yet most of them regarded Rolt as their saviour and he in turn made a great show of compassion for them, though now Tom suspected it was just that – a show.

Rolt's uncompromising views about Muslims had been no secret, but his sudden shift into politics had taken everyone by surprise. The whirlwind election campaign meant he had neglected Invicta. But was that the extent of Randall's grievance? Had he and others felt abandoned for a while? Was that enough to make him want to kill?

Rolt gathered up the last few papers from his desk. 'Well, I'm disappointed, but what can you do? You extend the helping hand and . . .' His voice trailed away. There had been more than a hint of self-pity in it. But it was revealing that he didn't seem to care much that a once loyal associate had attempted to take his life.

Tom took a slightly different tack. 'You used to cast yourself as a bit of an outsider, like them. Randall probably wasn't expecting you to throw in your lot with one of the mainstream parties. Maybe he felt – left behind.'

Rolt was clearly mystified. 'But I can be so much more effective now, instead of shouting from the sidelines. Besides, we've got bigger problems, with the country imploding.'

'I know that, but he may not have seen it that way.'

Rolt had once confided in Tom that deep down he thought of his supporters as damaged goods, looking for an outlet for their bitterness about the wars they'd fought and the lack of recognition they had received. The idea that *he* might owe *them* anything for their loyalty had been obliterated by his overweening vanity and hubris.

'But even to *think* of such a thing! The man must have completely lost it. Must have been the drink.'

Tom couldn't help himself. 'Well, it wasn't an impulsive choice. He came prepared. As well as the gas and the Glock, there was a loop of wire in his pocket *and* a Bowie knife. So he was well and truly bombed up.'

Rolt was starting to look bored, the full reality of what Tom was saying just bouncing off him. Suddenly he beamed. 'You tell it straight, no matter how uncomfortable it is, Tom. I've always liked that in you. Now, to business.'

He wasn't about to let anything get in the way of his appointment with destiny.

Tom shrugged. 'Well, that's just the way I am.' And because he couldn't resist it, he added, 'Good job you *didn't* stay at the hotel.'

Rolt bit his lip – Tom's comment seemed to spark off another worrying thought. Then he shrugged. 'Well, at least he's out of the way. One less problem to worry about, thanks to you.' He grinned. 'Good work, man.'

It wasn't good at all. It was shit work, not that Rolt would ever understand that. Tom felt like decking him. The strain of all the months he'd spent working under cover inside this snake pit had started to wear him down. He had been hoping to get out, but Randall's actions had changed that. Which made him wonder if the Security Service would continue to spy on the man who was about to become its political master.

'At least I'm in a position now to see it'll never get into the news. Imagine the headline! *Veteran's Bid to Kill Home Secretary.*' He let out a short laugh. Then his brow furrowed. 'No one must know, Tom. Ever.'

*Yes, that would be unfortunate, wouldn't it?* Tom thought, remembering Helen from *Newsday*. He glanced at his watch. 'You're due at Number Ten in twenty minutes, *Home Secretary.*'

Tom watched as Rolt gazed round the room that had been his HQ for the last five years, then up at his treasured Turner above the fireplace. It was an awesome rendering of a volcanic eruption in dusty reds and oranges, the night sky lit up by lava. This morning it merely reminded Tom of the fires he had seen burning all over Britain.

'I guess this is it.' Rolt sounded wistful.

Surely he wasn't having a sliver of doubt about crossing the political Rubicon? For a moment Tom was propelled back to their schooldays and his very first encounter with the teenage Rolt, an awkward loner who always looked as if he'd strayed into enemy territory. Now the former outsider was inside. Perhaps it would civilize him, curb his more . . . irrational tendencies. After all, one of Britain's defining features had always been an ability to neutralize extremists. They got into government from time to time, but never made it to where they could do permanent harm. But this era was different: cracks in the fabric of society had yawned open. Rolt had been talked up as some kind of saviour, yet all he had done was widen those cracks even further with his inflammatory rhetoric.

Tom glanced at the clock above the fireplace. 'The car will be on its way.'

Rolt strode over to his desk, pulled his tablet case towards him and zipped it shut. He was clearly nervous. 'Sorry I can't take you with me to Number Ten.'

'This is your moment. It wouldn't be appropriate.'

He nodded. 'You're right.'

'In a matter of hours you'll have a whole new team.' Tom offered his hand.

Rolt took it and gripped it hard, perhaps to conjure up some of the steel he had shown on the campaign trail. 'Thanks for everything.'

*And thank you for fuck all.* Tom let go of Rolt's hand and gave him a farewell wave.

And with that Rolt swept out of the room.

Tom turned and stared out of the window at the grey-white expanse of the park. He had served his country in the most unlikely way as a spy on the man who, in a few minutes, would be anointed Her Majesty's Principal Secretary of State for the Home Department. Yesterday he had been starting to think about where Fate would take him next. Back to his ex, Delphine, in France? Or somewhere much further away from all this shit? A stint at home with his folks, whom he'd barely spoken to in three months? Or, and he had suppressed this idea from the moment it had surfaced, back to the SAS? But that possibility was so fraught with emotional turmoil that pride wouldn't even let him say the words silently in his head.

Rolt's elevation should have been the end of his assignment. The Security Service had recruited him to get as close as he could to the man. Now that he was effectively their political master, Tom would be spying on his own ultimate boss. Surely in such circumstances he couldn't go on.

But the assassination attempt had changed everything. Just as he should have been getting out, he was suddenly in much deeper. And who was Rolt's mystery visitor? His gaze had settled on the small burn mark by the rug. It wasn't the smell of any old tobacco he had noticed when he came in, it was intensely foreign. Who drops his cigarette butt on Rolt's expensive flooring on the morning of his installation as home secretary yet hugs him in farewell? After all those months of shadowing, listening, monitoring the man's every move, two mysteries had come at once.

He cast his eye over the desk, as he always did when their meetings ended, in case there was anything useful Rolt had left behind, but he had cleared it. The drawers, as usual, had been locked. But on a small table tucked behind the door, there was an oblong wooden case he hadn't seen before. It was inlaid with intricately carved veneers depicting highly stylized crossed swords. The hinges were equally ornate and looked gold-plated, or even solid gold. He turned it over – *Heron*, it said on the bottom – and carefully unlatched the lid.

Lying on a bed of quilted purple silk was a sabre, the scabbard leather-covered, with gold markings. He lifted it from the box and drew out the blade. He recognized it, a Tartar Ordynka, not an original but newly forged, high-carbon steel with what looked like a solid gold guard and pommel, the wooden grip covered with deep brown hide. It was impressive yet hideously kitsch. A dedication was engraved on the blade: *To Vernon, for the next battle. Your friend, Oleg.*

# 6

## 09.30 (07.30 GMT)
## Aleppo, northern Syria

The temperature hovered around zero but Jamal could feel the sweat trickling down from his armpits all the way to his waistband. He gripped the strap of his AK with both hands and tried to keep his breathing steady by counting: in – one, two, three, four; out – one, two, three, four. Something he remembered from choir practice in Croydon, but that seemed a very long time ago, and a very long way from where he was now.

The wind whipped his face and made his eyes water. Eight of them were crammed into the back of the Toyota Hilux, in two rows of four, facing each other. Another three pick-ups followed in the convoy as it bounced through the shattered suburb towards the square where the executions were to take place, lurching and snaking across the roads in a vain attempt to avoid the numerous craters. None of his 'brothers' exchanged eye contact, which was just as well for Jamal. They had been told nothing, just to grab their weapons and some rations, get into the trucks and off. But they all knew. The whole district knew. And soon, if Jamal didn't screw up, so would the whole world.

*Dearest sister Adila*, he had texted, *God willing I will see you very soon. I have found a way.* It was a risk but telling her had made it more real. He was going home. All he had to do was get through the next three hours, keep his side of the bargain. And if he was found out? He shut the thought out of his mind.

He looked ahead at the pancaked buildings sliding by on either side, as if trampled by an angry, vengeful god. The place was a wasteland now, and all for what? Stumps of trees along what had once been an elegant boulevard in an upmarket suburb, the boughs either blasted away or chopped down for fuel in the perishing winter. Jamal had thought England was bad in winter but he had never experienced it without gas or electricity.

The residents with any sense had left long ago, for Jordan, Lebanon or Turkey. Some lucky ones had gone to America and Canada. Those who had stayed were made fools of by their courage. He saw them on the sidewalks, a hint of their past affluence shown by a leather coat or some tattered high-end trainers. But mostly they had now become indistinguishable from those who had rushed in to occupy the vacant properties of others who had fled, families from the villages convinced that Paradise on earth awaited them in the empty suburbs cleansed of corruption. What would his father have done? Would he have stayed or gone? Jamal didn't know, because he barely knew his father.

The pick-up slowed and squeezed through the gap between a bus on its side and a van with crude armour cladding, wreckage from one of last night's skirmishes. A crowd was picking through the spilled cargo from the bus's roof rack – the cases and bags of some group trying to flee the city. A child let out a whoop and held up a baseball bat, only to have it snatched out of his hands by a bigger boy.

Jamal's father was very devout. Growing up had been a constant struggle, trying to reconcile the values of home with those of school and the outside world. His father had had such high expectations. 'You're his first-born,' was his mother's explanation. 'He wants you to be an example to the others.' Jamal had won some battles, like playing football for the school, which had meant going away with the team, once as far as Wigan. But there always followed a long interrogation, not about the match but what had happened on the trip, even who he'd sat with. His father was so easily disappointed, it had become his default mode. Jamal's good grades and glowing reports were only to be expected, as far as he was concerned. 'Always room for improvement,' was his usual comment. Staying out late or meeting girls was strictly forbidden. Jamal's friends ribbed him for being so obedient.

The atmosphere in the house had got more oppressive. His brothers had told him he was making it worse for them, but their father was not so hard on them. In his last year at school Jamal rebelled – went clubbing, got drunk, smoked weed and even partied with some girls. But he never truly enjoyed himself – it was all just a fuck-you gesture to his father. His sister pointed this out to him. Adila knew him so well. She urged him to be patient: soon he would be going to college. How he wished he had listened to her. But his patience had run out. Going to Syria had been a last resort, a dramatic gesture to prove what a good Muslim he could be, prepared to give his life to help other Muslims, in accordance with Allah's desires.

In the wing mirror he caught sight of their commander, Abukhan's black eyes staring back at him. He told himself not to look away just yet. Above all else, show no fear. Give nothing away of his intentions. But he had come to hate those eyes. Four months ago he had looked into them for courage, for certainty, for reassurance of the rightness of their cause. All he saw now was hatred. Abukhan, a soldier since childhood in Chechnya, claimed to have made his first kill when he was six. He had never known peace, had no concept of it. His war was for its own end, a never-ending battle waged against any available enemy. The commanders higher up the ISIS hierarchy respected his appetite for killing – they even deployed him against their own, to dispatch other leaders who had resisted the call to accept ISIS's authority, or to exact vengeance on any who had strayed from the group.

Jamal and the three others who had travelled with him from

Croydon had carried with them such conviction; they were liberators, come to save the people from their oppressors, to carry out the holy orders as defined by their teacher, Emil, who had arranged their passage. Emil, the self-appointed cheerleader for the Syrian rebel cause, who rarely strayed beyond the street in Croydon where his barber's shop was yet claimed to have links with jihadis from Kazakhstan to Nigeria. The man seemed ridiculous to him now, which was a measure of how much Jamal had changed. What he had seen in Syria went way beyond anything they had been led to expect. And today would be no exception.

As they neared the square, he saw the people who had gathered. Another detachment was already there, holding them back. He could hear a strange keening coming from the women. As the pick-up slowed, he scanned the crowd, his heart hammering so loudly he was sure it could be heard outside his body.

The vehicle lurched to a halt. As Abukhan stepped out of the cab the sound died away. The crowd fell silent and stared. With his black headdress and long black robe under his parka, he was unmistakable.

Abukhan turned to them and beckoned. 'Come.'

# 7

## Westminster, London

Tom spotted Phoebe slipping into her office. She shut the door behind her but he opened it and followed her in. She should have alerted him that Rolt had left the hotel last night. 'You're trying to avoid me.'

She sighed and shook her head. She looked knackered. 'I'm so sorry.'

'Sorry's not good enough.'

MI5 had put her into Rolt's office several months before Tom, and it was she who'd been instrumental in his recruitment. Things had worked well and they'd watched each other's backs. But when Rolt's election campaign had got going, and he had insisted on having her almost constantly at his side, her dedication and stamina were tested to the limit. Woolf, their Security Service handler, was delighted, but the strain of being constantly on duty was clearly taking its toll on her. She was worn out and there were now tiny lines around her eyes.

But Tom was in no mood for dishing out sympathy. He shut the door abruptly behind him. 'So what the fuck happened?'

She came up to him and put out a hand as if to place it on his chest. He folded his arms, forcing her to retract it. He had last seen them together at the celebration party at around two a.m., after Rolt had delivered a perfunctory thanks to his election team. 'He whisked me away before I had a chance to warn you. I'm so sorry.'

'For all I knew *he* was in that hotel room – and possibly *you*.'

She looked sheepish, the implication hanging in the air. She reached out to him as a drowning woman might to a rock. 'Please, Tom. It's got really difficult these last few days. He's hardly left me alone for a second.'

For all these months Tom had been the only one she could let down her guard with. They had made a good team and had thought they had every corner of Rolt's life covered. It had brought them closer but he knew better than to get involved with someone on the job. Not only had she been disappointed, it had left her all the more vulnerable to Rolt's persistent attentions.

'A text would have done the job.'

Her shoulders sagged and she looked as if she was about to crumple, as if all her training had deserted her. Of course she should have told him that Rolt had left, but maybe she genuinely hadn't had a chance. And she couldn't have known that two other people would take the opportunity to use his room.

'Come on, Tom, you know what it's like. A moment's suspicion on his part could put my cover in jeopardy. I have to minimize that risk.'

Something about this didn't convince him. He had warned Woolf but kept the pressure on her to shadow Rolt's every move. Woolf wanted to know about everyone Rolt spoke to and, during the election campaign, the names of everyone of significance beating a path to his door, and his celebrity status had mushroomed. As Rolt's role in the election had become decisive a steady stream of influentials had sought him out, either to be seen and photographed with him or privately to express support. She could barely keep up. And when Rolt started showing her even more attention, Woolf was thrilled: it proved how well her cover was working, and he urged her not to hold back. The implications were not pleasant, for either Phoebe or Tom.

'Rolt was adamant he didn't want anyone to see us leave. He was in a really weird, jumpy mood. How could I possibly have known some lunatic was going to break in and—' She pushed a tear away with an index finger, then let her hands fall to her sides. 'Okay. So I lost my phone.'

Woolf had issued them with encrypted phones. Losing one got you a big black mark. If she really had run out of reserves, it was time to throw her a lifeline. There was nothing to be gained from giving her a hard time. He took the hand she had let fall. She trembled, almost flinched.

'Probably it would still have played out the way it did. Either way, Randall would have to be dealt with.'

She looked so relieved it was almost pathetic. Some of the light came back into her eyes. 'So what did Rolt say?'

'About what?'

'Randall.'

'Just indignant that it was one of his own men. But he wasn't as freaked out as I'd expected. It was as if in his mind he'd already left Invicta behind.'

Phoebe frowned. 'It was the weirdest thing, but when the vote came through, he actually looked frightened.'

'What happened after you left the hotel?'

They heard someone coming up the stairs. He put a finger against her lips until the footsteps had passed.

'We went to his flat.' She swallowed hard. 'He said he needed to be away from all those people. I think it had only just hit him, what it's going to mean – after all those years of playing the outsider.'

'What did you talk about?'

She shrugged. 'We hardly said anything. He kept checking his phone as if he was waiting for a message. Then he was on a call for quite a while in the next room.'

'Who to?'

She gave him a blank look.

'You don't know?'

'People in the Party, piling in to congratulate him.'

All her answers were vague. If fatigue had got the better of her, it would start to be a problem.

'And after that?'

'Why the interrogation? Just back off a bit, will you?' She looked away, her face reddening. She fumbled in her bag, pulled out a packet of cigarettes and lit one, even though it was strictly *verboten* – a small gesture of defiance.

'There are some things you don't *have* to do for your country, you know.'

She gave him a withering look, but he knew he had touched a nerve. She briefly gathered herself. 'You forget I've been trained for this.'

It was true: she was a professional spook – unlike him. But it was one thing to be a mole inside Invicta, and another altogether to have to stand beside Rolt in the full media glare as he transformed himself into a politician, who thought he needed a woman at his side. Was she being groomed for a bigger role in his personal life?

Her expression softened. 'I'm sorry, I know I haven't had to kill anyone or – anything, but it's been very difficult.'

He gave her a brotherly hug, and felt the fragility of her body against his as she lingered for a moment. 'Well, with a bit of luck you'll be out of it any day now.'

'Woolf hasn't said anything to me.' Her tone changed again. 'Anyway, never mind me. You must be feeling terrible, after what you went through.'

'Well, it's what *I'm* trained for, remember?'

She smiled, despite herself. But he hadn't finished. 'So, you stayed?'

She nodded. 'When I woke up he was gone. It must have been about seven.'

Tom folded his arms and perched on the edge of the desk. 'He was here when I arrived, about half past. And he'd already had a meeting.'

'That's early. Who with?'

He described the encounter in detail, including the cigarette burn, the farewell hug and the absurdly opulent gift with its mysterious note.

Phoebe blinked.

'Mean anything to you?'

She shook her head.

'Well, go through all the databases. See if an Oleg comes up. Go right back into his past.'

'Maybe that's all he was, some past business associate.' She sat down and pulled off her boots. The melted snow had formed two small puddles around them. 'You know how Russian oligarchs love to cosy up to the establishment, get passports for their families, their kids into Eton and so on. And now he's one of the in-crowd . . .'

'This one's probably not Russian – the gift suggests he's a Tartar from the Crimea.'

'Whatever.' She ground the remains of her cigarette into the side of a waste bin. When Tom had first encountered her she was the most dogged operator, with a ready answer for every question, desperate to make her mark. What a difference a few months had made.

'How come he's not shown up on our radar before? Woolf will want to be all over this when we tell him.'

Her face was now a mixture of exhaustion and dread. He would recommend to Woolf that he pull her out ASAP, before she became a liability.

'Look, he's about to inherit a whole new team in the Home Office. When he gets stuck into the job he'll probably forget all about you and the heat will be off.' Tom didn't believe for a second it would be that simple. In the last couple of weeks he had observed Rolt paying her more and more attention. He wasn't about to let her just melt away, not a man like him who was used to getting what he wanted. But Tom wasn't about to add to her woes by pointing that out.

'And with a bit of luck you can get on with your life.' She reached up and stroked one of his lapels. He squeezed her hand and took a step towards the door. She gave him a despairing look. 'I'm sorry I fucked up.'

'There is one more thing you can do. The sabre – there's no manufacturer's mark on the thing itself, but the name on the box is "Heron". Find out what that is and maybe it'll lead us to who sent it.'

# 8

**10.30 local time**
**Aleppo**

The sun had reached its mid-morning point, a weak winter sun that shone a cold, hard light on the proceedings. In front of the shattered remains of their school the girls were lined up, eighteen of them, hands bound behind them, either squatting or kneeling amid the rubble, covered from head to foot in black burkas. From a distance they resembled giant crows. The building had been destroyed months ago, the teachers all executed. But some of the girls had been discovered meeting in secret to study. Now it was their turn.

At least he couldn't see their faces yet. *Let me not see their faces, dear God.* But he knew he would have to soon. Abukhan, the commander, strode up and down in front of the girls, machete in hand, the skirt of his long black robe flapping in the wind. This was not by a long way the first beheading Jamal had been ordered to attend. Abukhan had required it as part of their training, a rite of passage to harden them until it became routine instead of extreme. He had taught them to fight with machetes, their training filmed for recruitment videos. The flashing blades were supposed to look more physical and appealing, even if day-to-day combat was with AKs and RPGs. When it was played back to them Jamal had been shocked to see himself in action, wielding the blade, shrieking and roaring as they were urged to do. That was the first time he realized, *This is not me.*

In spite of that, he had done well, the best of the British boys. Every new boy was made to carry out a beheading. They had all had to watch as poor Ziad, one of the four-strong Croydon crew Jamal had travelled with, tears streaming down his face, bore down on the neck of a shackled deserter, the knife shaking violently in his hand as Abukhan barked orders. Jamal had imagined it was done with a heavy machete, one blow and over, like in a movie. Quick, much like chopping wood. It was nothing like that. The blade was long and serrated, like a kitchen knife, and the process dreadful and unending. First the parting of the flesh, then sawing through gristle, then finding the place between the vertebrae – laborious work for the uninitiated – the blood oozing at first, then spouting in an arc as the carotid artery was severed. There was so much of it that poor Ziad had been drenched in it from the waist up.

Without moving his head Jamal glanced left, observing his comrades, in their identical Multicam parkas, their gaze dutifully fixed straight ahead, dead eyes that had witnessed several lifetimes' worth of terror in five short months. Knowing what was coming should have helped them prepare, but this was different. This was on a scale they hadn't seen before, and never before done to girls who might have been the same age as his own dear sister Adila, to be slain by their fathers.

He touched the space above his left ear and felt the lens, no bigger than the one in a phone camera, and noticed the cable to the recorder tense slightly under his headgear as he turned slowly towards the assembled audience. They were all males, men and boys as young as eight: fathers, sons, brothers, cousins, all forced here on the pretext of witnessing justice being done, allegedly in the name of Allah, but in reality to be left in no doubt that Abukhan's rule of terror in this district was now absolute, and that any disobedience would be met with the same penalty, keeping prisoners having been deemed a waste of precious resources.

In front of the gathering Abukhan paced up and down, blade in hand, addressing them in a low voice about the curse the girls had cast upon them, on their families, on the community, and how Allah was angry with them and demanded justice. Occasionally he looked at Jamal and the others, to check that they were being attentive. Once Jamal would willingly have taken a bullet for him, gladly given up his life. Not any more.

He turned his gaze back to the girls. *Face exactly where you want the lens to point, fix your eyes so they're looking straight ahead and only move your head when you want the camera to move. If you need to look down for some reason, keep your head up. Always think about where the lens is pointing.* Those were Emma's instructions, the video in exchange for his escape. *And, above all, when it happens, don't look away.* She was a journalist, interested only in the truth. He admired her calm, fearless focus; he wouldn't let her down. *You'll be a hero for this,* she had promised him. *Your family will be proud.*

They had met five months ago. He had just crossed into Syria driving an aid truck and had pulled over to wait for the rest of the convoy. Emma Warner had strode up, opened the door of the cab and got in.

'What you doing?'

'I can pay for a tank of diesel,' she said.

He didn't want her on board, didn't feel comfortable with a woman in the cab, but they were already short of cash and the Kurdish guide seemed okay with it. She was small, in her late twenties, olive-skinned with jet-black hair, and dressed like a local in a hijab, with a loose, long-sleeved, ankle-length dress. She seemed to blend right in among all the Kurds and Syrians. She spoke to the guide in Kurdish and to the others in Arabic, but when she addressed Jamal her English was posh, like a news reader's.

When she looked at him, he felt she could see right through him, as if she was saying, *You've never been here, have you? You don't know what you're letting yourself in for.* And she was right: he didn't.

Sixty kilometres inside Syria, they had a flat. He got the wheel off but there was no spare. The other trucks in the convoy wouldn't wait as it was already dark so the Kurdish guide went off with the wheel, hitching a ride on a pick-up going back towards the border.

While they waited she fired questions at him, to which he just shrugged.

'Okay, if you won't talk to me, how about we have sex?'

He blushed deeply. He was a virgin.

'Sorry if I've embarrassed you,' she said, 'but in this place you've got to take what you can when you can because tomorrow . . .'

She made a faint 'pkkh' sound and an exploding gesture with her hands.

He was relieved when they dropped her off in Ar-Raqqah, because she was starting to sap his resolve. 'Thanks for the ride,' she said, as she got down. 'Nice knowing you. Try not to die too soon.'

He watched her melt into the dawn crowd. He had never met a woman like her before – but, then, he hadn't met many women at all.

The second time was yesterday, right here in Aleppo. She was unrecognizable in a burka and *niqab* and he wouldn't have spotted her at all, except that her eyes locked on his – just for a second, but that was enough. Women here kept their eyes averted from men, and fighters especially, for fear of getting hit or arrested, so even that fleeting glance was a surprise. He was at a stall, buying water and cigarettes with two others from his platoon, his AK dangling from its leather strap.

She came towards him, eyes lowered now, and as she passed she brushed him with her elbow. Why? To show that she wasn't afraid? Was she mad? To be in this quarter of Aleppo, with all that was happening? She should have known he could order her to stop, then take her straight to the commander and certain death. Did she trust him not to? He turned away from his comrades to light a cigarette and watched her. After a hundred metres she glanced round to see if he was looking. He made an excuse to the others and followed her, keeping his distance. After they had gone a couple of hundred metres he realized she was heading too close to where the brothers were billeted. There were few people on the streets and it was unusual for a woman to be walking alone. She stuck out. He speeded up and went past her.

'You follow,' he whispered. Keeping a good distance in front, he led her several blocks to a deserted shoe shop and into the back room where they could be alone and not seen. As soon as they were inside he turned on her, furious.

'You're crazy. How did you know I wouldn't arrest you?' He pointed at his armband. 'Or worse.'

He could see only her eyes above the *niqab* but could tell she was grinning.

'I took a chance. I remembered you were a nice boy. Besides, I didn't ask you to follow me.'

She unpinned the *niqab*. Her face was thinner than before, which made her blazing eyes seem all the larger. She peered at him. 'You look tired, Jamal. Had enough of the killing yet?'

He looked away, his face heating up.

She kept her gaze on him, her expression grim. 'Is it true about those girls?'

He had already crossed one line and was about to cross another. He nodded. 'Tomorrow.'

'Are you part of it?'

'We've been ordered to watch. Everyone has.'

He felt her peering at him, through him, just as before. She could see exactly what he was thinking, knew that he wanted out.

'Help me get inside. I want to see it for myself.'

'That's impossible. There's no women allowed.'

'You're willing to watch those girls die and for no one outside here to know the truth?'

He didn't answer. She started to take off the burka.

'What are you doing?'

She grinned. 'The burka is the journalist's friend. You can hide all kinds of shit under here.'

From a small goatskin bag she produced the device, no bigger than a packet of cigarettes, with a coil of transparent cable that widened slightly at the end.

'See this?' She showed him the end of the cable. 'There's a lens in there.' She held up the body of the camera. 'It can record up to two hours. Here – take it.'

He stepped back. All videoing of beheadings was forbidden now. It deterred recruits. He could turn her over to Abukhan. She must know that.

But her eyes were insistent. 'Do this for me and I'll get you out. There's a driver with the Red Crescent. He knows a way to the border that avoids all the patrols. Yes or no? It could save your life.'

Or be the end of it, he thought. He shrugged, then nodded. She embraced him. 'When you get home you'll be a hero.'

Now there was complete silence except for the wind. None of the men spoke. The girls were all still, except for their trembling. Jamal was ready. He would not flinch, he would not look away, because Emma's camera was his way out of this hell. All he had to do now was wait, how long he didn't know, because Abukhan liked to draw out these proceedings and maximize the agony.

Holding the machete in front of him, Abukhan approached the gathering of men, elders of the community, parents. Two of the platoon who were positioned nearest raised their AKs in their direction. Abukhan approached one with a long grey beard, held out the machete. At first the old man shrank back but the others either side held him and pushed him forward. There was no choice. He took the machete, which shook violently in his grip. Jamal's heart was pounding so hard he was sure the others would hear it, but he kept his gaze fixed on the old man as he was led to the first of the girls.

Abukhan reached down and pulled roughly at her veil until her head was exposed. The girl's face was wet with tears, her mouth open as if emitting a silent scream. She looked no more than fifteen. Jamal's whole body was shaking with a mixture of rage and fear but he tensed himself to focus on what he had to do. The old man seemed to stumble. Abukhan gripped him and at the same time kicked the girl so she sank to the ground, then he held her there under his boot as he signalled to the old man to lift the blade. Jamal closed his eyes as it fell.

# 9

## 09.00
## Home Office, Marsham Street, Westminster

Sarah Garvey sat at her desk, eking out her last few hours in the job she loved. She was exhausted. After leaving her Surrey constituency, where she had scraped back in with a reduced majority, but a majority nonetheless, and having thanked her team for all their efforts, she had sped back to Whitehall with a blue-light escort to deal with the last pressing matters of state.

She had hoped the big freeze that had settled over the country would dampen the unrest. Not a bit of it. She glanced down the long list of level-four incidents, the ones deemed grave enough for the home secretary to be briefed on: twenty-eight in just one night. There had been a time when just one level-four had prompted a COBRA meeting. Not any more. She tossed the dossier back into the in-tray and smiled grimly. Good luck with that, *Vernon Rolt.*

Much more interesting to her was the MI5 report on the latest wave of British Muslims to have returned from Syria and Iraq, who were now incarcerated in various jails around the country. As far as most of the press and many of her colleagues were concerned, the best thing for them was to bang them up and throw away the key. She wasn't so sure. Some of those men had come home with a very different view of jihad; several had potentially good intelligence – if they could be debriefed before it went stale. She weighed the report in her hand. It wasn't supposed to leave the office. She dropped it into her bag.

Juliet, her PA, put her head round the door. 'Is there anything I can do?'

'Yes, fuck off!' She pulled off her glasses and rubbed her face. She'd noticed lately that it was taking longer to spring back into position. She sighed. 'Sorry.'

Juliet was well used to her boss's outbursts, which were usually rapidly followed by an apology. 'I completely understand, ma'am. We're all gutted.'

'Not as gutted as I am, I assure you. Just leave me in peace for a bit, while I clear up this last bit of sick.'

'The MI5 DG is on his way over.'

'To pay his last respects, I assume.' She pulled open a drawer and found a mirror. 'Yup, rigor mortis has set in.'

Her previously dark brown hair had greyed faster in the last two months than even she had thought possible. *That's all I've got to show for it*, she thought. *Witch hair and bags under my eyes the size of bloody holdalls.*

'And Henry wants to pop in.'

Garvey growled. He was her insubordinate but annoyingly capable intern, a constant thorn in her side. 'Well, tell him he can *definitely* fuck off.'

Juliet quietly closed the door.

As soon as she had heard that Rolt was being parachuted into a safe seat, she'd known she was for the chop. He had made it a condition of his standing for Parliament that if he got in he'd have her job, not that the prime minister had had the guts to warn her. He had left the Westminster rumour mill to do it for him. The irony was that, without Rolt on board, they would now have been in opposition. Part of her would actually have preferred that: she hated compromise. In fact, it was a wonder she had got this far – she was so stubborn. Of course, if she were a man she'd have been called 'determined'. When she confronted him about it, the PM was, as always, grovellingly profuse in his apologies. Watching him squirm was only minor compensation.

'You know, Sarah, that I've always held you in the highest regard,' he had told her, to which she couldn't resist answering, 'And you know, Geoff, that I've always found you much too slippery to hold at all.'

He had laughed politely, as he always did at her jibes, no matter how accurate they were. Laughter was his 'iron dome', the protective shield with which he deflected many an incoming barb. She knew that underneath the glibness he respected her honesty, even if he couldn't begin to match it.

'Compromise is the lubricant of government,' he liked to remind everyone around him, as if this was justification for weakness and vacillation.

Garvey eyed the whisky decanter, then the clock, then the decanter again. Nine forty-five: too early? She took a deep breath and turned back to the papers on her desk, but they were a blur. She considered her legacy. In the four years she had been in this chair, the country had nearly torn itself apart, polarized by Islamist terror and extreme-right-wing reprisals. And now the man who some believed had fanned the flames of the conflagration was about to take her place. She laughed to herself. The hardest part of the job? Realizing how little real power came with it.

Her gaze swerved back to the decanter. Maybe . . . But then came a familiar soft knock on the door. She sighed. 'All right, Henry, if you must.'

He entered, glided across the room, slid into the chair on her left and flipped open his iPad. He seemed especially animated that morning and she knew why. 'You're looking very smart today. Is that a new suit?'

He flushed. She always found something to needle him about.

'So what's the big occasion?' She gazed at him questioningly. They had never bonded. She had sensed quite early on that he didn't like women much, and she wasn't too keen on spoiled rich boys, gay or straight. He had made no secret of the fact that he was looking forward to having a man about the office.

'You've seen the footage?'

'What footage?'

He pursed his lips. 'I emailed you the link.'

She hadn't seen any footage. She had a habit of deleting Henry's numerous emails unopened. His lack of a social life meant he was horribly well up on the minutiae of events.

He prodded and swiped the iPad, waiting for it to boot up. 'I must warn you, it's pretty hardcore.'

She snorted. Patronizing little shit.

Being home secretary had given her brass balls. Nothing fazed her now. He should have known better but he was a recent arrival, foisted on her by Number Ten as a favour to his father, a party donor. His sense of entitlement infuriated her, but not as much as his apparently inexhaustible appetite for hard work, which made it harder for her to persecute him.

'I have to say, I've never seen anything like this in all my—'

She cut him off. 'In all your nine months in Whitehall.' It was probably longer but not by much. 'Well, let's get on with it. Where are we, exactly?'

'Chapeltown. It's in Leeds.'

'Ah, the Ripper's old stamping ground.'

Henry frowned. 'I thought that was Whitechapel.'

'The *Yorkshire* Ripper.'

The footage was shot from several storeys up. A shaven-headed white man, heavily tattooed and wearing only a T-shirt and underpants, was being manhandled by a group of men with dark hair and long robes, chanting.

'What are they saying?'

'There's a lot of *"Allahu Akhbar"* and "Death to the *kuffar"*, and the occasional "Kill the cunt" for a little local colour.'

'And do they?'

'What?'

'Kill him?'

Henry twisted his mouth slightly, as if chewing something unpleasant. 'He's in ICU at Leeds Infirmary. He's not expected to live. Practically the whole of Yorkshire's in lockdown in anticipation.'

'And why am I looking at this?'

'I thought you'd like to issue a condemnation. As part of your valedictory message . . .'

There was something loathsome about his righteous disapproval that irritated her profoundly, even when they weren't in disagreement. If the last months of public disorder had taught her anything, it was that the moral high ground became harder to defend as it shrank under them. He waited for the video to boot up, then passed it across.

'What provoked it?'

'He was accused of firebombing a *madrasah*, but there's no hard evidence.'

Fuck it. She snapped the iPad shut and pushed it back at him. 'Give it to your new boss as a welcome gift. I'm sure it's much more up his street. In fact, tell him it's my leaving present to him, thanking him for all he's done to make this country such a shit place to be anything but a white male . . . Never mind.' She felt her pulse throbbing again in her temple. The consultant had given her repeated warnings about her blood pressure and she had forgotten to pick up her beta-blockers. She breathed out heavily and leaned back in her chair. 'Anything else?'

'Another letter from your friend Adila.' He held it in the air between thumb and forefinger as if it was a soiled nappy. His weary tone made her want to reach across and poke his eyes out. She snatched it from him. It had been opened – no doubt he had already digested its contents.

*Dear Right Honourable Member Ms Garvey.*

It was probably the eighth or ninth communication she had received from her. There was something poignantly charming about an actual letter, on paper, written by a teenager in the twenty-first century. In the sea of misery that was currently her working life, Adila's thoughtful letters were a small but welcome ray of light.

*Please may I say that this is a sad day for me knowing that you are no longer to be our home secretary but I will hope that you may continue to show us the same wonderful attention that you have as our MP.*

Garvey clamped her lips together hard and told herself at all costs not to let so much as one millilitre of a tear appear in her eyes in front of Henry.

*I know you will have many important things to concern yourself with today and I want to thank you again for all the interest you have taken in the plight of Jamal.*

They hadn't even met. All Garvey had done was reply to her by text – as Adila had requested, terrified that her parents might discover their communications about her brother.

*I bring some good news of Jamal, in that he has sent an anonymous text saying that he is expecting to find a way to return home very soon. I do so hope, Ms Garvey, that you are able in some way to assist his passage should he encounter difficulties.*

Henry had been quick to point out that Adila's choice of language suggested the guiding hand of an adult, and had dismissed the letters early on as a con. Garvey wasn't so sure. As a very bright teenager herself, she remembered suspicious teachers accusing her of getting too much help from her parents. And Adila's father had already gone on record, denouncing his son to their local paper and vowing that if he ever came home he would turn him straight over to the authorities. The current strife had split families, workplaces, schools, even hospitals down the middle, opening up hideous divisions where there had been tolerance and unity. God, if only she knew – no, better she didn't know – what forces were ranged against her brother getting any humane treatment if he ever made it out of Syria alive and back to Britain.

*I am very sorry that I don't have more details and apologize again for*

*taking up your time, but remain truly thankful for all the consider-*
*ation you have shown so far. In closing, may I also say that I have just*
*heard that I have a place at medical school and look forward very*
*much to one day serving the country that has done so much for my*
*family. Yours respectfully.*

She read it through a second time, then carefully returned it
to its envelope. Henry was looking at her knowingly. He had
made no secret of his views about those who had gone to fight
in Syria.

'Something else I should pass on . . . ?'

The implication that a jihadi's sister must be his accomplice
hung in the air. Garvey knew it pained him that she had not
passed on Adila's details to the Security Service. She glared at
him and held on to it.

'The girl's my constituent. I'll have more time to look after
her now.' She gave him a chilly smile. She didn't know what if
anything she could do to help. For all she knew, Jamal might be
just another deranged zealot bent on self-destruction. She had
already locked horns with Halford, the Met commissioner, over
the treatment of returnees. No doubt he, too, was toasting her
departure this morning.

'Would you draft a letter to the chief of Border Security asking
him to notify me if the boy shows up?'

'I really rather think—'

'I don't need you to "really rather think", Henry.' A week ago
he wouldn't have questioned it. Already she could feel the
power slipping out of her grip. She leaned across the desk.
'Listen very carefully. You will go out there now and draft a
letter, bring it in for me to sign and have it dispatched by bike.
That's an order, even if it is the last one you'll get from me. And
if it's not done in five minutes I shall have you up in front of HR
for insubordination.'

She glared at him to press the point home. He stiffened, then
got to his feet, but still looked perturbed. Another thing she
wouldn't miss about the job: dealing with a generation that
wasn't used to being told what to do. How would they ever

manage to defend the country in future, these brats who thought the world owed them a living? Maybe bringing back national service wasn't such an extreme solution after all. She checked herself. *Jesus. I wasn't entirely joking.*

She gave him another ball-shrivelling look. He made for the door, and turned just as he reached it. 'There's, ah, a briefing over at Millbank I need to attend, if that's okay?'

Rolt had already scheduled a press conference after his anointing at Number Ten. She knew that because he had asked for all key staff to be present. 'After you've done the letter, you can skip right along and see your new idol in action.'

He blushed and looked down. He had been stupid enough to let slip his support for Rolt on Facebook and even more stupid to imagine that it wouldn't get back to her.

There was a loud guffaw from the outer office. Henry held the door as Stephen Mandler, the director general of the Security Service and one of the very few who might regret her departure, swept in. He bowed with an ironic flourish. 'Home Secretary.'

'For about another forty minutes. To what do I owe this unalloyed pleasure?'

He closed the doors carefully behind him, came up to the desk and took the seat Henry had just vacated. 'Something's come up which I think you may want to deal with – personally.' He sounded uncharacteristically weary, even troubled.

'Can't it wait for my esteemed successor? I'm sure he's keen to get his feet under the desk.'

'I don't think so. It concerns our friend Buckingham. It seems he shot someone.'

# 10

Garvey poured a generous measure into two tumblers.

'Really, Sarah, it is rather early.'

Mandler tried to keep his hands by his sides, to no avail. She thrust the tumbler at him so he had no choice but to take it. 'Shut up and drink. You can have one of those after.' She nodded at the tube of Trebor Extra Strong Mints she relied on for these occasions, then clinked her glass clumsily with his.

'So what shall we drink to?'

Garvey snorted. 'My imminent demise.'

Mandler sighed mournfully and took a surprisingly large gulp.

They had been a good team, if an unlikely one. His cerebral airs should have got right up her nose, but his appetite for mischief was a great redeeming feature. And he had been a quiet but staunch ally in the psychological warfare she had conducted with her adversaries in the Met, frequently slipping her titbits of intelligence to wrongfoot them. Best of all, they had conspired together to spy on Vernon Rolt, putting their man Buckingham in place right at his side – a surveillance triumph, though where it had ultimately got her, or the country, was hard to say. Rolt was in and she was out.

'I bet they're breaking open the champagne at Scotland Yard.'

'They do rather think Christmas is coming.'

'Water cannon, rubber bullets . . .'

'An HK36 on board every blue light.'

It was a mirthless exchange that rapidly petered out.

'So what about Buckingham?'

Mandler shifted in his seat. 'It seems he dispatched an armed intruder who found his way into Rolt's suite at the Ice Palace.'

She glared at him. 'Dispatched him with what, exactly?' Mandler's people weren't supposed to be armed.

'I've not been informed yet as to the specifics. Presumably he was carrying with Rolt's blessing as his *de facto* minder. Interestingly, Rolt himself wasn't there. Two of his election team had managed to get into his suite, evidently for . . . romantic purposes. The shooter had them cornered in the bathroom when Buckingham dropped him. It was pretty chaotic. The intruder had killed three others on his way in and fired off CS. Buckingham probably prevented what could have turned into a bloodbath.'

They allowed a few seconds' respectful silence for the innocent dead. Then Garvey shook her head. 'Shame.'

She knew Mandler would read her thoughts. 'Yes. If only Rolt had been tucked up in bed, as he should have been, it could all have been so different.'

There was another silence as Garvey reflected bitterly on how close she might have come to keeping her position.

'So if any of it gets out, Buckingham was just doing his job as Rolt's muscle. If anything, it reinforces his cover.'

Garvey took another sip of Scotch. 'So why are we even talking about this?'

'Well, here's the thing.'

Garvey noted the gleam in Mandler's eye that often appeared when he was about to impart something secret.

'You haven't asked me who the assailant was.'

'I assume one of our aggrieved Islamist zealots. No?'

Mandler's eyes sparkled with an almost childlike glee. She

63

liked that: even after all these years, the thrill of the great game hadn't left him. 'One of Rolt's own people, and one of the very first to join Invicta.'

Garvey absorbed this information slowly. 'How very intriguing. And was he acting alone?'

'He certainly must have had help getting in. Buckingham found a hotel security key card on him that had been made out in his name. And he definitely wasn't on the guest list for the party. Someone on the inside would seem to have arranged his entry.'

Garvey's eyes narrowed. She let out a low guttural chuckle. 'So Rolt will want *that* covered up. *Home Secretary's Loyal Lieutenant in Assassination Bid* isn't the sort of headline you want on day one, is it?'

Mandler smirked. 'You wish.'

She sighed. 'Well, I'm sure that particular nugget will come in handy – at some point.'

Then she frowned. 'But *why* would one of his own turn on him?'

'The way Buckingham sees it – and he should know – is that a good part of Invicta's original USP was Rolt's outlaw image, the man who stood apart, saying the unsayable. It's not so much that he's gone mainstream as that the mainstream's come to him. But that doesn't stop some of the old guard at Invicta feeling that in joining the government he's sold out. So we may have to brace ourselves for more.'

Garvey snorted. 'It doesn't take a bloody genius to see that he's responsible for whipping up a good part of all this aggro, talking about sending people "back where they came from". His proposals should be warming the hearts of his followers – ethnic cleansing, *de-Islamification*.' She spat the words with contempt.

Mandler wagged a finger. 'Yes, but it's more personal than that. Those chaps who came out of the services onto the streets, he gave them to believe they were all outsiders together. They may feel he's rather abandoned them.'

Another silence fell. Garvey had to remind herself that the clock was ticking. In a matter of minutes she would officially be a mere MP once more. Her thoughts drifted back to Buckingham. 'Do you suppose he would have pulled the trigger on the gunman if Rolt *had* been in the room?'

They gazed at each other for a moment. Mandler said, 'Interesting to speculate. Buckingham has no love for Rolt. In fact, he's probably chafing to get out.'

Garvey cleared her throat. 'Seems such a shame. Rolt thinks the world of him. His cover is rock solid. Only four of us know what he's really doing. I say leave him in place.'

Mandler raised his eyebrows. 'Buckingham's his own man. We can't *order* him to stay.'

'But surely his value to you as an asset has just shot up. Doesn't every self-respecting MI5 DG crave a spy in his political master's camp?'

'Well, I can't see a way of forcing him to stay in the saddle.'

'Then if I were you I'd bloody well find one.'

Mandler nodded half-heartedly.

'Do you really think there'll be others?'

'Other what?'

'Attempts on Rolt's life.'

Mandler delivered his default answer. 'Who knows? Most of Invicta's members have been trained to kill. If there are any more who've got disillusioned . . .'

'One can only hope.'

They exchanged a brief smile. In less than an hour Mandler would be answering to a new man. Well, fuck it. She poured herself a refill. If this was what it meant to be a functioning alcoholic, it had its compensations.

She had one more question. 'What do you really think about Rolt's plans? Do you really think any of it could work?' ·

'"Cutting out the tumour of terrorism, so British children can play safely on our gleaming white streets"?'

'Well?'

'Honestly?' He took a deep breath, swirled what was left of the Scotch and swallowed. 'I think it's going to make every-thing a great deal worse.'

# 11

## 12.00 local time
## Aleppo

Where was Emma? He had given her the camera twenty minutes ago; she'd told him to wait, promised to return with the driver in ten. Another ten and Abukhan would start to get suspicious about his absence, as would his comrades. Half an hour, and they would know he'd done a runner.

Overhead, a huge bank of cloud had blotted out the sun and turned the sky to the same dusty grey as the shattered buildings around him. The temperature had plummeted. He was still shaking. For more than an hour he and the others in his platoon had stood motionless as instructed, while one by one the girls were put to death. Every time he blinked, the terrible image of what he had just witnessed flashed up, seared into his brain for ever. He doubled over and threw up the meagre contents of his stomach.

The man who came out of the basement had on a bright yellow Puffa jacket and sunglasses. He didn't look like a local; nor did he have any of the natural wariness with which everyone in Aleppo armed themselves.

'Hey, Jamal. Let's go!' He spoke in English. He pressed a small translucent box into Jamal's palm.

'What's this?'

'The memory card. A copy of the film. She said for you to take it with you. You'll have to stash it. Come, there's no time.'

'But I thought she was going to upload it herself.'

'It's your insurance. So you can show it if you get any problems on your return home. Come.'

He grabbed him and pulled him along, a key dangling from his other hand. The motorbike was down an alley. Two boys who were guarding it stepped into the shadows as they approached.

'I'm Hakim, by the way. The border's no more than two hours. You should be in Turkey by nightfall.' He grinned and clamped his hand on Jamal's shoulder, then swung his leg over the bike and started it up. 'Jump on. No time to waste.'

Hakim tore out of the alleyway, across a courtyard, down a narrow path between a pile of rubble and a high wall, then out onto an empty street and headed east.

'You're going the wrong way!' Jamal shouted in his ear, above the wind and the rasp of the engine. Hakim swerved between donkey carts, bicycles and a few battered cars that were slowly making their way down the cratered road.

Hakim took a sudden left and yelled over his shoulder, 'It's a detour. There are convoys on the main road west. We'll go north first. Don't worry, just hold on.'

Jamal decided that he must know what he was doing and let him be. He had burned his bridges with the fighters; he would show the world the truth about the atrocities being committed in the name of Allah. If it got out that he had shot the video, people at home might come after him. He would have to take precautions. His family would help – if he could make them understand. He had missed them more than he could have imagined. He decided to focus on them, to think of nothing but his beloved sister. He was going home to her.

# 12

## 10.30
## 10 Downing Street

'"Selective *patriation*"? What in God's name does that mean?' The prime minister looked from one to the other until his gaze settled on Derek Farmer. 'Is that even a *word*?'

'If it wasn't before, it is now, Geoff,' said Farmer.

As the PM's spin doctor, he had some clout where this sort of thing was concerned, even if the minutiae of policy bored the pants off him. He glanced round the room. No one was looking at the PM.

'Well, thank you very much for that, Derek.' The PM gave him a reproachful look and tossed the briefing papers in the direction of the coffee-table, but they missed and slid into a heap on the floor. Giles Barker, his strategy chief, scrambled to gather them up and returned to his perch on the corner of the sofa beside Farmer, who was occupying most of it, reclining on a mound of all the cushions, his short fat legs splayed. If no one else in the room was feeling triumphant, he was. He had been an early champion of the 'Get Rolt Aboard' campaign. It wasn't that he cared much about the man's politics. Rather, he could see that without him they'd be toast. And, like the rest of them, he was now having to deal with the reality of what they had done.

The others in the room ranged from doubters to downright refuseniks. Farmer had sat through Giles's vociferous denunciations of Rolt as a neo-Nazi until he realized the PM had come around to the idea and grudgingly fallen into line. So much for strategy. Farmer chuckled inwardly.

Adam Mowbray, from the Home Office Policy Unit, was putting a brave face on the fact that in a few hours he would be answering to a home secretary with no previous political experience whatsoever. He had confided to Farmer that Rolt was bound to soften his rhetoric once he was in office and would soon be looking to him, his director of policy, for guidance. Meanwhile he would do his best to make friends with his new boss.

As for the PM, away from the cameras now, Farmer had never known a politician look so defeated in his hour of victory. But what they all knew in their hearts was that this wasn't their victory: it was Rolt's.

Someone had to fill the silence. Farmer was fucked if it was his job to do so. Mowbray plunged first. 'Rolt thinks it's pitched just right – tough but intuitive. "Selective" suggests that it is a *considered* measure, rather than being a *diktat*. As for "patriation", well, it has a certain gravitas. We should start with the known suspects, those who by and large everyone agrees are a menace to society, give them the choice of serving their term or "patriation" to whichever Muslim country signs up to our aid package.'

Farmer nodded approvingly. *That wasn't so hard, was it?* Mowbray had nailed his colours to the mast. He had appointed himself head cheerleader. But the PM was bridling.

'Yes, please take a generous helping of our Great British pounds with a side order of Islamofascist fanatics. We're effectively paying them to take our suspected terrorists – when they haven't even been convicted!'

Farmer, who had remained uncharacteristically quiet so far, knew it was time to give the PM a gentle prod and remind him on which side his bread was buttered. He leaned forward and reached into the pile of newspapers stacked on the end of the coffee-table. 'In his *Newsday* interview, Rolt points to those particular individuals who have made it clear enough that they're at odds with British society and British values, that they've effectively exiled themselves already. "Patriation" is simply a logical next step for those individuals – even a life-style choice.'

There was a nervous silence. He knew, as they all knew, that the scope of what could be said out loud had just widened.

'It's what a lot of the public want. It's why they voted for us.' He tapped the *Newsday* front page. Two photographs domi-nated: one of Rolt on a podium punching the air, the other a screen grab of a masked jihadi. Above the picture of Rolt was one word, '*IN*', and above the masked Islamist, '*OUT*'. Farmer grinned. 'I couldn't have put it better myself.'

He watched as the PM inevitably turned to Alec Clements, the cabinet secretary. It was to him that the premier always looked for the final word, as if he was the ultimate barometer of what could and couldn't be done. As always, Clements had bagged himself the only upright chair and sat, as he preferred, slightly apart from the rest of the group, his eyeline a few inches above those on the sofas. He appeared to be both presiding and remaining aloof. He had unbuttoned his waistcoat to give his ample belly some ventilation and was closely examining some-thing under the nail of his forefinger, giving the entirely false impression that he wasn't paying full attention.

'I rather think, Geoff, if I may come in here, that since there's no going back, we might as well concentrate on finessing the small print so we can whisk this through Parliament. At least then we can say, "Job done," and the Home Office can get on with executing the policy.'

They could always rely on Clements to home in on the main point. Farmer regarded him with a mixture of awe and fear, for his ability to glide along in a swan-like fashion, unflustered by the battles either out on the streets or inside the room. It had been Clements's idea to get Rolt to stand in the first place, but he had deftly contrived to manoeuvre the PM into voicing it. But now, rather late in the day, the PM was struggling with what was left of his conscience, his face reddening as he started to splutter.

'I don't think I like the word "execute" in this context. And I still don't see how the hell it's going to work! Are we talking about squads of police picking these guys off the street and putting them on the next plane to Syria? Bursting into mosques to round them up? Oh, yes, that should calm things down.'

Clements glanced up from his manicure. There was a hint of weariness in his tone. 'Yemen have already indicated they're quite keen. Lebanon's showing interest.' He looked at his watch. 'Anyway, the new man will be downstairs. Why don't we have him up and we can find out?'

You couldn't help but admire the way Clements manoeuvred himself away from direct conflict while at the same time goading them on. The PM stood up. 'I'm going to see him on my own for a few minutes. You lot can come back in when we're done.'

Clements stretched like a cat and got to his feet. 'He's booked himself a press conference at eleven so you'd better be quick.'

Farmer's enjoyment of the meeting came to an abrupt halt. *What the fuck?* He struggled to contain his dismay lest anyone think he wasn't on top of things. Still, there was nothing to be done but admit it. 'He just went ahead, I'm afraid, Prime Minister.'

'But he hasn't even been assigned a media handler yet.'

'I don't think he's the sort of chap who's going to wait for one, do you?'

The PM shifted awkwardly. The frantic election schedule had taken its toll on his back. 'Okay – everybody out. Send him in.'

There was a marathon gathering-up of papers and the room emptied until it was just the PM, with Clements and Farmer.

Farmer felt it was his turn to chip in with some supportive words. 'Really, Geoff, you should be celebrating. You're back. You've won.'

He offered the PM a winning grin. Clements beamed as well, though his smile was bereft of any warmth. Farmer could see the poor old PM's problem. He looked like a man who had been pushed into something. Farmer gazed at Clements. How did the man not only seem to thrive on crises but also accumulate ever more power and influence?

Farmer moved to the door just in time to see Rolt stride in, like a man in a hurry, by which time the PM had adjusted his features to his trademark wide grin. He watched as Rolt, also beaming, marched up to the PM, who shook his hand vigorously. 'Vernon. Welcome.'

'Prime Minister.' Rolt almost genuflected.

'Call me Geoff.'

They clasped hands and the PM laid a hand on Rolt's shoulder to remind him who was boss. Maybe he had made a pact with the devil. Maybe they would all go down in flames. He recalled Rolt's predecessor, Sarah Garvey, one person on his team who wouldn't compromise, wouldn't shut up, wouldn't spin her words for anyone. It was she who had warned Farmer that the PM's capacity for compromise would one day be his undoing.

Rolt took the chair Clements had just vacated and looked around approvingly, rather like a prospective tenant, Farmer thought, alarmed. 'What a very lovely room.'

Farmer noticed the sweat marks gathering on the PM's slightly flabby chest. Cartoonists had long ago spotted this unattractive tendency and were still drawing him grotesquely caricatured with huge man-boobs in a wet T-shirt competition. He flashed a warning look. The PM got the message and took the precaution of slipping his suit jacket back on. 'I feel a slight chill,' he said, with his best grin.

*You and me both,* thought Farmer, as he closed the door.

# 13

The operations manager for the building had a hunted look about him. 'I don't know how it happened, sir. It was all in order when I left last night.'

He and Tom were standing in front of a bank of monitors. At six a.m., it seemed, all the building's security cameras had been manually switched off and the barrier to the underground garage left open.

'I mean what with everything going on, who would do that?'

'Thanks.' He gave the manager a reassuring smile. 'I'm sure there's a perfectly simple explanation.'

There was: Rolt must have done it himself. He had been alone in the building, when Tom had arrived earlier, expecting a very particular visitor and wanting to make sure there was no record of him.

Tom went back to his desk and spent half an hour Googling Crimean Tartars, Ordynka swords, Ukrainians called Oleg – there were literally millions – and wealthy resident *émigrés* from Russia and the former eastern bloc. He even considered calling

73

Helen, the reporter who had been outside when he arrived in case she had seen anyone, but as the visitor had evidently come in via the garage there was no point: the entrance was in the mews at the back of the building. Besides, he didn't want to tip her off to anything that might turn out to be important. Meanwhile, he'd come across something else that intrigued him. Trawling a website for Crimeans based in London, he was distracted by a picture of a woman, pale and severe but striking, clearly not enjoying having her photograph taken. What also caught his attention was the caption: 'Xenia Dalton, proprietor of *Newsday*'.

A search produced very few entries – surprising, given her position. Her Wikipedia entry was sparse: she was born in Sebastopol, but there was no reference to a maiden name. Dalton was her late husband, whom she had met and married over there shortly before he'd brought her, his much younger bride, to the UK. Maybe Dalton was where she'd got the money to buy a newspaper, but it seemed unlikely: he turned out to have been an English language teacher from Margate, who had died after being mugged near their home.

He went and found Phoebe, who was pulling on her coat. 'Seen her before?'

She shook her head without really taking in the page.

'Sure?'

'Of course I'm sure. I'd remember – she's stunning. Do you want me to do some digging?' Her tone was less than enthusiastic.

'No, go and get some rest.'

The office was almost deserted. Rolt had given everyone the day off. There was nothing to be gained from hanging around.

Tom hunched his shoulders against a fresh flurry of snow as he made his way to Trafalgar Square. It was deserted, except for a few Chinese tourists photographing each other in front of the lions. He took out his phone.

'Ah, Buckingham, good of you to call.' Woolf sounded disturbingly upbeat.

'What are you so happy about?'

'Oh, you know, another day, another adventure. I'm just sitting on the late Fez Randall's sofa about to go through his hard drive. Care to join me?'

'Phoebe's imploding. She can't take much more of him. It's doing her head in. She'll become a liability.'

The silence at the other end of the line said it all. Tom pressed on: 'We agreed there would be an exit strategy in place for her if Rolt made home secretary.'

'Yes, of course. Just got to tie up a few ends first.'

Tom was being fobbed off. He didn't like it. 'What the fuck does that mean?'

'Twenty-four hours is a long time in our world, Tom. You let me worry about Phoebe.'

Over the months that Woolf had been his handler, Tom had developed a grudging respect for him, but he knew it would be naïve ever to let it develop into anything remotely like trust.

'The police want to talk to you about the shooting.'

'Well, tell them to fuck off.'

'They're getting ready to welcome the new home secretary. It would be a bit remiss of them if they were seen to be ignoring an attempt on his life.'

'When the fuck did you give a shit about protocol? And the last thing he wants is the Met crawling all over it. Make it go away. What's more important is whether or not Randall acted alone.'

'Indeed. That's why I'm here, going through his stuff.'

'There's something else.'

'What?'

'Rolt had a visitor this morning.' Tom described what little he could of the man he had seen, including the flattened cigarette butt and the Tartar sword in its fancy box.

'Intriguing. What does it say to you?'

'He gives Rolt expensive presents but chucks his fag ends on the floor, then demands a goodbye hug. The guy has something on him.'

'I like it.'

You could always count on Woolf's enthusiasm for a mystery.

'Look, I've got the DG on the other line. Why don't you join me at Randall's? I could do with your eyes on this place. Come on, you're bound to spot something we've overlooked.'

# 14

They had been on the bike for more than two hours. The aching pain from the ride over rutted and cratered roads had been numbed by the cold wind that battered Jamal's face, and his ungloved hands, wrapped round Hakim's waist, felt raw.

For the first part of the run they had kept to the main highways where they had encountered streams of refugees heading the same way, a few in heavily laden minibuses but most on bicycles or foot, who looked enviously at them as they shot past. As they neared the border, Hakim had branched off onto increasingly narrow and more heavily cratered roads that wound up into the hills. Jamal had lost all sense of where he was. He knew they were headed roughly north-east, but Hakim had told him they would have to take a route that avoided patrols and not to be surprised by sudden turns. He smiled a lot as he spoke and his calm self-assurance gave Jamal some comfort, though when he tried to make casual conversation about where he was from, Hakim shook his head. 'The less you know about me the better.'

He was right. Jamal understood that if he was caught on the

wrong side of the border, he would be questioned about how he had got there.

When they reached the foothills of the mountains the traffic thinned. As they neared the border Jamal's spirits lifted, until he reminded himself that even assuming he made it back to Britain, he was likely to face yet more hurdles, even with the video uploaded. He thought about Emma, how grateful he was to her for giving him a chance to redeem himself. He was desperate to know if the footage he'd shot was okay. When he asked Hakim, he just smiled and said, 'I don't know anything about that. I just take you to the border.' He was laughing when he told Jamal where he had to hide the memory card. 'Wrap it in a condom if you have one. If not, a bit of plastic bag. But not until after the bike.'

He clutched his buttocks and made a face. But Jamal knew what to do. A few weeks earlier they had captured an elder in a village they had overrun who insisted he had been robbed of all his possessions. Abukhan didn't believe him, and a full body search revealed a gold bracelet wrapped in cling film stuffed up his rectum. The copy of the film would be his insurance, in case anything had gone wrong with the upload. That and the two telephone numbers in London that Emma had given him.

Jamal's thoughts drifted to his family, above all Adila, the only one he had dared communicate with all the time he had been away. He was going to ask Hakim if he would text her when they parted, but something stopped him. A glimmer of worry. He had learned to be less trusting during his time in Syria.

He was still lost in thought when the bike suddenly slowed. The road ahead had levelled out but two pick-up trucks were parked broadside across the road forming a chicane. One had a grenade launcher on the back. There were several men, all with AKs, their faces masked.

'Say nothing. I will do all the talking.'

Hakim stopped and dismounted about ten metres from the roadblock. 'Stay with the bike.'

Jamal dreaded being recognized. What if they were from one of the militias his had fought with? He watched as Hakim walked confidently up to them, his palms forward. As he did, two men walked past him straight towards Jamal, their weapons trained on him. He had abandoned his weapon in Aleppo. Hakim had told him to. He was so used to it for his security, like the knives he and his brothers used to carry back home, that without it he felt naked. They came up close so the muzzles of their AKs were just a few inches from his chest, their fingers poised on the triggers. He could see the blaze of suspicion in their eyes. He felt his face flush with guilt for his betrayal of Abukhan, and of all his comrades. If they took him prisoner, returned him to his platoon . . . Better to die now.

Out of the corner of his eye he could see the other four gathered round Hakim, bent over something he had produced from his jacket. Emma had promised him he would be okay, but what was going on? The men round Hakim lowered their weapons but they continued to glare at Jamal.

Hakim walked up to the bike, waved at the group he had been speaking to, and they were off again.

'You made that look so easy.'

Hakim shrugged. 'Just lucky.'

'How did you do it? Did you bribe them?'

'Documentation.' His look told Jamal not to enquire any further. 'Not far now.'

Ten more minutes and Hakim came to a stop. The road curved sharply round and there was a big drop beyond.

'This is where we part.'

'What do I do from here? Where are we?'

'The rest of the route is on foot. You're nearly there.' Hakim pointed at a track that wound along a ridge. 'Only about five miles to the border.' He motioned for him to dismount, then reached back, unlocked one of the panniers on the side of the bike and pressed some kind of rough fabric into his hands. 'Take this. It should help a bit with the cold. You should have come better dressed but what's a little chill when there's freedom just over the mountain?' Hakim grinned.

Jamal marvelled at his calm. He wrapped the blanket around him. It smelt of petrol. 'How do I find my way?'

It was starting to get dark.

'Your eyes will adjust after a while. There is a track. It goes north-west. You haven't got the stars tonight so you'll just have to keep your eyes open for markers. There are wooden posts and some piles of stones. Don't be surprised if you come across others on the way. This is quite a popular route for those who know.'

'What about militias?'

'You won't be bothered up here. They don't control this area. Just make sure you keep moving – that's the best way of ensuring the cold doesn't get to you. You have your passport, cash?'

Jamal nodded. Hakim pointed into the failing light. 'Stay on the track. It will take you to a dry river bed. Follow it. You will see the frontier, mostly coils of razor wire. This section is seldom patrolled. Keep to the left of the river bed and you will be able to crawl underneath the wire. The first road you come to, go left. After three K there's a garage with a café next to it. Wait in there. Someone will come for you and take you to the airport.'

Jamal marvelled at this organization. Emma had come through for him, it seemed.

Hakim held out his hand. 'Good luck. You might even be famous after this.'

It was the only time Hakim had referred to his deed. Jamal took his hand. 'Thank you for all you've done for me. I'm in your debt.'

Hakim laughed. 'May God go with you.'

The bike burst into life with a roar, and he was gone.

Jamal was alone.

# 15

**13.00**
**Acton, West London**

Tom parked the Range Rover in a parallel street and walked round to the address Woolf had given him. Randall's house was at the end of a terrace of mid-nineteenth-century two-up-two-downs. He spotted Woolf's Mondeo, already entombed in a couple of inches of snow. He had clearly been there a while. Further down the street there was a white Transit, rusty, with a hubcap missing and a big scrape down the side but a noticeably fresh set of cold-weather tyres: transport for an MI5 plumbers' unit.

He pressed the bell on number forty-nine. A voice from inside asked him to identify himself.

'Buckingham.'

The door was opened by a man in a white disposable coverall. 'Go on up. Sherlock's in the bedroom sniffing the sheets.' He ushered Tom in and shut the door behind him.

'Want me to suit up?'

'Nah, we're pretty much done here. It's clean.'

After the chill outside, the house felt stiflingly hot. It smelt of stale sweat and fried food. Tom glanced into the kitchen-diner.

A single reclining chair was positioned in front of a large old cathode-ray TV, plugged into a VHS recorder. Randall wasn't exactly your up-to-the-minute internet-enabled assassin. The remains of his last meal were on a tray on the floor. Tom bent down, picked up a tumbler and sniffed. Sour milk.

Two more plumbers, packing up their kit, nodded at him.

'Any signs of booze?'

They shook their heads. 'Not so much as a sherry trifle.'

He mounted the stairs and pushed open the nearest door on the landing. Woolf was sitting on the unmade single bed, staring into space.

'Found anything?'

Woolf's face was ashen. 'Mandler's gone. He's been kicked upstairs.'

'What does that mean?'

Woolf slowly shook his head. 'SIC. Security and intelligence co-ordinator, based in the Cabinet Office. Right where Clements can keep an eye on him.'

Despite the heavy bags under his eyes from years of sleeping in cars and at desks, there was still something vulnerably boyish about Woolf. Right now he looked as if he'd just been told he had to resit his Latin exam. Tom sat beside him on the bed and stared at the same blank wall. Their operation had always been off-book, Mandler's pet project. What Mandler's move meant for Woolf was written all over his face. 'He was your mentor.'

Woolf nodded slowly. 'More than that. I'd have been out on my ear long ago if it wasn't for him . . .' He trailed off as he sank into his own thoughts.

The machinations of Whitehall didn't interest Tom much. He knew about Clements and his part in Rolt's elevation to the corridors of power, but beyond that the ferrets-fighting-in-a-sack element didn't seem to change, no matter who was in power. He tried to think of something useful to say.

'I suppose it's a sign of how things are going to be. You know Rolt – he doesn't like to hang around.'

'No, this is all Clements, cleaning the stables in preparation.

He always had it in for Mandler, and with Garvey gone he was a sitting duck.'

'If Clements wanted rid of Mandler, why didn't he just give him the boot?'

Woolf smiled grimly. 'It's not his style. He likes to keep his enemies close. Mandler loose on the streets, bitter and twisted, is a lot more dangerous than Mandler parked somewhere he can keep a close eye on him.'

'And his friends?'

'Clements doesn't do friends.'

This snapshot of Whitehall intrigue served one purpose for Tom: it was a reminder of how much more carefully he would have to watch his own back. But for now he erased all thoughts of Clements and looked round the sparse surroundings. No pictures, no trophies, just a pile of dirty washing tossed in a corner; a solitary ex-soldier's billet, with no one else's standards to live up to.

'Did Randall have anyone in his life? Any family?'

'They'd all cut him off. There's a woman in Thailand he was chatting to online. She thought he was going to marry her, but he pulled the plug about three months ago. And there's a stash of letters from another old girlfriend downstairs – unopened.'

He passed Tom a handwritten note in an evidence bag. 'It's to his son. They've not spoken for eight years.'

*Craig,*
*Be a good lad and watch out for your mum. She's a fine woman,*
*whatever she says about me. See you on the other side, maybe, one*
*day.*
*Dad*

Tom gazed at it. So, he hadn't expected to come out of the hotel alive. 'What else? What about his mates?'

'Zip. He took himself offline about three months ago. Had everything scrubbed.' Woolf smiled. 'Normally people can't stand it after a few weeks and go back online in another guise, but he junked everything, even his phone. There's not even a

83

landline in here. No cards. He's been drawing cash from his local bank branch. All the trademarks of a lone operator, I'd say. You agree?'

This wasn't like Woolf. He was usually obsessive about detail, the more obscure the better, the last to jump to conclusions. Tom sensed he was already detaching himself.

Woolf got up and rubbed his neck. 'Sorry I dragged you down here – bit of a fool's errand.'

Tom didn't respond. He looked out of the window. The snow had stopped. A youth was kicking half-heartedly at the side of a bus shelter. A post van was inching its way down the street, its driver, unused to ice, letting the wheels spin so it fishtailed on the freezing snow, hunting for traction.

'Randall was one of the *Freikorps*,' Tom said.

'The who?'

'My nickname for the original recruits to Invicta, when it wasn't much more than a shelter for homeless ex-squaddies who'd been spat out by the army, in debt and trying to get off the booze.'

Woolf frowned. 'Why that name?'

'German First World War ex-servicemen, enraged by the Armistice. They'd given their all in the trenches, only to be sold out by the lot that came in after the Kaiser. Or that was how they saw it. They banded together into paramilitary groups called *Freikorps*.'

'Embittered nationalists experienced with weapons. And was Hitler one of them?'

'He shared their belief that the German Army had not been truly defeated in the field, and that the politicians had sold them down the river.'

Woolf raised an eyebrow. 'You're full of surprises, Buckingham. I didn't have you down as a historian.'

'Some things stick in the mind. At the start, people like Randall were the bedrock of Invicta, lost souls with nothing left to live for and in need of rehab. As the organization took off it started to attract a wider constituency, officers, men with more of an eye for the sort of advancement that

Rolt seemed to offer. The *Freikorps* were a bit marginalized.'

Woolf was evidently unconvinced. 'How can you be so sure it's a matter of "they"? This is just speculation.'

Tom turned to face him. 'Guys like Randall view themselves as outcasts. Ironically, it's the sense of alienation that binds them together. We need to take a closer look at the others. Find out if it is just speculation.'

Woolf met his gaze, his earnest face on. 'Or give them a wide berth. If word gets out that you stopped Randall, if anyone was in it with him, it'll give them a pretty good reason to come after you. Maybe you should tell your friend the new home secretary to have the Met organize you some security.'

Tom gave Woolf a stony look. He couldn't think of anything more ridiculous than being watched over by cops. Besides, Woolf despised the Met. Was this a sign that he was cutting him loose?

'You could take a holiday – get right away. Restart your life,' Woolf added, with a bland smile.

Tom could almost hear the cogs engaging in his brain. Without Mandler's protection, he would have to press the reset button on his career. And snooping on the new home secretary wouldn't look too good on his CV. Had Tom become a liability to him?

Woolf yawned, displaying a fine set of slightly yellowed teeth. Clearly, in his mind, he was already moving on. Case closed.

'Have you talked to Phoebe?'

Woolf finished his yawn. 'She's staying in place.'

Tom's eyes widened. 'You're joking.'

'Nope, we just talked. I'm leaving her there in case we need her later.'

'She agreed?'

'Fact is, she doesn't get a vote. She's always been graded UNK, a contractor who doesn't show up on the books. Whoever comes in Mandler's place won't even know she exists.' The gleam of mischief had returned to his eyes. The idea of a spy in their boss's camp still amused him. 'Anyway, she's fine about it.'

'For a spook you're a fucking terrible liar. What do you make of Rolt's mystery visitor?'

Woolf shrugged. 'Perhaps he was just what Rolt said, an old business buddy.'

It was striking how quickly his curiosity had waned.

One of the plumbers appeared in the doorway. 'We're all done.'

'Thanks, Joe.' Woolf looked relieved to be interrupted. He got up, ready to take his leave.

Tom stopped him. 'What about Randall's movements? Did he have any transport?'

Joe the plumber glanced at Woolf, who gave him a nod.

'Nothing we can find that's actually registered to him. There's a burned-out Skoda in a disused warehouse a few miles away. The local cops assumed it was joy-riders. It belonged to an old lady in this street who died a couple of months ago. Randall used to do odd jobs for her. We've run a plate check and all it's come up with is a sighting somewhere near Carlisle two days ago.'

'Where near Carlisle?'

'Deep in the wilds of Cumbria,' said Woolf. 'But the number-plate recognition software's crap – full of errors and duplicates. I wouldn't get too excited about it.'

# 16

Hakim was right. His eyes would adjust. Jamal had only gone a few hundred metres when he saw the group coming up the track. His first thought was to hide, but where? The mountainside was barren. He could flatten himself on the ground and hope they didn't notice him. He pulled Hakim's blanket closer round him. His hands felt as if they were on fire now, and starting to swell.

There was nothing to do but stay in plain sight. Not to react, but behave as if this was his hillside more than theirs. The group stopped when they saw him. Young men his age, with small packs on their backs and ski jackets, staring at him, mouths open. He must have looked strange to them wrapped in the blanket. He envied them their padded coats. Everything about them said new arrivals – even from this distance he could smell their deodorant. He was propelled back to his first days in Syria: how he was made to give up everything he had brought with him until there was nothing left of where he had come from; how he had blocked out all doubt, smothering it with zeal. There was a terrifying innocence about them, just as he must once have shown.

One turned to the others. 'What do we do?'

They were speaking English.

'Dunno. Keep going?'

They started to move towards him. One waved.

'*Al salaam' aleikum*. We're friends. Come to help.'

The others sniggered at their comrade's attempt at a greeting. Jamal stared at their trainers – they had luminous streaks. One wore earbuds.

'*Wa alaykom el salam*,' Jamal replied.

'Fuckin' 'eck,' said the one who had uttered the greeting. 'How about that, then?'

They had distinct northern accents.

'Don't swear,' someone hissed.

'Have you come from the border?'

'Wow, you English, then?'

'Dutch.' Jamal wasn't taking any risks so close to freedom. 'How far is the frontier?'

'About a mile. You goin' home?'

Jamal nodded.

Another piped up: 'So you been fighting, then? How is it?'

*How is it?* How could he begin to answer that? They reminded him of how he was just five months ago, ready to sacrifice everything, convinced that the only true way was jihad. He wanted to tell them to turn round now, that everything they had heard from preachers or read or watched online was bollocks. That this wasn't about religion or freedom fighting. It was all about tribal violence, corruption and extreme brutality against women. They were staring at him, waiting for an answer.

Jamal shrugged. 'It's hard.'

'It's hard back home. We're not welcome no more.'

One of the others chipped in: 'Yeah, right, bro. The shit happening to us in Britain, this is gonna be home for us now.'

They all nodded, as if that helped them believe in the decision they had made.

One more mile.

'*Ma al salamah*,' said one. Peace be with you. Some hope. Jamal walked on.

# 17

**14.00**
**Home Secretary's Office, Westminster**

Henry stepped into the room. The PA had cleared the last bits and pieces from the previous occupant's tenure. He noted that the glasses and the decanter had been removed. That was good. The new man was teetotal. All that was left of Sarah Garvey was her scent, which clung to the air. It would soon fade.

He smiled. Good riddance. He was glad she was gone. It amazed him that she had lasted so long. She seemed to pride herself on being a rebel, winding people up, making enemies of other cabinet members and the police. The Met commissioner loathed her, would go to any lengths not to be in the same room as her. No wonder the country was in such a state. And the way she spoke to the prime minister! He opened each drawer of her desk. Nothing incriminating, no secret documents, just unused stationery. He straightened a few items, closed the drawers and put the chair in its rightful place at the desk. Only then did he notice the small envelope that had slipped into the gap between the cushion and the arm. He was about to drop it into the shredder by the desk, when he paused. It was the letter he had brought in that morning, from the girl who was her constituent, the one with the brother trying to get back from Syria. He weighed it in his hand, opened it again, reread the contents and put it back into its envelope.

Then he slipped it into his pocket and left the room.

# 18

A fresh fall of snow and thick grey cloud glowering overhead gave the Invicta campus more than a hint of Siberian gulag. A heavier-than-usual security presence at the gate made the atmosphere all the more oppressive. Tom waited in the Range Rover while two guards in the booth examined his pass. It was designed for only one occupant, so the other had to come out while they handed the document back and forth.

*Do I look like a suicide bomber?* Tom wondered, but then he reminded himself of Randall's own suicidal mission.

'Can't be too careful these days, sir. Extra checking 'cos of all the trouble.' The guard gave back his pass and signalled to the men on the gate to open up.

Tom nodded at him. 'Yep, you never know what's coming round the corner.'

Inside the gate, the drives and paths had all been cleared of snow and the sense of order that had impressed Tom on his first visit still prevailed. Apparently Rolt had ploughed the best part of the fortune he had made from his software businesses into creating this place out of an old army base, a haven for ex-service people to get cleaned up and prepare to re-enter civilian life. But a large number had grown to like life on the campus so much that they had managed to prolong their stay, like perpetual students. Perhaps some had even relapsed on purpose to avoid facing the outside world. Rolt hadn't objected: he had told Tom he liked the idea of his men being housed together in one place, enjoying the support of each other's camaraderie, even though it had stretched resources and put pressure on his seemingly limitless funds.

Tom left his car by the admin block and went into Reception. There was no one at the desk so he walked down the corridor towards the senior management offices.

The warden's office was empty, as were those of the field directors. He reached the last room and peered through the glass. Carter, the bursar, was at his desk, hunched over a screen. Tom knocked.

'Fuck off, I'm busy.' Carter, a paraplegic Basra veteran, was famously miserable.

He didn't look up as Tom stepped into the room. 'Sorry to disturb you.'

'Well, don't then.' Carter glared at him briefly then returned to the screen.

Tom knew it wasn't personal. And in a world of false courtesy and meaningless 'Have a nice day' platitudes, the brusqueness came as a relief. And there were no favourites where Carter was concerned: he treated everyone with the same contempt. He was good at the job and his memory for fine detail was legendary. When Tom had sat in on board meetings in Rolt's absence, he had watched with amusement as Carter tore into everyone round the table over various financial mis-demeanours, all of which he seemed to recite without notes and with terrifying, surgical accuracy. You might have survived the insurgents, his tone seemed to say, but woe betide you if you can't produce a receipt for that new pen.

Tom gestured at an empty desk. 'Could I log on to one of these? Need to look something up.'

'You can try. Only the whole fucking mainframe's down.'

A wasted journey. He'd wanted to give Randall's personal file a really good going-over.

'Where is everybody?'

'Hanson's taken them all off to Dartmoor.'

Hanson was the chief warden, a former Marine and one of the few Ruperts to have joined Invicta.

'What's that in aid of?'

Carter rolled his eyes. 'He's been giving them all hell about keeping in shape.'

'What – all of them?'

'Just the leadership and some of the long-termers.'

'First I heard of it.'

Carter's withering gaze settled on him. 'There's a lot you people don't hear about in the London office.'

Tom parked himself on the corner of an adjacent desk. He knew better than to ask for a chair. 'Did Rolt sanction it?'

'Fucked if I know. His lordship gave the warden *carte blanche* on spending when this election business blew up.'

He referred to it as if it were an unwelcome irritation in Rolt's schedule, rather than an unprecedented turning point in the fortunes of the nation.

'I thought things had been getting a bit tight.'

Carter gave him another withering look and returned to the screen. He was notoriously guarded about all matters financial.

'Sorry, didn't mean to pry.'

'Well, since you *are* here, you tell *me* something. What's going to happen now he's a fucking government minister? How's he going to square the new day job with all this?'

Since Rolt had become absorbed in the election campaign his fortnightly visits to the campus had been on hold, but the place had its own momentum and Tom wasn't aware that there had been any negative impact. 'You lot seem pretty good at keeping the ship on course.' He glanced nonchalantly around the room as he spoke. It was a hallmark of Carter's type that compliments only irritated them further.

'Paddling like fuck away from the rapids, you mean.'

This conversation wasn't going anywhere. He decided to plunge in. 'You know Randall? Used to be the boss's driver.'

'Gone. Had enough, I heard. A few of the old guard have in the past months.'

'Who else?'

Carter looked at him with exaggerated dismay. 'How should I know? No one tells me anything. Every time someone fucks off that's one less mouth to feed. Far as I'm concerned, the fewer the merrier. Now, if you don't mind, I'd like to get on with my job here. Why not fuck off and annoy someone else?'

Tom's attention was caught by a large wall map of the UK and a handful of locations marked as important. 'What's with the red flags?'

Carter followed his gaze. 'My personal hit list. Properties that are a drain on resources. Main one being the London office, I might add.' He gave him an accusing look.

'Don't blame me, I only work there.' As well as the main campus where they were now, there were three hostels used for training courses: one in Derbyshire, the one on Dartmoor where the senior management had gone now, and a third in the Lake District. It all added up to quite a portfolio. 'Are they all going to be sold?'

'Some, if I have anything to do with it.'

'Which first?'

'Derbyshire and the Lakes.'

'What do they cost to run?'

'Far too fucking much, is what. And if they're not maintained properly, and we're not using them enough, they go to seed. So we're obliged to keep them at least partially occupied when they're not in use for exercises. Turn the heating off completely and these old buildings succumb to damp and go to rat shit. And if the local dickheads think they're empty, you get burgled. Windows broken, graffiti . . .'

Tom stared more closely at the map. He had never been to these facilities. He thought about the car belonging to Randall's elderly neighbour that had shown up in Cumbria. 'Who's looking after the Lakes?'

Carter sighed heavily. 'As I think I tried to make clear, I just look after the figures. You'd have to see HR about that.' He leaned back and then forward again. 'Oh, no, you can't. They're on Dartmoor as well.'

The man could teach masterclasses in exasperation. He picked up a pencil and started to scribble something on a pad.

'How's the election gone down here? How do people feel about it?'

Carter threw down his pencil. It rolled off the pad and fell to the floor. 'Look, what do you actually want, Buckingham? Because, hard as it may be for you to comprehend, I've got quite a lot to be getting on with here.'

The phone on the other desk started to ring. He ignored it.

'Want me to take it?'

'No!'

'Only trying to help.'

'Well, don't.' Carter pushed himself away from his screen and wheeled over to the phone. He picked it up and listened, his face changing from mild irritation to thunderous annoyance. His questions came like bursts of rapid fire. 'When was this? . . . How many? . . . What's the extent of the damage? . . . Okay, okay. Stay there, I'm coming.' He glanced at Tom again. 'And, no, I *don't* need a push.'

'What's happened?'

'You'll see.'

# 19

**15.00**

Like many ex-service paraplegics, Carter had hugely powerful shoulders and upper arms, but the armoury was at least a quarter of a mile from the admin building, and a steady climb, more than any man could manage in a wheelchair, much as it clearly annoyed him to accept Tom's help.

The snow was starting to fall again, causing the lamps to come on along either side of the path. As they approached they saw Regan, the sallow-faced deputy armourer, waiting outside for them, pulling anxiously on a cigarette – which was forbidden, of course. Carter bellowed at him from twenty metres. 'Put that fucking thing out! When did this happen?'

Regan dropped the cigarette like a guilty schoolboy, and trod it into the snow. He was a small man, painfully thin, who, Tom knew, had lived rough for several years before joining Invicta. 'I've only just opened up.'

'Well, let's see, then.'

Regan hesitated, a worried glance in Tom's direction, irritating Carter. 'Get on with it – it's fucking cold out here.'

Regan held the door as Tom wheeled Carter in. For a moment even he was lost for words.

'This is what happens when people go away – nothing but fucking trouble.'

They looked along the racks. Thirty or more were empty. It was obvious to Tom that whoever had done this had come mob-handed and with the appropriate transport. 'Who was in charge of security last night?'

Regan nodded over his shoulder. 'There's some tyre tracks going up over the back field. They must have come through the forest gate, the bastards.'

He was making a big show of his disgust. Too big, Tom thought.

With all the security he found it hard to imagine that this was anything other than an inside job. If Carter was thinking the same, he probably wasn't going to say so in front of Regan. Tom glanced at where the door had been forced. Heavy locks top and bottom held it fast, but the damage was all midway down. Unconvincing. Tom fixed his gaze on Regan. 'Who else knows about this?'

He gestured at Carter. 'Mr Carter and you is all.'

It was obvious to Tom that he was lying. But Carter seemed to be taking him at his word. 'What about your boss?' Hartley, the senior armourer.

'Away with the bloody rest of them,' Carter growled.

'And there's no signal where they are,' Regan added.

Carter let out an exaggerated breath of frustration. Tom said, 'We call the cops, this'll be out all over the media. I'll break it to the chief. Now he's home secretary he can decide how he wants it handled.'

# 20

**15.20**

Back in his car, Tom called Phoebe. 'Are you at your desk?'

'Where else?'

He could tell from her voice that she had been crying. He didn't have time for any of that right now. 'Invicta has a hostel in the Lake District.'

'What's it called?'

'I don't know, it's near Keswick. The mainframe's down here so I can't find out any more. Can you access the records remotely? I want to know who looks after it. There must be a warden or someone on staff.'

'You after somewhere to go to ground? Woolf said you might have to lie low.'

'I don't do lying low. It's not my thing. He's talking through his arse. Give me whatever comes up – names, records, anything.'

'I'll call you back.'

'No, I'll hang on.'

Although she must have put down her mobile he could hear her cursing in the background as she moved to the other desk where the main computer was. A couple of minutes later she was back. 'It's called Lakeside Manor. It says here it's been sub-let to a school since September.'

'Who's responsible for it?'

'There aren't any names.'

'Okay, go into the staff database and search "Lakeside", see if any come up.'

There was another silence while she logged herself in.

'And what's the name of the school it's been let to?'

'Orchard College.'

He Googled it. No school of that name appeared. He could hear Phoebe tapping on her keyboard. 'Woolf says you're staying.'

She gave an empty laugh. 'Leaving isn't an option, apparently.'

'Well, if I said I was sorry to hear it I'd be lying. I thought I was done here. Now I'm not so sure. Things just got a lot more complicated.'

'Okay, it says here the last warden was called Evans.'

'Doesn't mean anything to me. Look him up – what's he doing now?'

'There's nothing listed for him, which means he might have left. What's the big deal about this place?'

'I don't know yet. Maybe nothing. What else have you got on Evans? When did he sign up?'

'He's got a very low number. Five. One of the first intake.'

The same as Randall.

# 21

**16.30**

On the drive back to London, a slow slog up a slippery M3, Tom reviewed the bits and pieces of what he had discovered. Randall could have been in Cumbria immediately before his assassination attempt at the hotel; the school to which Lakeside Manor had supposedly been let appeared not to exist; the armoury break-in had all the hallmarks of an inside job. Meanwhile, the Invicta management team was away, and Rolt had had a visit from someone he didn't want anyone to see who might or might not have links to the newspaper that had backed him. But that was all they were, bits and pieces, their only significance whatever Tom chose to attach to them with his own imagination. Woolf would probably dismiss them, but he was pulling back now that he no longer had Mandler's patronage. He had his own arse to watch. Tom realized he needed to get some perspective – a change of scene, which was why his much-postponed meeting with his father at his club was good timing.

Tom was greeted by the porter as if he'd seen him only recently, with the courteous neutrality characteristic of his kind. You could be someone's secret mistress or the Duke of

Wellington, whose illustrious ancestor gazed down at them from the wall opposite, and the greeting would be the same. The only difference was that this time Tom had remembered to wear a tie.

He found his father in the library behind the pink pages of the *FT*.

'My dear boy.'

Hugh Buckingham cast off the paper and rose stiffly from his chair. The last time Tom had seen his father he had been brimming with vigour, having, rather late in life, adopted a strenuous fitness routine. Today he looked noticeably older, as if it had been years rather than months. Tom felt a stab of guilt, made worse by the evident pleasure on his father's face at seeing him. 'Good to see you, Dad.'

Tom felt the urge to wrap him in a bear hug but, for two reasons, he didn't. First, they were in his club, surrounded by the other members, all male, who didn't go in for such displays of affection. Second, they hadn't even spoken to each other since their last disastrous encounter, and the ice had yet to be broken. Tom had been putting off meeting his father for weeks. Several times he had emailed him a date then cancelled, pleading that Rolt's election campaign meant he was left holding the fort while the boss was out on the road. Now the election was over there were no more excuses.

He took his father's hand, but gave it an extra squeeze as he had done on every occasion since the age of eight, when they had parted at the start of each term.

There was some moisture in his eyes, which Tom couldn't ignore. 'Steady on, Dad.'

'Of course.' Hugh wafted a hand in front of his face. 'Come, sit.' Hugh waved him to a chair. Tom sat. 'Well, I suppose congratulations are in order.'

For a moment Tom was flummoxed, then realized Hugh meant Rolt's new job. He waved away the compliment. 'Nothing to do with me.'

'Seems it was rather a foregone conclusion.'

'Guess it does look like that.'

Hugh sighed. 'Well, I've decided to give him the benefit of the doubt.'

'No, you haven't. You can't stand the man. You're just saying that for my benefit.'

Hugh smiled. 'You know me too well.'

'And you don't have to be polite to me of all people. Let's put what happened behind us.'

Hugh nodded eagerly. 'An excellent idea.'

They smiled, both knowing it would probably take a lot more than that. Hugh hailed a passing waitress.

'What can I get you, gentlemen?'

'Tea, please, Eileen.'

'We've got some scones today, Mr Buckingham, if you'd like.' She gave him a fond look.

He patted his stomach, as Tom had known he would. 'Not for me, sadly. The doc's been on at me about my GI.'

'Your what?'

'Glycaemic index – blood sugar and whatnot.'

The awful thought struck Tom that his father had diabetes. 'You haven't got—'

'No, no! Just Being Good.'

She looked hopefully at Tom, who shook his head, smiling.

'Just tea for two then. Very Spartan.' Hugh leaned back and Tom braced himself for the inevitable question.

'What's in store for you, now he's attained high office? Will you still be at his elbow or does the Party supply him with a whole posse of advisers and minders and whatnot?'

'I'm not sure yet.' He sensed an almost imperceptible sigh of disappointment. Why couldn't he just relax and take his father's enquiries for what they were, genuine interest and a desire to be of help? 'I'd tell you if I knew. I'm just not clear yet.'

When he was in the Regiment it was understood that Tom couldn't talk about his missions, even though his father would have loved to hear about them. But going under cover inside Rolt's organization was even worse; he couldn't risk his father knowing anything at all. He had to keep up his cover every minute of every hour of every day and it had widened the divide between them.

Hugh smiled bravely, like someone who'd just been told they hadn't won the Oscar. 'Well, if you're thinking of moving on there's lots to talk about. Plenty of opportunities out there.'

'Thanks, I'll bear that in mind.'

Hugh peered at him. 'You do look tired. I hope you've been looking after yourself. I expect you were up most of the night.'

'Why do you think that?' Tom asked irritably, the encounter with Randall still unpleasantly fresh in his mind. He felt immediately guilty and covered his embarrassment by smiling at the waitress as she arrived with the tea.

'You've got both milk and lemon there. All right, Mr Buckingham?'

'Marvellous, thanks.

'With all the excitement . . .'

'Oh, yeah, right. I am a bit wiped as it happens.' He observed his father watch the waitress depart with genuine gratitude. Hugh managed to go through life showing only goodwill to people – something Tom had only recently come to appreciate. Why couldn't he be more like him? Because every day of his life for the past six months he had been living a lie. It took its toll, no matter how often he told himself it didn't.

'Your digs still all right with Jez?'

'Very convenient.'

'He's a good chap. Always liked him. I expect he'd have something worthwhile to offer you, if you became available.'

Tom put down his cup. 'Dad. Go easy on the career counselling, eh? You know I'll tell you if I want any help.'

'Yes, yes. Sorry.'

Once again, there was an atmosphere between them. Tom needed to fill the silence. 'How's the City treating you?'

'Well, to be honest, it's been better.'

This was a surprise. He had never heard his father say his business activities were anything but 'booming' or 'going swimmingly'. Relentless optimism was one of his trademarks. 'Yeah? What's been happening?'

His father, normally so robust and unflappable, looked almost ashamed. 'I've had to . . . draw in my horns a bit. Couple of ventures went sour.'

Tom had always thought his father a past master at dodging a bullet.

Hugh waved a hand in the direction of the window. 'All the trouble – it's had quite an impact. In fact, your mother and I are thinking of downsizing.'

Tom looked at him in dismay: the idea of their selling the house – his childhood home – was unimaginable. Like most people once they've left home he hardly ever visited, but liked to know it was still there, a reassuringly fixed point on the compass. 'You always said the only way you were leaving Newland was in a box.'

'Well, one must adapt, you know. Adapt and survive.'

Tom did know – and he knew when Hugh was putting a brave face on something.

'We're not getting any younger, Tom. And the house really is too big for us. Then there's the garden – far too much. Your mother says she can manage it, but between you and me . . .'

There was something forced about his casualness. 'Bollocks, Dad. How much trouble are you in?'

Hugh shook his head, as if to dislodge something unwelcome. 'It's nothing out of the ordinary. Everybody's in trouble, these days. You've only got to look around you. Anyhow, we've had many good years. It's not as though we're going to be on the breadline. I just have to take what I can get.' He sipped his tea.

'But, Dad . . .'

Hugh registered the intensity of Tom's gaze and let out a long sigh. 'You always get uppity when I start probing about *your* work. Now it's *my* turn, okay? I'll tell you more when I'm good and ready. All right?'

Tom had touched a raw nerve. He could not remember ever having seen his father so agitated.

'Never mind all that. Your mother's worried about you.'

Tom knew that this was shorthand for them both being worried about him.

'She doesn't know what you're doing with your life any more.'

'Dad, I'm thirty-two. I'm a big boy, I can look after myself.'

'Look, I know you've made a point of never taking my advice, Tom, but nevertheless I'm going to give it. You need to think about the future.'

'Well, I'm probably going to have a bit of time out, regroup.'

Hugh's face came alive. 'Well, that's wonderful news, terrific. Mum will be delighted too – I can't wait to tell her. I assume that means you'll come and spend some time with us in the country.'

'Could we change the subject now, please?'

Silence descended. It was a full minute before Tom spoke. 'You still have any dealings with any of your oligarchs?'

'*My* oligarchs?' Hugh bridled. Several years ago he had advised on some very lucrative Russian-backed deals. But one had ended badly and Tom had warned him off doing any more, or thought he had. 'Why on earth are you asking?'

Tom knew it wasn't something he would want to be reminded of, but it was just possible that he might know something about Rolt's shadowy visitor. 'Bear with me, okay? I've got a first name – Oleg. He may be from the Crimea, a Tartar, perhaps. Goes around with a couple of heavies in tow.'

Hugh frowned, then leaned back and let out a snort. 'Well, that's not exactly narrowing it down! Have you any idea how many rich former Soviets are rattling around the nation's capital, let alone how many are probably called Oleg?'

It had been worth a shot. His father's connections with the City and high finance were second to none.

But Hugh's face now reddened with anger. 'And I resent the implication that I'm hobnobbing with gangsters. The people I deal with are all kosher.'

'Okay, chill, Dad. It was just a question.'

Hugh's forehead furrowed. 'Anyway, why do you want to know?'

Tom decided there was no reason to be evasive. 'Some

contact of Rolt's. Don't think he wanted anyone to meet him, though.'

Hugh's face remained blank.

'It was only a thought. Forget it.'

'My dear boy. I have to be discreet where clients are concerned. It doesn't do to go around fishing and it would make me sound ignorant.'

Tom put his hands up in mock surrender. 'I never mentioned it, okay?'

This wasn't going well. His father stared at him. 'Tom, what's happening to you? You grill me about this man, asking all sorts of questions, but you're never open with me about what you're up to. You've said nothing about your time with Invicta when it must have been jolly interesting being at the shoulder of Britain's most talked-about politician. And— Well, I just don't understand it.'

Tom looked at his father with regret. He would have liked nothing more than to confide in him. It would go a long way to repairing the rift that had opened up between them, and it would be a relief to unburden himself with someone he loved and trusted . . . He leaned forward and lowered his voice. 'I'm sorry, Dad. You're totally right. That's part of what's made it such a strain these last few months. Rolt's obsession with secrecy and security when, to tell you the truth, it's all been pretty bloody boring. Moving into politics has completely consumed him. He's obsessed with the Muslim threat. He's won popularity by whipping up fears about Islamist fighters coming back to blow up Britain, and once he gets his hands on some real power I think the rest of the government will have trouble restraining him.'

Hugh's eyes were sparkling again. A bit of honesty, not to mention intrigue, and they were back on track.

'So he's not going to "save us from civil war"?' Hugh made quotation marks with his fingers.

'He's more likely to cause it, if someone doesn't put the brakes on him. Plus he's got no empathy with his own men, the ones he's built his reputation on.'

It was rash, but he felt he owed his father something.

Hugh's eyebrows rose dramatically. 'Ah, I see. Well, I admit I'm relieved to hear the sun no longer shines out of his backside, but it does beg the question, why have you chosen to put so much of your energy behind him?'

It pained Tom that his father never missed an opportunity to question his judgement. He gave the older man a hard look.

'Sorry, sorry, I know, sensitive area. But, really, why not just leave? Jack it in, as you would say.'

Tom told himself not to rise to this and give his father a hard time. As much as he loved him, he had always resented any attempt to influence him. Even if he was able to come clean about what he was really doing inside Invicta, the worry alone would probably kill Hugh – never mind Tom's mother. Anyway, it wasn't an option.

'Okay, Dad, Rolt got me on the rebound from the Regiment. I was impressed with his organization and what it was doing for ex-service blokes. Maybe my head was in a different place then – and, anyway, I didn't know as much about him as I do now.'

'Well, perhaps your next decision will be a better one.'

Tom gritted his teeth, willing himself not to react.

'Speaking of which, I knew I had something to tell you. Your old CO turned up the other day, completely unannounced.'

'Ashton?'

Hugh nodded. 'It was a bit awkward, really. But we made a fuss of him. He was actually quite a nice chap.'

Tom's eyes narrowed. That was strange. The last time he had seen Ashton was at Brize, when he'd told him he was out of the Regiment. Not surprisingly, they hadn't spoken since. 'What did he want?'

Hugh shrugged. 'He didn't say exactly. Wanted to know how you were getting on out there in the big bad world. Said he'd like to see you some time. Though he didn't actually come out with it, I think he wants you to get in touch. You know, mend some fences.'

That was a surprise: Ashton had shown very little concern when he'd slung Tom out. 'You sure that was all?'

'Why not? He seemed genuine – didn't strike me as the sort to go in for light banter. Anyway, you'll be glad to hear I didn't give anything away. I know from bitter experience that you don't like me talking about you behind your back.'

Tom glanced at his watch. He'd had his fill of his father, but he didn't want to leave on another sour note. 'Look, Dad, it's been really good to see you.'

'Indeed it has, my boy. Do come and see your mother. She does miss you so.'

'I will, I promise.'

'And I'll keep my ear to the ground. If I hear of any strange men called Oleg bearing gifts I'll be sure to let you know.' He tapped the side of his nose theatrically.

Tom paused, the memory of the Ordynka on its garish purple bed fresh in his mind. 'I didn't mention anything about gifts.'

Hugh shook his head in mock despair. 'It's a saying – surely you know that. "Foes' gifts are no gifts: profit bring they none."'

'Yeah, yeah. Sophocles.'

'So you did learn something at school!' Hugh beamed. But even as they shook hands, Tom detected something in his father's manner that troubled him.

# 22

**17.00**
**Millbank, Westminster**

The press conference was packed. Rolt's triumph hadn't just got the attention of the British press, it was an international story. Reporters and TV news crews from every country with a free press – or otherwise – were crammed into the room and the halls beyond.

Derek Farmer and his deputy press strategist, Pippa Stevens, were late, having abandoned their cab in the freezing, grid-locked streets and struggled the rest of the way on foot. Walking was his least favourite mode of transport. His cab account, appetite for beer and lunch on expenses – always 'in the interests of putting the Party in a good light' or for a magazine 'gagging to do a flattering profile' of some MP or other – had taken their toll. If he had to hurry, his gut wobbled pendulously and his carb-inflated thighs chafed together. Pippa had no such problem, her long, slim legs hardened by years of hockey on the playing fields of Roedean. With fifteen years fewer on the clock than Farmer, and a genuine enthusiasm for the gym, she had a seemingly inexhaustible supply of stamina and looked young enough to be his daughter. Despite the freezing wind, by the time they arrived he was mopping the sweat off his face with the tissue she had handed him with ill-disguised revulsion.

They squeezed into the back behind a phalanx of cameras. Dick Allard from the *Telegraph*, a seasoned hack who'd seen eight home secretaries come and go, swivelled towards them as if his top half operated independently of the rest. 'Shouldn't you be up there, keeping him on a tight leash? Or *any* leash . . .'

Farmer gave him a bland, confident smile, hoping he looked as if he was in control and not like a child who'd been asked to walk a snarling bull terrier and accidentally let it loose in the playground. Allard's infallible radar would almost certainly have detected that Rolt was uncontrollable, but Farmer did his best. 'We've decided to let him have his head while he finds his feet.'

The journo gave him a withering look – *Is that the best you can come up with?* Still breathing heavily from the walk, Farmer knew that his excuse was crap but he was too knackered to think of anything better.

Beside him, Pippa glowed as if she'd just come from a spa. 'Yes, that's right, Dick. Not everyone constantly needs their hand holding. He's the Real Thing, not some manufactured PR product.' She smiled at Farmer.

Allard ignored her. He looked like a dog with a fresh bone. 'You're not going to get this genie back in the bottle – you do know that, don't you, Derek?' He looked at Farmer gleefully.

Farmer swallowed uncomfortably. The PM had wanted him to move over to Rolt's office and keep a close eye, but he wasn't about to give up his cushy place at Number Ten, not after all the work he'd put in to keep the bloody man in power. In any case, although he knew Rolt had saved their bacon, he had a nagging feeling that he was not only toxic but would soon have become a liability. He'd been in the game too long to fall for these populist 'Trust me, I'm not a politician' types, who always had to be paid off – or sacked, when they inevitably revealed their true nature. So he had offered the post to Pippa, sugaring the proposition with a juicy uplift in pay, but she'd reminded him wearily that she was going on maternity leave in a couple of months. That explained the tummy he'd been so careful not to mention. Bloody women – should have their eggs frozen before they came into these jobs, he thought. Or, better still, go back to the good old days when they could quite legally be let go. But his thoughts on that, like more and more of his thoughts these days, were best kept to himself. That was the difference between him and the likes of Rolt. He knew when to button it. And thus he would outlast them all.

So here they were, hurtling towards a live press conference, the country's most controversial new politician on stage, *unspun*. Allard was sickeningly right. They had not only had no control over him but, given his popularity, they might never get him to sing from the same hymn sheet. Hell, he wasn't even in the same church.

Rolt strode into the room to loud applause, waving and pointing at people in the crowd, like an American.

'Who the fuck does he think he is? Bill Clinton?' Farmer whispered.

'And who are *they*?' Pippa whispered back, nodding at a pair of heavy-set men with shaved heads who seemed to be with him.

Farmer peered at them. 'Probably some muscle from Invicta.'

Not far behind, the precocious intern, Henry Mead, was looking very pleased with himself. Farmer nudged Pippa. 'He's thrilled, the poncy little prick.'

There was a ripple of applause, which Rolt silenced with a sweep of his hand. Now he seemed to think he was the Pope. Farmer was also dismayed at the way the man seemed never to show the tiniest trace of fatigue. What the hell was he on? He hopped onto the podium. He had no notes with him and there was no autocue.

Rolt waited for the crowd to fall silent. Then he began, his voice low. 'First of all I want to thank the British public for giving me this opportunity to serve them.' He turned and looked straight at the cameras. 'From the bottom of my heart, I thank you. I will not let you down.'

'Fucking hell,' said Farmer, under his breath. 'It's like he thinks the entire bloody nation voted him in.'

'They might as well have done. He knows we wouldn't be back in if it wasn't for him.'

'And he's not going to let us forget it.' Farmer shifted his considerable weight onto his other foot; his shoes hurt and he was desperate to sit down.

'"The world is a dangerous place to live in, not because of the people who are evil but because of the people who don't do anything about it." Albert Einstein said that, a Jewish refugee from Nazi Germany.'

Farmer leaned closer, brushing her ear with his mouth and causing her to back away a little. 'In case he's about to be accused of being a Nazi, that's what that's for,' he whispered. But her attention was fixed on Rolt, along with the rest of the crowd's.

'There have been attempts to explain away the strife that has torn our country apart as the work of just a few extremists. Excuses have been made in the name of multiculturalism, calls for tolerance of different values, for broader minds. And where has it got us? That tolerance has merely allowed the open preaching of hatred. Words that are in direct conflict with democracy. Tolerance has not worked. And it stops here. Intolerance must be met with intolerance.'

His voice had risen several decibels, as if he was addressing a gang of tattooed men in the back room of a pub in Essex, not the world's press.

'They won't like being preached at,' whispered Farmer.

'He doesn't care about the press. He's talking straight to the people at home.'

Farmer knew that, as was so often the case, she was right.

Rolt gripped the lectern, then moved dramatically to the side, as if symbolically rejecting the old texts. 'To those who don't like this country's values I say, "Take your leave." To those who have gone abroad to fight for extremist causes, I say, "Don't bother to come back. You have forfeited your right to citizenship." I'm here in front of you today to make a pledge that very soon this land will be rid of all those who are not patriots, who do not love this country with their hearts and souls. Be under no illusion, whoever negates their allegiance to this country with some faith or connection to evil values like these, not only are they not welcome, they will forfeit their right to British citizenship.'

He paused for a few seconds, nodding to the crowd.

'Yes, it *is* that simple. And our country *will* once more be safe from terror. In the coming days and weeks I shall be devoting my time as your home secretary to piloting the legislation through Parliament that will end, once and for all, the right of individuals to live here, to enjoy Great Britain's freedoms – not to mention its generous welfare provision – who do not support its values one hundred per cent.'

He turned to the cameras again.

'And for any of you who are not willing to give your loyalty to this great nation of ours, and embrace its democratic values, I've got one simple message. Start packing.'

That was tomorrow's headlines sorted, thought Farmer, as a mixture of awe and fear spread through him, prompting more sweat. The atmosphere in the room was electric. Every word was great copy and would be quoted verbatim, a veritable banquet of sound bites. How the fuck was the PM going to control the man?

He had to hand it to Rolt: he knew how to connect with an audience, right over the heads of a hall full of cynical hacks. But he wasn't speaking like the new member of the government he now was. Allard was right. The genie was well and truly out. Be careful what you wish for, he thought as he leaned towards Pippa. 'The PM's going to love this – not.'

Pippa raised her neatly tweezered eyebrows. 'Well, he's made this particular bed, hasn't he? He'll have to lie in it.'

Farmer guffawed. 'Yeah, with Rolt's dick up his arse.'

She cringed.

Something about her head-girlish manner made him talk dirty – he couldn't help it.

They watched as Rolt started to leave the stage, apparently not intending to take questions. But all the scribblers and TV

113

reporters leaped to their feet, shouting and jostling with camera operators and photographers. Farmer felt a wave of relief as he saw that Rolt was not going to attempt to answer them, but then Allard got onto his chair and yelled above the cacophony: 'Home Secretary, can you tell us what else happened in the early hours of this morning, after your victory?'

Somehow this question – completely out of the blue as far as Farmer was aware – penetrated the wall of sound and stopped Rolt dead in his tracks. The room fell silent. He looked straight at Allard, his mouth half open, as if lost for words.

'What the fuck's he on about?' growled Farmer.

Rolt closed his mouth, then smiled. 'What happened last night? I'll tell you.' His voice was almost a whisper. He stepped back into the centre of the stage. 'An attempt on my life was what happened, the first shot in a war that I intend to win. Because, make no mistake, *we are at war*.'

He stood for a few more seconds as the cameras flashed, then stepped down.

The room erupted in a roar.

Farmer pressed his phone to his ear. The PM needed to know about this – if he hadn't already seen it broadcast live and passed out from the shock.

Pippa was giving him a thunderous look. 'What attempt on his life? What's he talking about?'

Allard looked round at them and grinned broadly as the heavies who had accompanied Rolt cleared the way for him to quit the room. The swarm of media followed, waving micro-phones and mini-recorders while some of the TV reporters set up hurriedly to deliver breathless pieces to camera as their colleagues pushed past.

Farmer felt his face heating, his pulse racing. Right now a heart attack would be a mercy. His usual *sangfroid* had deserted him. He grabbed Allard by the shoulder. 'Where did you get that?'

Allard smirked. 'Just doing my job, Derek.'

Farmer was struggling. He couldn't remember a time when he'd felt less in control.

# 23

**20.30 local time**
**Turkish-Syrian border**

The border was just as Hakim had described, except that it wasn't deserted. Twenty metres from the wire, blocking his path, four or five people stood in a tight cluster, lit by the head-lights of a small four-wheel-drive truck.

This is where it all goes wrong, Jamal thought. This is where I get recognized and sent back to Abukhan. Word could have spread about his disappearance. Their militia had links with other groups all over the north-west of the country. He was weak with hunger – he hadn't eaten since early morning and was starting to feel light-headed, as well as numb with cold. But this new threat gave him a useful surge of adrenalin.

A woman was kneeling on the ground. Three men were standing around her, while a fourth, smaller, maybe a child, was trying to get her to stand. But she wouldn't; he could see even at this distance she was hysterical.

There was no way of getting past them without being noticed. He could wait until whatever was happening played out. He was unarmed. He should keep his distance. But something about the scene compelled him to move closer. The woman on the ground in her hijab reminded him painfully of the girls that morning, their brief lives cut short by men who had no humanity.

In the truck, the driver was sitting at the wheel, smoking and gazing at his phone, showing no interest in the commotion. Jamal, screened from the group by the headlights, came alongside him. The driver glanced up at him, then returned to his screen. Jamal addressed him in Arabic.

*'What's happening?'*

The driver didn't look up. *'They want money.'*

*'For what?'*

*'They're saying they want their cut for bringing her through the border.'*

*'Did they?'*

The driver gave him a look and returned to his phone.

*'Are you with them?'*

He shook his head. *'I'm just the driver.'*

She was talking very fast in what sounded like French. Although he couldn't make out what she was saying, the emotion in her voice, the desperation, was only too clear. She was waving something in her hand, a small square. Reflections of the headlights bounced off it. As he came closer the group all turned to look at him, squinting through the headlight beams.

The woman waved at him and pointed at what he could now see was a photograph.

*'Mon fils!'* she cried. *'Je dois le voir.'*

The smaller figure tugging at her was a boy who could have been no more than eleven. They were both dark, Jamal guessed North African. He replied in French. *'Où est votre fils?'*

She was too distraught to answer.

He tried again in English. 'Where is he?'

'Hospital. Aleppo.'

He turned to the group. The men were all young, late teens. One was brandishing an AK, waving it around like a kid with a toy. They each had on thick padded gilets over their hoodies.

He addressed the gunslinger in Arabic. *'What's the problem?'*

*'Go away.'*

He waved the weapon at the path to the border, urging him to move on. Jamal could have gone through. The wire was just metres away. One of the gunslinger's pals had opened the woman's bag and was emptying the contents onto the ground, a pathetic scattering of a comb, two oranges, a piece of bread and a few banknotes, pushing the boy away as he tried to intervene.

'They take my money – I cannot go, cannot pay driver. Please. My son!'

Jamal held out his hand and she passed him the photograph. He held it up in the truck's headlamp beam. Étienne. Jamal recognized him instantly, even though the picture was a few years old. He had been in their platoon but had lost a foot to a landmine. The last he'd heard of him he was in an underground hospital somewhere outside Aleppo. When he looked again at the young boy and the mother there was no doubt. They were all so alike.

Jamal turned and walked a few paces back to the truck.

'*Hey, get going,*' the gunslinger yelled. Jamal ignored him. He and his pals were clearly preying on people coming through the border, taking whatever they could. He approached the driver.

'*You armed?*'

The man shook his head, but Jamal could see the grip of a handgun sticking out from under the dash. '*Not my fight, this. But if she doesn't pay me I'm not taking her.*'

Again, Jamal felt naked and useless without a weapon. The gunslinger was still waving his gun at Jamal, gesturing at the border.

'*Get going, now.*'

Jamal turned back to the driver. '*You wait. Don't go yet.*'

Jamal half raised his hands as he came back towards the group. 'Okay, okay.' He walked towards the gunman as if to go past him and on his way. But as he came alongside, with a lightning move he made a grab for the hand with the weapon. Gripping the barrel, he wrenched it upwards, twisting it sideways at the same time. He heard the forefinger crack but it squeezed the trigger. The round zinged past Jamal's shoulder and just missed the other two who dived for cover. The woman let out a piercing scream but she wasn't hit. Jamal's instinct was to jump back but he overrode it, keeping his grip fast on the gun hand, twisting it with all the force he could muster, until the weapon came free. The gunslinger dropped to his knees, let out a long, shrill screech, more like a bird than a man, and curled into a ball clutching his broken hand.

The driver, seeing the commotion, fired up the truck. Jamal whirled round and faced him.

*'No, you wait. You're taking them.'*

He revved the engine, saw the weapon in Jamal's hand and thought better of it. One of the gunslinger's mates still had the woman's bag in his hands. Jamal signalled to the boy to help his mother into the truck, then shouted to the other two: *'Pack that bag. Put everything back. And give it to me. Now!'*

The one holding the upturned bag was slow to move so Jamal stepped forward, pressed the muzzle hard against his left ear then fired a single shot above his head. Both of them bent down and scooped up the contents of the bag that were strewn over the track.

The boy was having trouble persuading his mother to get into the truck. She was still hysterical. *'Il a mon argent, tout!'*

Jamal turned back to the balled-up gunslinger. *'The money. All of it.'*

He didn't move at first. Jamal fired another round that went between the two others. They fell on their injured leader, yanking out the wad of notes buried inside his hoodie, and passed it to Jamal. He waved the money so the driver could see it, then gave it to the boy. 'Go now. Get away from here.'

The boy and his mother climbed into the truck. It took off at speed, the wheels kicking up a cloud of dust as the tyres scrabbled for grip, then bounced up the rutted track Jamal had just come down and disappeared into Syria. He didn't much fancy her chances of finding Étienne. Perhaps the driver had some clout with the men at the roadblock, but how many more thieves would demand her money before she reached her son? The whole thing sickened him.

He had temporarily lost focus. Suddenly the two came at him, one holding a knife. He was not much older than Étienne's little brother. A few seconds ago they'd been cowering. Now they seemed to have discovered some real balls. There was no alternative. Jamal aimed, and squeezed.

All he heard was the dead man's click of the weapon firing off the action but with no round to strike because the mag was empty. They must have known how many rounds were left. Jamal feinted as the knife man closed in, flipped the AK so he gripped the muzzle, and smashed the butt into the side of his head. As he went down the knife flew out of his hand and disappeared into the darkness. The second man hesitated, just long enough for Jamal to repeat the action with the AK.

They were all down. Four months ago, he wouldn't have had any idea what to do. Now out here alone, just a few metres from freedom, he eyed the three he had just felled, and realized with a shock how much in him had changed.

# 24

**19.00**
**Piccadilly**

Back at Jez's flat, Tom ran a bath, put the iPad on the laundry basket and started to watch a replay of the press conference. He'd known the incident at the hotel would leak out one way or another and couldn't help admiring the way Rolt had spun it. He'd let it run, not paying very close attention, until he noticed the two pumped-up security men standing to one side of the podium, almost off-screen. They weren't from Invicta, that was for sure. They reminded him of the two heavies who had blocked his way to Rolt's office that morning. He froze the image, then played it back several times and zoomed in on them, but the image broke up: the shot was too wide for him to be certain.

He searched through the hundreds of images of Rolt that had accumulated over the last few weeks of his campaign: visiting schools and hospitals, inspecting a street that had been virtually burned to the ground in riots, fending off a furious man in a white *jubbah*, being cheered by some old ladies and at several photo opportunities with the prime minister, who was doing his best to make it appear as if Rolt was his oldest pal. Phoebe was in several of the pictures, looking for all the world like the ideal politician's wife.

He dialled her number.

She sounded upbeat. 'I got hold of Heron. He's a real craftsman all right – thousand-quid toy chests, presentation caskets, that sort of thing.'

'Good. Any ornamental sabres?'

'Interesting. He wasn't about to divulge his client list but I charmed one name out of him. He's made several for the same customer.'

'And they are . . . ?'

'Superior Swords, of Hatton Garden.'

'Keep going.'

'Ah, well, there it gets a bit tricky. They don't disclose any data for reasons of commercial sensitivity, blah blah blah, so I had to get the techies to hack their bank account. I found five listed as Crimean Ceremonials. So, made for a company, not a person. Anyway, I pressed on. Are you bored yet?'

'Far from it.' This was Phoebe at her best.

'So the company that commissioned the daggers, or whatever they are, is UA Holdings. Just a property business, nothing odd or unusual about it at first sight.'

'Except?'

'It's registered in the Bahamas, one of a number of firms belonging to an umbrella company, which also owns Lancaster Media.'

'Surprise me.'

'Ultimate owners of *Newsday*.'

'Any other parties connected with the company, preferably with the first name Oleg?'

'It's all privately owned and that's as far as I got.' She was starting to tire of his torrent of questions.

'Okay, thanks. You get some rest.'

Having established that she was going away for the night, to visit an old friend, Tom reassured himself that she was safe for the moment and sank down in the water. He was no nearer to knowing who 'Oleg' was – but at least he now had another line of attack.

For the second time, he Googled Xenia Dalton. At one red-carpet event, the London première of a Hollywood blockbuster, she was standing just behind the prime minister: the same striking face, but more serious this time, the only woman there not hoping to get in front of the paparazzi. He zoomed in closer. She was beautiful in an understated way, with the sort of face that needed no makeup. He searched for more shots and found one of her being introduced to a royal. The only others showed her at a Crimean school surrounded by kids, opening an orphanage with an unpronounceable name, and at various functions – with no obvious man in tow, he noted. Finally there was one, from a couple of years ago, of her collecting an award from Amnesty International with Helen, the *Newsday* reporter who had tried to make a date with him that morning. Not a likely event for a supporter of Rolt to attend.

He searched the digital edition. Rolt wasn't the main story: he had second billing to an item about the mass execution of a group of schoolgirls in Syria – more fuel for the new home secretary to pour on the already incendiary situation. He made one more search, for any commentary about the paper itself, and found nothing except a small piece in the *Guardian*'s media section from some weeks before: *Newsday Veers Right*, remarking on the paper's surprise endorsement of Rolt. Underneath the piece was a profile of the recently appointed editor, a man named McCloud. Tom clicked off and placed the iPad on the chair next to the bath.

He was hoping to have the flat to himself for the evening, just to chill, get his head together after the day's activities and catch up on some much-needed sleep. The water was deliciously warm. The lack of sleep caught up with him and seconds later he was gone.

He woke with a jolt when he heard the front door slam. He must have been out for a good half-hour as the bath had cooled considerably. He flicked the hot tap on with his big toe. He could hear Jez and another voice – a woman giggling, followed by Jez's loud gusts of mirth. With a bit of luck they'd be gone in a few minutes.

But then the bathroom door was edged open.

'Ah, er, Tom? You there?' There was a note of hesitation in Jez's voice.

'Who were you expecting? Goldilocks?'

Jez slipped in and closed the bathroom door, swaying slightly, his eyes shiny from drink. 'So, ah, good day?'

Jez never asked how his day was. 'Ripping, thanks. How was yours?'

'Oh, you know. Same old.' He perched on the edge of the bath. Something was on his mind. 'Look, I know you're probably looking forward to a night in, but . . .'

Tom extracted a hand from the water and signalled for him to stop. 'Say no more.'

It was his flat. What could you do?

'Thanks, mate, you're a trooper. Can you sort something out?'

'Yeah, sure.' Tom stood up and reached for his towel.

'And have you got any, erm . . . ?'

'In the bedside drawer.'

'Cheers. I owe you one. Or maybe more, if I get really lucky.'

Tom was too distracted to pretend to laugh. He mulled over his options. Although he was knackered he also felt restless: the day had brought no solutions, only new questions, and he was impatient for answers. Even the meeting with his father, which should have been a relaxing interlude, had left him edgy.

He picked up the iPad and looked again at the images of Xenia Dalton, in particular the one of her accepting the award with Helen.

In one of his pockets he found the card she had given him and dialled her number.

'Hi, it's Tom Buckingham.'

'Tom! I'd given up hope.' She sounded thrilled.

'Never give up hope.'

'It's been mental since the press conference. The assassination attempt, anything you can tell me?'

'You don't let up, do you?'

'It's what I'm programmed to do. So, where do you fancy? Hawksmoor? Dukes? Nando's . . . ?'

He pretended to think for a few seconds. 'Actually, I have another suggestion.'

'Ye-es?'

He could almost hear her clothes loosening themselves down the line. 'What's your publisher doing tonight?'

It was not the suggestion she'd had in mind. 'Hosting a reception for one of her charities. Why?'

'I could make a donation.'

There was more than a hint of wariness in her voice: 'It's invitation only, far as I know.'

'I could help you out with what happened last night.'

'People can't just drop into her place on a whim. She's very private.'

'We could look in, say hello, then go on somewhere more exciting where I can fill you in on Rolt's dirty secrets.'

Another silence. He pressed on: 'You collected that Amnesty award together. It was a great dress by the way.' Maybe flattery would get him somewhere.

She gave a sigh of capitulation. 'Okay, I'll see what she says.'

'And then you can take me to dinner and ask me anything you like about Rolt.'

'And if I've lost interest in him by then?'

'We'll try to think of some other way to pass the time.'

She laughed. 'All right, leave it with me. I'll come by in a cab about eight. Give me your address.'

'No, I'll drive you. I don't fancy going anywhere by cab in this weather.'

She lived in one of the new buildings behind Paddington station, overlooking the canal.

# 25

He shaved and dressed, ignoring the drunken giggling emanating from the kitchen. On his way out he nodded to Jez and his date, who raised her glass. With a bit of luck she'd be too far gone to notice Jez's dilapidated boxers.

He took the lift down to the car park in the bowels of the building and fired up the Range Rover. Even in ultra low gear with the differential lock on, the car twitched and slithered as it struggled to gain traction on the frozen ramp. On Piccadilly, a sightseeing bus had evidently skidded and broadsided opposite the Ritz, at the junction with Berkeley Street: a gaggle of excited Japanese tourists were photographing each other in front of it while their chaperone urged them in the direction of Fortnum & Mason, perhaps for some restorative shopping. Tom mounted the pavement and steered round the chaos towards Hyde Park Corner.

He drove as fast as the conditions allowed, which was not very. More snow had fallen and frozen, which had frightened all but the most intrepid or reckless off the roads. He had to thread his way slowly between several abandoned cars along Park Lane, and at Marble Arch a bus on fire. The area was swarming with emergency services, and the yellowish flames looked unreal in the almost monochrome surroundings, like a special effect at the storyboard stage.

He called her from outside her flat and a minute later she was picking her way across the icy pavement in a pair of totally inappropriate high heels. He jumped out, opened the passenger door and helped her across a puddle of slush on the pavement.

'Such a gentleman.' She was swathed in a silver grey fox-fur coat and a matching hat. 'A present from Xenia. I have to tell everyone it's fake.' She lowered her voice guiltily. 'But it's actually *real*!' She got in, revealing a glimpse of bodycon dress in something shimmery and blue. 'I hope it doesn't change your view of me. Morally.'

'Morally, no. She did kill them all herself?'

She leaned across, enveloping him in scent. 'Have *you* killed a lot of creatures, Mr Buckingham?'

He smiled. 'Where to, milady?'

'Park Gate Place, Kensington.'

'So we're in?'

'Seemingly she was curious to meet you too. Word of warning, though, you should probably know she's not that big an admirer of Vernon Rolt.'

'That's not the impression given by the paper.'

'She's the owner and publisher, so not that involved with the day-to-day editing. That's down to Bill McCloud. He's real foot-in-the-door old school – poached from the *Mail*. What matters to her is for the paper to succeed as a business so she can pay for the stuff she really cares about.'

'So McCloud's the cheerleader for Rolt.' He slowed down and skirted the nervous drivers moving gingerly along the icy road. 'What else do I need to know so as not to put my foot in it?'

'She's a widow, but she kept the English surname – Dalton.'

'Where does her money come from?'

'Her father. He died some years ago.'

'In the Crimea?'

'That's something she doesn't talk about.'

A Transit in front of them braked suddenly, too hard, spun 180 degrees and slammed sideways into a phone box. Helen grabbed the dash to brace herself for a hard landing but Tom deftly twitched the wheel and took them safely past. She raised her eyebrows in exaggerated appreciation. 'Nice driving. Did they teach you that in the SAS?'

He nodded. She'd done her homework too. 'Anything else?'

She sighed. 'She keeps her life very compartmentalized. She's a very private person. And I don't mean celebrity private, I mean truly not keen on a high profile, more towards the recluse end of the spectrum.'

'No other blood relatives?'

She leaned towards him again. 'I hope this evening isn't going to be all work.'

He smiled at her. 'So do I. But I work for Rolt and you want to report on him. Your turn.'

She raised her eyebrows. 'O-kay. Is it true someone tried to assassinate him last night?'

Tom noted her use of 'assassinate' rather than 'kill'. Rolt had truly gone up in the world. 'Someone broke into his hotel room but he wasn't there.'

'Is it true that the assailant was *not* a Muslim extremist?'

'He was wearing a mask. What does *Newsday* get in return for supporting him and his agenda?'

'I don't know. You'd have to ask McCloud. He's very tabloid, not exactly into human rights.'

Tom looked mock-indignant. 'Some of my best friends read the tabloids.'

'Yeah, right. Okay, my turn. Can you confirm that the would-be assassin was a disaffected member of Invicta?'

That was a surprise. 'Why do you ask?'

'Why shouldn't I?'

Tom gave her a knowing look. 'Because if I said yes, you wouldn't print it – it would be too damaging to Rolt.'

She sighed. 'I think that's enough about work for now, don't you?'

# 26

The house looked Georgian, or even Queen Anne. But there was something not quite right about it. For one thing the ground-floor windows were uniformly black – as if there was a wall of brick behind the glass. And there were too many storeys for a house of that age. There was also a high perimeter wall that appeared to have been added recently.

'Looks like she takes her security very seriously.' He pulled up to the disproportionately large gates. There was a steel panel in the stone gatepost, which held a key pad, a microphone and a large touchscreen. He let down his window and the icy air rushed in.

Helen reached across and pointed. 'You put your forefinger against the screen so it can read your print, then type in your registration number and your first and last names.'

He did this.

'Good, then key in this code: ZZKLM5566S. That's a company code, and the machine remembers your print if you come again.'

'Now what? We wait for our burgers?'

'It's all automated. It checks we're on the guest list, and that your vehicle is registered to you and so forth.'

The perimeter walls were, like the gate, far higher than any he'd seen in London and that included those round Buckingham Palace. The CCTV cameras were also unusual.

'They're linked together with these infra-red beams,' Helen explained, 'which activate the screens covering that particular bit to alert them inside if someone goes through them. And – this is *really* high end – the place is laced with microphonic cables that pick up any sounds and vibrations from anyone coming near the house.'

'The postman must love it.'

'Oh, they don't have any deliveries here.'

'Isn't this overkill?'

'As I said, she's very private and doesn't like the place teeming with guards. With all this hi-tech security, she doesn't need to have any heavies hanging around. She doesn't trust them.'

After several seconds the gates opened – Tom saw they were far thicker than they appeared – and he drove towards the front door.

'Not there – bear left. See that yew tree? Just in front of that.'

Tom put the Range Rover where he was told, and opened his door.

'Uh-uh,' said Helen. She reached across him, lingering a moment, and pulled it shut.

'Where are all the other cars?'

'Aha! Wait and see. Trust me, you'll love this.'

He stayed put, feeling a bit foolish. Then his eyes widened as he felt the ground beneath them vibrate.

'Well, if anyone asks, I can say the earth definitely moved.'

She wagged her finger at him in mock disapproval.

There was an almost imperceptible jolt, and he realized that the ground around them was getting higher – no, they were descending. 'OK,' he said. 'I'm impressed.'

The whole front section of the drive pivoted downwards until, with a slight shudder, it came to rest level with a large underground garage. Tom expected to see a couple of Lamborghinis, maybe a Bugatti Veyron, but no: just a Jaguar XJ, a Mercedes G-Wagen and a couple of nondescript SUVs.

'All hers?'

She shook her head, then pointed at a classic Mercedes 230 SL parked apart from the rest.

'What now? Do we strap on jetpacks or is it a monorail?'

They headed for a narrow door flanked by CCTV cameras. So far that made twelve, and he'd only seen the front.

'Bulletproof,' she volunteered. 'They all are.'

Even newspaper proprietors weren't *that* unpopular. The woman was afraid of something a bit more menacing than her readers. 'What's she hiding from?'

Helen was busy going through the same routine with the key pads – using a different finger this time. The door slid open.

The building was three hundred years old on the outside, but that was just the façade. As soon as they were through the doors Tom saw it was newly built. He almost heard his mother's sharp intake of breath at such wanton modernization. The lift took them to a hall that was beyond minimalist: dove grey carpet with matching walls.

'Weird, isn't it? Like stepping through a wormhole.'

'Is it a home or an office? It's hard to tell.'

'Both. She does pretty much everything from here.'

'And this is all hers?'

'That's right.'

Standing by a black marble plinth that seemed to be a reception desk as styled for Cleopatra were two solid men in suits, one part head waiter to three parts roadblock. Tom gave them a cheery wave. 'Evening, gents.'

He whispered to Helen, 'I thought she didn't like on-site muscle.'

'They must be for tonight's reception. Normally it's deserted.' She took his arm and started towards the lift.

Tom turned back and went up close. The two men retracted their heads and puffed out their chests. 'Vladimir Putin takes the prime minister and his cabinet to dinner. The waiter asks,

"What'll you have?" Putin says, "I'll have the steak." The waiter says, "What about the vegetables?" And Putin says, "They'll have the same."'

There was just the flicker of a reaction, then one snorted and guffawed. The other smirked, thought better of it and changed his expression to one of disapproval.

The lift arrived and Helen pulled Tom in.

'Which worthy cause is this in aid of?'

'Orphanages in Crimea, apparently.'

The lift whisked them smoothly to the fifth floor, with just the minutest vibration of the silver fox coat to reveal they were moving.

'So she has a conscience, despite the wealth.'

Her pink lips tightened. He was pressing on a raw nerve. She frowned at him. 'You're not such a fan of Vernon Rolt yourself, are you?'

He weighed up the pros and cons of conceding this round. Maybe giving something back would be useful. 'Is it that obvious?'

'You hide it well, but I don't get the sense you're much of a zealot for his brand of politics.'

'On our first encounter, I thrashed the living daylights out of him.'

Her eyes lit up.

'In the boxing ring at school.'

She was about to ask a follow-up question when the doors opened to reveal a second pair of men almost identical to those downstairs.

'And they say good things never come in fours.'

The men waved wand scanners over them and nodded them through without cracking so much as a smirk.

'Hey, why aren't you at work?'

They both turned in the direction the strong Scottish accent had come from. A man in his late fifties, with a florid face and thin, sandy hair, was putting on a coat and scarf. He looked at Helen without any trace of warmth.

'Bill McCloud, my editor. Tom Buckingham, from Invicta.'

McCloud eyed Tom with amused disdain. 'Watch out for her. She'll have your trousers off before you can say "sexual harassment".'

Helen snorted. 'Don't mind him. He's drunk.'

McCloud scowled at Tom, his lips disappearing so his mouth became no more than a scrawled line across his weathered face. 'Your man's only been bumped off the front page once this week. Even he couldn't upstage a schoolgirl massacre in Aleppo. *Ciao.*'

He disappeared into the lift. Tom watched him go. 'Does he always talk to you like that?'

'It's scarier when he's sober.'

There were about thirty people in the room, all men, all in dark suits.

'It looks like an undertakers' convention. Who are these guys?'

She took his arm and propelled him forward. 'Donors to the charity, I suppose. Men of high net worth with deep pockets.'

Tom recognized one of them, Vic Sanders, an ex-SAS Rupert who had made a pile supplying security to oil installations. He caught Tom's eye and bounded over. 'Blimey, they'll let anyone in these days!' He pumped Tom's hand, evidently remembering him with a warmth and enthusiasm that Tom struggled to reciprocate. 'Where was it last? Helmand? Kandahar?'

'Godalming, I think. Davidson's wedding.'

'Shit, yes. Poor Davidson.'

Davidson had joined Sanders's outfit in Libya and been kidnapped. The Regiment mounted their own operation to spring him but he had died in the firefight with his captors. They shared an impromptu few seconds' respectful silence, which Tom broke with a question. 'So, what's your connection to Xenia?'

Sanders bridled. 'Ms Dalton to you, I think.' Then, clearly regretting his pomposity, he added, 'Well, that's how we mere mortals address her. I just come to drool like the rest of them. Pour a fortune into her fund in the hope she might . . . deign to look upon me.' His voice drifted off. Sanders had plenty of money but almost no charm.

'For the orphanages?'

'That's right.'

Tom lowered his voice. 'And what are they a front for?'

Sanders leaned closer. Tom caught a gust of wine breath as he spoke quietly into his ear. 'A word to the wise. This isn't the place to make cracks about things like that.'

The man Sanders had been talking to was now looking his way, frowning. 'You're Buckingham's lad, aren't you? SAS?'

Tom put on a smile. 'I work for Invicta now.'

'Ah, yes, good show.'

Part of his face seemed frozen and his left eye floated free of its twin. He put out his hand but the frozen-face man didn't seem to notice it. 'So you know my father, Mr . . . ?'

'Whitworth. We had a little venture with our Russian friends a few years back. It didn't quite come off. One lives and learns. Won't make that mistake again. Hugh not coming?'

'Why would he?'

Whitworth gave him a slightly surprised look. 'No reason. We're all very keen on your Vernon Rolt, aren't we, Sanders? We've got high hopes for him.'

Sanders nodded.

Whitworth wandered away.

Tom watched him go. 'So why's he here?'

Sanders eyed Tom as if he was a man who hadn't been let in on the secret. 'Dear me, you are out of the loop. Put it this way, Xenia's just the tip of a very formidable iceberg.' He pointed at Helen, who was beckoning. 'Uh-oh, looks like you're in demand.'

She scooped him up and propelled him quickly through the crowd. 'You'll get about five minutes. Less if you bore her, so be careful not to outstay your welcome. Don't shower her with praise or compliments, and keep in mind, she doesn't do small-talk.'

'I like her already.'

She gave him a warning look. 'And, really, don't try to flirt.'

They went through a pair of piano-black double doors into a smaller room with two full-length windows overlooking the park. Perched on her own on a very long leather sofa, Xenia Dalton was examining some papers on an equally long glass table. Her blonde hair was gathered into a loose bun that displayed to maximum effect a long, slim neck. Her face was pale, as were her eyes, an almost mauve shade of blue, but her eyebrows were darker and seemed set in a slight frown. She was talking into a phone but ended the call as they approached. She didn't get up but as she lifted her gaze to Tom her eyes widened slightly. She offered him a hand that was surprisingly chilly. 'Mr Buckingham. I'm so glad you could join us.'

'Thank you. Quite a place you've got here.'

Xenia picked up her glass and waved it at Helen. 'Would you give us a few minutes, darling?'

Helen disappeared back through the doors into the crowd.

Xenia put her head on one side and eyed him, frowning. 'So, why did you want to meet me?' Her English was completely fluent with only a hint of an accent.

He sat down on the sofa at a polite distance, about a dining table's length away. 'Oh, curiosity, mainly.' He gave her a winning smile, which she didn't return.

'I hear you watch Vernon Rolt's back most assiduously.'

Tom smiled at the compliment with more restraint this time. 'Do you know him well?'

'I know who *you* are. That you were thrown out of the SAS after an incident in Afghanistan and joined Invicta on the rebound.'

She'd completely sidestepped the question, which only made her more intriguing to Tom.

'Yeah, that's about right.' Well, it was, sort of.

'Are you one of those troublesome men who don't like to take orders?'

'I'm really quite obedient when the mood takes me.'

'And what does it involve, working for Vernon Rolt?'

'Nothing very thrilling. I'm a sort of glorified minder, really.'

'Don't be so modest. Surely you don't let all that expensive training go to waste.'

'Let's just say I help anticipate risks and . . . handle them. Try to keep him out of trouble.'

Her eyes widened. Was she sizing him up as a potential conquest, or something else? She already had more than enough muscle around the place.

He nodded at the copies of *Newsday* arranged on the table. 'It's done wonders for his campaign, all the space you've given him.'

She shrugged, as if she was barely aware of it. The paper she owned had gone all out to get him elected, and had greeted his appointment to the cabinet with undisguised euphoria. Her lack of interest was baffling. 'Sometimes one has to stoop a bit to keep the circulation up. My views aren't necessarily those of the editor.'

He smiled. 'Yes, I met him.'

A blank look from her. 'Do you doubt my sincerity, Mr Buckingham?'

'Tom. Not at all. It's just a surprise that you backed Rolt, yet you also win awards from Amnesty. How do you square that?'

'Newspapers are a business, human rights aren't. One pays so I can invest in the other.'

'Those men out there don't look like they go much on human rights.'

She ignored the comment, reached forward and spread out the front page about the murder of the girls in Syria. 'A freelance journalist I hired risked her life to get us this story. We're waiting for news of her. Forgive me if I seem a little preoccupied.'

'Dangerous place, particularly for a woman,' said Tom.

'You disapprove?'

'Good God, no. How else would we find out about these things?'

She nodded approvingly. 'Well, I'm glad we agree on one thing. And the more papers I sell, the more I can finance reporting like this.'

'So backing Rolt was all about circulation?'

She gazed into the darkness. The lights of the city were dulled by the heavy cloud that had descended. 'Sometimes, in order to survive, one has to make compromises. The challenge is to remain true to oneself in the process, and over time that can get harder. I think we both know what I mean, Mr Buckingham.'

Tom looked at her. Another time he would have come on a lot stronger. Quite where he had got to in terms of remaining true to himself was a question he had been avoiding for some time. The way she looked at him, with her eyes very slightly narrowed, was both seductive and threatening. He certainly did understand. Every day, working for Rolt while under cover, he was grappling with the same thing. But he also sensed that she was sending him a signal, that there was more she wanted to say but something was stopping her.

'I've lived in this country since I was eighteen.'

So, a change of subject.

'Why did you leave the Crimea?'

She seemed surprised at the question. 'The death of my father. We were very close.'

'And your mother, is she here?'

'She took her own life. Things became too much for her.'

'But you got out.'

She blinked. 'In a sense.'

She lit a cigarette, and blew smoke high into the air.

'It was love at first sight. So I stayed.'

'For your husband?'

'No – that was a childish crush that didn't last. For England. There are things about this country that are more precious than – than life itself.' She spoke with unexpected vehemence.

'Like what?'

'Freedom. Tolerance.'

Tom snorted. 'Doesn't feel as though there's a lot of either around right now.'

No response. She continued to gaze into the distance. Was his time up already? He pressed on: 'Is that why you have so much security? In case the masses rise up?'

She shook her head slowly. 'I have nothing to fear from the British.'

'Why did you agree to see me so readily? Helen said I should be honoured.'

A trace of a smile. 'I was interested to know more about Mr Rolt's plans.'

Tom frowned. 'Plans?'

'What he's preparing to do next.' She gave him what seemed to be a knowing look.

The only problem was he had no idea what she was talking about. 'Well, I suppose that's a matter for him to work out with the prime minister.'

She had leaned slightly closer, as if searching his expression for some other meaning. 'And do you think he's going to be able to satisfy his backers that way?'

'You mean Invicta?'

She shrugged. 'Maybe you are sworn to secrecy. Honour prevents you being candid.'

There was more than a hint of sarcasm in her voice. Tom was mystified. 'Is there something you think I should know?'

She looked away to the darkness outside. She was just as alluring from the side.

Damn. He wasn't about to give up yet. 'Rolt had a visitor from your part of the world this morning. I didn't get to meet him. Oleg, I think was his name. Left a nice present.'

One of the guards who had been by the door stepped into the room, approached and whispered in her ear, then waited for her response. She waved him away. '*Ckopo*. In a minute,' she hissed.

He seemed reluctant to go. Tom detected a distinct lack of deference. He gave the guard a cold stare, which was met with an insolent smirk.

Helen reappeared with another guard behind her. Xenia got to her feet. 'I'll leave you to your date. It was nice to meet you, Mr Buckingham. Keep looking out for your boss.'

She gave him her professional smile and offered her hand. He took it, felt its chill.

# 27

'How was that for you?' Helen steered him through the crowd towards the door.

'I'm not sure. The security need to learn some deference.'

She rolled her eyes.

'She seemed quite distracted.'

'She's worried about what happened in Aleppo. I mean, as well as those poor girls – the reporter's one of her oldest friends.'

He surveyed the crowd of suits, who were starting to move into another room. 'What's happening? Is Xenia going to talk to them?'

One of the guards approached Helen as if to hurry her towards the exit. Tom gave him a cold stare. Another guard joined him. The message was clear.

'Who's Oleg?' he asked her, as they headed out of the room. Helen gave a small sigh, as if she wanted to be done with talking about Xenia.

'I really have no idea.'

They ate at Hawksmoor. He ordered a T-bone that was just slightly smaller than the table. She had the turbot – with chips, which at least put her ahead of those tedious women who only ever ate salad. She was amusing, attentive and chatty, which was just as well since he was preoccupied by the conversation with Xenia. What did she know about Rolt that he didn't? Had he missed something, or had Phoebe? He had gone in search of answers and come away with even more questions.

When the bill arrived it was past midnight. Her flat was a treacherous two miles away through the slush. His was nearby . . .

But he would have to break it to her that he was too tired for anything. Maybe, if she stayed, he could make it up to her in the morning.

In the lift, she leaned against him and put her face up to be kissed. The doors opened, letting him off having to decide. He felt for his keys. With a bit of luck Jez and whatever her name was would be safely tucked away in the other room, releasing him from any social niceties. He unlatched the front door and they stepped into the hall. She made a move to kiss him again, then froze, her mouth open. He whirled round to see what she was looking at, as her hand shot up to cover her mouth. She turned white, doubled over and crumpled to her knees. Jez's bedroom door was open.

Now he saw the sprays of blood, such an unimaginable amount that it looked as if someone had chucked a bucket of it up the headboard and the wall. On the bed, Jez was face down, the back of his head blown clean away. Brain tissue spattered the pillow and the duvet. The woman was on her back, still half under him, her eyes wide open, with a glazed look of dismay, an entry wound on the right-hand side of her neck. Whoever had done it had been there only moments before. Or, Tom realized, his mind racing, could be still in the flat. Helen clung to him, trembling. He gripped her, then lifted her into the bedroom – the only place he could be sure was safe.

'Stay there.' He moved further inside. As he approached the woman, checking the carpet and bed for any empty shell cases, her eyes opened very wide. She wasn't dead – but soon would be. There was nothing he could do, but he went forward, and as her horrified gaze met his she raised a hand as if to stop him. Her mouth moved silently, then the hand flopped down and the little light left in her eyes went out. He wheeled round, grabbed Helen by the arm from behind the door where she had hidden, and pulled her into the room. She collapsed onto the floor beside the bed.

Helen was frozen with fear, holding her breath, probably ready to scream the building down. He gripped her tight and pressed his lips to her ear. 'Breathe out. Slowly.'

Nothing happened.

He looked at her hard. This was no time for pleasantries. 'Do it,' he hissed.

She nodded, and did as she was told.

'Good. Now, get under the bed. No matter what happens, do not move.'

'What?'

'Now.'

'I'm claustrophobic.'

Tom gestured at the bodies, still scanning the floor for any empty cases. 'Whoever did this may still be here.'

She got the message. He pushed her down and she wriggled out of sight.

There were no empty cases, which meant one of two things. If the weapon was a semi-automatic the shooter was being professional and had picked them up so there would be no forensics. But after what Tom had just witnessed, the shooter didn't appear to be that switched on. So the weapon might be a revolver, the professional killer's preferred choice because the empty cases stay in the chamber. So, a professional's weapon in an amateur's hands?

There was a reading light on the bedside table. He grabbed it, smashed the bulb and plunged the exposed wires into a tumbler of water. There was a loud electrical pop, a flash, then darkness. That was the lights dealt with. Nothing now but the dull orange from the streetlights below. He moved back towards the door and listened.

Jez's bedroom was opposite the front door. The hall ran to the left, with the door to the smaller bedroom, Tom's, on the same side as Jez's. Opposite that was the kitchen and, next to it, the bathroom. He had to be in there, unless he'd legged it down the fire escape outside the kitchen window.

Tom had about half a second to come up with a plan. He had left his weapon locked in the safe in his room – he'd assumed he wouldn't need it on a date. Jez, he was pretty certain, didn't keep one.

Still crouching in the doorway to Jez's room, he picked up a small carriage clock that was perched on a side table and chucked it down the hall. It made a solid clunk outside the three closed doors.

Straight away, two suppressed rounds slammed into the kitchen door, which told him the shooter was in the second bedroom, and that he was the type who would shoot before he looked. Tom listened out for the metallic clink of empty cases making contact with the floor. It didn't necessarily mean the weapon was a revolver, but it was another piece of information he would use to bring this shit to an end. One way or the other.

He picked up the table and chucked it in the same direction as the clock.

Another two rounds joined the first two in the kitchen door. With the two in Jez and his ladyfriend, that made six.

Tom picked up an umbrella leaning in the corner behind the front door, a classic old-fashioned one with a curved wooden handle. Then he opened the front door and slammed it so the shooter might think they had left. It was an old trick but better than nothing as he moved down the corridor. He was about to find out if the weapon was a revolver and the shooter had run out of rounds.

Shooting through the door was speculative. Whoever was firing wasn't a class act. They had given away their position. If Tom had been in the same situation he would have fired only when he had a clear target. That didn't make his opponent any less dangerous but it did give him more options as he flattened himself against the wall and edged towards his room.

The only other way out of that bedroom was through the window into the air shaft, with a three-storey drop. The drainpipes were too far from the window to reach unless the shooter was Spiderman. His only viable escape was past Tom to the front door. In the murk he saw the hazy shape of a head lean out. Just visible were the eye and mouth holes of a balaclava. Tom had the umbrella ready, holding it horizontally, at head height, parallel to the wall. He jabbed hard and almost got it into one of the eye-holes. The shooter yelped, crumpled and fired. The bullet passed Tom's temple so close he felt the air as he ducked. He had to stop another round heading his way. He threw himself onto the dark shape and they both went down, flailing in the darkness. Tom found the arm with the weapon at the end of it and snapped it back hard as a fist smashed into his left ear, then fingers clawed at his nose and eyes. Tom rolled them both over so he was on top but a head butt right on the bridge of his nose lost him a second and the shooter was up again, the pistol still in his now useless right hand. Tom lunged for him but the man dodged and fell into Jez's bedroom, landing half on the bed.

Two more rounds and Tom felt a hot stinging on the apex of his left shoulder. The shooter sprang up, smashed a knee into his crotch as he tried to recover from the pain and pushed past him into the hall. Then he was out of the front door. Gone.

# 28

## 01.00

Woolf met him on the landing, which was now choked with police. A couple of medics were looking after Helen.

'I'm so sorry, Tom. Poor fuckers. What shit luck.' Immediately the sympathy evaporated as professional necessity took over. 'Any ID?'

'Didn't get the balaclava off him.'

'Anything else?'

'Thirty-five, forty maybe. Hundred and forty pounds, five ten. Fit, though – very agile, well versed at working in cramped spaces. A crap shot, luckily. No empty cases but the rounds should be embedded about the place. Not that it matters. I doubt the weapon has a history. '

Woolf nodded at the bedroom. 'Better have a look.'

There was a very remote possibility that something in Jez's work might have provoked this, but as he and Woolf stood there in silent resignation, Tom knew that whoever had done this had in all probability come looking for him.

'Either they knew I did Randall or . . .'

'. . . you're a target because of your proximity to Rolt.'

Tom bent down, took out a pen and used it to pick up Jez's

Breitling, which had fallen on the floor beside the body. 'Well, that rules out burglary.'

He glanced at the team who were swarming over the scene. This wouldn't be secret for long. Woolf guessed what Tom was thinking. 'Don't worry, he's decreed a total blackout.'

'So he knows?'

As if on cue Tom's phone buzzed. He showed Woolf the screen: Rolt.

Tom didn't feel like talking to anyone, especially him, but Woolf urged, 'Go on. See what he says.'

Rolt seemed surprisingly calm. 'I just heard. I'm very sorry, Tom, and so relieved you're safe.' His voice sounded full of concern.

'Well, thanks. Good of you to call.'

'I'm going to deal with this situation, rest assured. And you're going to have a guard round the clock. It's all arranged.'

There was a new tone to his voice. How quickly the cloak of office had taken effect.

'How exactly?'

'They should be with you any minute. They'll take you to a safe house and keep a close eye. I must get going. Stay safe.' He rang off.

'Better do what the man says.'

Three men appeared in the hall. The M&S suits, practical shoes and earpieces said it all. Tom glared at Woolf. 'You knew about this?'

Woolf shrugged. 'He's the boss now.'

# 29

The wheels of the Airbus let out a sharp squeal as they touched the glistening tarmac and went from nought to two hundred miles an hour in one hundredth of a second. Either side of the runway a soft carpet of snow gave off a ghostly glow.

Jamal leaned his head against the window, peering out at the night. The engines roared as they reversed thrust to bring the aircraft down to taxiing speed. A mixture of relief and fear entangled inside him. Sleep had been in short supply as he'd made his way through the chaos of Syria into the comparative order of Turkey: whenever he closed his eyes, the memories flooded back, images that would stay with him all his life, as if they had been etched inside his eyelids, never to heal or fade.

'Cheer up – nearly home.'

He looked at the woman beside him. She had given him a big smile as she'd sat down in Istanbul – the first smile he'd seen in months – then fallen asleep before they were off the ground. How deeply, how peacefully she slept. What must that be like?

He gave her a weak smile. She leaned closer. 'I love my

145

homeland, don't get me wrong, but every time I get back to London I breathe a sigh of relief. Your family here?'

Jamal nodded.

She beamed. 'Aaah. Are they coming to meet you?'

'Maybe,' he lied.

He'd once imagined a hero's homecoming, his father proudly coming forward to embrace him now he knew what his son had achieved. His own naïvety shocked him. But he clung to the idea that he might find forgiveness, especially after what he had done for Emma.

The woman wasn't waiting for him to elaborate. Her eyes were glazed with excitement. 'My boy's coming to fetch me. He's a medical student – final year.' She oozed pride and nodded emphatically, as if to underline that her son had stayed the course, and she somehow knew Jamal was a dropout. 'And the Lord knows the world needs doctors.' She put a hand on his. 'He's already doing shifts at A and E in Chepstow. Sometimes he's on call up to thirty-six hours.' She shook her head mournfully. 'He says on Friday nights it's like a war zone.'

He peered into her eyes. *You have no idea what a war zone looks like,* he wanted to say. But he didn't. What overwhelmed him was this mother's pride and love for her son. He knew of women like her and sometimes he had wished his own mother was as proud of him. But he had never given her cause to be. Whatever she felt she had to keep to herself: that was how his father wanted it. He felt something welling inside him and she must have sensed it because she let her hand drop onto his.

He flinched. She frowned, glanced down and saw his fingers were purple and swollen. She moved her hand away. 'Have you been in a fight?'

'Frostbite.'

The ride on the bike and the trek to the border had taken its toll. The woman stared back, mystified, searching for a follow-up question, then perhaps deciding not to go there. Instead she beamed again. 'Well, you're safe now. Home sweet home.'

Home. He had never realized how much he would miss it. Everything he had taken for granted, even railed against as decadent and corrupt, now seemed uniquely precious. All that he had previously kicked against he saw now as something to be treasured: the most mundane things, like traffic keeping to the correct side of the road, postal collections and deliveries, fresh milk on the doorstep . . . all these now seemed like wonders of the world.

As the plane came to a halt on its stand there was a ripple of clicks as everyone undid their seatbelts, but an announcement from the captain asked them to remain seated for a few minutes while airport security boarded the plane. The cabin staff moved down the aisles pacifying those desperate to get off. A pretty stewardess glanced at Jamal, then quickly looked away. He watched through the window as the jet-bridge was manoeuvred into position and docked with the plane. As soon as the door opened, two uniformed police with MP5 carbines appeared at the door. With them was a third man in a hoodie with a shiny shaved head and small eyes. He looked more like a villain than anyone in law enforcement. Jamal tried to tell himself that their presence was some new measure on account of heightened international tension but, deep down, he knew there wasn't anything normal about this.

The three came purposefully down the aisle, the bullet-headed one in the lead, his eyes sweeping the rows of seated passengers. Then they locked on Jamal. 'Okay, Jamal, let's not make this any harder than it needs to be. Put your hands on top of the headrest in front of you and stand up.'

Jamal just stared at him. *He knows my name.*

At first Jamal didn't react. The armed pair closed round Bullet-head, who sighed. 'Do it now.'

He had kept his voice low as if he was trying to draw as little attention to himself as possible, but there was no point. The entire cabin was watching in stunned silence, the passengers in the rows ahead craning round to see what was happening as one of the armed cops gestured to the two other passengers in Jamal's row to move. The woman beside him shrank back, her hands masking her face as if she was about to be tear-gassed. The man in the aisle seat next to her, a young Caucasian no older than Jamal, gave him a look of disgust as he rose and moved out of the way. The Turkish woman remained glued to her seat, paralysed with fear. Bullet-head reached in and grasped her arm as if to lift her out of the way. She pushed him off and rose of her own accord, her shocked gaze still fixed on Jamal.

'Last chance, Jamal.'

'Okay, okay.'

He put his hands on the headrest and struggled to his feet. He had faced a lot of weapons in Syria, and had grasped enough about them to know that, unlike most firearms, the MP5s the police were carrying could be used inside the cabin: their mags would be loaded with low-velocity ceramic rounds that stayed in the target's body or would disintegrate if they hit any hard surface. All the same, they would be used only as a last resort. What worried Jamal more was the yellow Taser that Bullet-head had in his hand.

He'd known that, as a returnee from Syria, he was likely to be detained at Immigration, but he hadn't expected police to come onto the plane all tooled up. He told himself to do as they said and not give them an excuse to use the Taser.

'Stay there. Keep your hands on the headrest.' Bullet-head sounded almost matter of fact, as if this was just routine.

Jamal took a breath. Okay, be calm. They were probably pulling in everyone returning from Syria. He had his story – the true story. He had the film safely secreted. He could explain, and they would understand. They must. Maybe he'd even be thanked for what he'd done. That was what he'd told himself over and over on the brutal journey back. That was what would make it all worthwhile.

Bullet-head spoke again in a monotone, clear and firm. 'Do you have anything in the seat pocket or the overhead rack?'

He shook his head. He had left his few belongings in Aleppo. *Don't argue, don't resist. You have nothing to fear*, he told himself. To some people he would be a hero for what he had done. That was what Emma Warner had promised him. She would see to it that his story was told. She had given him her lawyer's personal number. He would help him. They let you make one call, didn't they? More than anything he wanted to speak to his sister, the only one of his family who would not have given up on him. But that would have to wait as Bullet-head wrapped plastic cuffs round his wrists and they closed with a rapid rasp.

He walked in single file between the two armed cops, Bullet-head bringing up the rear, but after they got to the aircraft door and stepped onto the jet-bridge, they took a sharp left through a narrow service door. The night air smelt of aviation fuel. They led him down steep steps to a waiting armoured van, where another two armed policemen stood guard. The cold bit into his face as he descended, stinging his chapped skin. At the bottom of the stairs he was searched and the pack of gum, passport and the few coins he'd saved for coffee at the airport were all placed in a transparent plastic bag. Then the two uniforms each took an arm and propelled him towards the open back doors of the van. Inside, another mesh door led to what looked like a cage with a small row of seats. It stank of disinfectant with an undertow of something worse.

'Stand still.'

One grabbed his cuffed and frostbitten hands ready to place him in a seat and belt him up. His whole body jerked as the knifing pain flashed through them. He stifled a yelp as he pulled them back towards him.

'Don't try to be clever, all right?'

He was doubling up with the pain.

Bullet-head was in no mood to mess about. 'Okay, have it your way.'

Something jabbed his arm. He shuddered uncontrollably and collapsed in a heap on the floor of the van. Bullet-head glared down at him. 'You're gonna wish you'd never come home, Sinbad. You are well and truly fucked.'

# 30

**08.00**

The bullet-headed cop introduced himself as Detective Inspector Brian Dawes.

'But you can call me "sir" for short.' He let out a staccato laugh.

Jamal made no response. He kept his eyes trained on the wall just above the cop's head. The room was painted a dismal grey, evidently designed to discourage any glimmer of hope.

'And over there is Detective Constable Chantal Richmond. If it offends you that there's a woman in the room, tough titty.' Dawes gave a low growl of mirth.

Out of the corner of his eye Jamal saw the DC close her eyes for a second, whether from the bone-dry atmosphere of the room or from long-suffering frustration with Dawes's brand of humour he couldn't tell. Her hair was very close-cropped and her eyebrows seemed to have been painted on. She stayed by the door, leaning on the narrow ledge below the window grille, her arms folded, her eyes trained on him. There was no clock and neither of them wore a watch that he could see.

He had lost all sense of time. After he was Tasered he had offered no resistance. He had barely slept or eaten in twenty-four hours and was utterly exhausted. He had been in the van for some time before they unloaded him. They had made him strip, then done a full body search and found the memory card. He had started to explain what it was but they weren't interested in hearing his side. The card was spirited away without comment.

As the armed cops stood by, a medic had bathed his frost-bitten hands and wrapped them in thick bandages that rendered his tender fingers almost useless. Jamal tried to explain about the damage but was told firmly to remain silent. He had been given tomato soup to drink through a straw, and a triple dose of Nurofen for the pain. His clothes and shoes had all been taken away. He sat there in a thermal vest and long-johns under a blue jumpsuit. The disposable slippers on his feet did nothing to insulate him from the icy cold floor.

Dawes didn't seem in any hurry. He leafed through a large file on his lap, whistling faintly to himself. 'Right, Jamal, let's go over some details, get a few things straight. You call yourself Al Britani, but your actual surname is Masri, correct?'

Jamal nodded. 'I don't call myself Al Britani any more.'

Dawes looked up, his eyebrows raised, twirling his pencil between his thumb and forefinger. 'Your father's name is Amir. Mother's name . . .' he frowned at his notebook '. . . Samba?'

It was wrong but Jamal didn't correct him.

'Just to keep you in the loop, Mr *Al Britani*, your family will also be taken in for questioning.' He gazed down again at his scrawl. 'Mani, Azil and Namir, your brothers . . .'

'And Adila?'

'Who?'

'My sister.'

Dawes glanced down again at the file in front of him and shrugged. 'Probably.'

Jamal felt the pain engulf him once more, like a toxic chemical coursing through his body. None of this should have been happening. He closed his eyes for a second, and when he opened them again Dawes had moved directly into his line of vision. Jamal leaned forward and took a breath. 'What about the video? You have it. It should be online – on TV.'

Dawes nodded slowly, his eyebrows raised.

'What does that mean? Yes?'

'Me policeman, you suspect. I ask the questions, you answer them. Got it?' Dawes glanced at Richmond.

'On what basis are you questioning me?'

Richmond took a breath and blew it out slowly. They both looked at him in mock-dismay.

'You haven't arrested me.'

'Schedule Seven, mate,' Dawes informed him. 'Don't need to.'

'What's that?' Jamal tried to keep his tone mild, with no hint of aggression.

Dawes sighed as if it was obvious, closed his eyes and recited, '"Under Schedule Seven of the Prevention of Terrorism Act, 2000, any individual can be detained for up to nine hours if there is a suspicion that they are, or have been, concerned with the commission, preparation or instigation of acts of terrorism."' He opened his eyes again. 'Do you understand?'

'May I?' He pointed at the pencil and pad on the table.

Dawes frowned, then brightened. 'You ready to write a statement? Where you've been, how you got there, what you did when you were there and with whom?'

Jamal reached forward slowly, picked up the pencil with his bandaged fingers and tried to close them round it. With some effort he produced a name in shaky capitals: ALISTAIR LATIMER, the lawyer whose name Emma had given him.

Dawes spun the pad round, glanced at it, snorted and pushed it away.

'He's a human-rights lawyer,' said Jamal.

Dawes sighed. 'I know who he is.'

'He should know I'm back.'

Dawes nodded excitedly. 'Mate, the whole world knows.' He reached into his case, pulled out a newspaper and flipped it open. 'You've got joint top billing.'

Jamal found himself staring at his own graduation picture.

Alongside it was the face of a man he didn't recognize standing at a lectern – very animated. Across the top was the banner headline, *PACK YOUR BAGS*, and beneath, *ROLT: IN*. Under Jamal's picture, the caption read, *AL BRITANI: OUT*.

'Who is this man?'

Dawes was grinning. 'Him? Vernon Rolt, the new home secretary, your worst nightmare. He's just made you public enemy number one.'

This was wrong, completely wrong. He felt a surge of nausea and looked away. Richmond unfolded her arms. 'Use the bin if you want to chuck.'

'This shouldn't be happening. I gave you the card. You have my evidence.'

He had shot the footage with Emma's camera, risked everything to capture the beheadings. Had something happened to it? Had he been tricked? How? Why? Who by? He was panting now, struggling to keep his composure. His head was spinning. He wanted very badly to lie down, and curl himself into a ball. No, he told himself. He had already been to Hell and got away. He must hold himself together, whatever happened. He slowed his breathing. 'I believe it's my right to see a lawyer.'

Dawes didn't respond. He put the paper down and went back to the file, flicking through the pages without reading them, as if browsing a catalogue, still whistling tunelessly. Eventually he closed it and pushed it away.

'Things have changed while you've been away, Jamal. And they're gonna change some more. People have had enough of your lot and all your human rights. They want *their* human rights. They're fed up with being terrorized by people who hate this country. We've had an election. And guess what, Jamal? It doesn't matter a fuck what you say. Vernon Rolt's going to make an example of you. By the time the new lot's finished with you, you're gonna wish you'd stayed in Syria.'

# 31

**15.30**
**Hendon, North London**

Tom woke from a deep but disturbed sleep in which the encounters with Randall and the intruder replayed themselves, blurred together in one titanic struggle. His eyelids felt as though they were made of lead.

When he realized there was another figure in the room they snapped open.

'Awright, Tom? Brought you a brew.'

He relaxed as he heard the voice, then a mug coming to rest on a surface close to his ear. Daylight oozing in round the edge of the curtains gave some shape to the large silhouetted figure bending over him. Tom hauled himself up onto an elbow, felt the sting from the flesh-wound. His head was thick with sleep. Outside he could hear the dull roar of fast-moving traffic. 'What time is it?'

'Tea time.'

'Yeah, but what *time*?'

'Three thirty.'

'*P.m.?*'

Almost a whole day wasted. Tom found the switch for the

bedside light, which illuminated the face of the tea bringer, who grinned. 'Reckon you had some kip to catch up on after the last couple of nights' excitements.'

As soon as his shoulder had been treated by the medics at the scene, a team of four had spirited Tom away from the flat. The damage had turned out to be little more than a graze, though the flesh had opened like a split in a grilled sausage, but there was no argument. He couldn't stay at the flat. The cops were there on the direct orders of the new home secretary and weren't about to let him out of their sight.

'Where are we?'

'Safe and sound.'

'Yeah, right. Does that have a postcode?'

'Hendon. That pleasant hum you can hear is the North Circular.'

'What's the plan?'

'Stay here until further notice. With a bit of luck we can get you moved to somewhere more comfortable.'

The sleep might have been necessary but time was ticking on.

'Where's my car?'

'One of the lads drove it up. I'm Vic, by the way.'

'Good to meet you, Vic.' He took a gulp of tea. Judging by the size of the window and the sounds outside, the flat was on the first or second floor.

'We can do you a fry-up or send out for something when you're good.' He gestured at the TV screen. 'The remote's on the side there. And you've got Sky Sports.' Vic zapped the screen into life. Rolt's face appeared. A crawler caption said something about 'Butcher of Aleppo'.

'What's this?'

Vic snorted. 'You couldn't make it up. Guy tops a bunch of school kids in Syria, then gets the plane home.'

Tom took the remote and leaned back on his undamaged shoulder. He wanted to give Vic and his crew the strongest possible impression that he was happy to chill.

As soon as he was alone, Tom leaped up and lifted the curtains. It was a low-rise block. He could see his car in a space

155

about forty metres away. But he didn't have the keys. In a wardrobe he found his jacket, felt for his pistol and two spare mags. As soon as the intruder had fled the flat he had gone to get it.

Taking out the Sig, he pushed the mag release with his right thumb and caught the thirteen rounds in his left before racking back the top slide to check the chamber. Once he knew it was clear he released the top slide, squeezed off the action, then pushed home the mag once more until it gently clicked into place. The weapon was now made safe. All Tom had to do was rack back and release the top slide to feed a round into the chamber to make ready. These drills had been drummed into him from the day he had joined the army. If you don't know the state of your weapon, you check it.

He had to get out of here. The attack in Jez's flat had just added to the pile of pressing questions to which he must find answers. Staying here would achieve nothing, but these guys weren't going to be talked round.

Still in his T-shirt and boxers, he ventured out to the bathroom where they had thoughtfully placed a new toothbrush and a rather small towel. The window was obscured with a frosted leaf pattern. He opened it to get a look at the other side of the building. Below the window in the service yard was a skip packed with tree prunings.

On his way back to the room he looked into the kitchen.

'All right, sir?'

So there were two of them.

'My glasses are in the car. You got the keys?'

The second guy stood up. He appeared to be the more junior. 'No worries. I'll get them for you. Orders are to keep you out of sight till further notice.'

Oh, well, then it had to be Plan B.

'It's Mike, by the way, sir.'

Tom grinned and shook his hand firmly. 'Tom will do fine.'

He watched Mike grab a jacket on his way out. He had to have the keys to the Range Rover on him. He heard one key going into the front-door lock, then a second. They weren't taking any chances.

On the kitchen counter he saw a couple of large loaves of sliced white, two boxes of teabags, two jars of instant coffee and two boxes of eggs. He opened the fridge door: bacon, sausages and five two-litre cartons of milk. Enough to last several days. Tom went back to the bathroom, had a shower, dressed and reappeared in the kitchen.

'No glasses,' said Mike, shaking his head. 'Couldn't see them.'

'Must've left them in the flat. Thanks anyway.'

Mike hung his coat in the hall. 'Want me to get someone to bring them up?'

'Nah. But I could do with some food.'

'At your service.'

Mike got to work on a fry-up while Tom sat and chatted with both men. They had joined the Met straight out of school, never wanted to do anything else, didn't like what was going on in the country and were hoping that the new home secretary would give them the chance to get stuck in and sort things out.

Tom agreed with everything they said, knowing only too well that it was all going to be a lot more complicated than that. But the task now was to relax them into dropping their vigilance.

The food was welcome. He demolished the lot and had another mug of tea with it.

'Why don't we get in a takeaway and watch something?'

'Mike's brought some DVDs.'

They gave each other a knowing look.

The films turned out to be *Mission: Impossible* and others in the same vein.

Five hours and three kebabs later, they were halfway through the second Tom Cruise when Tom got up to go to the toilet. He had already put on his trainers. He made for Mike's coat, found the keys to his Range Rover but not the front-door keys. Mike must still have them on him. Tom headed into the bathroom and locked the door, then put down the lid of the toilet and climbed onto it. A raw gust of icy air swept into the room when he opened the window. He hoisted himself up and put his feet through first. He could just squeeze out, twisting his body sideways. To drop he would need to turn right round and push himself away from the brickwork.

'Oh, fuck.'

The skip with its bed of trimmed foliage was gone. He cursed himself for not checking first. He gripped the sill of the window he had just come through while he searched for an alternative. The wastepipe was just below his feet, running down diagonally to a main pipe on his left. Flattening himself against the wall, he found a footing. But that committed him to going down. There was next to no chance of hauling himself back up to the window, and the drop from that height would still put him in hospital. He thought about dropping and making a grab for the pipe and ruled it out as too risky.

Then he saw, running vertically a couple of feet to his left, a satellite cable. He felt for it and worked his fingers under it. There was just enough slack between the fixings for him to get a decent grip. He gave it a tug to see how firm it was. It didn't come away. It might help get him to the main pipe. He put his weight on his one foot on the pipe, gripped the cable and lowered his left. He swapped hands on the cable, still trying to keep all his weight on the pipe, then slid himself down and along to the main wastepipe. With loud pings the two nearest cable fixings came away from the wall. He feared that would be it, but the cable held further up and he kicked with his right so that he swung close to the downpipe – but not close enough. His right hand gripped the cable, the thin plastic cutting into his fingers. A sliced hand and a broken back awaited him. He kicked again at the pipe and swung further this time, far enough to reach the downpipe with his left foot. He threw his last vestige of caution to the wind, let go of the cable and somehow got both hands on the pipe. From there it was just a matter of shimmying down.

He landed hard, winded and with a bloody hand, but he was free.

He reckoned he had about three minutes before they raised the alarm. By then he would be on the M1 heading north.

# 32

**17.00**
**Belmarsh Prison, South London**

The cell, on Wing Seven, was two metres by three. A window of thick, heavily scratched Perspex covered with steel mesh gave only a blurred view of a floodlit wall. As well as a shelf just wide enough to take a thin, narrow mattress, there was a TV on a plastic bench in one corner and a metal toilet in the other, with a small basin beside it.

'See these?' The officer pointed out the long lever tap handles on the basin. 'Abu Hamza was in here six years.' He made two hooks with his forefingers and flicked the cold tap on and off. 'Should have a blue plaque up for him.' He gave a mirthless laugh.

The process of just getting into the prison had taken nearly two hours. Fifteen doors and gates had to be negotiated. In the high-security unit, a grey solid block of a building – a prison within a prison – he was put through a series of security checks. First, he was told to remove everything he was wearing – even though it had all been given to him by the police who'd taken away the clothes he'd arrived in. Naked, he then had to walk through a metal detector before being subjected to an intimate body search. The soles of his feet, the spaces between his toes, his ears, his nose, his mouth and rectum were all thoroughly and humiliatingly examined. A sniffer device checked for any internal explosive devices. After getting dressed again he remained with two prison officers while they waited for clearance to go through a green metal door. Once through that he faced another locked door and a four-minute wait while he was scanned by CCTV cameras. After that, he was escorted out into the biting cold, an exercise yard, bright as day in the floodlights, surrounded by high fences topped with barbed wire and metal mesh for a roof. Two inmates were pacing the perimeter, watched by four prison guards. They all paused to stare at the newcomer.

The high-security unit was on two floors split into four spurs, each with twelve single-occupancy cells.

Two officers accompanied him. 'This was built for the IRA,' said the larger one, 'but we've had everyone and his dog in here since. All kinds.' He made it sound like a holiday resort.

'I need to see my lawyer.'

'You'll feel right at home here. We've got one in five claiming to be Muslims – some of 'em because they think the food's better. We got halal, vegan, all your multi-culti modern cuisine. Kosher, even, though there's not much call for that.'

He was in his late forties, overweight, with a faint asthmatic wheeze. The other one was younger, with a few spots on a neck that bulged over his collar.

'Normally, if you're a good boy, you get twelve hours in, twelve hours out. But any trouble and you'll be banged up for twenty-three.'

'What sort of trouble?'

They looked at each other and smiled.

'Oh, yeah, you been away, haven't you? Put it this way. It's not a good time to be a "brother".'

What did he mean?

'Used to be that your lot rubbed along fine with the others but since all the aggro on the streets . . .' The big one shook his head and smiled grimly. 'Still, you're a nicely brought up lad, aren't you? Mind your Ps and Qs and stay out of the skinheads' way. If you cause no trouble you'll get no trouble from us. But you give us any bother, you'll really know what shit is.'

Abruptly the cell door swung shut and Jamal was alone. After the cold of his walk to the Turkish border he should have been glad of the cloying warmth of the cell but it just added to his claustrophobia. He felt the rising panic.

A few minutes later the door was unlocked. Another officer came in while an orderly dumped a thin rolled-up mattress on the bed. On top of that was a thin prayer mat, a reminder to Jamal of how long it was since he had prayed. The orderly was dark-skinned, a thin beard along the edge of his chin. He gave Jamal a long look, turned and left.

'Okay, Jamal, just to the right of the sink, that's the direction of the Kabba. Everything for your comfort and convenience.' The officer gave him an empty smile and closed the door. Jamal heard the heavy metallic thud of the lock. A few minutes later the lights went out and the cell was lit only by a dull glow from outside. Jamal let the prayer mat fall to the floor. He unfolded the mattress. Inside were a grey sheet and a thin, uncomforting duvet. He was dead tired. He spread out the sheet and put the elasticated corners round the ends of the mattress. Then he opened the duvet, climbed onto the bed and pulled it over him. As he lay there the faint sound of the *Isha'a salat* came from the cell beyond the sink. Jamal turned over to face the opposite wall, as if that would block out the sound.

He pulled the duvet around him. As he did so he felt what seemed to be a label near the seam. But it was loose. He found the opening in the cover and felt inside.

It was a small piece of paper folded up several times. He unwrapped it. It was impossible to read what it said in the darkness so he held it up to where a sliver of light came in through the viewing hatch on the cell door: *Welcome, brother. Pray with us tomorrow.*

# 33

**19.00**

Jamal waited in the interview room. The shock of incarceration, the stale air and strange echoing sounds of the prison combined with his mounting dismay about the fate of the video to ensure that there was no chance of catching up on any much-needed sleep. His spirits had started to rise – not much, but knowing that the lawyer was coming had given him something to cling to, some hope that he would soon get out of this hell.

Down the corridor outside he heard keys clinking and voices. He got to his feet. At last he was about to meet someone he could call a friend.

The lock clicked and the door scraped open. Jamal could barely contain himself. He launched himself at Alistair Latimer as he entered, clasping his hand with both of his. The lawyer frowned at his bandaged hands and glanced at the officer who had opened the door.

'Want me to hang about?'

Latimer shook his head. 'It's okay, thanks. I'll take it from here.'

'Right you are.'

The officer gave Jamal a cautionary glare as he left, locking the door behind him. They were alone.

Jamal had not let go of the lawyer's hand. 'Thank you for coming. I'm so relieved you're here.'

Latimer was far younger than Jamal had expected, late twenties maybe, with black hair, a neatly trimmed beard and dark eyes that meant he could be from almost anywhere – just like me, thought Jamal. He had a thin nose and a slightly pointed chin, which, with his intense dark eyes, gave him a rather bird-like look. His expression was studiedly serious as if all his consciousness was absorbed by the job in hand. He extracted his hand from Jamal's, took off his coat and hung it over the back of the metal chair. Underneath he had on a slim-fitting black suit that was fully buttoned up and a T-shirt. Jamal tried to imagine him in a wig and gown, defending the righteous.

Jamal's words came out in a torrent. 'Emma spoke of you in the highest regard. She promised me that you would be able to help if I got into difficulty. What she did was so brave – well, we both took a risk, but for her, it was much more dangerous.' He let out a little laugh, as if to underline how much less dangerous he thought it had been for him.

Latimer looked at him stonily. 'Finished?'

Jamal went silent. Their time together was strictly limited, and here he was, wasting it. He raised his hands in apology. 'Sorry, it's just that – well, I've not had anyone I could – it's been – you know. You're the first person I've been able to *talk* to.'

Latimer flipped open his laptop. 'Shall we begin by looking at the video?'

Jamal nodded eagerly. 'Sure, whatever you need. I want to help you help me as best I can.'

Latimer booted up the machine and turned the screen so it faced Jamal. 'Let's watch it through, shall we, and then we'll talk?'

He could feel his heart pounding just as it had while he was filming, the tiny camera tucked in the fold between his left ear and his headdress, the device taped under his arm.

*All you have to do, Jamal, is look where you want to film and keep your head up, no matter what happens. Just don't look away.* Those had been her instructions. He had followed them to the letter, even though there were moments when he had had to close his eyes.

He felt Latimer's gaze on him as he started to watch as if he wanted to keep a very close eye on his reaction. Jamal braced himself. He remembered every second but knew the sheer brutality would be just as sickening on the screen as it had been when he was there.

At first he thought it was a mistake, that he was looking at one of the training videos. He was looking not at Abukhan but at *himself*, in close-up, wielding the machete. They had made it look as if he was the executioner. How had they done this? Why? He watched with a mounting sense of horror as waves of disbelief, shame, embarrassment and disgust washed over him. All the time Latimer remained silent, watching his face.

Jamal pressed his palms over his eyes, shaking his head. 'It's a lie, it's – it's fake!'

'I'd prefer if you watched closely right to the end, please,' Latimer said, his words slow and precise.

He obeyed, even though he could feel the bile rising inside him.

When it was finished, Latimer slowly closed the laptop and left it on the table between them. For a few seconds neither of them spoke.

'Those close-ups – they were done weeks ago. It wasn't even real, just an exercise. It's not me! You can see it's been changed.'

Did Latimer believe him? He was just sitting there, impassive. A hundred questions sprang into Jamal's mind.

Eventually the lawyer spoke. 'Yes, I think I know that,' he said. 'You and I know that, at least.'

What did he mean?

'So what did Emma . . . How did it get . . .' Tears welled in his eyes. He slammed his fists on the table, wincing at the pain. 'That was *not* me. I did *not* kill those girls.' His voice had gone up several decibels.

The door opened. 'Everything all right in here?'

Latimer turned. 'Yes, Officer. Everything's fine, thanks.'

The man looked doubtfully at Jamal as he shut the door.

Jamal lowered his voice, even though he was still shaking with rage. 'Those – that shot of me with the machete.'

'Yes?'

'They're from another— They made lots of videos when we were training. They've made it look like I was doing it, that I killed those poor girls.'

Tears were running down his face now, falling onto the table between them, his whole body convulsed in anguish.

Latimer remained very still, watching him. 'Yes, it does look very much like that, doesn't it?'

So he was agreeing. Well, that was something. Jamal wiped his face. 'Sorry.'

'I'm sure you are.'

Jamal took several deep breaths to try to bring his body back under his control, to unscramble his brain. And then it hit him. 'So what about Emma?'

Latimer reddened but didn't reply.

'How did the film – how did she . . .?'

The lawyer let out a short, ugly laugh. He faced Jamal. 'I thought you'd never ask. The fact is we don't know what happened to Ms Warner, Jamal, because she hasn't been seen since then.'

Jamal stared at him, speechless.

Latimer took out a small recorder, set it down on the table and leaned back, his arms folded. 'Perhaps it would be useful if you told me exactly what happened.'

Jamal told him about the filming, his exit from the site and handing the camera back to Emma.

'And then what?'

'I waited. Then the man came out who took me to the border. He gave me the memory card.'

Latimer was staring at him with barely suppressed contempt. 'It was blank by the way. Not as in wiped: it was never used. Describe the man who took you to the border.'

Jamal told him everything up to the moment they had parted.

Latimer stared at him with disbelief. 'When he got you through that checkpoint so easily, didn't that make you wonder?'

It had, Jamal remembered. 'But I don't understand. I did exactly what she asked, and gave her back the camera. What do you imagine happened to her?'

Latimer stared blankly at him for a few seconds before he answered. 'I think, Jamal, that I'd prefer not to imagine what happened to her.' His eyes had started to shine. 'Abukhan must have known. Did you say or do anything that could have tipped them off? Did you talk to any of the other fighters? Did you give them any cause for suspicion?'

Jamal shook his head. 'But why didn't they take *me*, punish *me*?'

Latimer smiled thinly. 'Oh, I think they are punishing you.' He leaned forward and switched off the recorder. 'Abukhan is punishing you for filming, that's what's happening, by telling the world you did it. Whether they will fully appreciate what a publicity coup they've handed the British government, who knows?'

Jamal frowned. 'I don't understand.'

Latimer hunched forward, pressing his palms against the table. 'The new home secretary's proposals have given them just the excuse they need to start getting rid of people.'

'But we were born here, me and my brothers and sister.'

Latimer leaned back. 'I'm afraid that will no longer count. Put bluntly, Jamal, I don't think either you or your family will be welcome in this country much longer.'

# 34

**19.30**
**Home Office, Westminster**

Henry hovered near the desk while the new home secretary pored over the letter. He was thrilled. Everybody wanted to speak to Vernon Rolt and he had got him all to himself. He wanted to make an impression early, to show him that he had an ally in the office, someone who was on side, keen to be part of the new team and ready for whatever was thrown at him. The outer office was still in shock after the brazen way Rolt had set about briefing the *Newsday* editor on the Syrian returnee. But Henry wanted to show he wasn't like the foot-draggers and tooth-suckers. Finding the letter to Garvey from the terrorist's sister couldn't have happened at a more opportune moment.

His new master was still reading. There was a powerful intensity to the man, as if he was capable of great concentration and deep thought. 'Very interesting,' he murmured.

Henry nodded, but Rolt was still focusing on the letter so he just stood by. What a difference twenty-four hours made. Garvey had been a law unto herself, careless of her public image, putting her own interests first, a source of ongoing exasperation to others when she wouldn't toe the line. She actually seemed to thrive on being awkward. Rolt was totally professional, attentive to whoever spoke to him and careful to remember names. Yet there was something beneath the polished exterior that slightly frightened Henry, as if a whole other side to him was lurking below the surface that might burst out if provoked.

Rolt looked up at him, his eyes blazing in a way that was both exciting and alarming. 'And this is a constituent of my predecessor?'

'That's right, Home Secretary.'

'So it's true what they've been saying, that she was soft on the Muslim community?'

Henry couldn't remember Garvey being 'soft' on anything or anyone, but he let Rolt draw his own conclusions from his silence.

'And from the letter we can safely conclude that either the girl had absolutely no idea what her brother was capable of or is in complete denial.' Rolt folded the letter and passed it back to him. 'Find out everything you can about the family. I think Jamal "Al Britani" is going to discover that he couldn't have picked a worse time to come home.'

# 35

It felt a long time to Jamal since he had prayed. He had done a lot of pretend praying in Syria, going through the motions. He couldn't reconcile what they were supposedly doing in the name of God with what he thought of as God's word, so he'd faked it to keep up appearances. But the words in his head were different from those that had come out of his mouth. This time was different. He prayed for Emma, then for his parents and brothers, and for his dear sister Adila. And finally he prayed for himself because he really was on his own now.

Latimer had made his position clear. He had said he would do what he could but Jamal had to understand that, without Emma, he had no witnesses, no one at all to corroborate his story. He had said he would look into having the film analysed, but he worried that even if he could demonstrate that it had been doctored, he doubted it would convince a jury that he was innocent since he had gone to Syria to fight and had apparently willingly joined an extremist group, who didn't exactly fit the description 'freedom fighters'.

'The fact is, the Home Office seems determined to make an

example of you. Their publicity machine has gone into overdrive.'

Jamal had thanked him profusely for whatever help he could give him but he could see that there wasn't much fight in him. The way Latimer looked at him, Jamal knew the lawyer blamed him for Emma's disappearance. He pressed his forehead hard against the mat as if to force God back into his soul.

'Brother, I know you.'

For a mad moment he thought the voice was from God, but then he heard the words repeated. He opened his eyes. The prisoner praying next to him was white, and bald, with a fringe of sandy-coloured beard running round his chin.

'My name is Isham. We applaud your work. You should not suffer in jail for this.'

Jamal didn't answer. He closed his eyes and tried to resume his prayer but the man repeated the words: 'Brother, you are not alone. There are many like you here, trust me.'

He didn't want to cause trouble or seem uncivil. He turned his head towards the man.

His eyes were pale blue. He grinned. 'Brother, there will be a way out. It is coming. I have been told to make room for you in our plans.'

Jamal decided to pay no attention, but his moment's reflection, his attempt to reach out for guidance, had been thwarted. He stood up, moved to the door and asked to go back to his cell. He had not sought trouble but it had found him all the same.

# 36

**23.30**
**Lakeview House, near Keswick, Cumbria**

Tom left the Range Rover in a ramblers' car park. The journey north had given it a thick film of brown road grime. Parked hard up against a huge copper beech with long, overhanging branches, it was almost invisible.

There were no distractions. His phone was off, the battery and SIM card separated so no one could pinpoint him, and he had bought a cheap pay-as-you-go from a service station should he need help, though where that help might come from was another matter. The Range Rover's GPS was also disabled and the numberplates covered with extra grime. No one knew he was there, not even Phoebe or Woolf. He felt unencumbered and free. He was going to do this his way, alone. He had made ready his pistol and shoved it into the front of his belt. The two spare mags he put in his left-hand jacket pocket, making them easier to get at for a reload.

He trekked up to the top of the ridge and surveyed the valley. It was long and narrow, shaded by the surrounding peaks. In the moonless dark, it had an eerie beauty. Patchwork fields curved up towards rocky outcrops too steep for the snow to settle. Clusters of trees dotted the landscape. A single-track road threaded its way up to the house, dry stone walls on either side. The only passing place was at a gate with a cattle grid. The snow had coated everything, gleaming white in the night-vision goggles and blotting out detail. He was better off using his own eyes, waiting for them to adjust to the dark.

An owl hooted, and a few moments later, its mate. Tom felt in good company. He dropped down to a half-demolished stone croft, presumably the remains of a shepherd's dwelling, with a decent view of the house and approach. The roof was gone but he had enough cover. He decided to wait there a while to see who else, if anyone, was there, and who might be coming and going.

In the yard in front of the house were two ex-Army Land Rovers with canvas tilts, presumably used on Invicta training exercises. They had a heavy coating of snow and looked as though they hadn't moved in a while. Next to them, under an awning, there was an elderly Vauxhall Astra with no snow on it but the same even film of grime from a long motorway journey, like the one he had just made.

As his eyes adjusted to the darkness he saw more: a single set of recent car-size tyre tracks on the drive, a dull light in one of the upstairs rooms, an orangey glow from the one beneath. Since he was alone he needed to know exactly how many were in there before he made any kind of move. He helped himself to a few swigs of coffee from his Thermos and demolished the roast beef sandwich he had bought at the service station on the M6.

Keeping at least a hundred metres between himself and the building, he made a complete circumnavigation to get a sense of its size, familiarize himself with all the exits and windows, and construct in his mind the likely layout inside.

It was a well-built, early-Victorian brick house of classic proportions, probably the sort of place he might have dreamed of owning one day. But under Invicta's ownership it had been turned into a hostel, its good looks disfigured by the institutional necessities of a wheelchair ramp and an ugly metal fire escape.

He took out the pay-as-you-go phone, put in the battery and called Phoebe. It was a gamble that she would take a call from an unknown number at three in the morning but you had to hope.

'Who is it?' She answered almost immediately, her voice tense and alert. Was she already awake?

'It's okay, it's me, Tom.'

A sigh of relief. 'Where are you? There's a big flap on. Woolf says you've done a runner.'

'Well, sort of. I need a favour: ID of a Vauxhall Astra owner.' He gave her the plate number. 'And if it's an Invicta staffer, can you look in the database for any more details on them?'

'You do know what the time is?'

'I know, I know.'

'It's not that I mind, just that if I do it remotely it'll show up that I logged in at this unusual time.'

'I can't worry about that. I need the information now.'

'All right. Call me back in ten.'

He called her back in five.

'The Astra belongs to Alan Evans, the early joiner with the low number. Are you thinking he's the shooter?'

'I don't know yet. I might wake him up and ask him.'

'He was a corporal in 2 Para at Colchester. Dishonourably discharged and sentenced to three years for nearly killing two other lads in a bar fight.'

'Good start. You got an image?'

'Looks like he's been in one fight too many.'

'Send it. Can you see this number?'

'Got it. And there's some kind of ongoing issue with his expenses. Seems he owes them over a thousand pounds. Plus there's a note on file that he had a "red lapse". What's that?'

'Means he fell off the wagon at some time, had to go back through detox.'

'Tom, I can hear the wind. I know you're outside and up to something.'

'What's happening with Rolt?'

'I didn't see him all day. He came back to HQ at seven, had a meeting with the editor of *Newsday*, then went off to dinner with him.'

'Bill McCloud. Did you get an introduction?'

'If you can call having my tits stared at an introduction.'

'Why the meeting?'

'The "Butcher of Aleppo". The man who killed those school-girls. They've caught him – he's in Belmarsh. Tom, what are you doing?'

'I'll check in later. Leave Woolf out of the loop for now, okay?'

He killed the call. The image of Evans came through: an angry face, the sort that went looking for trouble. He removed the SIM from the phone, moved silently down the field, vaulted a stone wall and gave himself a minute for a fresh recce.

He closed in on the house, climbing over the wall to bypass the bolted metal gate. He wasn't worried about leaving any ground sign. By the time it was noticed he should be gone. There were a couple of large wheelie bins next to an outbuilding, probably the former dairy or cold store. He stepped inside. It was empty, save for some planks and old tins of paint, a pair of wellingtons and an old, very crumpled porn mag: *Luscious Lolitas*. Nice. He lifted the lids of the bins. Among the Red Bull and Coke cans were numerous Newcastle Brown Ale emp-ties and a couple of quart-sized Scotch bottles. Invicta was dry, absolutely no exceptions. Separating the members from their chief weakness was one of its founding principles. And there were far too many empties for one person, even a serious drinker. On the plus side it was fair to assume that Evans would have had a few, giving Tom the advantage.

He approached the main building, keeping to the other side of the dry stone wall so his tracks wouldn't be too obvious now he was close to the target. The orangey glow from the ground-floor window he had observed earlier was coming from a TV: a football match. With a bit of luck, whoever was in there would have all their attention on the game. As he approached the window to take a closer look a shout went up: a near miss.

There were three of them round the table, their silhouettes

outlined by the light from the TV. There was no other light on in the room. Also just visible on the table were more bottles and cans.

One of the three said something and got to his feet. Perhaps he was going to take a leak.

Not quite.

The side door opened and a dark shape emerged near the ground. The door shut again and the shape travelled a few paces out into the yard before cocking a leg, the pit-bull, squat and obviously muscular even in silhouette, sniffing the air as it pissed. Tom kept frozen to the spot behind the wall. It was too late to duck and there was no point in doing anything else. There was nothing to be gained by moving or trying to hide behind the wall that was between them because scent can't hide. It was certainly pointless running. They might have crap eyesight but Tom knew only too well from years growing up with dogs that to start running would only trigger its prey drive. It would pursue and, if it had been trained to, attack. But for Tom, that wasn't the immediate challenge. He needed to bring the dog to him and keep the chance of compromise under control. Shooting the thing would be easy but the sound would give him away immediately. The pit-bull could out-hear, out-smell and outrun Tom. But he could out-think it. He would have to stand his ground and see what happened.

# 37

It wasn't long before Tom realized what was going to happen. His eyes were glued to the target but his ears had never left the dog. The pit-bull's panting stopped and no doubt its ears were going into overdrive too. For about three seconds nothing happened. Then came a growl, and a succession of rapid snarling barks as the animal hurtled towards him.

Tom prepared for the inevitable. It was pointless to try to evade an attacking dog so close. If he wasn't going to use his weapon he couldn't do anything about immobilizing the beast until it committed itself to an attack. The grim fact was he had to let it sink its teeth into him and take it from there. He presented his left arm, twisting it so that his knuckles pointed towards the oncoming attack to protect the veins in his hand and wrist. When the dog bit down, it would hit bone rather than vital blood vessels.

The animal moved at startling speed, a succession of blood-curdling snarls erupting across the night air as it thundered towards him. As it closed in, he made sure his footing was good to take the force he was about to have to absorb, if he was going to stay upright and win this fight.

The pit-bull leaped up, its jaws opening with a deep growl, lips pulled back to bare its teeth so it got a good bite first time.

He braced himself for the hit as the dog covered the last couple of metres before jumping up onto the wall. Tom saw its eyes roll back as it launched itself at him. He stood his ground and braced himself. He felt its saliva fly onto his face.

If there were other things going on, they were lost on Tom now. He couldn't hear anything but the snarling of his attacker. He felt the weight of the dog hit him, then its jaws closed on his arm. Its teeth sank through the thick sleeve of his leather jacket into the skin. There was blinding pain as its teeth drove into him but Tom didn't pull away. That's how most damage is done. Tom had to tell himself to let it happen. He had to make sure the animal had confidence in itself, that it sensed an easy victory. If Tom went with the flow, it would keep its teeth in one place, thinking it had him, and wouldn't thrash around. Forget the *Boy's Own* tales of grabbing a foreleg in each hand and splitting them apart: that only worked on Chihuahuas, and only then if you could get hold of the thing in the first place. In real life dogs were like apes: much, much stronger than they looked.

The dog thrashed, its hind legs scrabbling against Tom's legs and waist, trying to get him to the ground, engulfing him in the sickly meat breath that came blasting out of its nostrils and jaws. It got a deeper grip on his arm and he felt flesh being mangled.

Tom pushed into the jaws with his left arm. The animal was almost dangling now, suspended because it wasn't going to let go. Its growl changed tone as it shook its head from side to side, like a mad thing, trying to get a deeper grip, still striving to clamp its jaws together, but through Tom's arm.

Tom bent down and grabbed one of its back legs with his free right hand, twisting it backwards and to the side, trying to snap the bone. The limb twitched as it tried to kick away. The dog bucked its head, trying to rip at Tom's arm by jerking rapidly left and right. Tom started to pull the back leg up towards him. The dog was confused and very pissed off now, biting harder and frantically twisting its head as Tom struggled to keep hold of its leg.

He yanked hard on the thin calf bone, and this time it finally broke. The dog yelped but its jaws held tight. Tom got a firmer grip on the spindly bit below the break and pulled it up as hard as he could towards his chest, at the same time starting to turn. The dog yelped and Tom pirouetted, as if he was spinning a child in a game. He did three, four, five turns, and the dog rose with the centrifugal force, anchored by its teeth in Tom's arm and his hand on its leg. The dog had to make a decision, and it did: it let go of Tom's arm. But Tom didn't reciprocate by dropping the leg: he kept hold now with both hands and swung it round and round as violently as he could.

Still spinning, he managed to take two steps towards the corner of the wall. The dog was still twisting and bucking, as if it had just had an electric shock.

Once more, Tom spun round with the animal's front legs pointing outwards with the G force. The dog's head smashed against the stone. There was a thud, a weak yelp and the body relaxed. Tom's own momentum carried him another one and a half turns, his head spinning as he tried to get his bearings.

He let the dog drop to the ground, still holding the back legs to keep control. It might have lost the fight or been stunned, but it could still raise the alarm or even attack again. A moment later he let go of the animal, dropped to his knees, picked up a big lump of granite from the wall and brought it down with both hands onto the head. There was no blood, no opening of the skull, just the dull cracking sound of bone breaking under the flesh. He smashed it down twice more to be sure the animal was dead.

Tom dropped the stone, got back to his feet with his hands on his knees and gulped in oxygen, trying to slow his heart rate as the adrenalin dissolved back where it had come from and the puncture wounds started to rage.

He pulled himself up to a crouch, took off his jacket, yanked up his sweater, pulled off a strip of T-shirt and used it to make a temporary binding for the wound. There were gaps between the top stones of the wall – enough to see that one of the men was out already, holding what looked like an assault rifle, the butt into his shoulder. Tom couldn't see exactly what the weapon was but if it went bang, and something came out of the muzzle, that was a problem.

The man whistled, then listened. 'Frankie?'

Tom glanced at Frankie, then back at his master. Both he and the canine corpse were still obscured by the wall – but only as long as the man kept his distance. There wasn't likely to be much of a discussion if they did meet, so he needed to be ready.

A second man emerged from the doorway with a pistol. He slipped on the step, swore, caught his balance, swayed slightly then lifted his weapon vaguely in Tom's direction. Nothing else for it. Tom aimed through the gap between the stones and double-tapped, centre mass, taking the drunk down first. The first man whirled round as his pal collapsed and Tom dropped him in the same way.

He waited for the third to show. If he wasn't too pissed, this one would be taking a lot more care. Crouching low, with the stone wall for cover, Tom moved to his left so he had a better arc of fire on the doorway.

There was movement in the darkness just inside. The third man couldn't see his mates from either the doorway or the windows because they had both fallen in the snow close to the house. A long burst of something heavyish, probably a 7.62, came from the doorway. Chips of wall flew about as the bullets hit before ricocheting into the air with a high-pitched whiz. The man had decided he wasn't going to take his chances on the outside. Tom didn't return fire. No point until he could see his target. Let him stew. There was no hurry. Eventually curiosity would get the better of him and he would break cover.

Five minutes passed – a long time when you think you may be about to be shot. The third man was either very patient or shitting himself. You could tell a lot about a man's character from the way he handled a weapon. Spraying away like that showed nerviness, a failure to absorb training and a probable lack of any real experience of a fire-fight in which conserving ammunition is everything. Curiosity and impatience would override caution. And then the rabbit would emerge from his burrow.

Another five minutes passed. Then the third man stepped out, an HK G3 casually hanging from his right. He slipped on the snow and loosed off another burst, only it went straight down, shattering his left lower leg. Tom dispatched him with a double tap and set off towards the house.

He checked Evans's photo, which he had saved in the phone: dark hair and eyebrows, a thin nose that had been smashed up so many times it looked like Frankie had chewed it, and a small, thin mouth: undistinguished and unmemorable. He toured the three bodies, turning each of them over. None was Evans. Was this a wasted journey?

He changed mags before entering the house. He would have to clear it before he started to look round. It smelt of tobacco smoke, alcohol and dog: Eau de Single Country Bloke. There must be something among the contents that would prove of interest.

He stepped into the kitchen. An old, greasy Rayburn gave off some warmth but the room was in stark contrast to the trademark Invicta neatness. There was a full ashtray on the windowsill, the table was strewn with food remains, and the washing-up from at least one meal was piled haphazardly in and around the sink: definitely not what Carter had had in mind as maintaining the place. He counted three dinner plates.

The match was still on. Though he had been a passable forward, Tom had never bonded with the nation's favourite sport. He turned it off: the silence was a relief. He waited for a couple of minutes. Although there was no sound, he felt a presence. He was used to old houses seeming to be alive, letting out creaks and groans for no reason.

Clearing the ground floor first, he peered into the large wood-panelled living room, lit dimly by the last embers of the fire, taking care not to catch his foot on the frayed, unsecured rug. There were two more doors, one of which revealed some stairs down to what would have made a great wine cellar.

The circuit of the ground floor complete, he headed for the

first floor, taking his time, eyes and weapon pointing upwards, towards where he was going. The stone staircase was good for moving up noiselessly, unlike wood. But all the same he paused with each step. At the top he halted for longer, and listened. After a minute he became aware of the sound of breathing, short and rapid. To his left was what looked like the door to a fitted cupboard. It had no handle, just a keyhole. Good choice. If it hadn't been for the breathing he might have missed it.

'Come out very slowly, hands on the back of your head. Anything different and I will fire. You've got five seconds. Five . . . four . . . three . . .'

The door opened. The figure had only one hand behind his head; the other was in a sling. He had on nothing more than a T-shirt and a pair of boxers. His feet were bare. But on his face, which was contorted with a mixture of indignation and dismay, a livid bruise surrounded a scabbed-up wound. It had to be the man from the flat Tom had attacked with the umbrella. The man who had killed Jez and his girl.

'Evans. Good evening.' Tom kicked him over so he fell face down on the landing, a nice big 'Aargh' as he went. Then he leaned over him, his boot pressing down on the back of his head so that Evans's wound, with its newly formed scab, was pushed hard against the floor.

Evans squirmed and thrashed, like an insect pinned to a cork board by a curious school kid. Tom twisted his boot into the back of the man's head as if he was trying to screw it into the floor. 'So, how's the face?'

'The fuck? What is this?'

'What does it look like?'

'Fuck you, Buckingham.'

Tom pressed down a bit harder with his boot.

Evans let out another long furious groan of pain and frustration. 'Go on – just get on with it, then.' He spat the words through clenched teeth.

This wasn't revenge. This was the application of pain so Tom could get what he needed from him. 'We need to talk, you and me.'

'Fuck off.'

'Who sent you?'

'You fucking killed Randall, you cunt . . .'

Tom leaned harder on the wound, twisting his boot. Evans was in tremendous pain but doing a good job of not giving anything away.

'Who sent you?'

'No one tells me what the fuck to do. You fucking killed my best mate.'

He was writhing around on the floor, like a beached marlin. Tom pressed his boot down harder once more, then stepped off him. 'Hmm, well, I don't know about you, but I could use a brew. Let's go down to the kitchen, shall we? It's nice and quiet there.'

# 38

Keeping half an eye on Evans, Tom filled the kettle. He found two mugs at the bottom of a cupboard, tipped out the mouse droppings and washed them in some of the boiled water from the kettle. There was just enough milk. Evans sat and watched him petulantly.

'Too bad about Frankie. Only doing his job. Yours, was he?'

There was no answer from Evans, apart from a curt nod.

Tom eyed the empties as he reached for the teabags. 'Your mates were having quite a party. This a refuge now for all of you who've fallen off the wagon?'

'Fuck you.'

It could have been the demise of Frankie and his mates, getting caught barely dressed or being mocked for drinking that was pissing Evans off. He looked like a man who had been born angry, his features contorted into a mask of barely contained fury, which had reshaped what had once probably been an acceptable face. Tom had come across others like this in the forces, overstuffed with natural aggression but without the nous to channel it towards anything but their ultimate disadvantage. They attracted trouble like magnets, this sort. Every word that came out of Evans's mouth was accompanied by a rather limited range of expletives. Even by the repetitive standards of the army, it was tiresome.

'So what was on Randall's mind?' Tom put a mug down in front of him. 'Come on. We can have a nice civilized chat, or more fun and games where I stand on your shoulder. Your choice.'

There was no reaction.

Tom pushed the mug closer. 'Look, I get it. You're pissed off about Randall. But he was about to drop two civilians. What else was I going to do? Rolt wasn't even in the building. Just like you, Randall fucked up, but he was stopped and you weren't.'

Tom could see behind the angry face the wheels of Evans's brain slowly turning, only to be hijacked by another eruption of anger.

'Rolt fucked us after all we fucking did for him.'

'Okay, but how?' Tom had some sympathy for that view but this wasn't going to be a bonding exercise. It was going to take all his resources to get Evans to stop being aggrieved for two seconds and actually think.

Evans gave him another look of contempt. 'You cunts got no fucking idea.'

'You may well be right there. What don't we know?' Tom pushed the sugar bag towards him. 'Two spoons or three?'

Evans tipped a cascade of sugar into his mug and used the end of a dirty fork to stir it, while he delivered a speech Tom could have scripted for him about Westminster selling the country down the river, betraying the troops they'd sent in to fight bloody suicide bombers with one hand tied behind their backs because the politicians wouldn't provide what they needed to give it good and proper to the Taliban, then brought them home and pissed all over them. And now the country was being fucked over by fucking raghead scum while the government did fuck-all. The whole thing was depressingly predictable.

Then he fell silent, frowning at Tom with a weird gleam in his eye.

'What don't I know? Spit it out.'

Evans shook his head. 'Randall wasn't like us.' He gestured at the empties. 'He stayed on the wagon, wasn't going back to any of that. He worshipped Rolt. Reckoned he'd saved his life. He was devoted to him, never wavered. Getting the job driving him around in the Bentley, that was the ultimate. He was there for Rolt twenty-four seven.'

'I heard he was awkward.'

Evans looked at Tom as if he'd gone mad. 'Whoever said that's talking fucking bollocks! You couldn't have asked for a more obliging—'

'Never mind. Keep talking.'

'Then came the trip to Geneva. Rolt says to him, round dinnertime, "Get me to Switzerland for breakfast." No advance warning. Randall says of course. So he takes him through the Tunnel, drives him all the way down to Geneva for a meet.'

'Who with?'

Evans looked at him, pitying. 'You're Rolt's arse-licker and you don't know shit.' He nodded slowly, relishing the fact that he knew something Tom didn't. 'He's kept it from you an' all, hasn't he? Randall was the only one who knew.'

'Knew what?'

'That was when he found out, driving round Geneva while they talked in the back. Rolt closed the partition but Randall kept the intercom on. Heard the whole thing. Rolt begging and pleading . . .'

'Come on, then, begging who?'

Whether Evans was about to enlighten him or not, he never got to find out. Tom heard it first, the distant growl of an approaching engine, something making its way towards the house. 'Who's that?'

'Dunno.'

'*Who?*'

'I don't fucking *know*, all right?'

'Who else knows you're here?'

Evans didn't answer. Despite the snow the vehicle was moving fast. Tom leaned across the table and punched hard into Evans's shoulder to control him, then killed the lights and dragged him, whimpering, by his other arm towards the stairs.

'Who the fuck is that?'

'Fucking told you. I *don't know*.' There was a new note of desperation in Evans's protest. Maybe he was telling the truth.

Tom twisted both his arms. '*Who?*'

But Evans was starting to panic and they were out of time. Tom bundled him up the stairs and followed, keeping a firm grip on the injured arm. He had just seconds to decide whether to slot him right now so he could concentrate on the new threat coming up the lane, or keep him alive to use as a bargaining chip. He would have been better off staying on the ground floor, but he had the fire escape at the back as an alternative exit. All these thoughts were coursing through his mind as they reached the top of the stairs.

The engine noise was the distinctive grumble of a petrol V8. He glanced over his shoulder as the headlights came through the windows below and turned back to see Evans's hand held high, smashing something down on his head.

# 39

Tom came to with a blinding pain across the back of his head and the sensation of something warm trickling over his face. All he could see in front of him were flashes, pulsing from the pain. He had no idea how long he had been out: maybe no more than a minute. He struggled into a sitting position and found an old metal alarm clock that must have been Evans's weapon.

Evans was nowhere to be seen. Perhaps he had taken flight, but he was barefoot. Tom didn't fancy his chances on the hills. But then he heard voices coming from downstairs.

'What the fuck's all this, you stupid little cunt?'

With the aftershock of the blow still ringing in his ears, at first Tom couldn't place the voice: a similar vocabulary to Evans but deeper, muffled and heavily laced with incandescent rage.

There was no reply from Evans. Evidently he wasn't given a chance to respond because there followed a hard thwack, the sound of someone toppling over, then a scream, followed by retching.

'Look at this fucking mess. This is *so fucked up*. What were you fuck-heads thinking? Running around shooting people isn't how it goes, Evans. It isn't how we do this shit.'

Then the voice changed tone – and language. Tom strained to hear above the ringing in his ears.

'*Voz'mite organy i sobaku. Nichego za ne ostavit.*' Take the bodies and the dog. Don't leave anything behind. Russian.

Tom was by the closet where he'd found Evans. He didn't know who was down there, or how many. He had a strong desire to throw up and an even stronger feeling he was about to pass out again. Escape was out of the question. He felt for where the blood was coming from and found a pulpy area on his left temple. The closet door was open. Without getting up he shuffled backwards into it and closed the door. In the darkness he strained to follow the exchange coming up from below.

Evans had gone into pleading mode. 'Fucking give me a chance, will you?'

'No deal.'

Evans wasn't giving up. 'For fuck's sake—'

There was the dull thud of a suppressed shot and no more from Evans.

Tom heard a grunted exchange outside, also in Russian. Two men were evidently loading the dead into the vehicle, the engine still ticking over. Then, in the house, he heard footsteps on the stairs, one pair, which came right past his closet, down the landing, into each bedroom, back onto the landing, to the top of the stairs – and paused.

All Tom could hear now was the sound of his own blood pulsing through his body and his ears still ringing from the blow, distorting all other sound as if it were coming down a long pipe. He had his weapon pointed at where he hoped the guy's chest would be. Years of training and experience meant that he automatically squeezed the trigger very gently using only the top pad of his finger, until it had taken the first pressure.

The steps moved down the landing pausing at each door then back to the top of the stairs and paused again. Tom could hear the slow breaths of someone calmly taking their time. All his concentration was on the door inches in front of him, waiting.

'Okay. *Davayte ubirat'sya otsyuda.*' Let's get out of here.

The footsteps went back down the stairs.

Tom couldn't let them leave without getting a visual. He gave it another minute, opened the door an inch, listened some more, then emerged from the closet and moved into the bedroom that overlooked the yard, the night sight already in his hand. The vehicle was a Mercedes G-Wagen on low-profile rims. One of the Russian speakers standing by an open door lit a cigarette.

The English voice urged them on: 'Come on, do that later.'

The voice had been familiar – a standard-issue middle-England accent from nowhere in particular, but used to barking orders. Plus the impressive command of Russian . . . Now there was no doubt. In the blazing lights of the G-Wagen, he caught the profile of the man ordering the Russians back into the vehicle. Someone he knew – and knew well.

His old commanding officer from the Regiment – Ashton.

# 40

**05.30**
**Bampton Lodge, Charlbury, Oxfordshire**

Mandler's eyelids fluttered open. Something that had always stood him in good stead in this game: he was an excellent sleeper. He didn't need long either – five hours seemed to do it – and once he was out nothing usually roused him. The music was definitely coming from somewhere other than inside his brain. Brahms's Cello Sonata in E minor. Had he left the radio on? He squinted at the clock: 05.35. *Bugger.* His eyes closed again, but the music persisted. He peered at the other side of the bed but, of course, Miranda had gone to Val d'Isère with her old college friends. Of all the weeks for her to be away, just when he needed someone to moan at . . .

He turned over, plumped the pillow and closed his eyes again but little windows in his brain began to open, like a cerebral advent calendar.

The so-called 'promotion' had come completely out of the blue. Of course he should have seen it coming. Clements's connection with Rolt he was aware of: Buckingham had uncovered it in America on the Fortress operation, though both Clements and Rolt had come out of that mess with their reputations somehow unscathed. After that you'd have thought the wily old cabinet secretary would have realized how toxic Rolt was and given him a wide berth. Not a bit of it. When he'd heard Clements had proposed Rolt to the PM as a way of saving his political arse, he'd thought it was an April Fool.

He could feel his pulse speeding up. He must try to think of something else. The music was not at all unpleasant – but he really had no recollection of turning it on, though he'd had a couple at his club before being driven home. Oh dear, he thought. Is this what old age is going to be like? Unwelcome thoughts about other mishaps began to foment in his weary brain.

In fact it was he, Mandler, who had been made the fool of. He had remonstrated with the PM – what was he thinking of, parachuting in a man with no real experience of public life, let alone government at cabinet level? – only to find he had already made up his mind. But Mandler knew he had a bit of a blind spot where politicians were concerned. Always underestimated how low they might reach to save their arses. Garvey had warned him about the PM's weakness for compromise. Well, Mandler had known he was a marked man after that. He'd shown his hand, but now he was just too damn old to play those games any more. What angered him most was that the main casualty had had to be Garvey – the only one of the whole damn bunch with any integrity.

Now his pulse was really going: there would be no easy way of getting back to sleep. Nothing for it but to go down and turn off the music, though it was rather pleasant and soothing, now he had got himself all worked up. He swung his legs out of the bed, felt for his slippers and pulled on his ancient dressing-gown, which Miranda was always threatening to get rid of. He'd had it since Oxford. Some things were sacred, worth hanging on to.

The music was definitely coming from downstairs: the kitchen, in fact. There was a light on as well. Burglars? Should he get his Webley? The revolver had been in the family for generations; his father had used it during the Normandy landings. He opened the bedroom door. Miranda's Ming vase was still there. It was a shame in a way, since he had always hated it, but had never dared say so. Cautiously, he went down the stairs and pushed open the door, telling himself there was nothing to be afraid of: what kind of burglar chooses Brahms?

The answer was sitting at the head of the kitchen table, with a makeshift bandage wrapped round his arm.

# 41

'Sorry to barge in like this, sir.'

'So you bloody well should be. How did you get in? And what in God's name happened to your arm?'

'I was going to ring the bell, but the back door was open. You really ought to be more careful, sir.' Tom looked at the man who had been Woolf's boss and had engineered his infiltration of Invicta. Without the three-piece suit and wrapped in a distinctly dog-eared paisley dressing-gown he lacked some of his usual authoritative bearing.

'Do you realize what time it is?'

Tom glanced at the clock on the oven.

'And how did you even know where to find me?'

'Something's come up.'

It wasn't an answer but it was a reply. Mandler went towards the counter. 'Well, whatever it is, it'd better be damn good. This is highly irregular. And, technically, I'm not even in charge of you any more. In fact as of yesterday you're off the books – you do know that? Woolf said he told you to disappear for a while till things blow over.'

'I know, sir. And I have, sort of.'

Mandler shook his head. 'But you always plough your own furrow don't you, Buckingham?' The beginnings of a smile twitched around the older man's mouth. He sighed and steered towards the kettle. 'Well, now you're here, what's it to be? Builders' or Earl Grey?'

'Builders' will be fine, thank you.'

He filled the kettle and lifted a couple of mugs from the dishwasher, then turned back to Tom and frowned. 'It's not about money, is it? If you need a float to tide you over . . .'

Tom raised a hand to silence him. He launched into a detailed account that started with Rolt's mysterious visitor and ended with his sighting of Ashton. Then he downed some of the tea, which was more than welcome after the dash back from the Lake District and he waited for Mandler to emerge from thought.

It was a full minute before he responded. 'You do like to take things into your own hands, don't you, Buckingham?'

Tom said nothing. The answer was obvious. 'You don't have a biscuit to go with the tea do you, by any chance? Sir.'

Mandler frowned, opened a cupboard and produced a packet of Fortnum & Mason ginger thins, which he pushed across the table.

'Thanks.'

'I sincerely hope that reporter you had in tow isn't going to go into print.'

Tom shrugged. The events of that evening had been eclipsed by his excursion to the Lakes.

'You've taken a lot of liberties.'

Tom wasn't going to justify himself. He'd been in the game too long to expect any gratitude from Mandler, but he wouldn't have minded a glimmer of appreciation for his efforts. 'So, Ashton, what's all that about?'

Mandler focused again, frowning. 'You are absolutely sure about this, Buckingham? You're not trying to settle some old score . . .'

Tom didn't dignify that with a reply. Instead he just gave him a long cold look until he sighed and flapped the air with a gnarled hand. 'All right. I'm not at my best at this hour.'

'He's a serving soldier. Is it possible he's on some operation that you don't know about?'

Mandler bridled. 'I think it's fair to say that, in my position in the food chain, it's unlikely I would be unaware of an officer in Her Majesty's special forces, and—' He stopped himself.

Tom suspected he had just realized this wasn't the time for pomposity.

'Okay. Let's look at what we know. Ashton had no idea you were there. He'd come to see Evans and his merry men.'

Tom nodded.

'Or not so merry, as it turned out.' Mandler sniffed at his own joke. 'Did you really have to kill quite so many of them?'

Tom said nothing and contemplated his bandaged arm. His head was still throbbing from Evans's clock attack.

'So, the question is, was Ashton's action anything to do with Evans's attempt on your life?'

'"This isn't how we do this." Those were his last words to Evans.'

'So was he punishing him for making an attempt on your life—' Mandler broke off and frowned. '*Or* was he punishing him for *failing* to kill you?'

'If Ashton had any reason to kill me, he wouldn't have sent someone like Evans. I'd topped his best mate. He'd found out somehow, and was mad about it.'

Mandler nodded. 'Yes, I can see that. But what is Ashton's part in all this? Does he even know Rolt?'

'I think I'd know if he did.'

'And you're positive that the men he was with were Russian?'

'Russian speakers. They could have been Georgians, Estonians, Kazakhs, Tartars, Chechens, Tajiks . . .'

'Yes, all right, Buckingham.'

'Ashton I know speaks Russian.'

'Well, this is all very strange indeed. And are you thinking the meeting in Switzerland could have been with this Oleg fellow? Because that is pure conjecture.'

There was no way of knowing – short of asking Rolt.

Mandler got to his feet and stretched, but Tom hadn't finished. 'And whatever was said in the back of the Bentley, it was enough to turn Randall from loyal retainer into assassin?'

'Well, since he's dead, and so is Evans, we'll never know that either.'

There was a dispiriting hint of resignation in Mandler's tone. But, having come this far, Tom wasn't going to back off now. 'We need to find out what Ashton's agenda is. Maybe it'll take us closer to the identity of Rolt's friend.'

Mandler peered at him. 'I don't think that's at all wise.'

'I think it's time I met up with Ashton.'

Mandler gazed at him, mouth half open. 'Are you mad? You saw what he did to Evans.'

'*Heard* what he did, to be accurate. Sir.'

Mandler brushed a hand over his forehead.

'Ashton dropped in on my parents, was asking after me. So it's good timing, in a way. I'm just following up on his visit.'

'You do love trouble, don't you, Buckingham?'

# 42

Sarah Garvey was aware of a hammering coming from some-where but she had decided to ignore it. She was back in her old office but it was full of people, drinks in hand. Rolt was there, *in her seat*, and on each side, like maids of honour, the loathsome cabinet secretary, Clements, and that prick of an intern, Henry. Nearby was the greaseball, Farmer. All the slime poured into one room, celebrating Rolt's elevation.

Garvey was trying to listen to Buckingham's instructions. The weapon felt cold and greasy, just like her father's shotgun, and just as heavy. The handsome young former SAS trooper was showing her how to aim it. She could see his mouth moving but couldn't quite hear above the hubbub.

'What? What?' she kept saying.

'Twice in the temple, twice in the chest.' Buckingham's words got through at last.

And she remembered what her father had always said to her when he taught her to shoot: *'Don't think, girl. Just aim, squeeze – and kill.'*

She took aim at Rolt, but Clements was right beside him. She could take them both – and the others! But there was the knocking again, hauling her back into consciousness.

She raised her head an inch and froze. Her eyes snapped open. 'Damn and fuck.' She felt as if an ill-fitting metal helmet had been jammed onto her head. Her eyes focused on the near-empty bottle on the coffee-table, the tumbler at forty-five degrees in her lap. She looked at her watch. Oh dear. She had fallen asleep on the sofa, not for the first time, not by a long way, but she had never slept away a whole night.

The metal helmet seemed to have spikes that drove into her head when she moved.

'Ma'am? Visitor for you.'

She looked round. The place was empty. Then she remembered she still had security on the door. They had shouted through the letterbox. She levered herself up, the spikes forging deeper into her head. Gone were the days when she could drink any man under the table and rise for a breakfast meeting with her briefs mastered. She moved gingerly towards the kitchen to make some coffee, touching the furniture as she went to steady herself. 'Just give me a minute!'

This wouldn't do at all. Getting drunk as a skunk – in fact, she'd been pretty smashed the whole day before. Maybe once was allowed, just to get her through the post-election horror, the eviction from her office, the humiliating demotion, but this was not on. On the other hand, how could she face the prospect of the back benches in anything other than a state of intoxication?

To drown her thoughts, she picked up the remote and pressed the TV into life. Aerial shots appeared of a housing estate engulfed in flames. Well, at least that wasn't her problem now. Let's see what a shambles Rolt makes of it, she thought. She completed her journey to the coffee-machine and fumbled for the packet and a spoon, tipping some of it over the counter. When she looked again at the screen there was Rolt, holding up a newspaper. Headline: *The Butcher of Aleppo*, and beneath it, a frame grab of a figure brandishing a long blade.

She flicked on the coffee and went into the bathroom to check herself over. What a sight. She straightened her hair and gave her teeth a cursory brush with plenty of toothpaste. Not that she was likely to be kissing anyone in the imaginable future. The number of people with whom she was on kissing terms had dwindled over recent years to . . . How many was it? Oh, yes: none. Especially now she was just a common-or-garden MP. From now on when she came into a room, no one would look up.

She took a few deep breaths. The powerful mint flavour of the toothpaste coursing through her pipes helped her to focus. She moved towards the door, keeping half an eye on the TV.

'Who is it?'

She peered through the spy-hole. The protection cops outside were holding back a girl with long black hair half covered by a loose headscarf. She opened the door.

'Sorry to bother you, ma'am. This – person insists she knows you.'

She looked about fifteen, with big, dark anxious eyes, in clothes – the headscarf, smart black coat and boots – that seemed meant for an older woman. She had definitely never seen her before. She was about to tell them to send her away when it occurred to her.

'Adila?'

# 43

Adila sipped her green tea while Garvey sat very still, listening. It was the tears that made her look even younger than her eighteen years.

'I'm so sorry for just turning up on your doorstep like this, I really am, but I didn't know what else to do. I didn't dare phone or text. A neighbour helped me leave the house by going through her garden, and I just covered up with this.'

She touched the headscarf she had stuffed into her overflowing bag. Despite her tear-stained face, in her white shirt and straight black skirt, Adila had a business-like primness about her that appealed to Garvey. Also, she had insisted on taking off her boots at the door because of the snow. And now she sat opposite her on the sofa, bolt upright, her hands wrapped around the mug on her lap. She seemed so horribly vulnerable.

'All I know is he was detained at Heathrow, taken off the plane from Turkey and just marched away. I don't have any idea where he is. They won't tell us anything.'

Garvey glanced at the paper Adila had brought with her, the same one she had seen being held up by Rolt, with the headline *Butcher of Aleppo*. She pointed at the screen shot from the video. 'And this is definitely your brother?'

Adila's eyes welled up again. She nodded. 'But I can't believe he would do such a thing.'

'He was out there how long?'

'Four months, nearly five.' She balled the handkerchief in her fist and dabbed her eyes. 'Look, I know he did a bad thing, going there at all, but you have to understand there are so many who saw the Syrians being brutalized by Assad and the West doing nothing. But he was so shocked by the militants. Are they all going to be punished, treated as traitors?'

Maybe not on her watch, but things were different now.

'The group your brother was with, it's affiliated to ISIS. And beheadings aren't exactly about helping the oppressed.'

'He texted me: "They teach that jihad is not about mercy but extreme retaliatory violence to deter enemies. I cannot do this."' She took an iPad out of her bag and powered it up. 'Let me show you something. It's been taken down now but I managed to save it. Look.'

She ran the video down to a close-up of Jamal raising the machete and inched it forward over the cut to a wide shot of the girls. 'Look at the shadows: they're long in the shot of the women, but they're short in the image of my brother. The sun is much higher in the sky. It's a different time of day – or even a different time of year.'

'Show me again.'

Garvey scrutinized the shots as Adila moved between them. She didn't regard herself as technically savvy but she did understand shadows. The girl had done her homework. She was impressed. 'Okay. The first thing to do is get an expert opinion.' Before, she could have handed it to one of her staff, who would have had it rushed through. Not so easy now she was banished to the wilderness. She scrolled through her contacts until she found Woolf. 'I've got a favour to ask.'

She could hear the wariness in his tone. 'You know I'm Under New Management.'

'Yes, funnily enough. And you've got your arse to cover.' She mouthed, 'Sorry,' at Adila for her language. 'Just listen.' She started to tell him about the video but he cut her off.

'The little shit.'

A minute later her phone buzzed. A different number but it was Woolf calling her back. 'Sorry, had to go to somewhere a bit more private. Look, between you and me, the so-called Butcher of Aleppo video, we've already had it analysed. There's no question it's been doctored.'

Garvey nodded at Adila, whose eyes widened anxiously. 'Good. So we've got MI5's word for it?'

Adila leaned forward, almost rising out of her seat.

Woolf sighed. 'Ah, not as such. Rolt's just ordered us to bury the report – and he's got Number Ten to go along with it. He's adamant that this doesn't come out.'

Garvey felt her hangover come back with a vengeance as the anger rose inside her. 'I want that report.'

'It's more than my job's worth, ma'am.'

Garvey glanced at Adila again. She was all on her own, trying to do the right thing against forces whose power she couldn't begin to imagine. She hissed into the phone, 'If your job is about burying the truth, it's not worth a shit, is it?'

This time she didn't apologize for the language.

# 44

08.30
**Bampton Lodge**

Tom slept fitfully in Mandler's spare room. The old man had shooed him off to bed and told him not to move for at least twelve hours. During what was left of the night his dreams were crowded with the events of the last two days, a jumbled montage of incidents, each leaving behind it a trail of unanswered questions.

It might have been the sound of Mandler moving about, preparing breakfast to the sound of the *Today* programme that woke him, but it wasn't. When Tom's eyes snapped open it was because he had been recalling Mandler's reluctance for him to contact Ashton.

Why was that so unwise? What possible danger could there be, unless . . . He was on his feet now, heading downstairs in his shorts and T-shirt. Mandler was already out of the house and trudging through a fresh fall of snow towards his Jaguar. Tom shot through the front door, feet bare, onto the snow-covered gravel.

'You know exactly who Rolt's friend is, don't you?'

Mandler turned round and looked at him dismissively, taking

in his lack of proper clothing. 'Go back to bed, Buckingham. You're delirious.'

Tom followed him to the car, the ice stinging his feet. 'You've not been straight with me.'

He caught his arm. Mandler shook himself free with surprising force, climbed into the car and slammed the door. 'Get some more sleep.'

Mandler fired up the Jaguar and slammed it into drive. As it shot forward, Tom stepped back and watched. The slope up to the single-track road was steep. As the vehicle hit the incline, the rear wheels started to spin and the Jaguar fishtailed inelegantly as it fought a losing battle for grip. Tom folded his arms and watched with grim satisfaction as Britain's most senior spook tried and failed to make his getaway.

# 45

Tom adjusted the Range Rover's rear-view mirror so he could keep an eye on Mandler's expression. Ideally he would have preferred to eyeball him for this, but that would have meant another sit-down in his kitchen and time was ticking on.

'From the beginning, please. If you don't mind, sir.'

Mandler sighed heavily, like a deflating balloon. 'All right, Buckingham. But it goes no further, and if *any* of it comes back on me, I'll deny we ever had this conversation, understand?'

'Whatever you say.' Tom eased the vehicle slowly but steadily up the drive onto Mandler's lane, then stepped on it. The tyres bit satisfyingly through the snow and the vehicle powered ahead.

'Umarov – Oleg Emil Umarov, *Dr* Oleg Umarov. He's your man.'

'Okay. Go on, sir, if you wouldn't mind.'

Mandler let out another sigh. 'We have to go back to the last century, the nineties and the volatile post-Soviet days. Young Oleg had been on our books as something of a sleeper, one of those people we established contact with during the height of the Cold War on the off-chance that he might prove useful later. His Crimean Tartar heritage marked him out as a likely anti-Soviet. His father, Emil, was reputedly an awkward bugger

– fought with the Nazis during the war after they overran Ukraine, then joined up with Himmler's Tartar Legion. After the Soviets took back Crimea the whole Umarov family was packed off to a Siberian gulag, which was where little Oleg was born, and where Umarov senior died of a mixture of exposure and an excess of forced labour. Are you following this, Buckingham?'

'I'm all ears, sir.'

'Young Oleg turned out to be a lot smarter than Dad and played the system for all it was worth – talked his way out of the gulag by demonstrating amazing prowess at numbers and, armed with a doctorate in mathematics, which he completed at night school, secured himself a foothold in the Soviet machine. The disadvantages of his ethnicity were more than outweighed by his intellect, and he reached an influential position in the Soviet oil and gas ministry in Ukraine, where his brains earned him the charming nickname "Doktor Kalculyator".

'When we first got to him back in the mid-eighties, he was still playing the long game, despite having inherited his papa's fervent anti-Communism, and just biding his time. But he had never forgotten what the Soviets did to Emil, and was bent on revenge. So we popped him on the payroll and he fed us some scraps of intelligence. Come *glasnost*, *perestroika* and so forth, he did as every good servant of the centralized Soviet state with any brains was bound to do and metamorphosed overnight into a rampant capitalist, ruthlessly reaping the rewards of sudden privatization and becoming obscenely rich in an obscenely short space of time.'

Since Mandler was in full flow, Tom opted to stay quiet.

'As I said, we'd had him on a retainer of sorts since the eighties, naïvely thinking that when the time came he would do our bidding. But my predecessors hugely underestimated him. Oleg had his own fish to fry. What they didn't fully appreciate was that he wasn't just anti-Soviet, he was anti-*Russian*, anti-Kremlin, never mind who was in power, bent on revenge for their historic and unrelenting persecution of the Crimean

Tartars. All this just when we were extending the hand of friendship to our former Cold War foes.'

Tom braked hard as a Porsche Cayenne with two uniformed children in the back pulled out of a drive with no warning.

'You may as well slow down. This could take some time.'

'As you wish, sir.'

'So where was I?'

'Making up with Cold War foes.'

'Ah, yes. Not only was he incredibly effective at outsmarting his rivals, whenever the crunch came he had no scruples about liquidating both competitors and even collaborators whom he decided were getting too close to him. While he was still on our payroll, even though by now his income probably exceeded the entire Security Service budget, he had quietly become the covert banker of choice for any up-and-coming anti-Kremlin separatists. South Ossetians, Chechens, Uzbeks, he backed them all, helped them with not only finance but introductions to arms dealers. Although he was very discreet about it, very good at covering his tracks, our association with him was a ticking bomb, as far as SIS was concerned, and at one point we considered liquidating him. But then around the back end of 'ninety-five our interests – that is, HMG's and his – coincided over the need to quash some opposition to a pipeline we and he had an interest in crossing a certain region in the Russian Federation. Through some of his clients, he, ah – "helped", shall we say? – remove that resistance.'

'What sort of resistance?' In the mirror Tom saw Mandler's Adam's apple bob as he pressed a thumb and forefinger over his eyes. 'Is there a problem, sir?'

'Put it this way. As black ops go, they don't come much darker.' He let out a heavy sigh. 'Farmers, families, rural folk, blameless individuals whose misfortune it was to live in the path of this wretched pipeline, all wiped out. Torched to death, some of them, in their own church. And, to top it all, the fucking pipe never got built.'

Tom saw Mandler glance at him warily. He knew why. Some of what he was saying had an eerie familiarity. Only a couple of years ago, when he was still in the SAS, Tom had been at the sharp end of foiling an attack on the Channel Tunnel by a terrorist cell from the former Georgian enclave of South Ossetia. The incident, which had cost the life of one of his best friends in the Regiment, had left a very bad taste – and several unanswered questions. And his commanding officer on that mission had been Ashton.

'I'm sorry if this is bringing up some less than pleasant memories for you.'

'Just keep going with Umarov for now,' said Tom, tersely.

Mandler gave him a regretful look and continued: 'We were bloody lucky our involvement never came to light, but I always worried that it meant Umarov had something he could black-mail us with, if he ever chose to, knowing he liked to play the long game. Anyway, his tendency to go his own way and be a loner started to catch up with him. Friends weren't something he was good at making or keeping. Enemies were a different matter. By 2008–9 he was getting to be too much of a thorn in the Kremlin's side, a bit too big for his Tartar boots, so they arranged to have his assets seized. But our Oleg's style is all about staying a good few steps ahead of the pack. He'd seen this coming and already had most of his fortune stashed safely in Switzerland. When they came to arrest him they found that he had already bolted.'

'And you gave him a safe haven?'

'Actually, no. We would have been quite happy if Moscow had banged him up. We'd finished with him and the last thing we needed was any blowback. A long, perhaps indefinite, stretch at Mr Putin's pleasure would have been our preference.'

They had reached the M40, and its usual crawling mass of vehicles heading towards the capital. Tom accelerated down the slip road and wove across the traffic to take residence in the fast lane. 'So what happened?'

Mandler rubbed a hand over his eyes. 'He just went off our radar – not that we had any particular reason to keep an eye on him. The activities and whereabouts of a well-heeled, exiled oligarch weren't exactly top priority, though I must admit it always bothered me that he could blackmail us over the pipeline business, if he chose to. Anyway, it transpires he showed up in London only a few months ago. Just slipped in on the Eurostar bearing a Swiss passport that presumably his bankers had helped swing. What with all the current excitements, we didn't get wind of him until – well, the other day.'

'So was it him Randall drove Rolt to meet in Geneva?'

Mandler shrugged. 'Who knows? It's a possibility, that's all.'

'And you're saying this is the first you knew that he was here in the UK?'

'After you went to bed I made a few calls. It seems Umarov's been very quietly but rather rapidly acquiring a sizeable property portfolio across the capital.'

'How sizeable?'

'Very. He trades under a number of different and highly forgettable names. International Assets, AB Properties. United Investments.'

'And Xenia Dalton, how does she fit in with this?'

Mandler raised his hands and let them fall back onto his thighs. 'Ah, beautiful, tragic Xenia. Her father was Oleg's business partner before he was killed.'

'Killed how?'

'He was murdered, not unusual for Russian businessmen – or Crimean ones. It's not known by whom. Afterwards, Umarov took up with her mother – not a union Xenia supported. In fact, it was one of the reasons she left and came here. Knowing she was trying to escape Umarov's clutches, we fast-tracked her citizenship.'

'And the money she's ploughed into Newsday?'

'A legacy from her father.'

'And her relationship with Umarov now?'

'Put it this way, he almost certainly had her father killed. She built that fortress to avoid the same fate, only he's suddenly turned up here, and laid claim to her legacy. And it seems he's moved into the floor below.'

Tom's awkward conversation with Xenia now started to make more sense. 'So what's the deal with Rolt?'

'Well, you and Phoebe are the ones watching him . . .'

There was a flavour of indignation in Mandler's comment, which Tom ignored. 'And there's nothing you're keeping back from me?' Tom eyed him in the mirror. He looked pinched and careworn.

'No, you've got the sum total of it. What you know is what I know.'

Tom processed what he had heard. When Randall drove Rolt to Geneva something happened there that turned him off Rolt big-time, enough to want to finish him. Evans said he'd heard him begging. If it *was* Umarov in the car, what exactly was Rolt begging for? Mandler was staring into the murky distance, the traffic slowing as they reached London's western fringe. 'Let's come at it the other way. Ashton.'

Mandler said nothing.

'The Georgia mission, the one backed by Umarov, he was part of it, yes?'

Mandler nodded slowly.

'But you really have no idea what he's up to,' pressed Tom, 'what he was doing in the Lakes?'

He wasn't altogether surprised by Mandler's reply. 'Frankly, Buckingham, if anyone's going to crack that one, it's you.'

# 46

**10.30**
**Croydon, Surrey**

'Ma'am, I've got to say I don't think this is a good idea.'

Garvey and Adila sat motionless in the back of the Vectra, peering out through the misting windows at the mayhem in the street. The SO1 driver twisted in his seat to make eye contact with the former home secretary.

'I'm going to recommend we abort.'

He had to shout to make himself heard above the din outside. Garvey eyeballed him back. 'We're going to Adila's house and that's it. I want to talk to her family. If you don't want to drive us, we'll walk it. I'm not the home secretary any more, I'm just their MP. I get a bang on the head, the nation's not going to go into mourning.'

The driver eased the car forward. A glass bottle smashed against the windscreen, the stench of its contents seeping in through the air intake.

Garvey glared at the scene. On one side of the road a group of white thugs in bomber jackets was penned behind barriers with a battery of heavily armed police in riot gear, while on the other there was an equally angry mob of men with beards. A cop in full riot gear tapped on the driver's half-misted window.

'You lot can hoppit. Read my lips. No more media.'

The driver motioned with his thumb at his passengers. 'She's their MP, mate.'

Garvey flung her door open. 'I've had enough of this pussy-footing around.'

'Ma'am, this street's a no-go area. We can't be responsible—'

'No-go area? Since when? You're the police. *Nowhere* should be a no-go area for you.'

Garvey helped Adila out of the car. The cop was blocking her way. 'Look, ma'am, I don't think you quite understand.'

'Oh, I think I do. Now, are you going to escort us to this young lady's house or are we going in alone? Your choice. We're going either way.'

'I'll have to call this in.'

'You do that. Come on, Adila.' Garvey took her arm and together they walked up the middle of the street.

'Kill the cunt! Cut her head off!' shouted one of the protesters.

Garvey paused and turned to him. 'To which particular "cunt" are you referring? You want to kill me? Just you try.' She came up very close. He looked a bit less full of himself now, and his mates started laughing. A smoke bomb landed a few metres away.

Adila and Garvey kept walking. As they reached the front door of the house it opened and a couple came out, a man with a camera bag and tripod followed by a woman in heavy makeup, zipping up a laptop case. Four private security men in stab vests and hard hats encircled them as they went towards a people-carrier with blacked-out windows.

The woman reporter stopped when she saw them. Her face lit up. 'Adila, there you are! We nearly missed you.' She gestured furiously to the cameraman to set up. Garvey stepped between them. The reporter shook her head. 'You're too late, love. We've got the family exclusive. It's all in the can.'

Garvey went up very close to the reporter, causing her to take a step back. 'I am Sarah Garvey, this family's elected Member of Parliament. This is a live case with significant security implications. You're exploiting these people and I guarantee that your editor will receive an injunction within the hour.'

The journalist put her head on one side and gave Garvey a pitying look, her eyes gleaming with barely concealed pleasure. 'I'm sorry to disappoint you, Ms Garvey, but I think you'll find that the *new* home secretary's office actually called Mr Masri and *told* him to give us the interview.' The woman turned to Adila and switched her smile back on. 'So, Adila, a word on your brother. As a smart young student, I'm sure you'll be joining your parents in condemning Jamal's crime?'

Garvey felt her fists clenching. She took a deep breath and exhaled slowly. She could feel the blood pulsing in her temples. The temptation to flatten the smug bitch was almost overwhelming. Instead she took Adila by the arm, swung round and pushed past the cameraman who was still struggling with his tripod.

Adila pressed the bell. Nothing happened. After a few seconds, she pressed again. Then a third time. After the fourth try, the door opened. A man with a chinstrap beard, dressed in a long *jubbah*, stood there, his face like thunder. He glared at his daughter as she came to a halt. 'You traitor.'

'Father, this is—'

He slammed the door in her face.

Garvey went up to the door and lifted the flap of the letterbox. 'Mr Masri, this is your MP, Sarah Garvey. I'm here to tell you that your son is innocent until proven guilty and that I have it on very good authority that the video that was posted online has been faked. Please open the door so we can talk.'

'Jamal is no longer my son. He has brought shame on our family and destroyed our life. We have no future here.'

The crowd of white men had started chanting, 'Out, out, out!'

The SO1 driver had gathered a posse of heavily armoured local police, who encircled them. 'I'm going to have to get you out of here, ma'am. This is gonna get a lot worse in a bit.'

Adila pointed at the end of the street, where very slowly a large white vehicle was coming into view. 'What's that?'

Garvey knew very well what it was. One of the German-made Ziegler Wasserwerfer truck-mounted water cannon she had been persuaded to order by a delegation of chief constables. 'Unless your father has a very quick change of heart, which I don't imagine he will, we'd better do what the officer says.'

Garvey put an arm round Adila's shoulders and led her back to the car.

'I'm sorry, I overestimated my powers of persuasion.'

'My father doesn't bend easily.'

'He bent far enough to give those vultures an interview.'

'He's naïve – he doesn't understand how things work here. He doesn't realize they'll twist his words.'

Garvey was seething. *That preening little piece of shit, Henry. He's behind this.* But the news that Rolt had actually sanctioned the interview put a different spin on things.

Adila turned to her. 'Thank you for trying. I do appreciate this when you must be so busy.'

Surrounded by armed police and a baying mob, she still sounded as though she was thanking her for an invitation to tea. Garvey smiled to herself. For the first time in a long while she was far from busy. 'I've not finished yet, Adila.'

'If I could only see Jamal. Do you think there's any chance I'd be allowed to visit him? If I could even find out where he is . . .'

'Let's see, shall we?' said Garvey. 'Let's see.'

# 47

## 11.00
## Home Office, Westminster

Farmer waited in the home secretary's outer office. It was a long time since he had been there. He and Sarah Garvey had locked horns soon after she was appointed. It was his fault, mistaking her for someone who might bend to his will, like her more malleable fellow cabinet members. She had seen him off with a volley of abuse that even he would have been hard pressed to come up with. Thereafter he had kept his distance, but nurtured a grudging admiration for the old bat. He had been sorry to see her go. Unlike most of the others, she actually believed in something other than her own advancement.

Equally, he had been all for putting Rolt on their election ticket. It was a jammy idea conjured up by Clements, though you could never be entirely sure of the cabinet secretary's motives. All the same, Farmer had run with it, telling the doubters that it was a straight choice between getting into bed with Rolt and a return to opposition – possibly permanently. Now he was having misgivings, just as he was about to have his first one-to-one with the new home secretary. He would have preferred to be bringing happier news with him – all the better to make a good first impression. But what he had wasn't good, couldn't wait and had to be delivered in person, for his ears only.

The double doors opened and a school of junior ministers and senior mandarins swam past.

'You can go in now, Mr Farmer.'

Farmer put his head round the door. 'Home Secretary, do you need a minute or shall I come straight in?' He glanced at Henry, who was leaning over the desk, pointing out something to Rolt.

'No, no, come on in.'

'Derek Farmer, Number Ten press,' Henry explained, barely glancing up.

Farmer tried not to bridle. His correct title was director of communications for the prime minister's office.

'Ah, splendid. Good to meet you.'

Rolt stood up and offered his hand. Farmer took it and gave it one of his unthreatening shakes.

'Kind of you to see me at such short notice, Home Secretary.'

'No problem, if you've got a good reason. What can I do for you?' Rolt pushed back his chair and rested his elbows on the arms, his fingers knitted together.

Farmer glanced at Henry, who showed no signs of getting ready to leave. 'Ah, I think it would probably be better if . . .'

Rolt smiled blandly. 'Oh, no, don't worry. Henry and I have no secrets, do we?'

He gave Henry a friendly glance, which Farmer saw the little prick suck up with delight. Farmer took a seat, put on his grave prepare-for-bad-news face and opened the slim file on his lap. 'This is an evolving national security issue, which I'm not authorized to share with – with subordinates.'

It was balls, and Henry probably would guess it was, but Rolt ought to get the message.

He didn't. 'I'll tell you now, Derek, if I'm going to get done here what we need to get done in the little time we have, the fewer secrets there are between me and my staff the better. So why don't you give us the heads up?'

Farmer swallowed his sigh. He wasn't going to get off on the wrong foot here. 'Understood, Home Secretary.'

Rolt fixed him with a keen gaze. 'So, fire away.'

'It's about a journalist who's gone missing in Syria: Emma Warner, a highly regarded freelancer who does some of her own video reports for the web and TV. She's won various awards and whatnot.'

The name clearly meant nothing to Rolt. 'What's it got to do with the Home Office if she went missing in Syria?'

'Well, it's to do with Jamal.'

Rolt's eyes narrowed. 'Ah, yes, "The Butcher of Aleppo".'

Farmer winced at his use of the tabloid term, as if it was an official title. 'Currently detained in Belmarsh.'

Rolt gave a curt nod and glanced at Henry. 'Yes, until we can find a country willing to take him and his family.'

My God, he really was serious about this stuff. Farmer briefly lost his train of thought. 'Er, in his statement to his lawyer, a fellow called Latimer, Jamal claimed he had been recruited by Warner to do some secret filming.'

'Really. And?'

'It turns out that a body has been found. Or, to be more specific, some parts of a body have been recovered. A parcel containing her head and hands was delivered to the British Consulate in a town in eastern Turkey a couple of hours ago.' Farmer paused for the full impact of what he was saying to sink in.

Rolt frowned. 'And?'

'Well, it's – she's not been formally identified but the intelligence service inside the consulate are confident that it's the remains of the missing journalist.'

Rolt sighed. 'Well, that's very unfortunate but, as we all know now, it's just the sort of thing these people are capable of.'

Farmer nodded. 'Very true, Home Secretary. However, Latimer is also saying that the offending video featuring his client, which you are familiar with, has been technically examined and found to have been doctored.'

Rolt shrugged. 'So what? I've already heard this tale. Anyone mad enough to try to defend such a hideous criminal is bound to clutch at any old straw. I don't see the worry.' He eased his shirt cuffs out from inside the arms of his suit.

Farmer tried to pick his words carefully. 'Well, sir, the fact is . . . How can I put it? It's true.'

Rolt looked at him, disappointed.

Farmer decided to keep going. 'The news of Warner's death, coming just as there are suggestions that there's doubt about the footage, does throw more of a question mark over Jamal's guilt. And this could lead to speculation in the press. I mean, it almost certainly will.'

Rolt's expression changed to one of dismay. 'Then block it. Take out an injunction or whatever it is you have to do. A D Notice – isn't that how you deal with these things?'

Farmer took a breath. He could feel his face heating up. 'Sorry if I'm not getting you, Home Secretary, but are you saying that the truth about Emma Warner and the doctored video should be withheld?'

Rolt spread his arms. 'It bloody well has to be. The public are clamouring for action. This isn't the moment to be pulling back.'

Farmer noticed that Henry's eyes were also fixed on him, his head moving almost imperceptibly from left to right, and mouthing, 'No.' It was usually at this point in an exchange with a recalcitrant cabinet minister that Farmer rolled up his sleeves and gave his speech, reminding them of some compelling reason, usually personal, invariably embarrassing, why they needed to do exactly what Farmer was telling them to do and not question it. Not this time.

Rolt got to his feet. 'What we all have to come to terms with, Derek, is that we are in a state of virtual civil war. Society as we know it is coming apart. We have to act and we have to act fast. Normal service has been suspended. We are going to cleanse this country and eradicate the menace that is spreading through it. This is no time for inconvenient rumours and speculation.'

For the first time in his career Farmer was speechless. Rolt hadn't finished. He gestured at the phone on his desk. 'So do you tell the PM, or shall I pick up the phone and tell him what to do? Questions about this video or any other – imaginings about this woman journalist's death – must be erased from the record. Make them go away.'

There was a look in Rolt's eye that Farmer had seen before, at the press conference when he was replying to the question about the assassination attempt. Before, he would have dismissed it as typical of a politician getting carried away by the sound of his own voice. But this was something else.

Farmer folded the file in his lap and got to his feet. He could feel his face reddening with suppressed rage. There were a number of things he could have said, most of which he would have had to retract, probably followed by a swift tendering of his notice before he got the push. Perhaps that was Rolt's plan: evict the last members of the awkward squad who remained in the administration by provoking them into losing it. Farmer was famous for doing just that, and for his subsequent apologies, usually made through gritted teeth. But Rolt had done the seemingly impossible and shocked him into silence.

Farmer forced a smile. 'Good to meet you at last, Home Secretary. Thank you for your time.' And with that he headed for the door.

He hadn't got far into the outer office when he felt a gentle touch on his elbow. It was Henry. 'Ah, just to be clear, Derek. You understand he's not joking.'

There was a supercilious smile on the little shit's face.

'Oh, yes,' Farmer replied. 'I got the message loud and clear.'

'So you know what the home secretary needs to happen.'

Farmer looked at him, then nodded slowly. 'Oh, yes. I know what to do.'

# 48

**11.30**
**Central London**

Tom pulled into a side-street in Soho to drop Mandler well away from his usual stamping ground, as he'd asked. He was still processing what he had just been told. Mandler had identified Rolt's mystery visitor. He had admitted that Tom's old CO had been involved in a covert mission backed by Umarov. But he was no nearer to knowing what Umarov wanted with the new home secretary. With the proper resources the man could be located and surveillance started. But Mandler wasn't offering him any.

'Don't underestimate the extent to which my hands are tied, Buckingham. I'm under scrutiny myself. I'm afraid it may be down to you to put the pieces together.'

Those had been Mandler's parting words. Tom had watched him make his way down Greek Street, Britain's top spook, a cowed and frightened man.

The only person he could still count on for backup was Phoebe, though what condition she was in to carry on he wasn't sure.

She picked up straight away. 'Tom, I was worried about you.'

'I'll worry about me, you worry about you. What's happening?'

'It's all gone pretty weird. Rolt's shut down the office. Told everybody they're on leave pending further instructions.'

'And the campus?'

'On lockdown. No one in or out till further notice.'

'Something to do with the break-in?'

'I don't know. No one's saying anything. Did you find anything in the Lake District?'

'Just some dead wood. But I've got the name of Rolt's mystery visitor. Oleg Umarov. Ring any bells?'

Phoebe went quiet for a few seconds. 'I'll go back through all my reports, see what turns up.'

'Is Rolt finding time to keep in touch with you?'

'He's ultra-preoccupied with the new job. The guy who came back from Syria seems to be getting all his attention. It's all he talks about. Tom, I don't know what I'm supposed to be doing. Woolf's gone quiet on me as well. And you're in hiding. Where are you anyway? Where *are* you?'

There was more than a hint of desperation in her voice. He wasn't sure what impelled him to lie to her. 'Lying low, as instructed by the powers that be. Find anything you can that Rolt had on Umarov. Any reference, any call, any receipt or message or cigarette end. Anything at all that connects them. Call me when you've got something.'

He rang off, turned the car round and headed back out of London.

# 49

**14.00**
**Park Gate Place**

Xenia Dalton stood at the huge picture window that was one wall of her office and glared at the grey murk below. She kept her back to her visitor and spoke without turning round, using the native tongue that she would gladly have forgotten, if only she could.

*'I did what I was told. I backed Rolt. He's where you want him. Surely that's enough?'*

She placed her hands on the cold marble of the windowsill as if trying to absorb some of the strength from the fortifications she had built to protect herself, much good they had done her. She could see his shape in the reflection of the glass, just the silhouette, short, but with powerful, broad shoulders. She suppressed a shiver, reminded of what he had been like in her youth, and why she had run away. Then she adjusted her gaze so she couldn't see his shape at all. But she could feel his eyes on her.

She forced herself to turn and face him. His colouring was florid and the redness showed through the thin wiry hair that populated his scalp. His features seemed to be trying to conceal themselves: his mouth was lipless, his nose flat and broad, his eyes little more than slits. Although he had the colouring and stance of a man who had endured a lifetime of physical labour, his finely tailored suit told a different story. And there was the smell: the acrid Balkan tobacco smoke, the abnormally strong aftershave that smelt of sandalwood. She'd always hated that smell. Even now it caught in her throat. He lifted his cigarette to his mouth and sucked.

*'I told you Rolt would be a good investment. Now you are reaping the harvest.'*

She glanced at the page-roughs, the headline prepared by her editor, on paper, as she preferred, so she could handle it herself. But she didn't want to touch it. She knew the horrible truth about Emma, the woman whose brave mission she had financed. And she knew that what she was looking at was a complete lie.

## BUTCHER OF ALEPPO EXCLUSIVE – THE FAMILY SPEAKS!

McCloud's sole access to them had been sanctioned by Rolt. He had done the deal with the family himself, without consulting her, and sent a freelancer she didn't even know to talk to them. And the price? Flights for all the family to Lahore, one way.

*'I don't want this in my paper.'*

*'You supported Rolt. Think of it as a reward.'*

*'I had no choice, remember?'*

She could feel control of her paper slipping further out of her grasp.

*'Your mama always said you were an obstinate child.'*

She seethed inside at his even mentioning her mother but she refused to give him the satisfaction of seeing it.

*'This is all lies. I won't have it.'*

She caught the flash of anger in his cold pale blue eyes, scanning her from their hideouts beneath the heavy brow.

'You know perfectly well, my dear, that what's mine is yours and what's yours is mine. Everything I'm doing here is for you. So I think there has to be a little give and take, don't you?' He had switched to English, perhaps to show her how proficient he had become. He waved an arm in the direction of the window. 'I understand now why you like this country. Before I thought you were just a stupid runaway seduced by the bright lights and Western music. But now I've seen the ... possibilities, I agree. It has much potential, once order has been restored.'

The paper had been her project. She'd bought it from the administrators after it had gone bust, put it back on its feet and made it into a success. All with the money put away for her by her father. But Umarov didn't see it that way. As far as he was concerned, that was money *they* made when they were partners, in which he had a share. And now he was here, back in her life, gradually assuming control. She had hoped that after she'd given in to him over supporting Rolt he would be satisfied, and back off. How wrong she had been, how naïve.

There was a knock at the door.

'Not now!' she shouted.

The door inched open. McCloud put his head round. 'Sorry to butt in.'

'I said *not now.*'

Umarov swivelled round and raised his hand in greeting. 'Ah, Mr Editor McCloud.' McCloud gave Xenia a mock-apologetic look and stepped into the room. Umarov clapped his hands. 'Congratulations on your *eksklyuzivnyy.*'

McCloud came forward and shook his hand, Umarov gripping his forearm at the same time, as if he was a long-lost friend.

'I'm glad you appreciate it. Circulation's up another ten thousand, plus a million extra page views. What's not to like?'

Umarov gestured at the desk. 'Just a few differences to resolve.'

McCloud saw the paper on Xenia's desk and shrugged. 'It's all their own words, straight from the horses' mouths.'

Her humiliation was complete. She fought back angry tears but she could feel her face heating up, as if the years she had put between herself and the past had just shrunk to nothing. She was the petulant teenager again, powerless in her hateful stepfather's presence. 'It's all lies.'

The two men looked at her.

'I'm sorry you feel that way, Xenia.' There was no trace of apology in McCloud's tone.

She looked down at the page-rough that was laid out on her desk with its screaming headline. Somehow, she had to get even. The anger was boiling up in her now, ready to burst out. She picked up the page-rough, held it up for a second and, as the two men watched, she tore it into pieces.

# 50

Jamal stared at the note: *Empty your toilet bowl. 1 a.m.* He had found it under the drinking cup on his meal tray.

For the last day he had asked to be left in his cell. News had spread round the jail that the so-called 'Butcher of Aleppo' was in Belmarsh. It didn't matter that he was only on remand. The world of the prison was no different from outside. He was guilty. He was a target. Never mind that he hadn't been tried or even charged. He turned the slip of paper in his fingers. It was a piece of toilet paper, the message written in pencil.

Two hours ago the governor, Alan Thompson, had paid him a visit. Jamal stood to attention when he entered. Thompson gave him a pitying look and told him he didn't need to do that. 'I've got some good news. Your sister has been granted permission to visit you. It seems your Member of Parliament has taken an interest in your case and requested that I give you the news personally, so there's no danger of it getting lost or – forgotten.'

Jamal looked into Thompson's face to see if there was any indication of whether he thought this was a good thing or not.

But the man's features were devoid of expression. In spite of that, tears of joy welled in Jamal's eyes. 'Thank you, sir. Thank you very much.'

'You'll get twenty-five minutes in the communal meeting area.'

Twenty-five minutes. He must think what to say to make the most of it.

'Try to stay out of trouble between now and then, eh? You don't want to give the Home Office a reason to rescind.'

The governor left and Jamal was alone with his fears.

It was twelve forty-five. He hadn't been able to sleep. What would happen if he emptied the toilet? He had no idea.

He presumed it was from Isham. He was the only other inmate who had said anything to him that wasn't a volley of threats and abuse. He had avoided him in the prayer meeting but here, in the darkness of night, with the mounting sense of his own total solitude, he had begun to think that the offer of friendship was not to be rejected.

He had a plastic cup and a water bottle that was almost empty. He knelt down and began to scoop the water from the toilet bowl with the cup, pouring it carefully into the bottle. As the bowl emptied he became aware of a sound coming through the pipe. A sort of hum or chant, very distorted and indistinct.

'Hello?' he called softly.

'Brother.' The word came back so clearly it might have come from the next cell.

'Isham?'

'Brother.'

The voice was hard to recognize, transmitted in this way, but he was sure it was the man he had prayed beside.

'Are you praying, brother?'

'Yes, I am praying.' It was a lie: Jamal had intended to pray again but his pleas to God for help sounded pathetic and weak.

'Do you have hope?'

He didn't like to say no. 'My sister is coming. They've allowed her to visit.'

Isham went silent for several seconds. 'When does your sister come?'

Jamal told him. There was no response. After a few minutes of calling softly and no answer Jamal carefully replaced the water in the bowl.

# 51

**10.00**
**Newland Hall, Malvern Hills, Worcestershire**

*I'm at my parents'. Give us a shout.* Tom pressed send.

Ashton's reply came back in seconds. *The Flying Horse: 16.00.*

A pub about ten miles away.

Tom's mother was bent over the unstitched dog bite on his forearm. She knew better than to ask how he had come by it. He was seated at the kitchen table, her first-aid kit open beside him. He had arrived late last night, given her a hug, collapsed into his old bed and slept solidly for sixteen hours.

'So, will you be here for dinner?'

'Maybe. I'll let you know.'

She sighed. 'You turn up without any warning and I don't even know if you're just going to disappear again.'

'I know. I'm sorry, okay? It's like this right now.'

She squeezed his shoulder. 'Still, it's wonderful to have you back after so long. Sit still while I finish this. It's quite nasty. I suppose you're not going to tell me what happened.'

He smiled. 'Afraid I don't remember a thing. Must have had a few too many.'

She rolled her eyes. He knew she didn't believe him. It didn't matter. Long ago he had trained her to accept that he was always going to be economical with the truth about his life. But after the madness of the last few days it felt very good to be back in the comparative sanity of home.

'Tell me again what Ashton said.'

'Truly, only what I've told you. He was very civil, concerned to know that you were happy in your new role. We just made polite noises back. It was all we could say since we haven't a clue how it's—'

'All right, Mum.'

'He seemed keen to see you again but I think he was a bit reticent about making a direct approach since your departure from the Regiment. Think he wanted us to drop you a hint.'

'Well, consider it dropped. So where's Dad today?'

'He got called back to town. He's got some big deal going on he's rather excited about.'

'What sort of big deal?'

'He's been rather cagey about it, which is most unlike him. In fact, he's been like that for the past couple of weeks. I worry about him, sometimes even more than I worry about you.'

Hugh had been equally unforthcoming with him, but Tom wasn't about to add to his mother's worries. 'He can look after himself – he's never screwed up.'

She gave him a wry look. 'There's always a first time.'

After she had finished patching him up, he went into his father's study. On the desk there was a big old-fashioned Rolodex. Like many of his generation Hugh was almost endearingly wary of the digital world and still laboriously copied out the names and addresses of all his contacts onto small cards. Mandler's comment about Umarov building up a property portfolio had made Tom wonder if his father had come across him. He spun through the cards to U, but there was no Umarov. That was a relief. He put the Rolodex back in its place, then booted up the PC and had a few goes at the password. *Horace* worked: always the name of one of their dogs. He scrolled through his inbox and then his sent items until he started to feel grubby about what he was doing. Imagine if his father did the same to him. He shut the PC down and pushed the chair back from the desk. He was about to leave but something else caught his eye.

The box wasn't as big as the one he'd found in Rolt's office, and the Ordynka inside was less elaborately engraved. But the dedication said it all: *To Hugh, from your friend, Oleg.*

# 52

**15.45**

On the way to the pub, Tom tried not to think about what he had found in his father's study. He needed to rehearse the story of his apparent motivation for the meeting with Ashton but the thought that Hugh was in any way involved with Umarov was deeply troubling. Previously separate parts of his life had now become entangled.

It was Ashton who had thrown down the gauntlet by dropping in on his folks. Rolt was now in government and Tom's role as his right-hand man had been overtaken by events. It was coming up to time for him to move on; nothing more complicated than that. Oh, and an inclination, which Tom was not at all sure he was ready for, to put the past behind him.

He drew up outside the Flying Horse. It was closed for refurbishment. Ashton presumably didn't know either. He was about to text him when a black Mercedes G-Wagen rumbled into view, the same vehicle he had seen in the Lakes, which had been used to cart away Evans, his men and their dead dog. At the sight of it his blood ran cold. It turned into the car park beside the pub. The windows were blacked out so it was impossible to see if Ashton had company.

Tom stepped out of his car and walked up to the Merc as Ashton emerged from the front passenger side. So, he wasn't alone. Ashton was dressed much as he always was, thick sweater, chinos and boots. 'Hello, Tom.'

'Hello, boss.' Old habits died hard.

Ashton cracked a rare smile, took his hand and gripped it firmly. 'Good to see you.'

Two men, who might well have been the ones with him when he had murdered Evans, stepped out of the Merc.

'It's closed, by the way,' Tom said.

'I know,' replied Ashton.

One of the men approached him and patted him down carefully.

'Sorry about this, Tom. Can't be too careful at the moment. Strange days, eh?'

Tom's firearm was in the car. Carrying it would have looked odd. A warning bell sounded in his head. But then it was shut off, along with everything else, as he felt himself fall to the ground.

# 53

Something jolted him awake: something cold and wet on his face. He tried to reach up to remove it, but his arms were pinned to his sides. He was flat on his back, his feet higher than his head. He moved his head and realized with a jolt that it was wrapped in something.

'Who're you working with, Tom?'

Ashton's voice. Tom pulled furiously against the bindings.

'What the fuck is this?'

'Just answer the question, Tom.'

Ashton sounded faintly bored.

'You know who I'm working for. Vernon Rolt. Invicta.'

Ashton uttered something he couldn't hear.

The cold spread across his face, saturating the cloth wrapped round it and blocking his airways. Okay, he told himself. I can deal with this. Concentrate on what you're here for.

'I'll say it again. Who is it, Tom? Who's put you up to this?'

How ironic. Ashton's question was the very one Tom wanted to ask him.

The water saturated the cloth over his face. Try as he might, he could not stop his body going into convulsions, thinking it was drowning. He used all his concentration not to struggle. The more he tried to resist, the worse it would get.

*You are not going to drown*, he told himself. *That's not what they want.*

He felt the vomit rising in him and spreading across into his blocked airways.

There was only one way to deal with this. To relax. Yeah, good idea. Very funny. The water seeped straight through the cloth, into his nostrils and straight into the sinuses. No amount of head-shaking or snorting could stop it. The only thing to do was try to block everything, but how to do that and answer? There is only so long a human being can hold their breath. In the end the body takes over and with that sudden gasp comes an intake of water. The one thing Tom tried to cling to was the thought that Ashton wanted him alive. But he had seen off Evans. And they were both part of Invicta. Was this a purge? Don't be a fool, he told himself.

'Come on, Tom. Just give us the truth. Let's get this done.'

Who the hell else could he be working for? He could give up Mandler's name – except he knew Mandler would deny all: he had told him as much. Anyway, he was on his own. The old spook had said as much. He told himself to cling to that thought. Rolt was his only employer.

His body had gone into spasm, struggling for all it was worth to expel the water.

Someone lifted him up and he vomited the water out.

'Who are *you* working for?' He coughed. 'What's all this about? I work for Rolt – I've barely left his side for the last four months.'

He repeated it over and over, all the time arguing with the bit of his brain shouting at him to say Mandler's name and have done with it. There were moments when the names became confused in his mind as he fought to stay conscious.

He heard Ashton's voice very close to his ear, almost a whisper. 'This isn't working, Tom. Give it up, be a good man.'

They repeated the same routine with the water until he felt himself losing his grip on consciousness. But he forced himself, against every sinew inside his body, to hold on.

'Vernon Rolt, Vernon Rolt,' he repeated the name over and over.

Then he felt himself falling onto a hard cold surface, his pinioned arms unable to break the fall as he came down on his side. There he curled up in a foetal position as he attempted to empty his lungs.

'Okay, clean him up. *Ochistite yego.*'

# 54

Tom faced his former CO across a grey metal table. In front of him was a mug of coffee and an M&S sandwich still in its wrapper. Ashton had on a black parka now. The room was freezing cold.

'Sorry about that. Just a precaution.' Ashton gave him a wan smile.

Tom said nothing. His throat and lungs felt as though he had just inhaled a volcano.

'You know how it is.'

'No, I fucking well don't know how it is. For fuck's sake!' His outrage, even if not the result of innocence, was genuine.

'We just had to be sure you were still kosher, okay?'

'Who else could I have been working for? Al-Qaeda? ISIS?' He reached for the sandwich and ripped open the wrapper. Chicken and avocado, his favourite. He used to be ribbed about this in the Regiment. Ashton must have remembered. He bit into it. He had every right to be furious about the waterboarding, but he reminded himself he had walked into this for a reason. Now he was a step closer to finding out what Ashton was up to.

Ashton cleared his throat, leaned forward and rubbed his hands. A bit of him wondered if his old CO was enjoying this. 'What a difference six months makes, eh?'

'What's that mean?' Tom spoke through a mouthful of chicken.

'We're living in desperate times, Tom. You can see that as well as I can – maybe we all should have seen it coming. And desperate times call for desperate measures. You of all people should know that.'

Tom frowned. He didn't see why at all, but he said nothing and let Ashton talk.

'I would have thought that, from your viewpoint, at the elbow of our new home secretary, you would be in a pretty good position to see the big picture.'

Tom wolfed the rest of the sandwich.

'Let's not fool ourselves. This country is sliding towards anarchy. People are going to have to choose sides. It's already happening.'

'Happening where?'

'On the streets, in the corridors of power: people thinking the unthinkable.'

'But Rolt's got the right job to be able to sort it out, hasn't he?'

'And you think he will?'

'He won the election for them, that's for sure. He won't like it if they try to get in his way.'

Ashton went silent for a moment, sifting Tom's words. Then he started to shake his head. 'You always did have a streak of idealism.'

Tom felt faintly indignant. But Ashton's comment was an indication that his cover was still working. 'So you really think they're going to rush through his programme?'

Ashton prodded the table with a forefinger. 'The PM will put the brakes on, try to water it down, slow the legislative process. Meanwhile the country slides into chaos. And who wants that?' He leaned forward. 'Look, Tom, I know we've had our differences but that's all in the past. You and I, we're both on the same side.'

*Don't make this too easy*, Tom reminded himself. 'And you had to waterboard me first to decide that, yeah?'

Ashton put his hands up. 'As I said, just taking precautions.

238

Your man Rolt, what do you think of him, honestly?' He lowered his voice: 'It's all right. Whatever you say here stays in the room.'

Tom considered the question. He needed Ashton to open up. He needed to feed him enough to get him in the mood. 'I think he's a good man. He's done great work for ex-services blokes who've been dumped on the street.' He paused. 'He speaks a language that a lot of people understand and he likes to cut to the chase where others beat around the bush.'

Ashton sat back in his chair. 'Is there a "but"?'

'But politics is another matter. He's an entrepreneur, used to getting his way, running his own show and not having to justify himself.'

'Go on.'

Ashton seemed to like what he was hearing, but Tom didn't want him to get the impression he was being fed a line. The wall behind had a frosted window. There were people moving about behind it. 'Who are the goons?'

Ashton waved the question away. 'Contractors.'

'Where are they from?'

'Ukraine. Go on with your take on Rolt.'

'He's only where he is because of the votes he brought with him. You're right to be asking whether the rest of the cabinet have got the balls to allow him to follow through.'

Ashton's eyes were drilling into his. 'And where does that leave you?'

'I don't know yet. We didn't talk about what next. I'm not sure if he actually thought he'd make it.'

Ashton spread his hands on the table. 'I think your analysis is correct. And, as we speak, I suspect the prime minister is probably going into overdrive trying to stall him on the runway.'

He was waiting for Tom to respond. Time for another tack. 'There was an attempt on me. They got Jez instead.'

Ashton nodded. 'I heard.'

'It wasn't meant to be public.'

'I keep my ear to the ground. I heard you also stopped someone who was after Rolt.'

'Invicta's not the big happy family people think.'

Ashton shrugged. 'Just a few bad apples left over from when it started. My impression is the rest are all right.'

'You seem to know a lot about what goes on inside Invicta.'

Ashton studied him, evidently considering his reply. 'I ran into some of them down on Dartmoor. Just this week.'

Dartmoor and the Lakes: he had been getting around. Tom hid his surprise. 'And?'

'Good blokes. Itching to make a difference, give something back to society. That's the impression I got.'

Tom absorbed this as he balled up the sandwich wrapper. 'I'm free to go, right? No more fucking around?'

Ashton raised his hands. 'Of course, whenever you want.'

'You *are* working for the government?'

Ashton winced at the question as if it was ridiculous. '*People* in the government.'

'What's that mean?'

Ashton leaned forward again. 'The country's breaking apart, Tom. Someone's going to have to pick up the pieces and put it back together. That's not going to be about building consensus, weighing up the pros and cons. We're sleepwalking into chaos. The government's authority is slipping. People are taking things into their own hands. We have to do something before mob rule takes hold.'

'Some people think Rolt's partly to blame for that, stoking the flames.'

'Well, that's as may be. But we are where we are.'

'So what do you want with me? Why all this rendition-style bollocks?'

'I may have a proposition for you.'

'I'm still on the Invicta payroll, remember.'

'All the better.' Ashton got to his feet. 'The question for you, Tom, is this. When the shit hits the fan, are you going to be upwind or downwind?'

'So what is it, this proposition?'

Ashton was moving him towards the door. 'Keep your phone on and wait out.'

# 55

**14.00**
**Woolwich, South-east London**

Adila waited for the bus outside Woolwich Arsenal station. She looked at the others in the shelter. Were any of them going to Belmarsh as well? There was a woman with white-blonde hair whose two toddlers were whining. She handed them each a bag of crisps and silence fell. Adila smiled at her, reminded of a couple of women she had encountered on her work experience as a midwife. But the woman just looked away. That was how it was now.

Another woman in a hijab came towards them, very pregnant, with a limp. She didn't look old, but her face was haggard. Two men were with her. One steadied her. When she was safely perched on the narrow bench in the bus shelter they moved a few metres away from her and lit cigarettes. Adila smiled at her and the woman smiled back. She felt a little less alone.

When the bus arrived she helped the hijab woman on board. 'Thank you so much – you are most kind.'

'It's a pleasure.' Adila felt her heart warming and, for the first time in several days, allowed herself to think there was hope in the world after all. The two men put out their cigarettes and joined them on the bus.

She looked again at the instructions for visitors: *Give yourself plenty of time to get to HMP Belmarsh; please aim to arrive at least 45 minutes before the visit time. You must book in no more than 20 minutes after the start of the visits session, or you will not be allowed entry to the prison.*

She checked the identification she had brought: her passport and her hospital intern's ID card. She checked that she had remembered a pound coin for the locker. *No change is provided at the visitor centre*, the website had warned. She looked at what she was wearing and remembered the list of clothing that could 'breach security guidelines': hooded sweaters, ripped jeans, football shirts or anything with a national crest, low-cut tops or short skirts. How those could raise security concerns she couldn't imagine, not that she owned any such clothes. She had been warned that there was a biometric ID system where visitors' fingerprints and photos would be taken on the first visit, to be used as proof of ID for any later visits. She would also get an ultraviolet stamp on her hand to validate entry into the visits hall.

She had emptied out all the contents of her handbag that morning and removed anything that she thought might be a problem, even her pens, spiral notebook and makeup. She saw to her horror that she had left a nail file inside. She took it out and laid it on the seat. She would have to leave everything in the locker. She'd wanted so much to bring something from home, just a small memento, but because of her father's behaviour that hadn't been possible. She had had to spend last night with a friend. She believed she would be allowed home because her father usually relented with her. He favoured her over the boys – sometimes she resented it and wished he was as harsh with her as he was with them. Then they would be equal. But nothing was equal any more.

She noticed the blonde woman had a big transparent bag, containing nappies and bottles, and concluded she must also be a visitor. The few items that could be taken in included baby paraphernalia so long as it was all packed in a clear plastic bag.

She felt she knew what to expect. All visitors to HMP Belmarsh would be searched on their way to the visits hall with a metal detector, and what was ominously called a 'rub-down'. Shoes and coats were X-rayed.

When the bus stopped, the blonde woman yanked the toddlers onto their feet and steered them to the exit. Adila followed and, when she got to the door, noticed the hijab woman behind her, one of the men helping her off the bus. Her pregnancy wouldn't be the cause of her limp: it might well be rickets, Adila diagnosed, common in cultures where women were covered up from childhood, depriving them of vitamin D from sunlight.

After the first gate they moved down a covered walkway to a second door, which had been unlocked. They formed a queue with several other visitors, most of them women, waiting to be searched. Adila wondered how they would deal with the woman in the hijab, who was alone now. Something about her demeanour, the look of studied resignation, suggested that this was not her first visit. Nor was it the blonde woman's. She was greeted like an old friend by a female guard, who conducted a perfunctory search and ruffled the children's hair. Adila noticed a second female guard in a headscarf. That was something. The headscarf guard scowled as she beckoned the hijab woman, who scowled back. Certainly no love lost there. She waved Adila forward as well, looking her up and down. Adila was suddenly conscious of how smartly dressed she was compared to the other visitors.

'First time?' asked the guard.

'Yes, that's right.'

'Welcome to the monkey house.'

She passed a detector wand over the hijab woman. It made a loud beep. Several people looked round. The woman angrily pulled up the side of her garment to reveal a leg brace so all of them could see. 'Happy now?'

The guard sighed. 'Just doin' my job, darlin'. On you go.'

She beckoned Adila forward. After she had conducted the 'rub-down' and waved the wand over her, the guard pointed out the lockers. 'Bag in there, nothing with you in the hall, just your sweet selves.'

Adila locked up her bag and coat. Through thick wire-mesh glass she could see the visits hall. It reminded her of an exam room with rows of small tables, but with chairs on both sides.

Beyond a set of barred doors with frosted glass she could see blurred figures moving. She was about to see her brother.

# 56

Jamal waited in the line, his head down, hoping no one would recognize him from his photo in the papers. He felt a small tug on his sleeve and looked round. It was Isham. 'How are you doing?'

Jamal shrugged. 'I just want to see my sister. I just hope she's there.'

'If she wasn't you wouldn't be in this line. Only inmates with a signed-in visitor go through.'

'Who's coming to see you?'

Isham grinned. 'My wife.'

Jamal sank back into his thoughts. He didn't want to make idle conversation just now. He wanted to go over all the things he had prepared to say to Adila, that he was resigned to imprisonment for going to Syria and would freely admit his membership of what the British government classed a terrorist organization. But he emphatically denied even touching the murdered girls. He would explain to her how the camera worked and how they had also been filmed in training. She would believe him. He had never lied to her and never would. How lucky he was to have just one person left in his life like her.

The door opened and they filed in. Each of them was led to a table. Jamal saw Isham move towards a woman in a headscarf – she didn't look very pleased to see him. Then there was Adila smiling and waving across the room at a table near the back. He felt his heart almost burst with delight. He waved frantically. She started to rise out of her seat but a guard shouted to her to sit. Even from that distance Jamal could see her eyes were filled with tears of joy. He went towards her, his arms outstretched. He was no more than ten feet from her when he saw Isham's wife leap up from her seat and run shrieking towards the entrance where the visitors had come in. Two guards rushed towards her as she reached the barred door and grabbed her, just a few feet from Adila.

Before he had even consciously absorbed what he was seeing, Jamal's brain and muscles engaged. He knew what was about to happen: he had witnessed it many times in Syria. In a reflex action, he threw himself down and hid his face with his hands. He saw the flash between his fingers, felt the blast lift him, then all the sound in the room seemed to fade as everything went dark. His face slammed against the floor as he came to rest several metres away with debris raining down on him. The blast had knocked all the air out of him and when he tried to inhale he choked on dust. That was why, as soon as he saw the woman run, he had dropped down.

But where was Adila? Sounds were reaching him now. Wild, echoing screams. He felt hands on his back, pulling him to his knees and then his feet, a muffled voice in his ear. 'Come *now*.'

It was Isham, his arms wrapped round him.

'Adila. My sister!'

Jamal struggled out of Isham's grip and staggered in the direction of where Adila had been, but his path was blocked by bodies and debris, and it was impossible to see through the fog of smoke and dust.

'She's gone, brother, she's gone. This is your chance. Don't waste it.'

# 57

Jamal's legs felt like rubber. He couldn't stand properly, as if his balance had completely deserted him. The horror of his sister's death would be seared into his memory for ever.

'See? There's nothing you can do for her except save yourself.'

Isham was propelling him forward, half carrying him away from his sister's shattered body. They moved through a thick, choking grey fog, stumbling over soft obstacles that Jamal realized were the dead and wounded. Sounds came to him as if down a long pipe, dulled by a high-pitched ringing in his head and the *whoop-whoop* of an alarm. All the while Isham held him under the arms, propelling him along.

'Help me! I can't see!' someone screamed, but they sounded a long way off. There was a grey glow where the doorway was, daylight cutting through the choking smoke and dust.

'Keep moving,' Isham hissed in his ear. He seemed to know exactly what to do. They were slowed by the press of walking wounded, all trying to get through a narrow exit, the crush behind forcing them through. Then they were out in the open air, a yard. Some of the throng sank to their knees around them; others hovered, zombie-like, coated with grey dust, unable to absorb what had just happened.

Just as Jamal had begun to find some feeling in his legs, without any warning Isham pulled him to the ground.

'Face down! Now!'

Ahead of them, maybe twenty metres away, two more explosions ripped through the visitors' entrance gate and shrapnel from the blast hailed down.

Two seconds later he was back on his feet, Isham pulling him in the direction of the two blasts. A man in uniform lumbered towards them, bare-headed, his face a red mess. His arms reached towards them but the sleeves of his tunic were ribbons and he appeared to have no hands. Jamal's instinct was to stop and help. Still in shock, he turned.

Isham grabbed him. 'What are you doing? Don't you understand? Out there is your freedom. They are waiting for us.'

The visitors' entrance gate was gone, now just a crater a few feet deep. In the roadway beyond were more casualties, some lying down, others crouching or clutching each other. Jamal's eyes were so full of dust he could barely see. A pair of motorcycles swept towards them. Isham helped Jamal onto one and it immediately sped away. He gripped the waist of the rider, the cold biting into him, and buried his face in the man's back. The air was full of the sirens of emergency vehicles, a cacophony of distress. The bike snaked through the traffic, swerved left into a narrow street, then bumped down a ramp into darkness where it slewed to a stop.

Two men appeared, lifted Jamal off the saddle and put him beside a people-carrier. He heard the second bike come down the ramp and screech to a halt. Although Jamal's ears were still ringing he could hear whoops and cheers and 'Allahu Akhbar' as Isham greeted his comrades.

'No time to waste. Let's get going.'

Isham came up to Jamal and embraced him, his big pink grin beaming through the grey dust that caked his face. 'Welcome to freedom!'

Jamal's arms remained limp at his side. His beloved sister was dead, blown up by Isham's wife, and he had left her mangled corpse in the wreckage. This didn't feel like any kind of freedom. He was numb and shaking. He could barely stand. He gave in to Isham's embrace before being helped into the vehicle.

As they sped over the Dartford bridge, Isham was explaining with great relish that for months his wife had been fooling the guards with her limp, leg brace and bump. 'She gradually added to it over the weeks. They never suspected! The only time they tried to check, she complained angrily that she had been inappropriately touched. After that they were more careful!' Isham slapped his knee and laughed. 'And in the visits hall, when she jumped up and ran, we knew the guards would try to stop her, like moths to the flame. We counted on their foolishness.'

Another cheer went up from Isham's adoring crew.

'The explosions at the gate? That was two more martyrs. They waited until thirty seconds from the first blast. And the other two were already there with the bikes, just out of range of the blast. It worked. Man, it was so beautiful. Allah, praise be upon Him, has delivered us a great victory.'

His eyes blazed with fervour. Jamal had heard ranting like this in Syria, terrible atrocities recounted with great excitement. Over there he had come to expect it. But listening to this in the fast lane of the M25, it was almost impossible to believe. As for the idea of Adila being dead, that surely must be a dream, a dreadful nightmare from which he would wake. His mind, numbed by shock and disbelief, was unable to process this reality. He looked out at the green fields and trees sweeping by. The precious English countryside, which he had longed to see all those months, was now tainted for ever.

Jamal couldn't hold back any longer.

'My sister is dead. You killed my sister.'

He launched himself out of his seat but two of Isham's crew pinned him down.

'Brother, believe me, we feel your pain. But don't waste your anger on us. Direct it at those who put you behind bars, who caused you and your sister to be there, who are using you for their own ends.' Isham had swivelled round and held Jamal's face in his hands. 'Your sister has gone to the next place. My wife will look after her there. You can be sure of that.' There was a messianic gleam in his eyes.

'Brother, we applaud you!' shouted the driver. Then another cheer went up: 'The Butcher of Aleppo rides again!'

However repelled Jamal was, he forced himself to conceal his true reaction, just as he had learned to do in Syria. He had to think: was he free or had he just been taken hostage? He had to keep his cool and see how it played out.

Isham was still speaking: 'You're our bonus, our reward from Allah, praise be upon Him.'

Jamal managed a smile. The best thing he could do right now was to give Isham no reason to be suspicious of him. If they thought he was the 'Butcher of Aleppo', let them. He would try to get a sense of whose hands he had fallen into.

Isham told him he was six months into a seven-year sentence for bomb-making. He had been a TV-repair man, and before that a lab technician in a hospital. 'Where I learned my trade – chemicals and electricity. It's all you need. I've trained many more. The bombs today, all my design, my babies.' He said he was looking forward to getting back to work. He gripped Jamal's knee hard. 'Together we can plan our spectacular. I already have an idea.' He was looking eagerly at Jamal for agreement.

Jamal said nothing. He was out of prison, but at what terrible cost. And with a man who was quite happy – *happy* – that three people, including his own *wife*, had blown themselves up to facilitate his escape. Above all, Jamal had lost his dearest Adila. He looked intact, but a piece of himself lay in the ruins of Belmarsh. He knew now that there was such a place as Hell, and he was in it.

Up to now all Jamal had wanted was to clear his name. But Adila's death had changed everything. Now he felt only pure rage, and the desire for revenge.

# 58

## 17.00
## Whitehall

Farmer was struggling to keep up with the prime minister as he strode down the corridor in the bunker under Whitehall. Geoff had been in overdrive all morning, demanding briefings, calling in advisers, drafting statements, redrafting them, then shelving them when he had second thoughts. Twice he had told Farmer to stay out of a meeting, only to change his mind and call him in. He had sprinted from room to room at Number Ten as if he were on some kind of treasure hunt, only whatever he was looking for, he wasn't finding it. It looked like activity but in truth it was a kind of frenetic paralysis. Farmer could tell he was at a loss. Already spooked by the reality of having co-opted Rolt into his government, he now had to digest the fact that the bombs at Belmarsh had played straight into Rolt's hands. The first big crisis of the new administration – and it wasn't the PM whom the nation was waiting to hear from, but the new home secretary, a complete novice, and an uncontrollable one at that.

'I can't let him seize the initiative, Derek. You know that as well as I do.'

Farmer nodded. How right he was – for once. They'd ordered

a news blackout on the names of the escapees but Jamal's had been leaked and every paper in the land had a headline screaming about the jailbreak of the so-called 'Butcher of Aleppo'. Farmer was in no doubt that the leak had come from Rolt's office. No one would be interested in questioning the truth of the massacre video now. 'Find This Barbaric Executioner' and 'Nationwide Alert For Schoolgirl Killer' – all the papers were piling in.

They were a few metres from the entrance to the COBRA briefing room, the hubbub of the assembled company spilling out into the corridor, when the PM stopped abruptly and turned to his director of communications. 'We can't let him do this. I simply can't . . .'

Farmer couldn't remember when he had seen the man so far out of his depth: he really was starting to panic – at the very moment when he needed to stamp his authority on his administration and lead the country. 'If the question of emergency powers comes up, Prime Minister, why don't you say you're putting it on the agenda for the summit at Chequers?'

'How far away is that?'

'Er, this weekend?' Surely he remembered.

'And we've got the whole cabinet there?'

'Naturally, for your summit to agree policy strategy.'

Suddenly the sun came out in his face. 'Derek, that's an excellent idea!'

The PM hated to be put on the spot in an open meeting and welcomed any opportunity to postpone a decision. Farmer watched as he slipped into deep thought. For the first time that day he seemed calm, almost serene. The noise coming from the meeting room was getting louder. Farmer took him by the elbow. 'I think we should—'

'Of course, of course, but whatever happens in this room, I'm not going to be press-ganged into sanctioning emergency measures. No kneejerk reactions. We're going to do this in a calm and measured fashion.'

Then he put on his especially grave, prime-ministerly expression. 'This is not a state of emergency, Derek, it's a nationwide manhunt. Whatever additional security measures we decide to take in the longer term, I want that on the agenda for Chequers, okay?'

Farmer grinned. 'Absolutely, Prime Minister.' He marvelled at the speed with which the PM could hear an idea and make it his own.

As they rounded the corner into the COBRA room, the babble of the attendees showed no sign of dying down. It was packed. All the chairs round the table had been filled, except one for the prime minister, as had the others around the walls. Farmer shooed a junior aide out of the one just behind Geoff's so he was in whispering distance. He suspected he would be doing even more prompting than usual.

The PM tapped a pencil against his glass. No one heard so Farmer clapped his hands to get their attention. 'Pray silence for the prime minister!'

Geoff looked briefly startled. 'Thank you, Derek. Let's get started.'

Just then the door opened and Alec Clements, the cabinet secretary, came in, plonked himself down on the last remaining seat against the wall and folded his arms. Farmer had not seen him at all in the past twenty-four hours. Normally, in a crisis like this, Clements would be one of the first to be making his mark, pushing forward his advice whether it was asked for or not. It was he who had come up with the idea of recruiting Rolt. No doubt he was here to watch the sparks fly in the first encounter between the prime minister and the new home secretary in an open meeting.

Around the table were some of the most influential yet least known figures from inside the machinery of government. To the prime minister's right was the acting head of MI6, officials from the MoD and GCHQ, Halford, the Metropolitan Police commissioner, and the chief constable of the Transport Police. Several cabinet ministers were also in attendance, including, of course, the new home secretary, who had an almost childlike gleam of excitement in his eyes.

The prime minister nodded at the commissioner, who cleared

his throat and launched into a detailed update of the aftermath of the Belmarsh bombings and ensuing manhunt. Farmer couldn't help noticing it was very long on detail but devoid of any significant developments.

'Of the five inmates who took the opportunity to escape, three have been rounded up. As well as Jamal al Masri, also known as al Britani, we are focusing on one Isham al Aziz, formerly Ryan Chalmers, a white British convert from Bolton, who has a conviction for conspiring to make and plant explosive devices and is currently serving a seven-year sentence for doing so. We are following up on leads suggesting that they are at large together.'

'So the bottom line is you've no idea where these terrorists are?'

Rolt's words cut through the atmosphere like a knife. What a difference a few days made, Farmer mused. Rolt had more than found his feet: he was already going on the offensive. But far from looking stung, Halford nodded eagerly. Had this been rehearsed?

As he prepared to reply, Halford's gaze swung in the PM's direction. 'As things are at this time, I can't honestly disagree, but I've no doubt that, with the right powers and resources to draw down, we could make a lot more headway.'

Farmer saw the PM's cheeks redden. If he was coming close to being made a fool of in front of the massed ranks of the COBRA gathering, he was fighting not to show it.

'You can rest assured, Commissioner, we've directed all the law-enforcement agencies your way on this—'

There was an almost audible gasp as Rolt interrupted, pressing his hands on the table as he spoke: 'The sooner we start a programme of internment, the sooner public anxiety will be reduced. They've put up with enough trouble from the Muslims. It cannot go on.'

Behind Rolt, Farmer could see Clements, his eyes scanning the room, a small, wry smile on his face. Not for the first time he got the sense of the cabinet secretary as the puppet master, deftly and invisibly pulling a string here, a string there, silently goading on his new protégé. Rolt was already showing all the signs of being a loose cannon and Clements seemed to be enjoying the mayhem.

The prime minister's face turned even redder. 'I will not be party to any kneejerk policy decisions. Nor will I permit policy to be made on the hoof. The proper forum for any discussion of such measures is with the whole cabinet and we will be doing that this weekend.' He breathed out. It was pure flannel, Farmer knew, but it would do for now. The PM glanced at him, so he mouthed, 'Messages.'

'Meanwhile we need to concentrate on making sure we are sending the right messages to the public.'

Again, Rolt came back at him with indecent speed. 'As in "keep calm and carry on"?'

Farmer detected a faint ripple of amusement. Buoyed by this, Rolt continued: 'The extremist community is talking this up as a triumph against the state. What I'm getting back from the people I've been talking to is that we seem to be at a complete loss as to how to respond to what is virtually civil war.'

There was another almost audible gasp. But this time the PM was ready. 'The message is that we are on the case.' With a nod to Halford he went on, 'And the more police we can see out on the streets the better, even if some of them could be better used indoors.'

But Rolt hadn't finished. 'And the army?'

The PM looked at him over the half-glasses Farmer had warned him not to wear because they made him look older. 'We're not at that stage yet, Vernon.' He gave the nervous chuckle he was prone to when he felt cornered. The MoD people exchanged glances. Never before had Farmer felt his grip on authority to be so fragile. 'In fact, that's one of the items on our agenda for Chequers this weekend, along with any other significant move, such as declaring a state of emergency. For discussion,' he added firmly, lest Rolt was in any doubt.

Good, thought Farmer. At least he's firing back. It seemed to have silenced Rolt for now, but Farmer was watching him closely. This was the first big meeting the new home secretary had attended with the prime minister. Any other newcomer to the cabinet would have chosen their words very cautiously – in fact, they would have gone out of their way to make a show of support. Not Rolt. It had been a bold move to co-opt him, but he alone was probably the reason the chief was back in. And, as Farmer always feared, Rolt inside the government was going to be just as disruptive as he was outside – possibly even worse. He glanced at Clements. Usually the cabinet secretary liked to remind everyone of his presence by making some supportive noises. But he remained uncharacteristically tight-lipped.

The discussion veered off into a debate about a proposed forward deployment of military at RAF Northolt, which soon ran out of steam. But the MoD was directed to prepare a standby army presence, should the need arise. Now that those gathered understood that nothing of any substance was going to get done, they were all itching to get away. The PM had got away with it this time but he couldn't let them melt away without summing up, Farmer thought. He touched his elbow and frowned.

The PM frowned back, then twigged. 'I cannot overstate the gravity of the situation we find ourselves in. We must reassure the public about the operational actions we are now taking to find these men, among them an intense police and Security Service action to ensure we bring this man to justice. And I urge you all to scale new heights in your efforts to get on top of it.'

With that he stood up and marched out of the room. Farmer struggled to his feet and set off in pursuit. As he was leaving he caught sight of Clements exchanging glances with Rolt. That was all it was – a look – and anyone else might not have noticed it. But Farmer's job was to be the prime minister's eyes and ears, and what he had just seen he didn't like one bit.

# 59

## 21.00
## Malvern Hills, Worcestershire

Tom took his time driving back through the dark country lanes, which he knew like the back of his hand. Even with the roads in the condition they were in, he could have done it in half the time, but he wanted to be sure that the Fiesta was definitely following him. When he got to the bottom of his parents' lane the car speeded up, overtook and disappeared into the night. Evidently Ashton had decided to keep a watch on him. Reporting the latest developments to Mandler was not going to be straightforward.

It was almost midnight, but all the downstairs lights were on. And there was an unfamiliar car parked close to the front door, an Espace. As Tom got nearer and the security lights came on he could see that the vehicle was in bad shape. Several of the panels had been kicked in, the front valance was gone and a side window had been smashed. One rear tyre was flat. In the meticulously kept grounds of Newland Hall it was an incongruous sight. Tom stepped out of his car. He heard the dogs' deep baritone bark, welcoming him back. His mother met him at the door.

'What's that?' he said, nodding over his shoulder at the Espace.

'The Rashids – you know, with the village shop. They were attacked by some thugs from the pub, who smashed the place up, and their car. They were really in fear of their lives. The police didn't seem interested in helping them so I've decided to put them up. I hope you're not going to argue with me. And don't go up the stairs like a herd of buffalo – I'm hoping they've gone to sleep.'

She was wearing her resolute, don't-mess-with-me face. He gave her an admiring hug. 'Of course I won't. But have you told Dad? He's bound to worry about any trouble coming to the house, for your sake.'

'It was an emergency. Anyway, he's staying up in town. This deal he's got going on has become very drawn out. Sorry, I haven't even asked about your evening. How was Ashton?'

He rolled his eyes. His throat and lungs still ached from the waterboarding. 'Oh, you know. Same old.'

She peered at him. 'You look like you had quite a session. Are you sure you should have driven home?'

He feigned guilt. 'Probably not.'

She tutted. 'Has he got anything for you?'

He smiled. 'Maybe.'

At least that was the truth, for once. She smiled back, clearly still thinking about the Rashids, and how a sedate English country village could become the scene of an unprovoked, racially motivated attack reminiscent of Germany in the 1930s. 'They'd done nothing, you know. They were just closing up when those – bastards descended on them.'

She never used bad language. He pulled her towards him and stroked her head. Underneath the determination he could feel the anxiety in her shoulders.

'I think I could do with a cup of tea.'

'Let me make it for once, eh?'

They went into the kitchen and he settled her in a chair. The idea of anything happening to her, if she had been caught up in the attack, was unthinkable. The TV was on, tuned to the BBC News Channel.

'Never thought of you as a news junkie, Mum.'

'Well, you can't very well not be, these days. Especially when it's happening on your own doorstep.'

He filled the kettle. 'Any developments?'

'Only that those escaped prisoners seem to have vanished into thin air. I can't remember a time when I've felt more uneasy about what's happening to the country, and I don't mind telling you that I think Rolt's partly to blame. Instead of trying to calm things down he's stoking the fire just as much as the rioters and bombers. It's as if he actually wants to make things worse.'

She was usually much more careful about winding him up than his father was, but Tom knew that, since Rolt had moved into politics, she was deeply troubled by his association with him. He had never seen her like this. All his life she had let his father sound off about the state of the world while she kept her opinions to herself. Often he didn't even know what she thought. He realized she was glaring at him, as if he should take some of the blame, but then her expression changed. 'It's been a long day. Sorry.'

He put an arm round her. 'Don't be.' If only he could tell her . . .

She glanced back at the TV. 'Look, there he is again, hogging the cameras. It's as if he's trying to take over.' She shrugged off his arm and left the room.

# 60

For the fourth time in less than an hour he tried to get through to his father's mobile. It was past one a.m. but Tom wasn't going to give up.

Eventually Hugh picked up, plainly exasperated at being called so many times. He spoke in a low tone. 'This had better be important, dear boy. I'm right in the middle of closing a deal.'

He sounded frayed and drained. All the same, Tom was in no mood to apologize for disturbing him. 'Umarov. You lied to me.'

There was a pause. Tom heard a door open and close. Evidently his father was in search of somewhere more private.

'Sorry, I didn't quite get that. What did you say?'

'You heard. What are you doing with him? I need to know.'

Hugh's voice was hushed but his anger was only too apparent. 'Tom, that really is my business and, as it happens, it's at a very delicate stage. And how on earth did you find out?'

Tom weighed the Ordynka in his palm. 'I'm sitting in your study, looking at his fancy gift. Do you have any idea what you're getting into?'

'Tom, what I'm "getting into" is not only going to make me financially secure and save your mother and me from bankruptcy, it could also benefit you in the long run – that is, unless someone comes along and tries to bugger it up. And how *dare* you go through my private things?' He almost spat the words. Tom had never heard him so angry. 'I've put up with your secrecy all these years. I've bitten my tongue the whole time while you've gone off risking your neck. You've no right to be lecturing me, or indeed calling me a liar. No right at all! How honest have you been with me about your dealings with Rolt, eh?'

What did he mean by that? Tom left a silence for him to fill. When Hugh spoke again his tone was softer. 'You may see me as an old fool, but I know you better than you think. Now, if you'll excuse me, I have to get back to work.'

The line went dead.

# 61

**07.30**

Tom's early jog took in the perimeter of his parents' land. The grey murk that had descended on the country almost a month ago showed no sign of clearing, and a fresh flurry of snow was falling. Not great weather for a run, but he wanted to clear his head and think. He also wanted to check just how much attention Ashton was paying him before he decided his next move. Sure enough, the Fiesta was parked a hundred metres from the gate to the driveway, its windows misted, the two people inside just shapes, though as he came past he smelt the distinctive whiff of Russian tobacco.

Tom made no attempt to conceal himself, but did the opposite, running past the car as if not bothered by it at all. After the difficult call with his father, he had stayed up well into the night, writing a detailed report in longhand for Mandler. In any other situation he would simply have waited for further orders, but this wasn't any other situation. In fact, in all his time in the Regiment he couldn't think of a moment like this. He had no obligation to continue. Rolt was in government, Woolf had been redeployed and Mandler – despite his exalted position – was in no position to watch his back. But he had come this far.

He had been shot at, mauled by a dog, smashed over the head – twice – and waterboarded. And he was still no nearer to finding out what Ashton was planning or what exactly his connection was to Rolt and Umarov. But Tom knew he had made up his mind: Ashton wasn't going to open up unless he made him some sort of commitment. Whatever he was proposing, he would have to go along with it, if he was going to find out any more about his plans.

Before he left for his jog he had dispatched his mother to Mandler's house with the report, to deliver it in person. Buried in the text was a time for them to RV at his father's club, somewhere in plain view they might have every reason to be, and where he hoped he might also find Hugh.

Using his mother was a desperate measure. He had never involved her in any of his work before, but there was no one else he trusted who wouldn't be followed. Besides, since he had discovered his father's connection with Umarov, all the old boundaries between home and career had been blown away. To his surprise, she had willingly agreed, though he had promised to explain when he could. *If* he ever could. Her instructions were to wait while Mandler read it through and told her if he wanted to meet. He had correctly anticipated that Ashton's goons would be keeping tabs on him, so his only option was to behave as if it was a normal day.

When he got back to the house the Rashid family were in the kitchen, feeding their three children. Six months ago he had been into their shop and was greeted like an old friend. Now they all looked up nervously. 'Your mother said it would be all right . . .'

'Good morning, all. Absolutely right she did. Do you have everything you need?'

'Yes, thank you. We're sorry to inconvenience you. Your mother has been so kind.'

Mrs Rashid had done the talking; her husband was still looking at Tom warily. Tom gave him a warm smile.

'I'm only too glad we can help. It must have been awful. Stay

263

as long as you need – we've got more than enough space. It's no problem at all. I'd better get cleaned up. See you later, kids.'

He had adopted what he hoped was a breezy, reassuring tone. But as he went back into the hall Mr Rashid followed. 'Do you think we should make arrangements to leave?'

'No, honestly, you're welcome to stay as long as you need.'

But then Tom grasped what he had really asked, and it sent a chill down his spine.

# 62

**09.00**
**Watford**

Jamal awoke from a deep, chemically induced sleep. After a few minutes, he raised himself a little and saw that he was not alone. Five men, not those who had helped in the escape, were seated close to his bed, watching him. As soon as they saw he was awake, the oldest, who was dressed in a light brown *jubbah*, nodded at one of the others, who got up and left. Then he leaned forward.

'You must be hungry after your long sleep. Refreshment is coming.'

For a moment, Jamal thought he was back in Syria. The walls that surrounded him were windowless and built of breeze blocks. The floor was concrete with a couple of rush mats. Then he remembered the rest of the journey. They were in Watford, on an industrial estate, in the back room of a plumbing company. He stared at the men blankly, still trying to disentangle what was a terrible dream and what was real, until it all clicked into focus with a terrifying jolt. There was no dream. It was all horribly real. He had left his beloved sister, the only one who had not shunned him, dead in the ruins of the prison. A great mass of grief and anger surged up inside him.

A woman entered the room. She was completely covered. She bowed as she approached, put a tray beside the bed and scuttled away.

He looked down. There was a mug and a teapot, a bowl, a carton of milk and, incongruously, a Kellogg's variety pack. One of the younger men came forward, poured the tea and added some milk. Jamal drank, and instantly felt nausea rising. He put the mug back on the tray. The door opened again and Isham appeared. All the men stood up and there was a lot of embracing and back-patting. Then he turned to Jamal and opened his arms. Isham was freshly showered, his ginger hair glistening, and had on a brand new ankle-length *jubbah*, the creases where it had been folded still showing in the fabric.

'And here we are, *Alhamdulillah*.'

Jamal didn't move. All he could feel was anger boiling inside him. He hadn't asked for any of this. He would have stayed inside prison and fought to clear his name, however hard and drawn-out that would have been. But that option was gone – and with it his beloved sister. He looked at Isham, smiling down at him as if he was some kind of trophy.

Months under the ever-suspicious gaze of Abukhan had trained him to mask his true feelings almost as a matter of course. He got to his feet shakily and accepted Isham's embrace. '*Alhamdulillah*,' he replied.

The group broke into applause.

'You are a great prize, Jamal. All our brothers are celebrating your escape. Yours will be the example for all who are prisoners of the *Kuffar*.' The loss of his wife had not dented his jubilation. 'First you will bathe and then we will dress you in new robes and you will record a video. Your supporters will be waiting to hear from you. You must show them that you are free and ready to fight again. You must issue a call to arms.'

Despite Isham's northern accent, pink complexion and gingery hair, he hadn't only adopted the beard and dress of the Muslim: his pattern of speech mimicked that of someone whose first language wasn't English. Evidently his supporters in the room, who were all Asian, were buying it. But Jamal had been here before, back home in Croydon, when he had fallen under the spell of the man who had originally recruited him to go to Syria. Britain was full of self-appointed zealots oozing hate-speak that masqueraded as religious belief. But there was something about Isham that marked him out. The others were buffoons, all mouth and posturing. Isham was a cut above. Horrific as it had been, the prison break had been meticulously organized.

The idea of trying to clear his name seemed absurd now. He still wanted to know what had happened to Emma; maybe he could find out from Latimer, the lawyer he had seen in Belmarsh. For now, he needed to play along with Isham and be his 'prize', but only so far. He decided that the fewer words he said the better. He should show no remorse. If he was their hero he would behave like one. He had observed Abukhan asserting his authority with silence: the fewer words he said, the more they counted.

He held Isham to him, then broke away and turned to the smiling group, his hand touching his heart. 'Brothers, I thank you.'

# 63

'This is the man who's trying to destroy you.'

Jamal didn't hear him at first; he was too stunned by what he was seeing. In the news report, a tight-lipped police spokeswoman refused to confirm the number of casualties or the names of anyone who was missing. But Vernon Rolt, the new home secretary, left no one in any doubt that Jamal had escaped, describing him as an enemy of the state, a mass killer bent on destroying Western values – even the most dangerous man in Britain.

Isham tapped the screen. 'Welcome to the new reality. It's nothing less than a declaration of war on Islam.' He smirked. 'This is your next target. And we are ready.'

Jamal was working on the basis that the best method of handling Isham was to play along with his plans, for now. Perhaps this was how he could escape his fatal embrace, maybe the only way. But he also realized that something in him had changed. He must avenge Adila's death, and Isham was showing him where to direct his vengeance.

'But he's the home secretary. How do I even get near him?'

Isham's eyes blazed. He leaned closer and spoke in a whisper, even though they were alone. 'We have the means to get right up close. You will see.' He made a gesture with his hands, miming an explosion.

Jamal said nothing. Whether this was pure fantasy or not, he didn't know. The Belmarsh escape had been audacious but also planned with great precision. Isham was a fanatic, whose only thoughts were about his personal war on the British Establishment, his dream to see the black flag of the caliphate flying over Buckingham Palace. Jamal's time in Syria had convinced him of the folly of the Islamist cause and the waste of life it involved. Now, seeing Rolt on national TV calling him those terrible things had rekindled his sense of outrage.

Isham gestured at the image of Rolt on the screen. 'This man is using you to further his cause. We will show him what folly that is. You will declare war on him.'

Jamal folded his arms and gave him the dead stare that he had learned in Syria from Abukhan. No expression, just stillness. 'No video.'

'But, brother, we must alert the world so your escape can be celebrated. They are saying you are unaccounted for. The world needs to know you have triumphed.'

Jamal remained still. In the twenty-four hours he had been in Isham's presence he had got the measure of the man. But Isham knew nothing about him. He just believed what he had read in the papers about the Aleppo massacre. He didn't know the real Jamal at all. 'If I am to do this, I want no video. Let people think I am dead.'

# 64

**10.30**
**Pimlico, London**

Sarah Garvey eyed the lawyer sitting opposite her. He definitely wasn't her type, that was for sure. His buttoned-up collarless shirt said it all, and his brown suede shoes. *Never trust a man in brown shoes*: one of her father's pet sayings. Not only that, just about everything he stood for made her flesh creep. Yet here he was, Alistair Latimer, human-rights lawyer, friend of terrorists, here in her own living room at her invitation.

She picked up the teapot. 'Milk and sugar?'

'Just plain, thank you. Lemon if you have some.'

Her father would have had something to say about that as well. She found half a lemon in the kitchen and sliced off the mould. She had called Latimer out of the blue and had had to convince him it wasn't a hoax. He had refused to meet her anywhere public or at either of their offices, and wanted it understood that if asked he would flatly deny that they had ever met and expected her to do the same. 'Whatever works,' she had told him. He was her last chance to help Jamal and she owed it to Adila's memory to try.

'Well, this is a turnaround, eh?' She'd thought a touch of levity might help things along. He stared at her blankly as she plopped the slice of lemon into his tea. 'You and me, of all people, getting together like this.'

He stared into his tea. 'I'm glad you find something to amuse you in these difficult times.'

Pompous twat. And that was a low blow. She had lain awake all night, unable to sleep, thinking about Adila. It was she who had pulled strings and smoothed it with the governor so the girl could visit Jamal . . . 'Well, let's just say that it's an interesting sign of these difficult times, is it not, that we find we have a common interest?'

'Do we?'

She felt like slapping him but held it in check. All through her tenure as home secretary, Latimer had been a persistent thorn in her side. High-profile cases against crazed murdering jihadis, men with blood on their hands who should have been bang to rights, had collapsed in court, thanks to his relentless chipping away at the Crown's case, prising open tiny cracks in the prosecution's arguments until they were laid bare, yawning wide for all the court to see. He had particularly undermined the credibility of the Metropolitan Police, humiliating its officers as they were repeatedly wrong-footed in trials.

Much as she would have preferred to hold this nasty little man personally responsible, much as she would have liked to denounce him as a friend of terrorists and an enemy of the state, she knew that the problem was not him but the police themselves. When it came to dealing with the huge escalation in terrorist acts and bloody reprisals, they were grotesquely under-resourced. Although there was no love lost between her and Halford, the Met commissioner, she had some sympathy for him in his struggle to meet the expectations of an ever more anxious public.

But they had underestimated the impact of Latimer, the terrorists' brief of choice in front of juries wishing to see the streets cleared of terror. By the time he had finished, the prosecution's case was usually in tatters and the judge had to direct them to deliver a not-guilty verdict. And after it was over, he would stand outside the court oozing pious self-righteousness as he delivered his lefty rubbish to the media about defending the downtrodden and oppressed. She eyed him with a mixture of awe and contempt as he took a sip of tea and placed the cup carefully back in its saucer.

She cleared her throat. 'Well, let's get on with it, shall we?'

She downed the contents of her cup in three gulps and refilled it. The teapot shook slightly in her hand so that the top rattled. A Scotch would calm that. Maybe if she just nipped into the kitchen . . . *For God's sake, woman, get a grip.*

'I know you tried to help Jamal's sister,' he said.

'Much good it did her.' She reached into her case and drew out one of the two manila folders she had procured, marked MOST SECRET. She placed it on the coffee-table between them, spun it round and pushed it towards Latimer. His eyes widened.

'The Secret Service report on what happened in Aleppo, suppressed on Rolt's orders. Go on, take a look. I think you'll find Jamal comes out of it rather well.'

He opened the folder and scanned it. 'Your friends in government appear to be hell-bent on the destruction of our civil liberties . . .'

'Not my government, not my friends,' she snapped.

He gave her a weary look. 'Okay, whatever.'

Biting her lip, she pressed on: 'It's pretty comprehensive. It looks as though Abukhan, Jamal's militia commander, was tipped off just in time. Emma Warner was intercepted as soon as Jamal handed back her camera. And Abukhan arranged Jamal's passage out of the country.'

Latimer frowned. 'But why? Why didn't he kill Jamal too?'

'Presumably because he wanted to teach the Western media a lesson, and to punish Jamal in a different way by having him blamed for the massacre. Or maybe for the same reason he had Emma's remains deposited at a British consulate – because he's a fully paid-up out-there fucking nutcase.'

She had his attention now. 'Who tipped him off about Emma?'

She shook her head. 'They don't know.'

Latimer examined the report. Again, as she watched him, she

was plagued by doubt. What was she thinking of, showing secret documents to a card-carrying enemy of the state? Well, to hell with it. Having fallen this far, out of cabinet and into the wilderness, what did it matter if she plummeted even further? She had obtained evidence of Jamal's innocence from SIS, but he was involved in an audacious jailbreak in which several people had died. It was the knowledge of Rolt's complicity in suppressing that information which strengthened her resolve. She had Derek Farmer to thank for it, another unlikely ally in what felt like her own personal vendetta against her successor. She had to keep in mind that what she was doing would ultimately be for the greater good.

No doubt Latimer felt he was crossing a line of his own even meeting a former home secretary. And now he was looking at her as if she had gone mad – which might not be far from the truth.

'He is a fugitive from justice. You are aware of that?'

Garvey ignored the patronizing tone. She reached into her case and produced the second folder, also marked SECRET. 'The interim report on the Belmarsh bomb, the contents of which have also been blocked by the Home Office. It's not chapter and verse but it points pretty conclusively to the first bomber inside the visitors' area as being the wife of Isham al Aziz. The two accomplices who blew themselves up outside the visitors' entrance have yet to be identified. This was a well-planned attack that must have taken weeks to prepare. Neither Jamal nor his sister could have had anything to do with it. For all we know, al Aziz might even have taken Jamal hostage.'

As Latimer buried himself in the closely typed text uncertainty infected her again. She had made her name for herself as a toughie, a hawk, the twenty-first-century equivalent of a hang-'em-and-flog-'em advocate, a believer in the value of tough prison regimes and long sentences. But not at any price. The more she had come to understand the workings of law and order during her time as home secretary, the more she had discovered the extent to which fair play had been squeezed out of the system, and found herself in a minority of one in cabinet as

she railed against the steady erosion of the nation's most treasured freedoms. Then had come the ultimate ignominy of having
to make way for the man who would dismantle the rights of the
accused altogether. In Rolt's new world, you were guilty until
proven innocent. And that was not acceptable.

Latimer put down the folder without comment. Was she
getting through to him? 'So, do you know where he is?'

His nostrils flared slightly as he took a deep breath, as if she
had just woken him from a trance. He looked at her in horror.
'Even if I did I would hardly be likely to divulge—'

'Okay, okay.' Irritating man. She cut him off. 'Let me rephrase
that. If he were to contact you, you could indicate that there is
an interested party, in Parliament, prepared to support him.'

Latimer closed the folder, put it on top of the other and moved
them back across the table. Garvey prepared herself for a
further humiliation. The man clearly thought she was out of her
mind, sharing secret documents with him, talking about helping
Britain's most-wanted fugitive.

'What do you know about Isham al Aziz?' she asked.

Latimer shrugged.

'Let me fill you in. He and Jamal are cut from very different
cloth, and not just because Isham's a white convert. At the time
of his arrest he was in the midst of assembling a suicide vest in
a garage full of hydrogen peroxide and didn't appear to be
running a hairdresser's, so he was bang to rights. But he still
tried to make the most of his day in court to denounce the
government and call for the raising of the ISIS flag over
Buckingham Palace. The judge had to have him removed. He
has tried to style himself as the ISIS caliphate's ambassador to
Britain, not that anyone's particularly noticed in Raqqa. But for
him Jamal is a game-changer. He will be considered a great
prize, which will raise Isham al Aziz's profile considerably with
the affiliated Islamist groups, not just here but all over the
extremist blogosphere. He's going to make the most of Jamal
while he can, especially if we don't try to help him.'

Latimer put his hands together and rested his chin on his
fingertips. 'At the time we met, I have to say I had my doubts

about him. Based on what you have here, and what's in those reports, I think he did something very brave in Aleppo.'

'So what do you think? Some kind of deal to get Jamal out of his predicament and al Aziz back in the bag?'

Latimer let out a long, weary sigh. 'Jamal may not have been part of the plan to break out of Belmarsh, but the fact that he absconded doesn't exactly help his case.'

Garvey gripped the edge of the table. 'Look, given what we now know about what happened in Syria and the claim that the home secretary *personally* ordered the suppression of the details of the tape and the fate of the journalist Emma Warner, then surely you could try to build a case that mitigates Jamal's decision to escape. Indeed, it might help if we could argue that al Aziz effectively forced Jamal to abscond with him.'

No reaction. Garvey peered at him. Perhaps he was getting the message. Perhaps she hadn't gone mad after all. 'So you think you can help him?'

He gave her a disapproving look. 'You're asking me to aid and abet a fugitive from the law, an accused terrorist.'

Garvey gritted her teeth. 'Oh, for God's sake, man, you've made a career out of helping terrorists.'

He placed his fingertips on the folders again, then spoke in an icy whisper: 'I'm not sure you've thought through the ramifications of all this. If it ever got to court, what you have here is potentially enough to destroy the current home secretary's reputation. But in the current climate that's a very big if.' He paused and prodded the folders again. 'Furthermore, certain people would be extremely upset if they found out these had got into the wrong hands.'

She pushed the folders towards him and grinned. 'Good.'

'There's the matter of who's going to pay for all this. We're hardly going to be applying for legal aid.'

Garvey glared at him. 'Well, don't look at me.'

Latimer paused and sucked his bottom lip. 'There is another interested party.'

'What's that mean?'

'Someone else with an interest in Jamal's fate.'

# 65

'I'm sorry, sir. We haven't seen Mr Buckingham for the last two nights. But he hasn't checked out. Maybe he's gone back to the country and it's slipped his mind.'

The porter's hangdog expression betrayed just the minutest hint of irritation. He liked to run a tight ship.

Tom smiled. 'Probably my mistake.' It wasn't. His father had gone AWOL. 'Anyway, he's got my regimental tie and I need it for a do tonight. I don't suppose you could let me have the key to his room?'

The porter pursed his lips. 'I'm afraid the rules are that no one is allowed into a member's room without being accompanied by the member himself.'

He knew that any high-horse stuff wouldn't work. Neither would bribery. They were hard as nails, these old geezers, and didn't take shit from anyone. Perhaps if he appealed to his sense of propriety. 'I'm not sure I can show my face if I don't have the right tie . . .'

The porter looked at him over his glasses and sighed.

Two minutes later he was standing in his father's room. All

that was left was a half-completed *Times* crossword and some socks. He had packed and gone – but where?

The porter was looking over his shoulder. 'Well, as I said, he hasn't signed out. That's not like him, sir.'

Tom turned. 'I'm sure he'll show up soon enough. Sorry to have troubled you.'

Back in the lobby he stepped into one of the club's charmingly archaic and seldom used phone booths, and dialled Mandler's number. Tom had put the covert message in the letter to meet him here but there was no sign of him either. He got a continuous tone: unobtainable. He dialled his main office number. The same. He dialled his home number. No answer, and no outgoing message.

Because he couldn't think of anyone else to try he dialled Woolf.

'I can't really talk, Tom. We've got a big flap on with these escapees.'

'What's happened to Mandler? He's gone off the grid.'

'No idea. He's been kicked upstairs, remember?' The din of a busy office almost drowned his reply. 'Garvey wanted to speak to you, though. She's his ally. Why don't you ask her?'

'What does she want?'

In the background someone was shouting Woolf's name. He hung up.

Tom tried Garvey's mobile. The former home secretary was the only other person to know about his true role inside Invicta.

'Tom Buckingham, what a pleasant surprise.'

She sounded pissed. That was all he needed. He asked her if she knew where he could find Mandler.

'How should I? But listen, Tom, I need to pick your brains. How about a drink?'

He could hear ice cubes clinking. 'I'm sorry, I can't right now.'

'Well, give me two minutes.'

Four minutes later he was still listening as Garvey went into breathless detail about Jamal al Masri, the Belmarsh escapee whose sister had died in the blast and how he was being hounded by Rolt who was suppressing the truth about his bravery in Syria. Tom didn't have time for it, but it confirmed that Xenia Dalton had been right to be worried about the fate of her reporter in Aleppo.

'This boy's being stitched up through a combination of spin and censorship. I want anything Rolt says or does that nails him as the liar and bastard he is. I need it, okay, Tom? I'm going to bring him down if it kills me.'

Tom managed to get rid of her as politely as he could.

On his way back to the front desk, his phone buzzed. Let that be Hugh or Mandler. He took it out. The porter put his fist to his mouth and coughed. Mobile phones were strictly forbidden in the club. 'Oh, sorry, just reading a text.'

'No difference, sir, I'm afraid.'

'Okay, okay.'

Tom stepped outside. By the time he got to the revolving doors he had read the contents. Just a postcode, and the message:

*19.30. Bring your toothbrush.*

It was from Ashton.

# 66

**14.30**
**Junction 5, M1 motorway**

All three southbound lanes had stopped moving completely for the police to do their check. Jamal put his feet on the dash. Bashar, at the wheel, was gently rocking to the music coming out of his earbuds, an almost imperceptible, tinselly sound, just audible enough to be irritating. As they headed to London, he had glanced at Jamal every few minutes and grinned, excited to have been chosen to drive such a famous passenger. Now he was looking nervous and took out his earbuds.

'Put them back on and turn up the volume. It'll help distract you.'

Bashar complied.

Jamal watched the police as they moved among the vehicles. Such was the volume of traffic they couldn't hope to search every one. Instead they were picking them at random – or not quite at random, taking a good look at every male with black hair or a beard. But this was like no vehicle check Jamal had ever seen. Those doing the questioning were accompanied by two more carrying MP5 carbines. A few cars up, two other officers were going through the contents of an aged Volvo estate, which they had laid out in the slush on the hard shoulder, ignoring the turbanned driver who was remonstrating with them.

Jamal had been given a freshly prepared ID with a photo that matched his new appearance. He had shaved off his beard and one of Isham's people had cut his hair and trimmed his eyebrows. The effect was alarming but it did the job of changing his appearance, along with a pair of thick-framed, plain-lensed glasses and an earring. He barely recognized himself, so with any luck no one else would either.

He had his whole speech ready about their destination, the plumbing job they were going to, with a phone number that could be checked, and there was an answerphone message on the line that matched the name of the company on his ID. There was even a landing page uploaded on the web. Isham might be a fanatic but you couldn't fault his attention to detail. He had gathered round him a small army of loyal helpers with all the right skills, young men radicalized by the tension on the streets. Bashar told him he now saw no future for himself except as one of Isham's soldiers.

'I envy you going to Syria, brother. I want to so much. But Isham wants me to stay here and serve him.'

Jamal nodded, noncommittal. Syria had been such an eye-opener, but he was equally shocked at how much Britain had changed.

The night before, Isham had shown him the vest. It was much more compact and sophisticated than the bulky devices he had seen in Syria, but there they could be hidden under much looser garments. 'Winter is good because everybody's wearing thick clothes,' he had said. 'Nobody is surprised to see someone wearing a padded coat. And in this weather it's not so surprising when people keep them on indoors.'

The explosive was spread evenly over the surface of the chest and thicker at the small of the back. It was heavy, because of the layer of small, jagged lumps of metal shrapnel.

'But everything in your pockets – coins, watch, belt buckle, glasses – becomes shrapnel too,' he'd told him. He had even shown him pictures of the bomb his wife had worn, which he had designed before his arrest. 'Try it on. Let's see how it fits,' he had urged, and Jamal had obliged. Isham had shown him how to route the wires down one sleeve so the activator, a small squeeze-sensitive switch, could be hidden under his cuff, ready to be drawn down into his palm at the right moment.

'Now imagine you're about to meet Vernon Rolt, shake his hand. "Hello, you say to him. I am the Butcher of Aleppo." Then bang.' Isham laughed uproariously. 'It will be so glorious, even better than my wife's triumph.'

'But don't you miss her?' Jamal had ventured, unable to contain the thought.

Isham was clearly mystified. 'I am free to continue the work. What else matters?' And without any further comment, he produced a fat folder and spread the contents in front of them. On top was a photograph of Rolt. 'Everything you need to know. It's all here. The plan of his building, how to get access, where you can hide. We've been collecting information, building up the detail, for a long time.'

'How come?'

Isham smirked. 'A mole – a disgruntled ex-soldier with a grudge against him. He gave us all we need to gain access: key codes for the underground car park, service lift combinations, the lot.'

Isham smoothed his hands proudly over the papers. Already Jamal was starting to understand what made him tick. But already he could see a fairly obvious flaw. Rolt was home secretary now. Why would he use his old office? But he chose to keep that thought to himself. If this was what would get him back to London, so be it.

The police waved on the three cars in front of them.

'That means they're going to pick us.' Bashar's voice was shaking.

'What's the matter? You never talked to a cop before?'

He shook his head.

'Just keep listening to your music.'

It was a shock to Jamal how most of Isham's crew had lived

entirely cloistered lives, having almost no contact with white people. Perhaps it explained why they were able to take Isham, a white convert, so seriously.

The cop motioned for Jamal to wind down the window. He obliged, keeping eye contact. Here it was the opposite of Syria, where it was all about showing deference to whoever had set up the roadblock to be sure you looked like you knew you were inferior. An icy blast rushed into the cab.

'All right in here? Keeping warm, are we?'

The cop clapped his gloved hands together. Jamal grinned and raised the Thermos. 'Like a cup?'

The cop looked over his shoulder into the van. 'You got everything and the kitchen sink in there.'

'Don't like to be unprepared. You'd be surprised what we find on these jobs.'

The one with the MP5 stared at them, stony-faced. Bashar was gazing straight ahead, nodding to the beat, but looking guilty as fuck.

'What's up with the kid?'

'He needs the toilet.'

'Sure you haven't got a spare in the back?'

They all had a laugh except Bashar.

'I'd better take your card. The missus is always on at me about putting in a new kitchen.'

'Just Google J&R Plumbers. Don't hold your breath, though. We're booked up till June.'

'Must be good, then.'

Jamal nodded. 'Oh, yeah, we're good.'

The cop jerked his head in the direction of the open road in front of them. 'On you go, then.'

Jamal wound up the window. He turned to Bashar. 'Not too fast now. Take it nice and easy.'

Bashar looked like he had just had a reprieve from the hangman.

'Don't relax too much. That may not be the last we see of them.'

# 67

**17.30**
**Hertfordshire**

Monkton Grange was bordered by a high brick wall, from a time long gone when there were the means and cheap labour to create such barriers. Tom knew the name. It had once housed a notorious prep school that had been shut down following a scandal. As a boy he remembered seeing the pupils in their grey blazers with their matching blank grey faces. To the left of the gates a sign said SOLD.

Whoever had occupied it most recently had fitted an intercom. He pressed it and waited. Nothing. The night was still and very cold, and it looked as if more snow was coming. There were several things that could have preyed on his mind, like the whereabouts of his father, and Mandler, and just what the hell he was getting into. But none of that was useful.

He buzzed a second time. Still no answer. There was no point in freezing out there, so he got back into the Range Rover to wait. A pick-up appeared, coming towards the gates from the inside. It pulled up and two men in jeans, Rab Summit jackets and Gore-Tex boots got out. He recognized them straight away from the Invicta campus: Morton and Sharp, relatively recent recruits, unlike Randall and Evans, ex-infantry fitness freaks who specialized in Iron Mans and other such modern forms of voluntary torture.

Tom nodded at them. 'Evening, all.'

They opened the gates. 'Go straight up to the house. The boss is waiting for you.'

The drive was bordered by tall poplars, several of which had fallen. Claimed by the ivy and bramble that had taken charge of the verges they looked like strange, camouflaged defences. Parked in front of the grim-looking Victorian pile were two people-carriers and the Mercedes G-Wagen. What also caught his attention, parked well away from the house and visible only by its own interior lights, was an executive type white helicopter, an S-76.

As he came up to the house an outside light went on and a door opened. It was Hanson, the warden. He was dressed civilian but practical: strong boots, sweatshirt, cargos, stuff he could easily move about in.

'Thought you lot were in Dartmoor.'

Hanson gave him a wry look. 'Some people think we still are.'

'Why all the cloak-and-dagger?'

'You'll see. Come on in.'

They stepped into a big, wood-panelled hall. Through one door Tom could see folding army cots, green nylon with aluminium cross legs, scattered about the place with multi-coloured sleeping-bags crumpled on top. Washing and shaving kits lay next to bergens, along with green body armour, some of it being used as improvised headrests on the cots. Empty mags for both 5.56 assault weapons and 9mm shorts lay beside it or in the pouches attached to the body armour. All that was missing were the weapons but Tom knew where they would be.

From one of the other rooms came the sounds of ten or more men eating off paper plates and drinking from plastic beakers. A black bin-liner was taped around a door handle with a hand-written cardboard sign fixed above it: *All crap in here.*

It was familiar. Tom had been in enough holding areas before an operation to know one. It almost made him feel nostalgic.

Hanson waved him in the other direction. 'We've got a briefing at twenty-one hundred but the boss wants to see you first. He's set up shop down there.'

Tom followed him along the creaking wood-floored corridor.

In a small side room, Ashton looked up from a desk where he was studying some documents. He got to his feet when he saw Tom. 'Ah, hello again. Glad you could join us.'

Tom nodded and saw the weapon bundles on the other side of the room: large green nylon roll-outs, a bigger version of the sort of bag a chef would keep his knives in. These held assault weapons and the shorts, the easiest way to move weapons around. The padding protected not only the weapons but, more importantly, the optics. 'Good to be here.' He gave Ashton's hand a firm shake and added a confident smile to show willing.

'You had no trouble getting away?'

'I'm not exactly overworked right now.'

Ashton waited for Hanson to leave them, then faced Tom, his face set with a to-business look. 'So you decided to come after all.'

'Were you in any doubt?'

'Well, I did think we might have put you off, what with all the, er, vetting.' He cracked a faint smile.

Tom grinned. This wasn't the moment to give him any cause for suspicion. 'Seemingly not. So, what's the deal?'

Ashton was still standing. He folded his arms and adopted his trademark addressing-the-troops stance, face stern. 'Before I get into any detail, understand this. Once I give you the briefing – that's it. No backing out. No fucking around. You're in. You got that?'

This was the moment, Tom realized, where he crossed over. If he felt a flicker of doubt he didn't show it. 'I don't do backing out and I don't fuck about. You should know that by now,' he said tersely.

The beginnings of a smile twitched at the corners of Ashton's mouth. 'Okay. That's good.'

He sat down and gestured at another chair. Tom tried to scan the documents on the desk as he sat. But Ashton rested his forearms on them and knitted his fingers together. From now on he had to be on high alert, absorbing everything he could, while he could.

'What you need to know, and I want you to keep in mind all the way through, is that what you're about to do – there's a lot of support for it. By that I mean from people who matter, the powers that be, inside Westminster.' He straightened up in his chair. 'We've got backing in the MoD, high up, same in the Met, in the Civil Service, those who've come to the end of the road with the current status quo, who recognize that things can't go on as they have been any more, that something's got to change and it has to be drastic.'

'So what is this, then?'

Ashton shrugged. 'Call it what you like. I'd call it saving our arses.' There was a cold gleam in his eyes.

Tom kept his face neutral. 'And how does Rolt fit into this?'

Ashton leaned back and spread his hands. 'He's got the right ideas but, let's be frank, you know as well as I do, the prime minister only let him get this far so he could save his own political arse. Now the election's over he's going to drag his feet on all Rolt's strategies, and time's running out.'

'You're going to replace the PM with Rolt?' Tom couldn't help his tone of surprise.

Ashton pointed at him. '*We* are, Tom. Be clear about that.'

Neither of them spoke for a few seconds. Ashton was studying his face to gauge his reaction. 'You'll get fine detail on the whole mission when I give my formal orders to the team but your role is very particular.'

'Okay.'

'This job is all about stealth. The weapons are just to show we mean business. I very much hope we can get it done without a shot being fired in anger. You'll all have Tasers to dominate the area if there's a problem with any of the security round the target. It's about a show of force, no more than that. If we fuck up in any way, we're done for. It'll be the end of Invicta, the end of Rolt. You understand that? There's no exfil, no second chance.' He nodded at Tom. 'But you've been there before, haven't you? You know the score.'

*Get to the fucking point*, thought Tom. But it was also time to show Ashton some enthusiasm. He smirked. 'You bet. So fill me in.'

'I'm putting you up front on this because Rolt knows and trusts you. He'll do what you say. He knows your background, knows what you're capable of. I'll be honest – it was he who said he wanted you in. In fact, he insisted.'

Ashton was still scrutinizing Tom as if even now he hadn't made up his mind about him. 'You came through pretty convincingly the other day. But I'm still not one hundred per cent. I've never totally bought you signing up with Rolt. I think you're too smart for that.'

Tom came straight back. He needed to dispel that notion right now. 'He helped me after you binned me from the Regiment, remember? I owe him a lot.'

Ashton didn't even blink. 'And he thinks he owes you after what you've been through dealing with Invicta's "rogue elements". You won't have any more trouble there, by the way. They've all been dealt with.'

Yes, thought Tom, and I was just a few metres away at the time when you slotted Evans. It was time to move him on and get some answers. 'So who's funding all this?'

'Supporters.'

It was time to try out a name. 'Oleg Umarov?'

Ashton's eyes narrowed. Evidently he wasn't expecting him to come up with that. 'You got any problem with him?'

'I've never met the man.'

An unexpected light came into Ashton's eyes. 'Well, if you've got any doubts you can ask your father when it's all over. Umarov's keeping him close by at the moment. Very close.'

Every muscle in Tom's body tensed. Was this some kind of threat?

Ashton gave him a chilly smile. 'Let's say it gives me confidence in you. I know how important your old man is to you.'

He leaned back in his chair and continued: 'And I gather that if the deal they're working on goes through, your family's financial troubles will be over.' Ashton raised his eyebrows and nodded. *Think about that.*

It was clear he wanted Tom to be under no illusion: he had him by the balls.

Not for the first time, but with much more force now, doubt surged through Tom, laced with anger. Here he was, right out on a limb with no safety net, no backup, no Mandler, about to lead a coup against the very government he was working for, with his own father as a hostage. It was an insane situation, and he had walked right into it. He had no one to blame but himself.

Tom kept his face blank. All his time in the Regiment he had harboured suspicions about Ashton. As the boss, he was respected for his commitment and his resilience, but he wasn't altogether liked, and there were others who felt they could never totally trust him. Tom had never deliberately given Ashton cause to dislike him, but there had always been a lingering hint of doubt. Perhaps it was a chip on his shoulder, an irritation that Tom, a public-schoolboy from a well-heeled background, had not gone the officer route. Perhaps it was because people naturally liked him and Ashton was jealous of that.

But why should Ashton know anything about his father's business affairs? Tom fought with himself not to react. The surprise visit to his parents didn't seem so surprising now. He forced himself to ignore the barely veiled threat. Nothing would be helped by an outburst. The more he kept his cool, the more he could focus on what was about to happen.

# 68

**18.30**
**St James's Park**

Jamal sat in the van in the mews behind Invicta, the plans and notes Isham had given him laid out on his lap. There were the codes to the underground car park, the codes for the lift up to the office floors, and a plan of the rooms where Rolt and Tom Buckingham usually worked. He had photographs of them, of their PA, and of the rest of the staff. Isham was nothing if not meticulous. To Jamal's intense relief, the offices were empty. All the lights were off and the security screens that protected the windows overlooking the mews were shuttered. Bashar was tapping the steering-wheel, nodding to whatever was coming through his earbuds.

'Shall I take you to where you're going to stay?'

Isham had arranged a room for him in a safe house belonging to one of his contacts in Leytonstone.

'I want to do a proper recce. I need to check out the park in front and find a good place where I can watch the building undisturbed.'

Bashar nodded eagerly, as if he understood exactly what Jamal was talking about. On the journey down from Watford

Jamal had done all he could to give his young driver no cause for concern about his precious passenger.

'The van will become too conspicuous if you hover around here. You can leave me and I'll make my own way.'

'But Isham insisted I don't leave you.'

Jamal gave him a cold look – he was getting quite good at it. '*I* am insisting, okay? This is *my* mission. I need to do what I need to do.' He gave Bashar a fatherly smile. 'Go on home, and thank you for driving me.' He offered Bashar his hand. 'God be with you.'

# 69

**19.00**
**Monkton Grange**

Ashton unrolled a large drone photograph of a stately home, marked up with various colours. Tom recognized the house instantly but said nothing.

'Chequers. The prime minister's official country residence.'

Tom's eyes widened appropriately.

'Just the cabinet are there, no minions, no mandarins or special advisers. It's one of the PM's strategy brainstorms, a.k.a. "What the fuck do we do now?"' Ashton grinned and poked the photograph with a ruler. 'Pretty much all you need to know is on here, a complete layout of all the systems and processes.' He snorted. 'Courtesy of a Regiment exercise six months ago to test the security. And, of course, all the blind spots where we can do what we need to do.'

Tom peered at the photo, training all his concentration on it.

'Basically, it's leaky as fuck. No one acted on our recommendations. They've literally done nothing, except add a panic room under the kitchens. Penetrating the perimeter will be a piece of piss.' He shook his head pityingly. 'Even with all the aggro going on around the country, all they've done is increase the headcount.'

'What protects it?'

'Now that the police have enough on their hands on the streets it's farmed out to contractors, would you believe? Harcore. All their people have done time on diplomatic protection in places like North Africa and Iraq so they're not knuckle-draggers.'

'They armed?'

'Of course.'

'How many?'

'Twenty-odd. It can vary, but only by two or three.'

Tom scrutinized the layout, absorbing as much as he could while Ashton continued.

'As you know, these things are all about speed, aggression and surprise. If it goes to plan, the first thing they'll know about us is when they're on the ground with Taser barbs in them, getting plasticuffed.'

'And if they're quicker?'

'Well, that's the first reason we're going in bombed up.'

The awful possibilities hung in the air. Ashton lowered his voice. 'That's why I'm briefing you separately – because you're at the front of this. You'll be going in with the documentation, which is being prepared now – hence you'll be dressed as you are.' He nodded in the direction of the hall. 'The Invicta guys out there, they'll make sure you get to the PM and deliver the paperwork.'

He turned back to the drone photo. 'There'll be three groups, one for each of the entry points – the gatehouses, on the perimeter. As soon as all groups are at their start lines, I'll give the go. Electronic counter-measures will do their job as the teams move in, take the three gatehouses and dominate the space and security. Some of each group will just push past and head direct to the house. You'll be with them. But only you'll make entry. They'll provide a cordon around the house so the PM and cabinet can see you mean business.'

Tom swallowed. *Mother of fuck: was this really happening?* But his job now was to get with it. 'So the less this looks like overt coercion the better, I'm guessing.'

'Right. Nothing should have to happen at gunpoint. The cabinet need to feel they've still got a modicum of free will.'

Tom continued to look as if this was all quite normal.

'And don't expect Rolt to react straight away. You're not coming in as his man, so no high fives or clapping each other on the back, okay?'

As if, thought Tom.

'Keep it cool and businesslike. All your attention will be on the PM. You produce the first document, and give it to him. On it are the signatures of those who have already put their names to this. It's up to him whether he shares that list with the cabinet straight away. Once he's seen the names it should be obvious to him that he's toast. After he's read it, get it back off him and pass it to Rolt, then let him circulate it. Don't make them feel rushed. But let them know they've got five minutes to digest it. Make it clear that the place is surrounded and no one goes in or out until it's done. While they're reading it you present the second document to the PM. That's his resignation letter, formally handing over to Rolt, with the cabinet's unanimous support. No one leaves until you have that signed. That's the second reason why everyone is bombed up. If anyone tries to do anything brave, they'll be stopped.'

Tom struggled to believe what he was hearing. He strove to keep his features relaxed, as if this was the sort of thing he'd been expecting all along.

'There'll probably have to be a show of hands to convince the PM. Several of those sitting round the table have already been sounded out. Any likely dissenters are in the minority, so I don't think there'll be any quibbling.'

Ashton clapped his hands and rubbed them together. 'Once that's done we'll have a new premier.'

*A coup, right here in Britain?* He made it sound as though they were buying a new car.

'And that's legally binding?'

'Effectively. The PM's position will no longer be tenable.

What's left of his credibility will be shot. Rolt will have had his vote of confidence. There will be a few more formalities but this gives him the tools to get the job done.'

The words 'tools' and 'job done' struck ice into Tom's heart. Once the democratic foundations had been hacked away, what terrible vengeance was planned? He needed his own plan, fast. 'And once it's done, what then?'

'You saw the helo outside? We fly Rolt back to London, keep him at a secret location until we get the all-clear from our people at Number Ten and the press are assembled outside for him to make his entrance.'

Tom pored over the drone photo, still trying to digest what he was hearing.

'Okay. When do you give orders?'

# 70

Tom watched as the Invicta crew started to shake out for the op. It was half surreal, half completely familiar, as if he was back in his old life. All fifty-eight of them were carrying out their battle prep of themselves and each other, Velcro being readjusted, a plate of Kevlar body armour front and rear, ammo pouches being threaded through webbing straps, plus a polymer holster for a secondary weapon, a Sig 228. Each man also wore thigh holsters carrying their Taser so that the armour wouldn't get in the way of the weapon when it was drawn down. M4 assault weapons, the American newer and lightweight version of the Vietnam vintage M16, hung from slings on shoulders or were being made safe with thirty-round mags. Several of the guys with gloves on had cut the tops off the fingers so they could grip weapons and kit more easily.

This was no rag-tag crew of Wild Geese: these were the smartest and fittest Invicta had to offer, the opposite end of the spectrum from Evans and Randall. Ashton had drilled them well. Everything Tom was seeing oozed professionalism, which was both good and bad. Good, because he could predict their behaviour more easily; bad, because it would be harder to confuse or divert them.

Two of the team were bent over thirty-litre daysacks, carrying out final checks on trauma kits. Plastic bottles of plasma replacement were being repacked along with their giving sets. It was reassuring that, if things did go noisy, someone on the team would be ready to plug holes and replace lost fluid. Another man was making checks on an electronic counter-measures kit. The daysacks with ECM gizmos would create the vital bubble of static over the target so all communications coming in or out could be blocked at will. They would also take care of the landlines to achieve total isolation.

Tom could only guess that this was what Dartmoor had been all about. He also concluded that the apparent theft of weapons from the Invicta campus had been to divert attention away from what they were being used for. The longer he watched, the clearer it became that this had been prepared over a good while. But if Rolt had been involved in the detail, Tom and Phoebe would surely have got wind of it. The more he thought about it, the more he was coming to realize how much Rolt was merely a part of the plan, rather than its true instigator.

He carried on watching as they checked each other over in case there was a pocket or pouch that hadn't been buttoned or Velcroed and made sure that the grab handle on the back of the armour was accessible. If a man went down and needed dragging out of the line of fire, the handle would be crucial. Others were jumping up and down checking for any rattles from the kit. The snow had started again but no Gore-Tex was being worn now: it produced too much rustling noise, and noise meant compromise.

This was all Ashton, the fanatical attention to detail that had made him such an effective CO and why he was respected rather than liked.

'Looks good, doesn't it?'

Hanson was at his side. There was energy coming off him as if he had been given a whole new lease of life.

'Yep.' Tom nodded.

He imagined them going through Ashton's hoops, the table-top rehearsals, markings on the ground at first so the teams could develop a sense of where they would be in relation to each other. There would have been walk-throughs, then more realistic rehearsals with kit and in real time, practising the attack, then interrogating the what-ifs to cover every eventuality, a man down, the ECM not working. And if there was any opposition . . .

The atmosphere was electric. Tom knew all too well that, for most of them, their time in uniform had been the best years of their lives, and that everything since had been about trying to come to terms with life outside, with the fact that it was over. Invicta had been more than a halfway house. It had picked them up after they'd been spat out, dusted them down and shown them how to start again, how to be of value and make a contribution. But the chance to do something like this, to take part in an actual mission that would have a dramatic impact on the nation, to – as they all saw it – serve their country again, was a dream come true. They were about to make history.

And what was uppermost in Tom's mind was how he was going to stop it happening – not only how to derail it, but how to do so without making himself the scapegoat on all sides. Mandler was unreachable; he had made it clear that he suspected something was about to happen, but had no idea what or when. Had he found out? Was that why he had gone off the grid? Tom's mind was racing. A coup against the British government was about to be launched and he was the only one outside the conspirators who knew anything about it. He was on his own.

Ashton emerged from another door at the end of the hall, closed it behind him and came towards his men, nodding at Tom as he passed. Tom noted the light fade under the closed door, then brighten. Someone else was in there. Tom had already sensed that Ashton hadn't been alone in the room he had just left. He went towards the door, listened, heard the almost inaudible sounds of a person moving about, and knocked.

There was no answer. He opened the door. A small, ruddy-faced man with short spiky silver hair looked up from a tablet, through a fog of cigarette smoke.

'Good evening.' Tom smiled and walked in nonchalantly, as

if it was the most obvious thing to do. The man said nothing, just gazed at him, his eyes almost invisible under a heavy over-hang of brow. Although they had not come face to face before, he had no doubt who this was. 'Oleg Umarov? I'm Tom Buckingham.'

The man's expression relaxed. 'Ah, yes. Tom Buckingham.' He repeated the name as if it was already familiar, nodding slowly. 'Quite a reputation you have.'

Umarov spoke with a thick guttural accent, but seemed at ease with the language. He got up slowly and came towards Tom, looking at his outstretched hand as if he was making up his mind whether it was safe to touch. Eventually he took it and gave it a curt shake. 'And you know my name. You are well informed.'

'I have to be. Watching Vernon Rolt's back means I need to know all I can about him.'

Umarov looked unimpressed. 'Well, I prefer not to be noticed.'

For a second neither of them spoke. Tom looked on as Umarov continued to size him up.

'So you are ready?'

Tom nodded.

'Vernon Rolt has become a very important person in this country. Don't you agree, Tom Buckingham?'

Time for a display of solidarity. Tom offered up a smirk. 'We are about to make him *the* most important.'

Umarov nodded approvingly.

'And what's in all this for you?'

Umarov frowned. Perhaps he wasn't used to being put on the spot. But while he was in the room with the ringleader, Tom thought, he might as well milk it for all it was worth.

Umarov lit a cigarette and blew out a long plume of smoke. 'I like this country. It has great potential still, but the futile experiment with multiculturalism has failed. It's become a distraction and now it's blown up into something they can't handle. The process needs to be reversed. Vernon has caught the public's imagination. Now he needs the tools to finish the job. To clear the decks and start again. Do you think he's up to it?'

Was this a trick question? Tom just stared at him.

'When he came to me he had money trouble. I helped him out but I told him that in return he should raise his game.' Umarov waved a hand towards where the sounds of the assembled men were coming from. 'Let's say I opened his eyes to the possibilities.'

Tom couldn't help himself. 'Do *you* think he's up to it?'

'Now he knows he has no alternative, yes.'

While he was saying this, Umarov had moved closer. Although he was several inches shorter, his presence seemed to fill Tom's vision. 'I can see why your father is so proud of you.'

Tom felt a cold chill down his back at this reminder of how far into his life Umarov's tentacles already reached. Mandler had left him in no doubt as to Umarov's reputation and now the man was talking about Tom's father as if he knew him well. He decided to ignore the comment, pretend he hadn't even heard the threat wrapped up in it.

Umarov's eyes glinted. 'I hope you aren't going to disappoint us all tonight.'

'Why would I do that?'

He produced a thin smile. 'Only if you were a fool.'

# 71

**20.00**
**Charing Cross Road, London**

Jamal sat in the Pret A Manger just off Leicester Square. For 'Britain's most wanted' it was a crazy place to show himself – except that here in plain view he was probably better off than in one of Isham's safe houses. He kept his face down and away from most of the other customers but noted how many of them had his colouring. It should have made him feel at home, but all he could think of was that all of them were under threat. He now knew that Vernon Rolt's plan was nothing short of ethnic cleansing. How could this happen in the country that had welcomed his parents, where he and his siblings had been educated, where Adila, who in Pakistan would have been married off at fourteen or younger, had won a place at medical school? It was an abomination. All thoughts of clearing his own name had left him now. There was one thing he could do and it was stop Rolt. And Isham had given him the means.

The thought of Adila dead had changed everything. Jamal drew his bag closer and considered the device inside with which Isham had entrusted him. Rolt had singled him out for persecution, used the lies about him to further his own cause.

Abukhan had been the leader he had come to hate, but Abukhan had not had anything against him personally. Vernon Rolt was another matter.

Alistair Latimer slid into the seat opposite without looking at him. Jamal glanced at his face. All his muscles were taut. Latimer took the lid off his coffee and, as he blew on it, spoke in a low whisper. 'Don't say anything, don't look at me. Just listen.'

Jamal did as he was told. Latimer's words came rapidly in a low hiss. 'You realize I'm breaking the law even speaking to you, let alone meeting you, after what's happened? My career is finished if this is discovered. You understand that, okay?' He broke off and glanced Jamal's way. Jamal tried hard not to return his gaze as Latimer continued: 'However, there may be a way we can help you to get justice.'

Jamal turned his face a fraction towards Latimer. 'I don't want justice.'

'You want to know what happened to Emma? You'll want justice when I tell you.'

Jamal listened while Latimer told him about the way her remains had been delivered, how the news had been suppressed. 'If it wasn't for Rolt the truth would be out now. Don't you see what he's done to you?'

Jamal nodded. 'Yes, I see that very clearly.'

Latimer was staring at him now. 'Please, Jamal, don't do anything rash. You can help us expose what Rolt has done, but it may take time. There's someone who wants to meet you – the person who sent Emma to Aleppo. She also can help you or, at least, give you a safe place to be, here in London.'

Jamal lifted his head and looked out of the window at people outside, hurrying by in the cold. 'Is anywhere safe now?'

# 72

To the south there was a sweep of open parkland, while to the
north the house was protected by the rising ground of Beacon
Hill and Combe Hill, the highest points of the Chilterns. On a
clear day it was possible to see seven counties, from the Berkshire
Downs to Salisbury Plain to the Cotswolds. But right now they
couldn't see shit. The cloud cover had blocked out the half-
moon and the snow had shut visibility down to less than fifty
metres. Good, thought Tom, that wasn't a bad thing. More
murk, better cover. But he still didn't have a plan.

As they drove towards their target all he could think about
was how to stop this. In theory, he could throw a spanner in the
works at any time, never mind the danger. But it wasn't the
consequences for himself that concerned him so much as what
might happen to his father. Now that he had come face to face
with Umarov, all lingering questions about his involvement
had been answered. And Ashton's veiled threat about
Hugh had been reinforced. Tom had got himself into an
impossible position – effectively having to choose between his
country and his father. Added to that, he wasn't just a

302

'deniable': his only connection with his true masters had gone silent, number unobtainable.

He cursed his own curiosity for getting him into this. Mandler hadn't ordered him to go this far – in fact, he had made it clear he would be on his own. But Tom hadn't reckoned without having him to call on. What had they done with him? Was it Clements's doing? It wouldn't surprise him. Clements had taken an early interest in Rolt and it was he who had suggested putting him on the Party's ticket with a safe seat. Tom felt the sealed documents in his pocket. Was Clements's own name on that list? Perhaps he was too cunning to show his hand.

The snow was coming down harder now. The Discovery shuddered, its wipers working at top speed, as the driver corrected a skid. The atmosphere among the men with him, which had started off so buoyant at the euphoria of being back in the game, had been overtaken by a quiet, nervous anticipation.

Somehow he *had* to subvert the proceedings. He gained some advantage from being in the lead. Assuming he wasn't compromised, and breaching the security in the grounds went according to plan, he would be the first into the house while the rest cordoned it off. He had memorized as much as he could of Ashton's plans of the place. Perhaps there was a way he could separate the PM from Rolt long enough to brief him without arousing Rolt's suspicions.

He tried to think himself more deeply into Rolt's mindset. Ashton was right that Rolt trusted him absolutely. Months of undercover work had ensured that he knew the man as well as anyone did. He would be nervous, that was for sure. The thought also occurred that he, too, was in awe of his Crimean backer. Would this be happening if Umarov hadn't willed it?

Bigwigs arriving at Chequers went in through the imposing lodge gates and up Victory Drive, so named by Winston Churchill. They were heading towards one of the two tradesmen's entrances, the less conspicuous east gate, which was bordered by trees. The driver pulled off the road and the vehicle bounced a few metres down a woodland track before coming to a stop.

The doors opened and they all jumped out. It was completely quiet and very cold as they moved in single file towards their start point. All the different teams had one and nothing would happen until they were in position and Ashton gave the go. Snow was still falling and crunched under their boots until the target came into view. The one light they could see in the distance coming from the grounds was blurred by mist, the house itself a distant ghostly image picked out by the lights in its windows. It looked so vulnerable, and the key members of the British government were inside, about to be taken hostage.

The assault group stood at the start line, plumes of vapour circling up from their breath into the grey snow-filled darkness. There was no more checking of kit, no smoking, no talking. Tom felt the documents Ashton had given him, protected by a thin plastic folder. He scanned the area. The huge old oaks over-looking the wall he'd seen in the drone photo had once famously provided a perch for a particularly enterprising tabloid paparazzo to get shots of the visiting Italian prime minister and his companion in their guest room. After the furore, the trees had been deemed a security threat and moves made to cut them down, until local conservationists mounted a vociferous protest. The trees had survived.

Hanson got on to the radio attached to the front of his body armour and called in to Ashton. Once the other two groups were ready, Ashton would give the go. He spoke in a low tone: whispering would make too much noise.

'Zero, this is Zero Three at the start line. Over.'

Every man was still and quiet, waiting for the only thing that mattered: Hanson getting the go in his radio earpiece.

Tom couldn't hear the reply, but it was clear that the radio traffic was taking too long.

Hanson squeezed the pressel and spoke. 'Roger that.' Then he let go of the radio. 'Shit,' he muttered through his teeth.

'What's happening?' Tom murmured.

Hanson put his mouth next to Tom's ear. He replied in a low tone, clear and professional: 'Zero One's come off the road about fifteen miles out. They're trying to retrieve the wagon.'

Tom calculated. Zero One was the main call-sign of the team tasked with taking the main gate. Ashton had covered a delay like this happening in his orders. The cabinet would probably go into dinner at half seven or eight. They'd be eating and talking round the table until nine thirtyish, then carry on in the drawing room. There was still time for Zero One to get in position because the cabinet would still all be in one place until ten thirty or so. But after that, some of them were bound to split off and go to their rooms. Others might even head home or go back to London.

Instantly, Tom saw an advantage for himself. 'Give me the radio. I've got an idea.'

Tom plugged in the earpiece. 'Zero, this is Zero Three. Over.'

Tom's earpiece buzzed with the digital voice of Ashton. 'Zero, send.'

'This is Tom. It makes sense for me to make entry now, then be on standby outside the house. What if Zero One doesn't make it in time? What if we have problems at the main gate when you give the go? No matter what happens, I'll be ready at the house to carry out what I have to do. Otherwise the whole thing could fail. Over.'

He released the pressel and waited. A couple of long seconds passed before Ashton came back.

'No. All call signs will stay on their start lines and go as planned. I don't want any chance of compromise before we move. Acknowledge, Zero Three?'

Was there some underlying wariness? Tom wasn't going to give in that easily, but if what he had in mind was to work he couldn't afford for Ashton to get suspicious.

'The mission's all that matters. I can make it happen, no matter what, if I go in now. ECM will help get me in, easy. Over.'

There was another pause. Tom could have ignored Ashton and gone for it without making the call but he needed two things to happen. He needed to behave as if he was part of the team, thinking ahead, trying to achieve the mission, and he also needed Ashton to get the ECM up and working so he could pass the perimeter undetected.

Tom's earpiece crackled into life once again. 'Tell me how you plan to make entry.'

Tom explained. There was another pause. Then came Ashton's reply. 'Roger that, go for it. However, do not enter the house until the cordon arrives. Remember, you all need to be together for this to work. Acknowledge.'

'Roger that. Stand by.'

Tom handed the radio back to Hanson who gathered the team round him so each man's head was almost on top of another. Tom explained what was about to happen.

Then he and Hanson headed to the right of the gatehouse to the edge of the wooded area. Hanson turned to him. 'How does this work?'

'You'll see.'

Hanson helped him up into the lower branches of one of the oaks; it must have been three hundred years old. He climbed steadily until he reached the level of the parapet above the brickwork and discovered his first problem. Since the security review a generous helping of razor wire had been applied to the parapet – presumably as an alternative to felling the trees. Great. In the distance, the lights of the house beckoned in the damp, snowflaked air. Tom managed to part the wire just enough to inch his head between the coils until he could see down the other side of the wall.

Immediately below there was sign: prints in the snow from the foot patrols. Keeping his head down among the wire, where he was unlikely to break any infrared beam or motion detector protecting the perimeter, he gave the agreed signal that he was ready – a simple snap of his fingers. A second later he got one back from the base of the tree. All Hanson had to do now was get on the radio to tell Ashton he was in position, and to activate the ECM, but for no more than twenty seconds. Any longer might suggest there was a breach. The razor wire cut into his clothes and skin as he bent it back and moved through it. But there was no choice: he had to get over the wall.

He also had to hope that in this weather the patrols had their heads tucked well inside their hoods or were back inside, relying on the CCTV. Either way, he was about to find out.

He disentangled himself from the wire, climbed over and dropped, propelling himself out as far as he could, to land on the already displaced snow. Immediately he moved to his left, towards the gatehouse, in the footprints left by the patrols.

Next to the gatehouse a 110 Land Rover was parked up with about a centimetre of snow on it, the crew inside, hunched around a gas fire, enjoying a brew.

Once he was on the service road, Tom got into his stride and legged it up to the western end of the house. From memory, and his recollection of the drone photo, it was where the deliveries came in and unloaded – close to the kitchens.

As he approached the house he changed course to try to get confirmation that the cabinet were having dinner. Coming up close to the windows he moved along until he found one with a curtain open just a crack. Shapes crossed the gap and blocked his vision, then moved. A steward in a white shirt was serving and, just visible behind him, people he recognized from the cabinet were sitting at the table.

He moved back towards the service road and followed it into a kitchen yard. There were four huge wheeled bins, stacked crates of empty bottles, and flattened cardboard under an awning waiting to be recycled. He stood in the shadow between two skips to get a good view into the kitchen and watched.

The stewards were Royal Navy – the only one of the three services that supplied the Chequers serving staff – all in pressed white shirts and ties, the females in straight black skirts.

It didn't take him long to see which of them was the boss. She was small, maybe early thirties, with light brown hair pulled back in a bun. She checked the plates that the chefs were placing on a long glass preparation counter and hustled the staff along. He couldn't remember the navy's ranks; her epaulettes showed an anchor surrounded by laurels and crowns.

Tom moved out from the shadow between the bins and headed for the door. Then he took a deep breath and bowled into the kitchen as if he belonged there. The smells of sweet and savoury instantly made him hungry. It was hours since he had eaten.

He scanned the room and looked at the oldest of the chefs, a guy in his fifties, his hands covered with breadcrumbs.

'Who's the boss?'

He wore his grave, self-important face in the hope of countering the rips in his jacket and wet jeans, radiating confident authority as he waited for an answer. His look broadcast that he felt at home where he was, that he knew these people, they were his tribe, and he had a reason to be there. If that wasn't enough, his accent should swing it. To a navy man like the chef, who was gazing back at him, uninterested, Tom could only have sounded like an officer.

The chef pointed at the female with the anchors on her shoulders. 'She's in charge of the service. I'm in charge of the kitchen. Who do you want?'

'I want her. Thanks.'

He lifted a hand to attract her attention, but she was already looking at him – and not much liking what she was seeing. He gave her his best this-is-important-so-listen-up expression, and reminded himself that the further behind the enemy lines you are, the safer you are. It's just the getting there that's the problem.

Tom called to her over the din of the kitchen, stern but not hostile. 'I need you a minute. It's important.'

In most other walks of life that would have gone down like fresh turd but this was the forces.

She glanced at the head chef, who shrugged, and headed towards him through the landscape of stainless steel and bubbling pans to his position by the door. As she came forward he moved back out into the yard.

He stopped a couple of metres by the bins but this time not in shadow. Then he prepared to give her his best officer voice, but she got in the first shot. 'Who are you?' She was from the northeast, and sounded just as she looked: short, sharp, and to the point.

'My name's Tom. That's all you need to know – apart from I'm friendly forces. Who are you?'

'Chief Petty Officer Warren.'

'What's your first name?'

'Gemma.'

'OK, Gemma, listen in: this is very important.'

He wanted her to recognize him as from a military background. He pointed at her to emphasize the words, but did so with an open palm and straight fingers. In the military it was a sign of respect, and she would know that.

'I work for the Security Service, MI5, whichever you call it. I don't have any ID on me so don't ask. But what I do have, in fact what *we* have, is a national security threat that is going to need your help. Roger so far?'

Tom waited for her to register. The woman was switched on: she was frowning but she wasn't flapping.

'OK. I'm not going to tell you what the situation is, for your own protection. But you must do as I ask or we'll all be in a world of shit.'

Tom sensed her hesitation. He needed to climb aboard her now and get control of her. He lifted his hands and gripped her shoulders to be sure she didn't decide to make a run for it. 'Gemma, all I need you to do is get the PM to step out of the dining room. Nothing else.'

Her eyes drilled into his, demanding more.

'I need to get him away from the rest so he hears it first. No other cabinet, no security, just him.'

He gave her a cold stare to drive the words home, but at the same time leaving her with the sense that it was her choice, that he was asking, not ordering, so she still had some sense of control. Since she looked like the sort of woman who didn't take shit from anyone it helped that these were times of heightened tension and unprecedented events.

Her eyes narrowed. 'If it's so fucking important, Tom, why are you bothering with me? Why don't I just get security and you get them to sort it out? Eh?'

She moved her head from left to right, looking at nothing in particular, and put her hands on her hips. She exhaled hard and her vapour mixed with all the others gushing from the wall pipes.

'Gemma, I can't tell you anything else. I'm trying to keep this as low key as it needs to be. The PM's got to know about it first so it can't be filtered through security. There's about to be some shit and he needs to know so he can make his decisions. I'm asking you to help me do that.'

And because she had to be thinking it, he added, 'If I was here to kill him, I would have just gone for it.'

Tom took a step back, but he had to keep the momentum going. 'I need an answer, Gemma.'

She took a deep breath and looked back up at him. 'Fuck it – all right.'

She turned to move, then stopped. 'What if I don't?' Her face suggested she'd known the answer before she'd even asked.

'Just do it, Gemma. OK?'

She stared hard at him with a mixture of anger and disgust. 'You fucking people.'

She stepped forward, so he had to move out of her way, and headed back towards the kitchen door.

# 73

None of the kitchen staff looked up as the two of them re-entered: a good sign. Gemma wasn't letting any pressure show as she carved her way through the chefs and the boiling stoves.

She reached the serving counter. A line of stewards was preparing to go into the dining room, each in the process of collecting a dessert plate in each hand. One frowned at Tom. Gemma gave him a look and he turned away. 'Don't worry about him, worry about me. Whose turn is it to serve the PM?'

'Ma'am.' A young blond man who could have been a teenager stepped forward.

Gemma took the dessert from him, an enticing apple tart. Tom's mouth watered. *Not tonight.*

She had to get a move on. He needed to make contact with the PM immediately. He had no idea – and no means of finding out – when Invicta were going to start screaming across the grounds to put in the cordon. But he couldn't rush her. She was the boss of her domain and he had to respect that.

Her crew were all waiting for her to give the word.

'OK, everybody into the corridor. I'll follow you in.'

As the stewards shuffled to the far right-hand corner of the kitchen and the double doors with their faded In and Out signs, Gemma turned to Tom. 'Right, you come with me.'

He did as instructed, but she wasn't heading for the swing doors. Instead she turned towards a service corridor. At the end of it there was an open door into the main entrance hall.

'Wait here while I tell him. *If* he agrees, you'll see him coming out of those doors to the right, in the hall.'

She turned and went back the way she had come. He scanned the hallway, his head the only part of him exposed beyond the semi-opened door. The hall was inviting, like that of an old country-house hotel, with an ancient flagstone floor and the whiff of woodsmoke coming from a fireplace the size of a goal mouth. A chandelier sparkled in the mirror. Mum would like this, he found himself thinking, and quickly doused the thought before it led on to his father.

There was a resonant, ponderous ticking from a tall grandfather clock against the opposite wall that seemed to be getting louder – something he recognized as a trick of the mind.

Below the sound of the clock he could hear a gentle hubbub of chatter echoing along the hall, the clink of cutlery on china and the odd guffaw, coming from the double-height oak doors down to the right. In another mirror opposite the doors he could see a section of the table. He was tempted to step further out to get a glimpse of how it was going with the PM but he resisted.

His heart sank as the clock ticked on. What if this didn't work? He didn't have a plan B or a plan C. In fact, he was pretty much making up plan A as he went along. He decided to move. He wanted to see for himself, have an early warning, if Gemma was going to help him or not.

There was movement in the dining room as the stewards glided in with the dessert and took up their positions behind the diners. Gemma must have given them a signal, as they all stepped forward at the same moment.

He heard nothing from her but after another agonizing ten seconds the PM's voice wafted towards him.

'Carry on. Back in a sec.'

Success?

Gemma appeared first, followed by the PM brushing crumbs

312

off his chest. He frowned at the sight of Tom's damp and torn clothing. Gemma lingered, watching.

'Sir, Tom Buckingham. I work for Stephen Mandler. Is there somewhere we can speak in private?'

# 74

'What did you say your name was again?'

The documents were still in Tom's outstretched hand. The prime minister was ignoring them. His eyes bulged, as if they were about to launch themselves clean out of his reddened face. Evidently he'd had a few and was not focusing the way Tom needed him to. Gemma had disappeared back into the dining room. They were alone in the hall. Tom repeated his warning.

'You are about to be surrounded by Invicta troops, sir. They think they're staging a coup to replace you with Rolt. They're going to force you to resign. I need to take you to the panic room now. With you safe there, nothing can happen.'

The prime minister seemed to be taking his time to absorb what he was saying. Tom had seen this sort of reaction before, that rabbit-in-the-headlights look, the denial people could slip into when confronted with immediate danger. There were a thousand ways this was going to go tits up, but he knew that if he stopped to consider any of them it would be a waste of precious seconds – and, in any case, the way it would go wrong would be the thousand and first. He had staked everything on working the same magic he had done with Gemma. He tried to put the documents into the PM's hand but he took a step back. Tom grabbed his arm to try to force him to take them.

There was more movement at either end of the hallway. Not wanting to look shifty, Tom kept all his attention on the prime minister. Finally he spoke.

'There's only one flaw in your story, though, Tom.'

'Sir?'

From the corridor where Tom had followed Gemma, two men in suits appeared, pistols drawn, while a third came from the dining room. The prime minister's face relaxed into a look of mild disgust.

'Stephen Mandler was relieved of his duties earlier today. With immediate effect.'

Tom dropped the documents and stood exactly where he was. He'd figured Gemma would speak to security but had hoped that the PM would have got the message.

The third suit had his Taser up. Tom knew this wouldn't be the time to do or say anything. One movement, one word or combination thereof would be taken as a threat, and he would be shot. He knew all too well that these situations were very black and white. If the life of their principal was in any way at risk they were entitled to shoot.

He kept still and prepared to accept what was about to happen as the third man advanced between the two with the pistols, and fired the Taser.

# 75

Tom glimpsed a streak of yellow arc through his peripheral vision heading towards his thigh, closely followed by fifty thousand volts.

Then his whole being shuddered as if having its own private earthquake: the shock vibrated through all the cells in his body, short-circuiting his nervous system, and he dropped in a helpless heap. He knew he was face down on the carpet – his face was buried in it – but he couldn't remember getting there.

He tried to lift his head up off the carpet. In the haze of his brain he knew he must establish whether or not the PM had seen the documents. They would prove he was telling the truth.

'Read them, Sir, please.'

His voice sounded thick and blurred, as if he was speaking through a wet flannel. He felt a large foot bearing down on his back as his arms were straightened out behind him, then heard the ratchet sound as he was plasticuffed. Two hands roughly patted him down, more with anger than efficiency. They would be seriously in the shit for letting him anywhere near the boss, and were evidently making up for their carelessness by being extra hard.

More security now appeared on the scene. One reached

down, picked up the documents and escorted the prime minister away.

'This is a bad idea, guys. You're going to be in even more shit in a few minutes. Will you just hear me out?'

'Shut up, cunt.'

He took that as a no.

They grabbed him and pulled him back onto his feet, then half dragged, half frogmarched him through a narrow door and down a stone spiral staircase to a basement passage. No one spoke. All he could hear was their laboured breathing as they manhandled their prisoner.

'Please listen to me. It's all going to kick off outside and they're going to need every one of you.'

For that he got a fist in the temple and nearly dropped again as they came out into a yard where a people-carrier was waiting, the engine running. One of the suits was shouting at the driver: 'Fantasist! Only got right into the fucking house, didn't he?'

'All right, load him in.'

They had a job to do, and listening to reason wasn't in the brief. Tom's body was still quivering from the shock of the Taser. He knew better than to fight it. Give in to it and the body had a better chance of recovering faster, so the opportunity to escape would come sooner. Except that sooner was still too late.

# 76

**22.00**
**Soho, London**

Jamal had remained in Pret A Manger after Latimer had gone, his mind a cauldron of remorse and rage. He had heard suicide bombers being prepared in Syria, having it drilled into them that their lives were over, there was nothing to live for but the act of war. Now he knew how they'd felt. But he wasn't going to squander his last opportunity. He needed to focus again. Use the resources he had. He followed Latimer's instructions. He made his way to the street in Soho where he had been told to wait. The BMW was there, lights on, the engine ticking over. As he came up alongside the driver's door the window opened a couple of inches.

'Get in.' A woman's voice.

He opened the door and entered the warm, leathery cocoon. The woman at the wheel was pale, almost ghost-like. 'Hello, Jamal.' She offered him her hand. 'I'm Xenia. Emma's friend.'

The car glided forward and out into the evening traffic. Jamal clutched his bag to him with its combustible contents inside and said nothing.

He saw the Mall and Buckingham Palace, just a ghostly shape

without any floodlights. Parked outside the gates were Husky and Pathfinder armoured vehicles and a line of police mini-buses with riot grilles over the steamed-up windows.

'Quite a lot has changed while you've been away.'

'Was I the last person to see Emma?' Jamal asked.

She nodded. 'I financed her assignment in Syria. She was very committed to her work.'

'I'm so sorry she died. I don't know how it happened.'

'It's okay. We know it wasn't your fault.'

He looked over his shoulder, checking to see if anyone was following.

'You can relax for now. It's not likely anyone will bother us.' She accelerated away from Hyde Park Corner towards Knightsbridge. 'There'll be a police cordon at the end of my street, but they know me. Don't be alarmed.' She handed him some dark glasses.

'Really?'

She nodded. 'They'll make you look more like my bodyguard.'

They travelled in silence until she made a left turn and slowed as two armed police came into view.

'Sit up. Don't cower and don't try to avoid their gaze.'

Miraculously, the police waved them through.

The residence was surrounded by a wall and tall gates, which opened automatically as they approached. Jamal had never been in a building anything like it before. It looked more like a fortress than a house, bristling with security devices.

'You should be safe here.'

They descended to the underground car park where they left the car, and travelled to the fifth floor in a lift that was all mirrors. Jamal saw himself standing beside this impossibly beautiful woman clutching a bag with Isham's bomb in it, as if he was in a dream.

She showed him to a room with a large double bed, and an adjoining bathroom almost as big that was all white marble. It was as if he had died and gone to some other place, not necessarily Heaven. A servant came and offered to take his bag but he refused to let it out of his hands. He looked out of the window at the rooftops and the street below. He was safe, which he had not felt in a long time.

# 77

**22.30**
**M40 motorway**

Tom examined his options: there weren't very many. Basically he was limited as long as he was surrounded by the four with him in the Ford Galaxy people-carrier, one each side of him and two in the front. It wasn't clear where they were going. No one answered when he asked. But they were on the M40 heading for London. He had put up no resistance after the Tasering, partly because he couldn't – his muscle tissue had contracted. After that subsided, he remained limp, to fool his escorts into lowering their guard sufficiently to give him something to work with: if an opportunity presented itself there would be maximum surprise.

As he was being driven out of Chequers Tom had looked to see if Ashton's main gate team had actually made it to the start point. If they'd halted this vehicle he might have had one final chance of stopping Ashton but if they were there they hadn't shown themselves, and the Galaxy sped on.

On the motorway, sleet and mist slowed their pace, reducing all three lines of traffic to a steady thirty-five. He didn't much like how close the driver was keeping to the vehicle in front but right now that was the least of his worries. His wrists were bound behind his back with plasticuffs. He didn't have his seatbelt on, which made him vulnerable if the driver didn't watch his distance but it offered an opportunity if the right moment arose.

He assumed that at some point he would be handed over to the police. With Mandler apparently gone, his only contact left was Woolf, though in the current climate it wouldn't surprise him if he denied all knowledge of him. And where was Phoebe now? There was nothing more he could do for the prime minister. By now most probably all the call signs would have carried out the attack. Ashton would have been the one to walk in and make the PM sign the documents.

There was complete silence in the vehicle until the front passenger with the goatee facial hair heard his phone buzz and put it to his ear.

'Yeah, I can hear you . . . The fuck?'

That put the rest of them on the alert.

'You having a laugh?' Goatee's voice went up an octave. 'You want us back there?' He pulled the mobile from his ear and examined the screen.

'Fucking cut off.'

'What's going on?' asked the one on Tom's left.

'Some kind of incident. Wait out.'

Goatee tried to get the caller back.

'You wanna stop?' the driver asked Goatee, turning his head towards him just as the brake lights flashed on the truck in front of them. Before even consciously thinking what he was about to do, Tom tensed his calf and thigh muscles and launched himself at Goatee. The driver lifted one hand off the wheel to stop him, his attention distracted by the commotion as the two either side of Tom made to grab him. Tom used the force from the man on his left who had grabbed his shoulder to drop behind the back of Goatee's seat just as the driver realized what was happening in front of him and slammed on the brakes. Tom couldn't see what was happening but felt the steering being yanked left.

The impact didn't feel like much, but the angle at which the people-carrier hit the truck twisted it ninety degrees as the air-bags deployed. All Tom could do was hope that whoever was behind was better at keeping their distance or he would be responsible for a massive pile-up. That thought had barely formed when it came. Not as big an impact but just enough to put the already tottering people-carrier on its side.

Above the high-pitched whistling in his ears, caused by the detonating airbags, he heard a mixture of groans, swearing and car horns. With the people-carrier on its side, Tom unexpectedly found himself on his feet. He was standing on the tarmac in the aperture where the side window would have been, in a pool of broken glass.

Headlights from the traffic behind lit up the interior. The man who had been on his left had been thrown forward by the impact and had come to rest curved over the headrest of the seat in front of him on top of Goatee, who was groaning under him. The man on his right had demolished the driver's seat and the pair of them were slumped half out of the windscreen and not moving.

There was nothing Tom could do for them while his wrists were cuffed so he worked his way past the third row of seats to where the rear window had burst out of the tailgate. Then he backed himself up to the edge of the window frame and worked the plasticuffs up and down against the sharp metal edge until they snapped apart. Already a crowd of other motorists was forming around the front of the vehicle and someone was ministering to Goatee through the space where the windscreen had been.

Tom made his way back into the vehicle and reached the man who had been on his right, suspended in his belt, his eyes half open but barely focusing. He lifted a hand but let it fall as Tom reached into his coat for a weapon.

Tom checked the chamber of the Glock, keeping it out of sight. 'I'll get it back to you when I'm done with it.' He lifted a phone out of another pocket, checked that it was still working and didn't need a password, then retraced his route through the passenger cabin and out of the tailgate.

323

'You all right, mate?'

Tom heard the question through the high buzzing in his ears from the airbags. The man talking to him was a truck driver, with a big orange first-aid kit in his hand. 'Bit dazed, that's all. Them in there need the help.'

The traffic on the London-bound carriageway was stationary, the motorway ablaze with headlights glowing in the mist and sleet.

'Where am I?'

'About three miles from Gerrards Cross.'

In the distance he heard sirens. That wasn't going to be useful. He moved across the lines of cars to the hard shoulder and into comparative darkness. It was freezing cold and he had no coat. He surveyed the scene from the comparative gloom of the verge. A row had broken out between a man whose Mercedes had been lightly rammed by a woman's Mini. The driver had gone up to her door and was giving her a piece of his mind about female motorists. She was politely asking him not to be so abusive, when another woman shouted from another car, telling him more purposefully to back the fuck off. Meanwhile, a second man was heading towards them.

'Hey, you fuck off out of this,' said the Merc man.

'Don't you fucking talk to me like that, cunt.'

As the Merc man squared up to the other, Tom skirted round the cars and past the Merc's open door. The key was still in the ignition, the engine still running. He stepped in, rammed the shift into Drive, let off the handbrake, swerved onto the hard shoulder, pulled round a couple of the other cars that had also stopped there, and sped off into the night.

After he had put about ten high-speed miles between him and the pile-up he came off the M40 and stopped in a lay-by. He had tried to warn the prime minister and failed. He had done nothing to derail Ashton's plan; for all he knew he had helped it. Well, fuck it, he thought. I did what I could. All he cared about now was his father.

He took out the phone.

Hugh Buckingham wasn't picking up. Maybe it was the

unfamiliar number Tom was calling from. He sent a text: *Dad call Tom on this NOW.*

Then he tried Woolf. 'It's Tom Buckingham. Remember me?'

Woolf sounded breathless, as if he'd been running. 'Have you any idea what's happening?'

'I might – but you go first.'

'Some flap on at Chequers – I haven't heard much detail yet. Some paramilitaries have surrounded the house. Most of the cabinet are in the panic room but Rolt isn't with them. The assumption is he's the target.'

'That's an interesting interpretation. Let me give you mine.'

Tom gave Woolf his headlines.

'Mother and father of fuck! Where are you now?'

'Pass. What's this about Mandler? The prime minister said he's been dumped.'

'Something to do with a past misdemeanour. Tom, seriously, you'd better watch your back. With Mandler gone, I'm not sure who's going to vouch for you.'

'Well, that's helpful. Where's Phoebe?'

'She's gone off the grid. I thought she might be with you. Something else you should know, Tom. We raided a place in Watford a few hours ago and picked up one of the Belmarsh fugitives.'

'Jamal al Masri?'

'No, the other one – Isham al Aziz, the convert. There was a mass of material on Rolt, plans of Invicta's HQ and stuff on you too. One of Isham's lieutenants has told us Jamal's in London and has got an IED with him. You'd better go to ground until it's blown over.'

Some chance. Tom killed the call and considered his diminishing number of options. He tried his father again.

'Tom, I'm sorry, I can't talk right now. I'm right in the middle of something.'

He sounded frail.

'Where are you, Dad?'

'Look, I'm really not— '

'Are you at Umarov's place? If you are, I want you to get out of there right now. Walk away. Go outside, get in a cab and disappear.'

There was an agonizing pause.

'Dad?'

'I'm afraid I couldn't do that even if I wanted to . . . I'm sorry, Tom, I should have listened to you.'

The phone went dead.

# 78

Tom kept his foot flat down all the way, headlights on full beam to encourage any slower traffic in the fast lane to make way. The Merc had seen better days, and a metallic clattering from the engine warned that an expensive service was imminent, probably more than the car was worth, so, really, he was doing the owner a favour by taking it. But these thoughts were only background noise: he had to focus on finding his father.

He came off the Westway and checked his speed. The car would have been reported stolen by now so he'd better not get pulled over. From the Holland Park roundabout he retraced his route to Xenia's place. As he approached, he paused to rehearse the keying-in routine that had got him through the gates and into the underground car park before. He drew up to the key pad, lowered the window, pressed his forefinger on the touch screen, then tapped in the code and the number of the Mercedes. Nothing happened.

Fuck.

He didn't want to make a scene and crash his way in. If he could get to Xenia without raising any alarm he had a chance of preventing anyone freaking out. His father had to be in Umarov's quarters, almost certainly with some security. He needed to go in as if he was meant to be there. But, knowing what he did now about Xenia and her stepfather, that didn't seem like a viable option.

He reversed away from the gate, parked, killed the lights and took out the phone, struggling to remember Helen's number. He tried to picture the card she had given him, willing the digits to load into his mind. He dialled what he thought was her number, then tried again switching the last two digits.

Her voice came through, crisp and clear.

'Hi – it's Tom.'

They hadn't spoken since they'd found the bloodbath in Jez's flat – not the ideal end to a first date.

'Oh, yes? I wondered when you'd call.' There was a distinct chill in her tone.

'Look – it's been difficult. I had to go away.'

She sighed. 'Can't you do better than that?'

'I'm trying to make a follow-up visit to your boss. You're not in a position to give me her number, are you?'

Silence.

'I could give you the biggest and best scoop of your career. A world exclusive . . .'

'Tom, it's so nice of you to suddenly remember me, but you're a bit out of touch with recent events. Xenia's not responsible for the paper any more, and McCloud sacked me this morning. As for your designs on her, well, good fucking luck.'

The phone went dead.

While he was considering his next move as he redialled her, a van with the *Newsday* logo on it pulled up behind him and hooted. He backed up so the van could get in. Helen had powered down her mobile and the message service kicked in. Tom killed the call and pulled the Mercedes up close behind the van. As soon as it moved, Tom went with it, following it through the gates with barely an inch between them, in the hope that the sensors might register them as one vehicle.

It worked. He was through. The van drew up by a loading dock. Two men got out and started unloading boxes. They didn't pay him any attention. He found the lift at the back of the car park, tapped in the same code he had seen Helen use and heard the whirr of it coming his way. He hung back in the shadows and only stepped in once he had seen that it was clear.

The reception area where he had met Xenia was on the fifth floor. There was a sixth button so he pressed it, imagining that if you were going to live in a building like this you would want to be as high as possible. He checked himself in the mirrors. He was a mess. Dusty from the smash in the people-carrier, nicks and grazes from flying glass and a bruise on the side of his head, which must have had something to do with the impact. When he made an abortive attempt to tidy his hair, bits of glass fell out. As the lift approached the end of its upward journey he felt for the weapon, prepared for whatever would be waiting for him.

When the doors opened Xenia was standing there, frowning. 'Wouldn't it have been simpler to call?'

He smiled. 'There wasn't time.'

'I see. What happened to your face?'

'A problem I was hoping you'd be able to help me with. May I come in?'

She stepped to one side as Tom moved into the hallway. He came straight to the point. 'My father is in this building. I need you to help me get him out.'

'Your father?'

'Mid-sixties, white hair, going a bit bald, half-glasses. Are you going to help me?'

She frowned. 'I don't understand.'

He owed her an explanation, maybe, but he didn't know how long he had or what it would take to get Hugh out. 'Just show me how to get onto the right floor.'

'I don't go to the other floors any more so, I'm sorry, I won't have seen him.' She was looking at him warily, measuring him.

'Is there a security presence?'

She shook her head. 'That's why I had it built this way, so I wouldn't have to be surrounded by protection.'

She was being cool, borderline obstructive. Tom needed to get her onside, fast.

'When we met, you asked me what I thought Rolt's plans were. At the time I'm afraid I didn't fully appreciate what you were asking. Perhaps we were both being too guarded. Anyway, I know what they are now.'

There was no answer from her, as if it no longer mattered. He didn't want to get heavy except as a last resort. 'Helen told me about the paper. I'm sorry. After all you've done . . .'

She sighed and started walking towards an area with large white sofas.

He followed. He thought he heard movement down one of the corridors. 'Are you alone up here?'

'Oh, yes,' she said, over her shoulder. 'Tell me what you know and then we'll see about your father.'

# 79

Jamal's moment of tranquillity was short-lived. He watched the exchange from the shadows of the corridor outside his room. He couldn't hear what was being said but the man was unmistakable. His picture had been in Isham's dossier of intelligence about Vernon Rolt. Jamal even remembered the name: Tom Buckingham, Rolt's right-hand man.

This woman was too good to be true. For a brief few hours he had thought he was no longer on his own, that there were people who believed him. But why should anyone help him after what he had done? No, this was an elaborate trap and he had walked right into it. Latimer and this woman had conspired together to deliver him into Rolt's hands via one of his henchmen. But why?

Not that Jamal cared why. Despair mixed with disgust had taken over any rational thoughts he might have had. This was a humiliation too far. This time he wasn't going to let himself be hoodwinked. He returned to the room, unpacked his bag and laid the suicide vest on the bed.

# 80

Xenia deserved a proper explanation of what had happened, Tom thought, but right now all his concentration was focused on reaching his father. He knew now that behind the mask of reclusive newspaper magnate she was a tragic figure, a prisoner of her own past, whose misfortune had been to cross paths with one of the most ruthless oligarchs ever to emerge from the former Soviet Union. Through his past association with the British Security Service, he had a free pass to do whatever he liked – even, it seemed, to change the government.

But Umarov wasn't the priority. In his heart, Tom didn't care about him or Rolt. He had done what he had done and it had fucked up. All that mattered to him now was what happened to his father.

He kept his speech to Xenia short and sweet, but in order to build a bridge to her he explained the real reason for his being involved with Rolt: as a spy for the Security Service. 'Somehow we failed to discover the connection with your stepfather.'

Her whole demeanour had changed since their last meeting, as if some of her spirit had been sucked out of her.

'That's a shame. But I appreciate he has a special status with your masters, so perhaps it was naïve to think he could be stopped.' There was more than a hint of bitterness in her tone.

She gestured at the floor. 'They have changed the codes so I can't get onto the executive floor any more.'

'Your own building. Isn't this all humiliating for you?'

She gave him an empty look. 'I was stupid to think he might leave me alone. He wants everything I have. He thinks it's his by right. I know that even if I try to run he will pursue me. His resources are limitless and his obsession is overwhelming.'

She stood up, moved towards the window and leaned her head against the glass. 'I was such a fool. I built this place to protect me from him and here he is, right inside, like a parasite. Even after he had my father killed, that wasn't enough. He had to have everything that had been his, including my mother and now me.'

Tom saw this could take some time. Much as it helped to have her on his side, time was ticking on. 'I need you to get me down there.'

'There are the service stairs. But the codes on those doors will have been changed as well.'

'Show me.'

He followed her through a kitchen to a door by the rubbish chute. The precast concrete stairs, with a simple steel tube banister, were in stark contrast to the luxurious surroundings of the apartment. 'Let me look at the key pad. Maybe there's something I can do.'

'Are you armed?'

He nodded. 'But only for when I've exhausted all the other options.'

He examined the key pad. He didn't want to break the door down and set off an alarm. All he needed was to go in, find his father, tell him he had to come with him, help him on with his coat and leave. Unless anyone tried to stop them . . .

He felt anger rising again at the thought of Hugh held hostage in this concrete mausoleum. But emotion was the last thing he needed right now. He needed focus.

He could hear a muffled conversation, a clinking sound. A party? In the circumstances, it seemed bizarre. He turned to Xenia. 'Why don't we just knock?'

After a few seconds the door opened. It was Rolt.

# 81

Rolt took one look at Tom and spread his arms. 'Here he is – the hero of the hour! Come in!' Tom stepped into the room as Rolt tried to embrace him. 'My God. We thought you'd been taken away by the heavy mob!'

There was a manic gleam in his eye. For someone who took such pride in his appearance he looked distinctly dog-eared. But, then, it had been a long day. Tom scanned the room: desks and screens that looked as if they had been hastily erected, and several men in striped shirtsleeves, City types, two of whom Tom recognized from the fundraiser.

'Where's my father?'

'He's here, don't worry. Let me get you a drink.' Rolt was urging him forward. He saw Xenia. 'And won't you join us too?'

'Why aren't you at Number Ten?' Tom asked him.

'Just waiting for the all-clear. Should be any minute now.' He raised a tumbler of orange juice to them. 'I can't join you in case I have to broadcast to the nation.'

He spoke in a jovial tone, as if he'd done the whole thing for a joke. But Tom ignored him because his attention was caught by the appearance of another man, with silver hair, stooping very slightly as he moved slowly towards a desk in one corner:

his father. Not far behind him was Umarov who, when he saw Xenia, stopped dead.

Tom marched across the room to his father. Hugh looked up. There was a heartstopping delay before he focused. 'Oh, hello, dear boy. What on earth are you doing here?' A wan smile appeared on his face. 'Just putting the finishing touches . . .'

Tom stepped up to him and embraced him. 'It's okay, Dad. I'm going to take you home.'

'Well, I . . .' Hugh looked into his son's eyes, uncomprehending.

Tom's pent-up rage roared to the surface. He could feel his restraint slipping. He needed to hold on, just get away, but here was Umarov. *Forget him. Leave it, just go,* he told himself. *Keep focused, don't lose it.*

Umarov caught his glare and smirked. 'It seems you've proved yourself. Ashton wasn't sure you'd come through in the end. Your father is very proud of you, aren't you, Hugh?'

Umarov's eyes swivelled towards Hugh as Tom moved forward.

But before Tom could react he was distracted by a shout from across the room – and the figure standing at the door to the service stairs he had just come through.

He didn't immediately recognize the face, but that was because all his attention was concentrated on the device strapped to the young man's chest.

# 82

What Woolf had been telling Tom now all slotted into place. This was Jamal al Masri, the so-called Butcher of Aleppo, the man who had supposedly busted out of Belmarsh, whom Rolt had made into the poster boy to help whip up hysteria for his campaign, the man Sarah Garvey had been trying to help.

Tom made eye contact with Jamal immediately, hoping it would create a window, an interval he could work in. All his concentration was on him. It was as if Rolt, Umarov, Xenia and even his father had been vaporized and it was just the two of them. In return, he needed Jamal to focus only on him and not be distracted. The device on Jamal's chest looked very convincing. Tom had no reason to doubt it, since it was being worn by a man who had just blown his way out of prison. And the fact that he had not attempted to conceal it must have been to make the point: he wanted them all to know what he was about to do. Rolt was now cowering behind a screen: much good that would do him when the moment came for Jamal to enter Heaven. If anything, it would probably slice his head off.

Tom took a couple of steps forward, hands down, palms open, facing out so Jamal could see they were empty. 'Hello, Jamal. I've heard a lot about you. Sounds like you've been on quite a journey. I like your timing. You couldn't have picked a better place to show your face.'

Jamal said nothing. Tom could see his forehead was glistening with sweat and his features twisted with anger. One hand twitched. A wire attached to the device dangled from the remote switch in his palm.

'For God's sake, Tom, take him down!' Rolt's strangled cry rang out across the room.

Tom replied slowly, without taking his eyes off Jamal, 'Actually, Vernon, whatever I do won't make any difference. As I'm sure Jamal knows only too well, from his time in Syria, he has the advantage. By the time I draw my weapon, before it's even out of its holster, he can have activated the device. He holds all the cards. What happens next is Jamal's decision. Right now he controls the room. Our lives are in his hands. There's nothing any of us can do. Isn't that right, Jamal?'

Out of the corner of his eye, Tom saw Rolt's mouth open and close a couple of times as if he had found the words he was never short of – but then realized they weren't right and discarded them. He was shaking; he looked at Umarov as if he might find something there. But Umarov's concentration was on Jamal, as was everyone else's. Tom caught sight of his father looking even more haggard, now a frail, vulnerable man, who had done nothing to deserve any of this. He banished all thought of Hugh as he focused back on Jamal.

'So, Jamal, I'm sure Vernon Rolt needs no introduction. He's the man who's made it his personal mission to destroy your name, no matter who he's had to silence along the way. He's your man, your target – but you're in double luck tonight, because the real power in the room isn't him at all. It's the man standing just to his right, the short one, Dr Oleg Umarov. He's the one who bankrolled Vernon Rolt's grab for power and who's looking forward to cashing in his winnings.'

Tom paused, but only to take a breath.

'As for the other people in the room, Xenia is the one who holds your interests closest to her heart. She's been a lonely and tireless supporter of people like Emma Warner, who gave their

337

lives trying to bring the truth out of Syria. Xenia knows about the courage you showed there, and what you've sacrificed to tell the world the truth, only to have your brave exploits criminally misinterpreted.'

Tom then pointed at Hugh. 'And over there, Jamal, is my father, Hugh Buckingham. Yes, my own dad is right here, a hostage. Without any doubt the most important man in my life.'

Tom had no idea where the words were coming from, but he kept going. All the time he was maintaining eye contact with Jamal.

'Jamal, I know you've had your differences with your father. And I know he has misunderstood what you've done, but only because he has been fed a bunch of lies by people like Rolt. Me and my dad, we've had our differences. He'll tell you that he neither knows nor understands what I've been up to, won't you, Dad?'

Hugh nodded tentatively, probably thinking his son really *had* gone mad now. Jamal was quite still, just the device moving as his chest rose and fell rapidly with his quick breaths, a small wire hanging from a cuff that disappeared into his right fist. Well, at least I have his attention, thought Tom. Though whether any of this guff was getting through to him . . . He just had to keep going and hope.

'What does your dad really know about you and your courage, Jamal? What's he ever going to know about how you risked your life to get those pictures? Detonate your device now and, yes, you rid the country of the man who's doing the most to break our society apart. But, then, your father's never going to know what you sacrificed. You know why? Because if you choose to do that, for the rest of his life and for generations to come you will be the Butcher of Aleppo who supposedly massacred those poor girls, then blew himself up in a fit of revenge. That lie will outlive you.'

Jamal was shaking now, struggling to control the rage and anticipation boiling inside him. Tom saw his hand twitch again.

'You went to Syria to show your father what you were made of. You wanted him to be proud of you, to understand you. And it didn't turn out that way. But you can change that, Jamal. If we were to explain to him what you did, your courage in Syria, how you risked everything to get those pictures, then he would not only understand, he would be proud.'

Was this working? Tom could only hold on to the fact that they were all still breathing. But how long could he keep it up? He needed an outcome. And as he pressed on with his speech, he started to craft one.

'And your sister, Jamal. Adila, God rest her soul.'

Jamal flinched at the mention of her name as Tom took a step towards him, still speaking, his hands passive.

'What would Adila want most for you now? Vengeance? I don't think so. She died for you, died wanting to clear your name, because she believed in you, knew the truth in your heart.'

Tom pointed at Rolt. 'But because of all the noise coming from this man, no one could hear it.'

The genie was out of the bottle now, Tom's own feelings laid bare after all the months of dissembling. The brakes were off. The relief was immense, mixed into a toxic fuel of raw anger on behalf of the man facing him who now held their lives in his hands.

Tom saw on Rolt's face a mixture of indignation and terror as the full reality of his predicament became clear to him. He glanced back at Jamal, who was still standing there, tense and sweating. All this time one compartment of his brain had been evaluating the other option, whether as a last desperate measure he could get a head shot in time, if he could distract Jamal long enough to draw down. It had to be a head shot because for all Tom knew the explosives could be detonated by a high-velocity round passing through it. He would have to get closer to guarantee one round one kill. But he also knew that the person he felt closest to in the room right now was Jamal. They'd both tried to do the right thing, both been fucked around, abandoned and left out in the cold. Tears were running down Jamal's face now. At least Tom knew his words were getting through. But it wasn't a guarantee that he could save the day.

It was as if nothing else existed outside what Tom could see in front of him. If there were any noises coming from anyone to either side of him he couldn't hear them. The only thing registering in his brain was Jamal.

'You've sacrificed so much, Jamal. You went to Syria for the best of reasons. And once you'd discovered what was going on there, you did the best and most courageous thing you could. You risked your life trying to get the truth out. Only these people,' Tom indicated Umarov who had stepped behind Rolt, as if for some kind of cover, 'made sure the truth didn't get out. They wanted you as public enemy number one to justify their own evil agenda.'

Umarov now had his phone in his hand, as if he could summon up his security to take control – or maybe it comforted him to hold it, to maintain the illusion that he had some choice left. Tom turned back to Jamal.

'So detonate, take your revenge. This is your opportunity. The key perpetrators of your downfall are right here in the room. They'll be vaporized. It's a once-in-a-lifetime opportunity. But before you do it, I ask you this. Remember your sister. She wanted your name cleared, so the world could know your courage. She wanted you to live, to be free. I don't know if there's an afterlife, but I do know that if I live, as long as I'm alive, I'm going to remember what I know you did and what Adila did for you. You die now, you will always be the Butcher of Aleppo, who blew up his own sister to get out of jail – the truth will never come out. But if you walk out of here tonight, alive, your sister's dream can come true.'

Jamal was shaking his head as Tom took another step and now was alone, in front of everyone and closer to Jamal.

'I can't do that. I can't.'

'You can. You have the choice. Your life. Your name. Your father.'

Tom could feel himself running out of words. He could sense something inside him trying to get his attention. His reason was exhausted and with that came anger – just a hint of what lay inside him, unadulterated uncontrollable rage, almost too unmanageable to channel. He had been trained for situations like this, to be at his calmest, most measured, most focused, only they didn't usually involve his own father.

Jamal was looking at Rolt and Umarov. 'I can't let them . . .'

Tom was almost in a state of hypnosis as he looked into Jamal's eyes. 'Jamal, you don't have to.' He turned to face the way he had come, sucked in his stomach and brought up the Glock with his right hand. Without using his left for support, he raised the weapon so the only thing between his vision of Rolt was the pistol's rear and foresight. Rolt's image blurred as he focused on the foresight and squeezed.

Time had slowed, so even as he shifted his position, he saw Rolt's right cheek open up and the eye immediately above disappear into its socket. The impact snapped his head with sufficient force to send the rest of him toppling over on to a desk.

Without waiting to see the result, Tom swung left, took two steps and focused on what he could see of Umarov as he tried to take cover. He fired twice into the top of his head. It was all over in less than two seconds.

Xenia swayed, steadying herself against the wall, but she didn't look away. Her eyes never left Umarov as the last of his life seeped out of him.

Tom tucked the weapon into his belt and turned back towards Jamal. His hands had dropped to his sides and his chin had lowered itself into his chest. Tom went up to him, took his hand and gently lifted the detonator out of his palm.

# EPILOGUE

Luckily for Derek Farmer, the first tweets about explosions at Chequers had sounded so hysterical and outlandish that the rest of the Twittersphere didn't pay them much attention. They had given him just enough time to get to his bunker at Number Ten where he had remained for the rest of the night, his phone pressed continuously to his left ear until the whole side of his face was blotched red from the heat coming off it. His fingers scuttled across his keyboard, banging out a deluge of releases and updates. His rule: when the shit hits the fan, chuck back as much as you can. By four a.m. he had done the rounds of all the key media outlets until he'd had them singing from his hymn sheet.

Yes, he had conceded, there *had* been an assault on the prime minister's country seat, *not* by rabid Islamists but, get this, by *white* British men from Rolt's own organization, apparently a rogue group with delusions about their leader taking over. Yeah, yeah, he agreed with one editor. You couldn't make it up! What a story, they exclaimed, and all the time his fingers were tightly crossed that the rest of this God-almighty clusterfuck would never see the light of day.

Getting Geoff to broadcast live down the DSL line from the Chequers panic room he had to admit had been a master stroke on his part. He came over nice and clear, just as if he was at Number Ten or Broadcasting House. That pretty much skewered the wild tales circulating that he really had handed the country over to Rolt at gunpoint.

Quite how it *had* actually played out at Chequers, Farmer had yet to discover; maybe he never would. After the PM's triumphant return to Number Ten at around six a.m., all Farmer could get out of him was that he had 'pulled a blinder', having fooled Rolt into thinking he *had* surrendered so the fucker would clear off back to London and, as it turned out, to his doom, while the Invicta heavies dispersed, thinking 'job done'. The deep sceptic lurking in Farmer suspected a heavy helping of post-rationalization had been smothered over the bare facts but, hey, if it had put his boss in a good mood then what the fuck? Politics was all about making a virtue out of a load of shite.

Rolt's demise? Well, that would always be a mystery, and probably one so hot it would be subject to the hundred-year gagging rule. The Security Services had that one buttoned up good and proper, so fast Farmer suspected they must have had a hand in it. Someone was trying to put it about that an MI5 operator had assassinated Rolt *and* his shadowy Crimean backer, but that was too far-fetched to get any traction. The location – a fortified oligarch's lair with more security than Downing Street – never mind for now that it was also the home of a newspaper proprietor, did the trick perfectly. All that paranoia and bullet-proof security convinced the media to do a quick U-turn on Rolt and go big on lurid tales of his dodgy Russky associates. *Home Secretary Bought By Terror Banker!* screamed one headline. Strangely, the spooks were only too willing to dish the dirt on Oleg Umarov, strictly off the record, of course, to help paint him as a man for whom few tears would be shed.

Even so, a few awkward bastards like those bra-less muesli eaters at the *Guardian* would be determined to keep poking the embers in search of a conspiracy, and in time more would come out; it was inevitable. Perhaps they could be stalled with an inquiry or even just the promise of one, something like Chilcot, which would go on and on for years and years, so that when it finally did report no one would remember who Rolt was or give a shit. By then he would have receded into history, an aberration who had flown too close to the sun.

When Farmer finally closed his laptop for the night and stepped out for a well-earned fag, Alec Clements, the cabinet secretary, was in the corridor, waiting to congratulate him on a job well done.

'But wasn't it you who first suggested Rolt to the PM as his ticket back into Downing Street?' Farmer took no small pleasure in reminding him.

But Clements gazed past him with the slightly out-of-focus look he had when his mind had moved on to other matters. 'As Harold Wilson said, Derek, a week is a long time in politics.'

Barely an hour after the prime minister's call, Sarah Garvey strode triumphantly into the Home Office in Marsham Street, to reclaim her old office, like de Gaulle liberating Paris, albeit with a teensy hangover. First to congratulate her on her rehabilitation was *über*spook Stephen Mandler.

'Buckingham said you went off message. What happened?'

Mandler's face was in sphinx-mode.

'Oh, for fuck's sake, Stephen.'

He sighed. She knew he was a gossip at heart.

'Someone wanted me out of the way in case I got wind of the Rolt plan and tried to foil it. One condition of my being reinstated is that it will never come to light.'

Garvey couldn't be doing with this. 'Clements.'

He became even more opaque, as if he were trying to blend in at Madame Tussaud's. 'I couldn't possibly comment.' He sipped the celebratory single malt he had brought along to toast their rehabilitation.

'So what about the man we have to thank for saving us all from oblivion?'

Mandler allowed himself a smirk. 'You'll like this. The PM wanted to apologize to him in person for handing him over to the heavy mob in Chequers. And you know what Buckingham said? "Tell him I'm helping my mother wash the dogs."'

'Nice. What'll he do now? Are you going to give him a proper job?'

Mandler gave her a wry look. 'I don't think he does proper jobs.'

They moved on to Jamal. In exchange for her constituent's silence about that night, the matter of his possession – and, indeed, very near deployment of Isham al Aziz's IED – would not be disclosed at any trial on grounds of national security. Mandler would see to it. If nothing else, Garvey felt she owed it to the memory of Adila that, after all he had been through, the lad should finally get a fair deal. The truth about his bravery in Aleppo, his hounding by Rolt and his virtual abduction by the bomb-maker Isham al Aziz should ensure, with a following wind, that he would soon be a free man and the ideal candidate for Garvey's returnee rehab programme.

She detected Mandler's eyes twinkling, as they always did when he was about to throw her a particularly choice morsel of intelligence.

'Something else that might be grist to your mill: Jamal's commander, Abukhan, fought in Chechnya before he decamped to Syria. And guess who bankrolled him when he was fighting the Russkies?'

'Motherfucker.'

'So in all probability it was Umarov who tipped him off about Emma Warner.'

'To fuck up Xenia, the crusading stepdaughter. No one's going to want to put Jamal away after that.'

And they drained their glasses in something almost like a toast.

'Another?'

Mandler frowned at her over his half-glasses. 'Sarah, it's not even elevenses.'

After it was over, Tom had taken his father straight home and stayed close by his side for the next forty-eight hours. No phone calls or emails, just backgammon, reading and gentle walks. A lot of the time neither of them spoke, but Tom wanted to be sure that he was coping, especially since the effects of trauma like that could be delayed. His own work had never crashed into his family life before and it had shaken his father badly. His mother, they had agreed, would be spared the details. The version Tom gave her, which wasn't all that far from the truth, was that Umarov's people had taken Hugh hostage – without harming him at all – and that Tom had freed him. Enough said.

As he knew she would, Mary Buckingham took the explanation at face value and did a good job of conveying her gratitude and admiration to her son for getting his father out of trouble. But Tom could tell by the look in her eyes that she suspected she was being given a varnished version of the truth. She deserved better. And she would get it, one day, maybe, but not yet.

When he wasn't with Hugh, who didn't want to go near the TV, Tom sat with her watching the BBC to try to make sense of the last few days. Also, he was curious to see which version would be aired.

Number Ten, you had to hand it to them, had done a pretty good job of spinning it their way. According to them, elements within Invicta had indeed attempted to take the cabinet hostage at Chequers, but had been thwarted by the Security Service. The fact that the prime minister had wasted no time in taking the credit, going on air so soon after it had all kicked off to say that order had been restored, had helped put a lid on it. Never had people been so relieved to see their prime minister's bland features on their screens.

'Will we ever know what happened to Vernon Rolt?' Mary asked Tom, with feigned casualness.

He sighed. 'Well, I think it was as they said. It turned out he was mixing with the wrong crowd – he'd mortgaged himself to Umarov and it all got out of hand.'

She moved slightly so she was directly in his gaze. 'And he got shot?'

Tom looked at her steadily. 'So it would appear.'

His mother's gaze lingered on him a moment longer than was comfortable. 'Well, good riddance.'

On the second morning, Hugh had appeared by Tom's bed-side and said he wanted him to know that he understood Jamal had left him with no real choice: frankly, Rolt and Umarov had been as bad as each other and the world would be a better place without them.

'Guess that sums it up pretty well,' Tom replied, relieved.

Later, when he was seeing him off, the old man looked hard into his eyes. 'I've often been rather unforgiving about your choice of work, imagined there was something better for you. Well, I'm sorry, Tom. I was wrong. And I was a fool to get involved with Umarov. I should have known better.'

'You and half of London. Don't beat yourself up too much, Dad.'

'I won't forget this, ever. Even when dementia has set in!'

'Will you be all right financially?'

'Oh, yes, fine. We're going to hang on here for a bit, then we'll see. Don't worry – we won't move without telling you.'

It was only just getting light. Westminster Bridge had been closed since midnight, armed police guarding each end. Floodlights had been erected that lit up the seaward side, and two police launches bobbed on the icy water beside the platform the divers were working from. Several unmarked vans were parked along the bridge and an ambulance was on standby.

'Shouldn't be long now,' murmured Woolf, as he clapped his ski-mitts together for warmth and gazed at the river. Overhead, a milky sun was trying to penetrate the cloud which seemed to have taken up permanent residence over the city. 'You don't have to wait.'

'I'll wait,' said Tom.

Woolf nodded. 'Good job Garvey bent your ear about Jamal.'

Tom shrugged. 'I'd have had to improvise otherwise. But with guys like him, sadly, it's so often the same story.'

His gaze fell on the cops guarding the bridge, in full kit with their MP5s. Quite who or what they were expecting was anyone's guess. He wondered when things would ever return to normal – or, indeed, if there would ever be a 'normal' any more. Maybe with Rolt gone there might be.

'I'm sorry you were left out there on your own.' Woolf's embarrassment was leaking out from behind the poker face.

'It's not the first time.'

'You sure you want to wait? Could be a while.'

Tom nodded.

The night before, Tom told Phoebe to meet him at Invicta. It was strange going back in. Rolt had been a stickler for tidiness and the place had been trashed. The police and Security Service had been all over it. All the computer hard drives were gone; filing cabinets yawned open. No cupboard had been left unrummaged. And every surface had been dusted for prints as if it were a crime scene. Strangely, the only item that had been overlooked was the Ordynka, still resting in its wooden box.

Phoebe had made an effort to look her best, in heels and a low-cut burgundy suit, with a gold brooch in the shape of a feather pinned to her lapel. Tom noted that she had more makeup on than he had seen her wear before. But it did not mask the strain and fatigue on her face.

He was standing in Rolt's office, gazing at Umarov's garish gift, weighing it in his hand, when she came towards him. 'Tom, I'm so glad you're all right. You have no idea.' She kissed him on each cheek. She felt hot and was trembling a little.

He didn't speak at first, just smiled and nodded, curious to see what she would say next. 'Nice brooch,' he said.

'It was my mother's. My father gave it to me after she died.' Her gaze floated around the room. 'Well, I'm glad we can finally put all this behind us.'

Tom didn't say anything.

She walked up to Rolt's desk and trailed her fingertips in the dust left by the search team. He watched her intently, taking his time. She looked up at him. 'Was there something – is there something you wanted to say?'

Tom examined the blade of the Ordynka. 'Just a question.'

She looked at him, a wariness in her gaze. 'What question?'

He didn't respond, just looked at her. His face must have said it all because after a few seconds' silence her eyes filled with tears. She blinked nervously and looked away. Eventually she spoke. 'How did you know?'

'Someone had to have warned Umarov about me. Not a straight "He's under cover," or they would never have let me near Chequers. More a hint, maybe, that I couldn't be completely trusted. Enough for them to threaten me that my father . . .'

He paused to swallow the anger. 'Enough for them to effectively take him hostage.'

Despite the foundation, blotches of red appeared on her cheeks. Tears tumbled out of her eyes and fell with faint plops onto the desk. 'Rolt and I, we were always together, so much of the time . . . It just sort of happened.' She wiped away some of the tears. 'Then he got it into his head that MI5 had a source inside his organization. There was I, always fiddling with my phone, so he accused me. It never entered his head it could be you.'

'So you saved yourself by informing on me.'

She flinched as he said the words, even put up a hand as if she thought he might strike her. 'I was terrified of Umarov. I knew his reputation.' Her face was a mess of tears and despair. 'What are you going to do?'

He considered his answer. 'Oh, take a break. Keep an eye on Dad for a bit.'

She was steadying herself against Rolt's desk. 'I meant now.'

Tom put the Ordynka back in its box, closed the lid and went to the door. Before he left he turned and looked at her one last time. 'Live my life. I've got a lot to live for.'

Then he left and closed the door behind him.

On the bridge, Woolf waved Tom forward to the balustrade. 'Okay, they're ready. You sure you want to watch?'

'Yes, I am.'

A couple of the cops made room for him; one breathed out a

long mournful sigh as the cables tightened and the crane powered up.

The hair was a matted mess, grey with sediment; the skin looked as if it had been bleached white. She had attached a weighted diving belt round her waist, insurance against a change of heart.

Woolf was at his shoulder. 'Okay?'

'Okay.'

'Officially we still have to confirm ID.'

But Tom didn't need to wait. Her burgundy jacket still had the brooch on its lapel. He turned to Woolf. 'Make sure the brooch doesn't disappear. It mattered a lot to her.'

# ABOUT THE AUTHOR

From the day he was found in a carrier bag on the steps of Guy's Hospital in London, **Andy McNab** has led an extraordinary life.

As a teenage delinquent, Andy McNab kicked against society. As a young soldier, he waged war against the IRA in the streets and fields of South Armagh. As a member of 22 SAS, he was at the centre of covert operations for nine years, on five continents. During the Gulf War he commanded Bravo Two Zero, a patrol that, in the words of his commanding officer, 'will remain in regimental history for ever'. Awarded both the Distinguished Conduct Medal (DCM) and Military Medal (MM) during his military career, McNab was the British Army's most highly decorated serving soldier when he finally left the SAS.

Since then Andy McNab has become one of the world's best-selling writers, drawing on his insider knowledge and experience. As well as three non-fiction bestsellers – including *Bravo Two Zero*, the bestselling British work of military history – he is the author of the Nick Stone and Tom Buckingham thrillers. He has also written a number of books for children.

Besides his writing work, he lectures to security and intelligence agencies in both the USA and UK, works in the film industry advising Hollywood on everything from covert procedure to training civilian actors to act like soldiers, and he continues to be a spokesperson and fundraiser for both military and literacy charities.